Once you're in,
you're in W9-BTM-550

"This is Len Deighton country. *The Tourist* is a complex, contemporary espionage story told with wit and sagacity, and it offers up a dozen or more intricate characters who keep the action on target. While the international intrigue and cross-country chase are the stuff of traditional Hitchcockian entertainment, Steinhauer once again demonstrates how his economical prose can turn unrelenting paranoia into an exciting ride."

—*Boston Globe*

"*The Tourist* is an incredibly multifarious and multi-layered novel. . . . Steinhauer . . . goes above the straightforward thriller to show the consequences of a spy's existence on every level. . . . Olen Steinhauer has composed a hugely complex successor to *The Spy Who Came in from the Cold*. Unlike most espionage tales written in the years since that classic work first saw print in 1963, however, he manages to give his characters—even the most reprehensible ones—a human side and a degree of warmth. Spying is a nasty business that chews up and spits out the people involved in it. *The Tourist* shines a light on the moral costs."   —*January Magazine*

"Only le Carré can make a spy as interesting."

—*Kirkus Reviews*

"Steinhauer manages to push the genre's darker aspects to the extreme . . . without sacrificing the propulsive forward momentum . . . [Weaver] is the perfect hero for such a richly nuanced tale."   —*Booklist* (starred review)

"Superbly accomplished at both plotting and characterization . . . compelling and hard to put down . . . highly recommended." —*Library Journal* (starred review)

"A first-class spy novel—wry, intelligent, layered . . . the kind of thing John le Carré might have written if he knew then what we know now."

—Lee Child, *New York Times* bestselling author

"*The Tourist* is an absolutely superb contemporary espionage novel in the great tradition of the old masters of the genre. Olen Steinhauer is a wonderful storyteller who is smart, observant, and witty. *The Tourist* has what it takes to become a classic."

—Nelson DeMille, *New York Times* bestselling author

"Olen Steinhauer's *The Tourist* is a complex, fast-paced spy novel populated by dozens of striking characters, each with an unexpected, shifting place in the puzzle."

—Thomas Perry, *New York Times* bestselling author

"Every now and then a writer of thrillers or mysteries emerges who deserves to be compared with the best."

—*Chicago Tribune*

"*The Tourist* . . . raises a lot of questions, but only answers enough to keep the story moving briskly and the reader's curiosity stoked through to the end." —*Penthouse*

"Outstanding." —*Publishers Weekly* (starred review)

"Milo Weaver [is] a spy to die for."

—Marilyn Stasio, *The New York Times Book Review*

ALSO BY OLEN STEINHAUER

The
TOURIST

OLEN STEINHAUER

St. Martin's Paperbacks

THE TOURIST

Copyright © 2009 by Olen Steinhauer.
Excerpt from *The Nearest Exit* copyright © 2010 by Olen Steinhauer.

For information address St. Martin's Press, 175 Fifth Avenue, New York, NY 10010.

ISBN: 978-1-250-01841-0

Printed in the United States of America

Minotaur hardcover edition / March 2009
Griffin edition / February 2010
St. Martin's Paperbacks edition / September 2012

St. Martin's Paperbacks are published by St. Martin's Press, 175 Fifth Avenue, New York, NY 10010.

10 9 8 7 6 5 4 3 2 1

For Margo

ACKNOWLEDGMENTS

Thanks to William Desmond, my French translator, for repairing my poor attempts at his language.

My agent Stephanie Cabot helped make all this possible, with her generous ear, her astute advice, and her unlimited energy on my behalf. Her colleagues at the Gernert Company showed amazing zeal with this book, for which I'm deeply grateful.

Kelley Ragland at Minotaur once again found the forest in the trees. Few things in this world beat an editor who not only cares, but understands.

As ever, without Slavica so little of this could have happened. She gives faith when it's needed, gives a kick when it's necessary, and supplies the affection we all, not just novelists, need to keep going.

THE END
OF TOURISM

MONDAY, SEPTEMBER 10, TO
TUESDAY, SEPTEMBER 11, 2001

1

Four hours after his failed suicide attempt, he descended toward Aerodrom Ljubljana. A tone sounded, and above his head the seat belt sign glowed. Beside him, a Swiss businesswoman buckled her belt and gazed out the window at the clear Slovenian sky—all it had taken was one initial rebuff to convince her that the twitching American she'd been seated next to had no interest in conversation.

The American closed his eyes, thinking about the morning's failure in Amsterdam—gunfire, shattering glass and splintered wood, sirens.

If suicide is sin, he thought, then what is it to someone who doesn't believe in sin? What is it then? An abomination of nature? Probably, because the one immutable law of nature is to continue existing. Witness: weeds, cockroaches, ants, and pigeons. All of nature's creatures work to a single, unified purpose: to stay alive. It's the one indisputable theory of everything.

He'd dwelled on suicide so much over the last months, had examined the act from so many angles, that it had lost its punch. The infinitive clause "to commit suicide" was no more tragic than "to eat breakfast" or "to sit," and the desire to snuff himself was often as strong as his desire "to sleep."

Sometimes it was a passive urge—drive recklessly without a seat belt; walk blindly into a busy street—though more frequently these days he was urged to take responsibility for his own death. "The Bigger Voice," his mother would have called it: *There's the knife; you know what to do. Open the window and try to fly.* At four thirty that morning, while he lay on top of a woman in Amsterdam, pressing her to the floor as her bedroom window exploded from automatic gunfire, the urge had suggested he stand straight and proud and face the hail of bullets like a man.

He'd spent the whole week in Holland, watching over a sixty-year-old U.S.-supported politician whose comments on immigration had put a contract on her head. The hired assassin, a killer who in certain circles was known only as "the Tiger," had that morning made a third attempt on her life. Had he succeeded, he would have derailed that day's Dutch House of Representatives vote on her conservative immigration bill.

How the continued existence of one politician—in this case, a woman who had made a career of catering to the whims of frightened farmers and bitter racists—played into the hands of his own country was unknown to him. "Keeping an empire," Grainger liked to tell him, "is ten times more difficult than gaining one."

Rationales, in his trade, didn't matter. Action was its own reason. But, covered in glass shards, the woman under him screaming over the crackling sound, like a deep fryer, of the window frame splintering, he'd thought, *What am I doing here?* He even placed a hand flat on the wood-chip-covered carpet and began to push himself up again, to face this assassin head-on. Then, in the midst of all that noise, he heard the happy music of his cell phone. He removed his hand from the floor, saw that it was Grainger calling, and shouted into it, "What?"

"Riverrun, past Eve," Tom Grainger said.

"And Adam's."

Learned Grainger had created go-codes out of the first lines of novels. His own Joycean code told him he was needed someplace new. But nothing was new anymore. The unrelenting roll call of cities and hotel rooms and suspicious faces that had constituted his life for too many years was stupefying in its tedium. Would it never stop?

So he hung up on his boss, told the screaming woman to stay where she was, and climbed to his feet . . . but didn't die. The bullets had ceased, replaced by the whining sirens of Amsterdam's finest.

"Slovenia," Grainger told him later, as he drove the politician safely to the Tweede Kamer. "Portorož, on the coast. We've got a vanished suitcase of taxpayer money and a missing station chief. Frank Dawdle."

"I need a break, Tom."

"It'll be like a vacation. Angela Yates is your

contact—she works out of Dawdle's office. A familiar face. Afterward, stay around and enjoy the water."

As Grainger droned on, outlining the job with minimal details, his stomach had started to hurt, as it still did now, a sharp pain.

If the one immutable law of existence is to exist, then does that make the opposite some sort of crime?

No. Suicide-as-crime would require that nature recognize good and evil. Nature only recognizes balance and imbalance.

Maybe that was the crucial point—balance. He'd slipped to some secluded corner of the extremes, some far reach of utter imbalance. He was a ludicrously unbalanced creature. How could nature smile upon him? Nature, surely, wanted him dead, too.

"Sir?" said a bleached, smiling stewardess. "Your seat belt."

He blinked at her, confused. "What about it?"

"You need to wear it. We're landing. It's for your safety."

Though he wanted to laugh, he buckled it just for her. Then he reached into his jacket pocket, took out a small white envelope full of pills he'd bought in Düsseldorf, and popped two Dexedrine. To live or die was one issue; for the moment, he just wanted to stay alert.

Suspiciously, the Swiss businesswoman watched him put away his drugs.

The pretty, round-faced brunette behind the scratched bulletproof window watched him approach. He imagined he knew what she noticed—how big his hands were, for example. Piano-player hands. The Dexedrine was making them tremble, just slightly, and if she noticed it she might wonder if he was unconsciously playing a sonata.

He handed over a mangled American passport that had crossed more borders than many diplomats. A touring pianist, she might think. A little pale, damp from the long flight he'd just finished. Bloodshot eyes. Aviatophobia—fear of flying—was probably her suspicion.

He managed a smile, which helped wash away her expression of bureaucratic boredom. She really was very pretty, and he wanted her to know, by his expression, that her face was a nice Slovenian welcome.

The passport gave her his particulars: five foot eleven. Born June 1970—thirty-one years old. Piano player? No—American passports don't list occupations. She peered up at him and spoke in her unsure accent: "Mr. Charles Alexander?"

He caught himself looking around again, paranoid, and gave another smile. "That's right."

"You are here for the business or the tourism?"

"I'm a tourist."

She held the open passport under a black light, then raised a stamp over one of the few blank pages. "How long will you be in Slovenia?"

Mr. Charles Alexander's green eyes settled pleasantly on her. "Four days."

"For vacation? You should spend at least a week. There is many things to see."

His smile flashed again, and he rocked his head. "Well, maybe you're right. I'll see how it goes."

Satisfied, the clerk pressed the stamp onto the page and handed it back. "Enjoy Slovenia."

He passed through the luggage area, where other passengers from the Amsterdam-Ljubljana flight leaned on empty carts around the still-barren carousel. None seemed to notice him, so he tried to stop looking like a paranoid drug mule. It was his stomach, he knew, and that initial Dexedrine rush. Two white customs desks sat empty of officials, and he continued through a pair of mirrored doors that opened automatically for him. A crowd of expectant faces sank when they realized he didn't belong to them. He loosened his tie.

The last time Charles Alexander had been in Slovenia, years ago, he'd been called something else, a name just as false as the one he used now. Back then, the country was still exhilarated by the 1991 ten-day war that had freed it from the Yugoslav Federation. Nestled against Austria, Slovenia had always been the odd man out in that patchwork nation, more German than Balkan. The rest of Yugoslavia accused Slovenes—not without reason—of snobbery.

Still inside the airport, he spotted Angela Yates just outside the doors to the busy arrivals curb. Above business slacks, she wore a blue Viennese blazer, arms crossed over her breasts as she smoked and stared through the gray morning light at the field of parked cars in front of the airport. He didn't approach her. Instead, he found a bathroom and checked himself in the mirror. The paleness and sweat had nothing to do with aviatophobia. He ripped off his tie, splashed water on his cheeks, wiped at the pink edges of his eyes and blinked, but still looked the same.

"Sorry to get you up," he said once he'd gotten outside.

Angela jerked, a look of terror passing through her lavender eyes. Then she grinned. She looked tired, but she would be. She'd driven four hours to meet his flight, which meant she'd had to leave Vienna by 5:00 A.M. She tossed the unfinished smoke, a Davidoff, then punched his shoulder and hugged him. The smell of tobacco was comforting. She held him at arm's length. "You haven't been eating."

"Overrated."

"And you look like hell."

He shrugged as she yawned into the back of her hand. "You going to make it?" he asked.

"No sleep last night."

"Need something?"

Angela got rid of the smile. "Still gulping amphetamines?"

"Only for emergencies," he lied, because he'd taken that last dose for no other reason than he'd wanted it, and now, as the tremors shook through his bloodstream, he had an urge to empty the rest down his throat. "Want one?"

"*Please.*"

They crossed an access road choked with morning taxis and buses heading into town, then followed concrete steps down to the parking lot. She whispered, "Is it Charles these days?"

"Almost two years now."

"Well, it's a stupid name. Too aristocratic. I refuse to use it."

"I keep asking for a new one. A month ago I showed up in Nice, and some Russian had already heard about Charles Alexander."

"Oh?"

"Nearly killed me, that Russian."

She smiled as if he'd been joking, but he hadn't been. Then his snapping synapses worried he was sharing too much. Angela knew nothing about his job; she wasn't supposed to.

"Tell me about Dawdle. How long have you worked with him?"

"Three years." She took out her key ring and pressed a little black button until she spotted, three rows away, a gray Peugeot winking at them. "Frank's my boss, but we keep it casual. Just a small Company presence at the embassy." She paused. "He was sweet on me for a while. Can you imagine? Couldn't see what was right in front of him."

She spoke with a tinge of hysteria that made him fear she would cry. He pushed anyway. "What do you think? Could he have done it?"

Angela popped the Peugeot's trunk. "Absolutely not. Frank Dawdle wasn't dishonest. Bit of a coward, maybe. A bad dresser. But never dishonest. He didn't take the money."

Charles threw in his bag. "You're using the past tense, Angela."

"I'm just afraid."

"Of what?"

Angela knitted her brows, irritated. "That he's *dead*. What do you think?"

2

She was a careful driver these days, which he supposed was an inevitable result of her two Austrian years. Had she been stationed in Italy, or even here in Slovenia, she would've ignored her turn signals and those pesky speed limit notices.

To ease the tension, he brought up old London friends from when they both worked out of that embassy as vaguely titled "attachés." He'd left in a hurry, and all Angela knew was that his new job, with some undisclosed Company department, required a steady change of names, and that he once again worked under their old boss, Tom Grainger. The rest of London station believed what they'd been told—that he had been fired. She said, "I fly up for parties now and then. They always invite me. But they're sad, you know? All diplomatic people. There's something intensely pitiful about them."

"Really?" he said, though he knew what she meant.

"Like they're living in their own little compound, surrounded by barbed wire. They pretend they're keeping everyone out, when in fact they're locked in."

It was a nice way to put it, and it made him think of Tom Grainger's delusions of empire—Roman outposts in hostile lands.

Once they hit the A1 heading southwest, Angela got back to business. "Tom fill you in on everything?"

"Not much. Can I get one of those smokes?"

"Not in the car."

"Oh."

"Tell me what you know, and I'll fill in the rest."

Thick forests passed them, pines flickering by as he outlined his brief conversation with Grainger. "He says your Frank Dawdle was sent down here to deliver a briefcase full of money. He didn't say how much."

"Three million."

"Dollars?"

She nodded at the road.

Charles continued: "He was last seen at the Hotel Metropol in Portorož by Slovenian intelligence. In his room. Then he disappeared." He waited for her to fill the numerous blank spots in that story line. All she did was drive in her steady, safe way. "Want to tell me more? Like, who the money was for?"

Angela tilted her head from side to side, but instead of answering she turned on the radio. It was preset to a station she'd found during her long drive from Vienna. Slovenian pop. Terrible stuff.

"And maybe you can tell me why we had to learn his

last whereabouts from the SOVA, and not from our
own people."

As if he'd said nothing, she cranked the volume, and
boy-band harmonies filled the car. Finally, she started
to speak, and Charles had to lean close, over the stick
shift, to hear.

"I'm not sure who the orders started with, but they
reached us through New York. Tom's office. He chose
Frank for obvious reasons. Old-timer with a spotless record. No signs of ambition. No drinking problems, nothing to be compromised. He was someone they could
trust with three million. More importantly, he's familiar
here. If the Slovenes saw him floating around the resort,
there'd be no suspicions. He vacations in Portorož every
summer, speaks fluent Slovene." She grunted a half-
laugh. "He even stopped to chat with them. Did Tom tell
you that? The day he arrived, he saw a SOVA agent in a
gift shop and bought him a little toy sailboat. Frank's
like that."

"I like his style."

Angela's look suggested he was being inappropri-
ately ironic. "It was supposed to be simple as pie. Frank
takes the money down to the harbor on Saturday—two
days ago—and does a straight phrase-code pass-off.
Just hands over the briefcase. In return, he gets an address. He goes to a pay phone, calls me in Vienna, and
reads off the address. Then he drives back home."

. The song ended, and a young DJ shouted in Slovenian about the *hot-hot-hot* band he'd just played as he
mixed in the intro to the next tune, a sugar-sweet ballad.

"Why wasn't someone backing him up?"

"Someone was," she said, spying the rearview. "Leo Bernard. You met him in Munich, remember? Couple of years ago."

Charles remembered a hulk of a man from Pennsylvania. In Munich, Leo had been their tough-guy backup during an operation with the German BND against an Egyptian heroin racket. They'd never had to put Leo's fighting skills to the test, but it had given Charles a measure of comfort knowing the big man was available. "Yeah. Leo was funny."

"Well, he's dead," said Angela, again glancing into the rearview. "In his hotel room, a floor above Frank's. Nine millimeter." She swallowed. "From his own gun, we think, though we can't find the weapon itself."

"Anyone hear it?"

She shook her head. "Leo had a suppressor."

Charles leaned back into his seat, involuntarily checking the side mirror. He lowered the volume as a woman tried with limited success to carry a high E-note. Then he cut it off. Angela was being cagey about the central facts of this case—the *why* of all that money—but that could wait. Right now he wanted to visualize the events. "When did they arrive at the coast?"

"Friday afternoon. The seventh."

"Legends?"

"Frank, no. He was too well known for that. Leo used an old one, Benjamin Schneider, Austrian."

"Next day, Saturday, was the trade. Which part of the docks?"

"I've got it written down."

"Time?"

"Evening. Seven."

"Frank disappears . . . ?"

"Last seen at 4:00 A.M. Saturday morning. He was up until then drinking with Bogdan Krizan, the local SOVA head. They're old friends. Then, around two in the afternoon, the hotel cleaning staff found Leo's body."

"What about the dock? Anyone see what happened at seven?"

Again, she glanced into the rearview. "We were too late. The Slovenes weren't going to ask us why Frank was buying them toys. And we didn't know about Leo's body until after seven. His papers were good enough to confuse the Austrian embassy for over eight hours."

"For three million dollars you couldn't have sent a couple more watchers?"

Angela tightened her jaw. "Maybe, but hindsight doesn't do us any good now."

The incompetence surprised Charles; then again, it didn't. "Whose call was it?"

When she looked in the mirror yet again, her jaw was tighter, her cheeks flushed. So it was her fault, he thought, but she said, "Frank wanted me to stay in Vienna."

"It was Frank Dawdle's idea to go off with three million dollars and only one watcher?"

"I know the man. You don't."

She'd said those words without moving her lips. Charles felt the urge to tell her that he did know her boss. He'd worked with him once, in 1996, to get rid of a retired communist spy from some nondescript Eastern European country. But she wasn't supposed to know about that. He touched her shoulder to show a little sympathy. "I won't talk to Tom until we've got some real answers. Okay?"

She finally looked at him with a weary smile. "Thanks, Milo."

"It's Charles."

The smile turned sardonic. "I wonder if you even have a real name."

3

Their hour-long drive skirted the Italian border, and as they neared the coast the highway opened up and the foliage thinned. The warm morning sun glinted off the road as they passed Koper and Izola, and Charles watched the low shrubs, the Mediterranean architecture, and the ZIMMER-FREI signs that littered each turnoff. It reminded him just how beautiful this tiny stretch of coast truly was. Less than thirty miles that had been pulled back and forth between Italians, Yugoslavs, and Slovenes over centuries of regional warfare.

To their right, they caught occasional glimpses of the Adriatic, and through the open window he smelled salt. He wondered if his own salvation lay in something like this. Disappear, and spend the rest of his years under a hot sun on the sea. The kind of climate that dries and burns the imbalance out of you. But he pushed that aside, because he already knew the truth: Geography solves nothing.

He said, "We can't do this unless you tell me the rest."

"What rest?" She spoke as if she had no idea.

"The *why*. Why Frank Dawdle was sent down here with three million dollars."

To the rearview, she said, "War criminal. Bosnian Serb. Big fish."

A small pink hotel passed, and then Portorož Bay opened up, full of sun and glimmering water. "Which one?"

"Does it really matter?"

He supposed it didn't. Karadžić, Mladić, or any other wanted *ić*—the story was always the same. They, as well as the Croat zealots on the other side of the battle lines, had all had a hand in the Bosnian genocides that had helped turn a once-adored multiethnic country into an international pariah. Since 1996, these men had been fugitives, hidden by sympathizers and corrupt officials, faced with charges from the UN's International Tribunal for the Former Yugoslavia. Crimes against humanity, crimes against life and health, genocide, breaches of the Geneva conventions, murder, plunder, and violations of the laws and customs of war. Charles gazed at the Adriatic, sniffing the wind. "The UN's offering five million for these people."

"Oh, this guy *wanted* five," Angela said as she slowed behind a line of cars with Slovenian, German, and Italian plates. "But all he had was an address, and he demanded the money up front so he could disappear. The UN didn't trust him, turned him down flat, so some smart young man at Langley decided we should purchase it ourselves for three. A PR coup. We buy ourselves the glory of an arrest and once again point out the UN's incompetence." She shrugged. "Five or three—either way, you're a millionaire."

"What do we know about him?"

"He wouldn't tell us anything, but Langley figured it out. Dušan Masković, a Sarajevo Serb who joined the militias in the early days. He's part of the entourage that's been hiding the big ones in the Republika Srpska hills. Two weeks ago, he left their employ and contacted the UN Human Rights office in Sarajevo. Apparently, they get people like him every day. So little Dušan put in a call to our embassy in Vienna and found a sympathetic ear."

"Why not just take care of it there? In Sarajevo?"

The traffic moved steadily forward, and they passed shops with flowers and international newspapers. "He didn't want to collect in Bosnia. Didn't even want it set up through the Sarajevo embassy. And he didn't want anyone stationed in the ex-Yugoslav republics involved."

"He's no fool."

"From what we figure, he got hold of a boat in Croatia and was going to wait in the Adriatic until 7:00 P.M. on Saturday. Then he could slip in, make the trade, and slip out again before he'd have to register with the harbormaster."

"I see," Charles said, because despite his returning stomach cramps he finally had enough information to picture the various players and the ways they connected.

"Want me to take care of the room?"

"Let's check the dock first."

Portorož's main harbor lay at the midpoint of the bay; behind it sat the sixties architecture of the Hotel Slovenia, its name written in light blue against white concrete, a surf motif. They parked off the main road and wandered around shops selling model sailboats and T-shirts with PORTOROŽ and I LOVE SLOVENIA and MY PARENTS WENT TO SLOVENIA AND ALL I GOT . . . scribbled across them. Sandaled families sucking ice cream cones and cigarettes wandered leisurely past. Behind the shops lay a row of small piers full of vacation boats.

"Which one?" asked Charles.

"Forty-seven."

He led the way, hands in his pockets, as if he and his lady-friend were enjoying the view and the hot sun. The crews and captains on the motor- and sailboats paid them no attention. It was nearly noon, time for siestas and drink. Germans and Slovenes dozed on their hot decks, and the only voices they heard were from children who couldn't fall asleep.

Forty-seven was empty, but at forty-nine a humble yacht with an Italian flag was tied up. On its deck, a heavy woman was trying to peel a sausage.

"Buon giorno!" said Charles.

The woman inclined her head politely.

Charles's Italian was only passable, so he asked Angela to find out when the woman had arrived in Portorož. Angela launched into a machine-gun Roman-Italian that sounded like a blast of insults, but the sausage woman smiled and waved her hands as she threw the insults back. It ended with Angela waving a "Grazie mille."

Charles waved, too, then leaned close to Angela as they walked away. "Well?"

"She got here Saturday night. There was a motorboat beside theirs—dirty, she tells me—but it left soon after they arrived. She guesses around seven thirty, eight."

After a couple more steps, Angela realized Charles had stopped somewhere behind her. His hands were on his hips as he stared at the empty spot with a small placard marked "47." "How clean do you think that water is?"

"I've seen worse."

Charles handed over his jacket, then unbuttoned his shirt as he kicked off his shoes.

"You're not," said Angela.

"If the trade happened at all, then it probably didn't go well. If it led to a fight, something might have dropped in here."

"Or," said Angela, "if Dušan's smart, he took Frank's body out into the Adriatic and dropped him overboard."

Charles wanted to tell her that he'd already ruled Dušan Masković out as a murderer—there was nothing for Dušan to gain by killing a man who was going to give him money for a simple address with no questions asked—but changed his mind. He didn't have time for a fight.

He stripped to his boxers, hiding the pangs in his stomach as he bent to pull off the slacks. He wore no undershirt, and his chest was pale from a week spent under Amsterdam's gray skies. "If I don't come up . . ."

"Don't look at me," said Angela. "I can't swim."

"Then get Signora Sausage to come for me."

Before she could think of a reply, Charles had jumped feet-first into the shallow bay. It was a shock to his drug-bubbly nerves, and there was an instant when he almost breathed in; he had to force himself not to. He paddled back to the surface and wiped his face. Angela, on the edge of the pier, smiled down at him. "Done already?"

"Don't wrinkle my shirt." He submerged again, then opened his eyes.

With the sun almost directly above, the shadows beneath the water were stark. He saw the dirty white hulls of boats, then the blackness where their undersides curved into darkness. He ran his hands along the Italian boat at number forty-nine, following its lines toward the bow, where a thick cord ran up to the piles, holding the boat secure. He let go of the line and sank into the heavy darkness under the pier, using hands for sight. He touched living things—a rough shell, slime, the scales of a paddling fish—but as he prepared to return to the surface, he found something else. A heavy work boot, hard-soled. It was attached to a foot, jeans, a body. Again, he fought to keep himself from inhaling. He tugged, but the stiff, cold corpse was hard to move.

He came up for air, ignored Angela's taunts, then submerged again. He used the pilings for leverage. Once he'd dragged the body into the partial light around the Italian boat, through the cloud of kicked sand, he saw why it had been such a struggle. The bloated body—a dark-bearded man—was rope-bound at the waist to a length of heavy metal tubing: a piece of an engine, he guessed.

He broke the surface gasping. This water, which had

seemed so clean a minute before, was now filthy. He spat out leakage, wiping his lips with the back of his hand. Above him, hands on her knees, Angela said, "I can hold my breath longer than that. Watch."

"Help me up."

She set his clothes in a pile, kneeled on the pier, and reached down to him. Soon he was over the edge, sitting with his knees up, dripping. A breeze set him shivering.

"Well?" said Angela.

"What does Frank look like?"

She reached into her blazer and tugged out a small photograph she'd brought to show to strangers. A frontal portrait, morose but efficiently lit, so that all Frank Dawdle's features were visible. A clean-shaven man, bald on top, white hair over the ears, sixty or so.

"He didn't grow a beard since this, did he?"

Angela shook her head, then looked worried. "But the last known photo of Masković . . ."

He got to his feet. "Unless the Portorož murder rate has gone wild, that's your Serb down there."

"I don't—"

Charles cut her off before she could argue: "We'll talk with the SOVA, but you need to call Vienna. Now. Check Frank's office. See what's missing. Find out what was on his computer before he left."

He slipped into his shirt, his wet body bleeding the white cotton gray. Angela started fooling with her phone, but her fingers had trouble with the buttons. Charles took her hands in his and looked into her eyes.

"This is serious. Okay? But don't freak out until we know everything. And let's not tell the Slovenes about the body. We don't want them holding us for questioning."

Again, she nodded.

Charles let go of her and grabbed his jacket, pants, and shoes, then began walking back up the pier, toward the shore. From her boat, her chubby knees to her chin, the Italian woman let out a low whistle. "Bello," she said.

4

An hour and a half later, they were preparing to leave again. Charles wanted to drive, but Angela put up a fight. It was the shock—without him having to say a word, she'd put it together herself. Frank Dawdle, her beloved boss, had killed Leo Bernard, killed Dušan Masković, and walked off with three million dollars of the U.S. government's money.

The most damning piece of evidence came from her call to Vienna. The hard drive of Dawdle's computer was missing. Based on power usage, the in-house computer expert believed it had been removed sometime Friday morning, just before Frank and Leo departed for Slovenia.

Despite this, she clung to a new, hopeful theory: The Slovenes were responsible. Frank might have taken his hard drive, but he would only have done so under coercion. His old SOVA buddies were threatening him.

When they met with Bogdan Krizan, the local SOVA head, she glared across the Hotel Slovenia table while the old man gobbled a plate of fried calamari and explained that he'd spent Friday night with Frank Dawdle, drinking in his room.

"What do you mean—you visited him?" she said. "Didn't you have work to do?"

Krizan paused over his food, holding his fork loosely. He had an angular face that seemed to expand when he shrugged in his exaggerated Balkan manner. "We're old friends, Miss Yates. Old spies. Drinking together until the early morning is what we do. Besides, I'd heard about Charlotte. I offered sympathy in a bottle."

"Charlotte?" asked Charles.

"His wife," Krizan said, then corrected: "*Ex*-wife."

Angela nodded. "She left him about six months ago. He took it pretty hard."

"Tragic," said Krizan.

To Charles, the picture was nearly complete. "What did he tell you about his visit here?"

"Nothing. I asked, of course, many times. But he'd only wink at me. Now, I'm beginning to wish he'd trusted me."

"Me, too."

"Is he in trouble?" Krizan said this without any visible worry.

Charles shook his head. Angela's cell phone rang, and she left the table.

"There's a bitter woman," said Krizan, nodding at her backside. "You know what Frank calls her?"

Charles didn't.

"My blue-eyed wonder." He grinned. "Lovely man, but he wouldn't know a lesbian if she punched him in the nose."

Charles leaned closer as Krizan dug into his calamari. "You can't think of anything else?"

"It's hard when you won't tell me what this is about," he said, then chewed. "But no. He seemed very normal to me."

Near the door, Angela pressed a palm against one ear so she could better hear the caller. Charles got up and shook Krizan's hand. "Thanks for your help."

"If Frank *is* in trouble," said Krizan, holding on to him a moment longer than was polite, "then I hope you'll be fair with him. He's put in a lot of good years for your country. If he's slipped up in the autumn of his life, then who's to blame him?" That exaggerated shrug returned, and he let Charles go. "We can't keep to perfection one hundred percent of the time. None of us are God."

Charles left Krizan to his philosophizing and reached Angela as she hung up, her face red.

"What is it?"

"That was Max."

"Who?"

"He's the embassy night clerk. In Vienna. On Thursday night, one of Frank's informers sent in information about a Russian we're watching. Big oligarch. Roman Ugrimov."

Charles knew about Ugrimov—a businessman who'd left Russia to save his skin, but kept influential contacts there as he spread his diversified portfolio around the world. "What kind of information?"

"The blackmail kind." She paused. "He's a pedophile."

"Might be a coincidence," Charles said as they left the restaurant, entering the long socialist-mauve lobby, where three SOVA agents stood around, watching out for their boss.

"Maybe. But yesterday Ugrimov moved into his new house. In Venice."

Again, Charles stopped, and Angela had to walk back to him. Staring at the bright lobby windows, the final pieces fitted together. He said, "That's just across the water. With a boat, it's ideal."

"I suppose, but—"

"What does someone with three million dollars in stolen money need most?" Charles cut in. "He needs a new name. A man with Roman Ugrimov's connections could easily supply papers. If persuaded."

She didn't answer, only stared at him.

"One more call," he said. "Get someone to check with the harbormasters in Venice. Find out if any boats were abandoned in the last two days."

They waited for the callback in a central café that had yet to adjust to the postcommunist foreigners who now shared their thirty-mile coastline. Behind the zinc counter a heavy matron in a coffee-and-beer-splattered apron served Laško Pivo on tap to underpaid dockworkers. The woman seemed annoyed by Angela's request for a cappuccino, and when it arrived it turned out to be a too-sweet instant mix. Charles convinced her to just drink it, then asked why she hadn't told him that Frank's wife had walked out on him.

She took another sip and made a face. "Lots of people get divorced."

"It's one of the most stressful things there is," he said. "Divorces change people. Often, they get an urge to start again at zero and redo their lives, but better." He rubbed his nose. "Maybe Frank decided he should've been working for the other side all along."

"There is no other side anymore."

"Sure there is. Himself."

She didn't seem convinced of anything yet. Her phone rang, and as she listened she shook her head in anger—at Frank, at Charles, at herself. Rome station told her that on Sunday morning a boat with Dubrovnik registration tags had been found floating just beyond the Lido's docks. "They say there's blood inside," the station chief explained.

After she'd hung up, Charles offered to drive—he didn't want her Austrian habits slowing them down. In reply, Angela showed him her stiff middle finger.

He won out in the end, though, because once they were among the tangled hills of the upper peninsula, she started to cry. He got her to pull over, and they switched seats. Near the Italian border, she tried to explain away her hysterical behavior.

"It's hard. You work years teaching yourself to trust a few people. Not many, but just enough to get by. And once you do trust them, there's no going back. There can't be. Because how else can you do your job?"

Charles let that sit without replying, but wondered if this was his own problem. The idea of trusting anyone besides the man who called him with assignments had long ago been proven untenable. Maybe the human body just couldn't take that level of suspicion.

After showing their passports and crossing into Italy, he took out his cell phone and dialed. He talked a moment to Grainger and repeated back the information he'd received: "Scuola Vecchia della Misericordia. Third door."

"What was that?" Angela asked when he hung up.

He dialed a second number. After a few rings, Bogdan Krizan warily said, "Da?"

"Go to the docks across from the Hotel Slovenia. Number forty-seven. In the water you'll find a Bosnian Serb named Dušan Masković. You've got that?"

Krizan breathed heavily. "This is about Frank?"

Charles hung up.

5

It took three hours to reach Venice and hire a water-taxi—a motoscafo. By five thirty they were at the Lido docks. A sulking young Carabiniere with a wishful mustache was waiting by the abandoned motorboat—the Venetians had been told to expect visitors, but to not set up a welcome party. He raised the red police tape for them, but didn't follow them aboard. It was all there—the Dubrovnik registration papers, the filthy cabin littered with spare engine parts, and, in one corner, a brown splash of sun-dried blood.

They didn't spend long on it. The only things Frank Dawdle had left in that boat were his fingerprints and the chronology of the killing. Standing in the middle of the cabin, Charles held out two fingers in an imitation pistol. "Shoots him here, then drags him out." He squatted to indicate where the oil on the floor had been smeared, with faint traces of blood. "Maybe he tied that metal tubing to him on the boat, or maybe in the water. It doesn't matter."

"No," said Angela, eyeing him. "It doesn't."

They found no shell casings. It was possible the casings had fallen into Portorož Bay, but it was also possible that Frank had followed Company procedure and collected them, even though he'd left his prints. Panic, maybe, but that, too, didn't matter.

They thanked the Carabiniere, who muttered "Prego" while staring at Angela's breasts, then found the motoscafo driver waiting on the dock with an unlit cigarette between his lips. Behind him, the sun was low. He informed them that the meter was still running, and it had passed 150,000 lire. He seemed very pleased when neither passenger made a fuss.

It took another twenty minutes to ride back up the Grand Canal, the bumpy path taking them up to the Cannaregio district, where the Russian businessman, Roman Ugrimov, had just moved in. "He's into everything," Angela explained. "Russian utilities, Austrian land development—even a South African gold mine."

He squinted in the hot breeze at a passing vaporetto full of tourists. "Moved to Vienna two years ago, didn't he?"

"That's when we started investigating. Lots of dirt, but nothing sticks."

"Ugrimov's security is tight?"

"Unbelievable. Frank wanted evidence of his pedophilia. He travels with a thirteen-year-old niece. But she's no niece. We're sure of that."

"How do you get dirt on him?"

Angela gripped the edge of the rocking boat to keep balanced. "Frank found a source. He really is quite good at his job."

"That's what worries me."

He paid the driver once they'd reached the vaporetto stop at Ca' d'Oro, tipping him handsomely, and they broke through crowds of milling tourists to reach the maze of empty backstreets. Finally, after some guesswork, they found the open area—not quite a square—of Rio Terà Barba Frutariol.

Roman Ugrimov's palazzo was a dilapidated but ornate corner building that rose up high. It opened onto Barba Frutariol, but the long, covered terrace that Angela gazed at, shielding her eyes with a hand, wrapped around to a side street. "Impressive," she said.

"A lot of ex-KGB live in impressive houses."

"KGB?" She stared at him. "You already know about this guy. How?"

Charles touched the envelope of Dexedrine in his pocket for comfort. "I hear things."

"Oh. I don't have clearance."

Charles didn't bother answering.

"You want to run this, then?"

"I'd rather you did. I don't carry a Company ID."

"Curiouser and curiouser," Angela said as she rang the front bell.

She showed her State Department ID to a bald, cliché-ridden bodyguard with a wired earplug and asked to speak with Roman Ugrimov. The large man spoke Russian into his lapel, listened to an answer, then walked them up a dim, steep stairwell of worn stone. At the top, he unlocked a heavy wooden door.

Ugrimov's apartment seemed to have been flown in direct from Manhattan: shimmering wood floors, modern designer furniture, plasma television, and double-paned sliding doors leading to a long terrace that overlooked an evening panorama of Venetian rooftops to the Grand Canal. Even Charles had to admit it was breathtaking.

Ugrimov himself was seated at a steel table in a high-backed chair, reading from a notebook computer. He smiled at them, feigning surprise, and got up with an outstretched hand. "The first visitors to my new home," he said in easy English. "Welcome."

He was tall, fiftyish, with wavy gray hair and a bright smile. Despite heavy eyes that matched Charles's, he had a youthful vitality about him.

After the introductions, he led them to the overdesigned sofas. "Now, please. Tell me what I can do for my American friends."

Angela handed over her photograph of Frank Dawdle. Ugrimov slipped on some wide Ralph Lauren bifocals and tilted it in the failing evening light. "Who's this supposed to be?"

"He works for the American government," said Angela.

"CIA, too?"

"We're just embassy staff. He's been missing three days."

"Oh." Ugrimov handed back the photo. "That must be troubling."

"It is," Angela said. "You're sure he hasn't come to see you?"

"Nikolai," said Ugrimov, and in Russian asked, "Have we had any visitors?"

The bodyguard rolled out his lower lip and shook his head.

Ugrimov shrugged. "Nothing, I'm afraid. Perhaps you can tell me why you think he would come here. I don't know this man, do I?"

Charles said, "He was looking into your life just before he disappeared."

"Oh," the Russian said again. He raised a finger. "You're telling me that someone at the American embassy in Vienna has been looking into my life and works?"

"You'd be insulted if they didn't," said Charles.

Ugrimov grinned. "Okay. Let me offer some drinks. Or are you on the job?"

To Charles's annoyance, Angela said, "We're on the job," and stood. She handed over a business card. "If Mr. Dawdle does get in contact with you, then please call me."

"I'll be sure to do that." He turned to Charles. "Do svidaniya."

Charles repeated the Russian farewell back to him.

Once they were down the steps and in the dark street, the air moist and still warm, Angela yawned again and said, "What was that?"

"What?"

"How'd he know you spoke Russian?"

"I'm telling you, I need a new name." Charles looked up the length of the street. "The Russian community's not so big."

"Not so small either," said Angela. "What're you looking for?"

"There." He didn't point, only nodded at a small sign at the corner indicating an osteria. "Let's take a long walk around to there. Eat and watch."

"You don't trust him?"

"A man like that—he'd never admit it if Dawdle came to him."

"Watch if you want. I need some sleep."

"How about a pill?"

"First one's free?" she said, then winked and stifled another yawn. "I have embassy drug tests to contend with."

"Then at least leave me one of your cigarettes."

"When did you start smoking?"

"I'm in the midst of quitting."

She tapped one out for him, but before handing it over said, "Is it the drugs that do it to you? Or the job?"

"Do what?"

"Maybe it's all the names." She handed over the cigarette. "Maybe that's what's made you so cold. When you were Milo, you were a different person."

He blinked at her, thinking, but no reply came to him.

6

He spent the first part of his night watch at the little osteria, looking down Barba Frutariol, eating a dinner of cicchetti—small portions of seafood and grilled vegetables—and washing it down with a delicious Chianti. The bartender tried to start a conversation, but Charles preferred silence, so when the man rattled on about George Michael, "certainly the greatest singer in the world," he didn't bother contradicting or agreeing. The man's banter became dull background noise.

Someone had left behind a copy of the day's *Herald Tribune,* and he mused over the stories for a while, in particular a statement by U.S. Secretary of Defense Donald Rumsfeld that "according to some estimates we cannot track $2.3 trillion in transactions." A certain Senator Nathan Irwin from Minnesota, breaking party ties, called it "a damned disgrace." Not even that could hold his attention, though, and he folded the paper and put it aside.

He wasn't thinking about suicide, but about the Bigger Voice, that thing his mother used to discuss with him during her occasional nocturnal visits in the seventies, when he was a child in North Carolina. "Look at everyone," she told him, "and see what guides them. Little voices—television, politicians, priests, money. Those are the little voices, and they blot out the one big voice we all have. But listen to me—the little voices mean nothing. All they do is deceive. You understand?"

He'd been too young to understand, and too old to admit his ignorance. Her visits never lasted long enough for her to explain it well enough. He was always tired when she arrived in the middle of the night to rap on his window and carry him out to the nearby park.

"I am your mom, but you won't call me mom. I won't let you be oppressed, and I won't let you oppress me with that word. You won't even call me Ellen—that's my slave name. My liberation name is Elsa. Can you say that?"

"Elsa."

"Excellent."

His early childhood was punctuated by these dreams—because that's how they felt to him: dreams of a ghost-mother's visitations with her brief lesson plans. In a year, she might come three or four times; when he was eight, she came nightly for an entire week and focused her lessons on his liberation. She explained that when he was a little older—twelve or thirteen—she would take him away with her, because by then he would be able to understand the doctrine of total war. Against whom? Against the little voices. Though he understood so little, he was excited by the thought of disappearing into the night with her. But he never did. After that intense week, the dreams never returned, and only much later would he learn that she'd died before she could bring him into the fold. In a German prison. By suicide.

Was that the Bigger Voice? The voice that spoke from the stone walls of Stuttgart's Stammheim Prison, convincing her to remove her prison pants, tie one leg to the bars on her door, the other to her neck, and then sit down with all the enthusiasm of a zealot?

He wondered if she could have done that had she kept her real name. Could she have done it if she had still called herself a mother? He wondered if he could have survived these last years, or chosen so casually to end his life, if he had kept hold of his own name.

There he was again, back to thoughts of suicide.

When the restaurant closed at ten, he again checked Ugrimov's front door, then jogged westward, sometimes frustrated by dead ends, until he'd reached the waterside porticos of the Scuola Vecchia della Misericordia. The third door, Grainger had said, so he counted to three, then, despite his stomach again acting up, lay flat on the cobblestones to reach over the edge of the walkway, down toward the rancid-smelling canal.

Unable to see, he had to do it by feel, touching stones until he felt the one that was different from the others. By now, these selected cubbyholes were over fifty years old, having been added to the architecture of postwar Europe by the members of the Pond, a CIA pre-cursor.

Remarkable foresight. Many had been discovered, while others had broken open on their own from poor workmanship, but occasionally the surviving ones proved invaluable. He closed his eyes to help his sense of touch. On the bottom edge of the stone was a latch; he pulled it, and the stone separated into his hand. He placed the lid beside himself and reached inside the exposed hole to find a weighty plastic-wrapped object, sealed airtight. He took it out, and in the moonlight ripped it open. Inside lay a Walther P99 with two clips of ammunition, all like new.

He replaced the stone's cover, returned to Barba Frutariol, and worked his way around the area, circling the palazzo as he wandered dark side streets, always returning at different angles to watch the front door or peer up to the lights along Roman Ugrimov's terrace. Sometimes he spotted figures up there—Ugrimov, his guards, and a young girl with long, straight brown hair. The "niece." But only the guards passed through the front door, returning with groceries, bottles of wine and liquor, and, once, a wooden humidor. After midnight he heard music wafting down—opera—and was surprised by the choice.

While the mewing cats ignored him, a total of three drunks tried to become his friend that night. Silence worked on all except the third, who put his arm around Charles's shoulder and talked in four languages, trying to find the one that would make him answer. In a swift and unexpected surge of emotion, Charles thrust his elbow into the man's ribs, cupped a hand over his mouth, and punched him twice, hard, on the back of his head.

With the first hit, the man gurgled; with the second, he passed out. Charles held the limp man a few seconds, hating himself, then dragged him down the street, across an arched bridge spanning the Rio dei Santi Apostoli, and hid the drunk in an alley.

Balance—that word returned to him as he crossed the bridge again, trembling. Without balance, a life is no longer worth the effort.

He'd been doing his particular job for six—no, *seven*—years, floating unmoored from city to city, engaged by transatlantic phone calls from a man he hadn't seen in two years. The phone itself was his master. Weeks sometimes passed without work, and in those periods he slept and drank heavily, but when he was on the job there was no way to stop the brutal forward movement. He had to suck down whatever stimulants would keep him in motion, because the job had never been about keeping Charles Alexander in good health. The job was only about the quiet, anonymous maintenance of the kindly named "sphere of influence," Charles Alexander and others like him be damned.

Angela had said, "There is no other side anymore," but there was. The other side was multifaceted: Russian mafias, Chinese industrialization, loose nukes, and even the vocal Muslims camped in Afghanistan who were trying to pry Washington's fingers off the oil-soaked Middle East. As Grainger would put it, anyone who could not be embraced or absorbed by the empire was anathema and had to be dealt with, like barbarians at the gates. That was when Charles Alexander's phone would ring.

He wondered how many bodies padded the murky floor of these canals, and the thought of joining them was, if nothing else, a comfort. *It is because of death that death means nothing; it's because of death that life means nothing.*

Finish the job, he thought. *Don't go out in failure. And then . . .*

No more planes and border guards and customs people; no more looking over your shoulder.

By five, it was decided. The prescient glow before dawn lit the sky, and he dry-swallowed two more Dexedrine. The jitters returned. He remembered his mother and her dreams of a utopia with only big voices. What would she think of him? He knew: She would want to beat him senseless. He'd spent his entire adult life working for the procurers and manufacturers of those insidious little voices.

When, at nine thirty, the George Michael fan unlocked the osteria again, Charles was surprised to find himself still breathing. He ordered two espressos and waited patiently by the window while the man cooked up a pancetta, egg, garlic, oil, and linguine mix for his dour, sickly customer. It was delicious, but halfway through his plate he stopped, peering out the window.

Three people were approaching the palazzo. The bodyguard he'd seen yesterday—Nikolai—and, close behind, a very pregnant woman with an older man. That older man was Frank Dawdle.

He dialed his cell phone.

"Yeah?" said Angela.

"He's here."

Charles pocketed the phone and laid down money. The bartender, serving an old couple, looked angry. "You don't like the breakfast?"

"Leave it out," Charles said. "I'll finish it in a minute."

By the time Angela arrived, her hair damp from an interrupted shower, the visitors had been inside the palazzo for twelve minutes. There were four tourists along the length of the street, and he hoped they would clear out soon. "You have a gun?" Charles asked as he took out his Walther.

Angela pulled back her jacket to show off a SIG Sauer in a shoulder holster.

"Keep it there. If someone has to get shot, I better do it. I can disappear; you can't."

"So you're watching out for me."

"Yeah, Angela. I am watching out for you."

She pursed her lips. "You're also afraid I won't be able to shoot him." Her gaze dropped to his trembling gun hand. "But I'm not sure you'll even be able to shoot straight."

He squeezed the Walther until the shaking lessened. "I'll do fine. You get over there," he said, pointing at a doorway just beyond, and opposite, the palazzo's entrance. "He'll be boxed in. He comes out, we make the arrest. Simple."

"Simple," she replied curtly, then walked to her assigned doorway as the tourists, thankfully, left the street.

Once she was out of sight, he reexamined his hand. She was right, of course. Angela Yates usually was. He couldn't go on like this, and he wouldn't. It was a miserable job; it was a miserable life.

The palazzo's front door opened.

Bald Nikolai opened it, but remained inside, his tailored jacket arm holding the bloated wooden door so that the pregnant woman—who Charles could now see was very beautiful, her bright green eyes flashing across the square—could step over the threshold and onto the cobbles. Then came Dawdle, touching her elbow. He looked every one of his sixty-two years, and more.

The bodyguard closed the door behind them, and the woman turned to say something to Dawdle, but Dawdle didn't answer. He was looking at Angela, who had emerged from her doorway and was running in his direction. "Frank!" she shouted.

Charles had missed his cue. He began running, too, the Walther in his hand.

A man's voice shouted from the sky in easy English: "*And her I love, you bastard!*" Then a rising wail, like a steam-engine whistle, filled the air.

Unlike the other three people in the street, Charles didn't look up. Distractions, he knew, are usually just that. He hurtled forward. The pregnant woman, eyes aloft, screamed and stepped back. Frank Dawdle was stuck to the ground. Angela's flared jacket dropped as she halted and opened her mouth, but made no sound. Beside the pregnant woman, something pink hit the earth. It was 10:27 A.M.

He stumbled to a stop. Perhaps it was a bomb. But bombs weren't pink, and they didn't hit like that. They exploded or crashed into the ground with hard noises. This pink thing hit with a soft, wretched thump. That's when he knew it was a body. On one side, spread among the splash of blood on the cobblestones, he saw a scatter of long hair—it was the pretty girl he'd spotted on the terrace last night.

He looked up, but the terrace was again empty. The pregnant woman screamed, tripped, and fell backward.

Frank Dawdle produced a pistol and shot wildly three times, the sound echoing off the stones, then turned and ran. Angela bolted after him, shouting, "Stop! Frank!"

Charles Alexander was trained to follow through with actions even when faced with the unpredictable, but what he saw—the falling girl, the shots, the fleeing man—each thing seemed only to confuse him more.

How did the pregnant woman fit into this?

His breathing was suddenly difficult, but he reached her. She kept screaming. Red face, eyes rolling. Her words were a garbled mess.

His chest really did feel strange, so he sat heavily on the ground beside her. That's when he noticed all the blood. Not the girl's—she was on the other side of the hysterical woman—but his own. He could see that now. It pumped a red blossom into his shirt.

How about that? He was exhausted. Red rivulets filled the spaces between the cobblestones. *I'm dead.* Off to the left, Angela ran after the dwindling form of Frank Dawdle.

Amid the indecipherable noises coming from the pregnant woman, he heard one clear phrase: *"I'm in labor!"*

He blinked at her, wanting to say, *But I'm dying, I can't help you.* Then he read the desperation in her sweaty face. She really did want to stay alive. Why?

"I need a doctor!" the woman shouted.

"I—" he began, and looked around. Angela and Dawdle had disappeared; they were just distant footfalls around a far corner.

"Get a fucking doctor!" the woman screamed, close to his ear. From around that far corner he heard the three short cracks of Angela's SIG Sauer.

He took out his telephone. The woman was terrified, so he whispered, "It'll be all right," and dialed 118, the Italian medical emergency number. In stilted, too-quiet Italian from just one painful lung, he explained that a woman on the Rio Terà Barba Frutariol was having a baby. Help was promised. He hung up. His blood was no longer a network of rivulets on the ground; it formed an elongated pool.

The woman was calmer now, but she still gasped for breath. She looked desperate. When he gripped her hand, she squeezed back with unexpected strength. Over her heaving belly, he looked at the dead girl in pink. In the distance, Angela reappeared as a small form, hunched, walking like a drunk.

"Who the hell are you?" the pregnant woman finally managed.

"What?"

She took a moment to regulate her breaths, gritted her teeth. "You've got a gun."

The Walther was still in his other hand. He released it; it clattered to the ground as a red haze filled his vision.

"What," she said, then exhaled through pursed lips, blowing three times. "What the hell are you?"

He choked on his words, so he paused and squeezed her hand tighter. He tried again. "I'm a Tourist," he said, though as he blacked out on the cobblestones he knew that he no longer was.

Part One

PROBLEMS OF THE INTERNATIONAL TOURIST TRADE

WEDNESDAY, JULY 4 TO THURSDAY, JULY 19, 2007

1

The Tiger. It was the kind of moniker that worked well in Southeast Asia, or India, which was why the Company long assumed the assassin was Asian. Only after 2003, when those few photos trickled in and were verified, did everyone realize he was of European descent. Which raised the question: Why "the Tiger"?

Company psychologists, unsurprisingly, disagreed. The one remaining Freudian claimed there was a sexual dysfunction the assassin was trying to hide. Another felt it referenced the Chinese "tiger boys" myth, concerning boys who morphed into tigers when they entered the forest. A New Mexico analyst put forth her own theory that it came from the Native American tiger-symbol, meaning "confidence, spontaneity, and strength." To which the Freudian asked in a terse memo, "When did the tiger become indigenous to North America?"

Milo Weaver didn't care. The Tiger, who was now

traveling under the name Samuel Roth (Israeli passport #6173882, b. 6/19/66), had arrived in the United States from Mexico City, landing in Dallas, and Milo had spent the last three nights on his trail, camped in a rental Chevy picked up from Dallas International. Little clues, mere nuances, had kept him moving eastward and south to the fringes of battered New Orleans, then winding north through Mississippi until late last night, near Fayette, when Tom Grainger called from New York. "Just came over the wire, buddy. They've got a Samuel Roth in Blackdale, Tennessee—domestic abuse arrest."

"Domestic abuse? Can't be him."

"Description fits."

"Okay." Milo searched the cola-stained map flopping in the warm evening wind. He found Blackdale, a tiny speck. "Let them know I'm coming. Tell them to put him in solitary. If they've got solitary."

By the time he rolled into Blackdale that Independence Day morning, his travel companions were three days' worth of crumpled McDonald's cups and bags, highway toll receipts, candy wrappers, and two empty Smirnoff bottles—but no cigarette butts; he'd at least kept that promise to his wife. In his overstuffed wallet he'd collected more receipts that charted his path: dinner at a Dallas-area Fuddruckers, Louisiana barbecue, motels in Sulphur, LA, and Brookhaven, MS, and a stack of gas station receipts charged to his Company card.

Milo shouldn't have liked Blackdale. It was outside his comfortable beat of early twenty-first-century metropolises. Lost in the flag-draped kudzu wasteland of

Hardeman County, between the Elvisology of Memphis and the Tennessee River's tri-border intersection with Mississippi and Alabama, Blackdale didn't look promising. Worse, it was as he drove into town that he realized there was no way he could make his daughter's July Fourth talent show that afternoon back in Brooklyn.

Yet he did like Blackdale and its sheriff, Manny Wilcox. The sweating, overweight officer of the law showed surprising hospitality to someone from the most-despised profession, and didn't ask a thing about jurisdiction or whose business their prisoner really was. That helped Milo's mood. The too-sweet lemonade brought in by a mustached deputy named Leslie also helped. The station had a huge supply on tap in orange ten-gallon coolers, prepared by Wilcox's wife, Eileen. It was just what Milo's hangover had been pleading for.

Manny Wilcox wiped perspiration off his temple. "I will have to get your signature, understand."

"I'd expect nothing less," Milo said. "Maybe you can tell me how you caught him."

Wilcox lifted his glass to stare at the condensation, then sniffed. Milo hadn't showered in two days; the proof was all over the sheriff's face. "Wasn't us. His girl—Kathy Hendrickson. A N'Orleans working girl. Apparently she didn't like his kind of lovemaking. Called 911. Said the man was a killer. Was beating on her."

"Just like that?"

"Just like that. Picked him up late last night. I guess that's how you guys got it, from the 911 dispatch. The hooker had a few bruises, a bloody lip. They were fresh. Verified his name with the passport. Israeli. Then we found another passport in his car. *Eye*-talian."

"Fabio Lanzetti," said Milo.

Wilcox opened his calloused hands. "There you go. We'd just squeezed him into the cell when your people called us."

It was about two inches beyond belief. Six years ago, unbalanced and living under a different name, Milo had first run into the Tiger in Amsterdam. Over the ensuing six years, the man had been spotted and lost in Italy, Germany, the Arab Emirates, Afghanistan, and Israel. Now, he'd been trapped in a last-chance motel near the Mississippi border, turned in by a Louisiana prostitute.

"Nothing more?" he asked the sheriff. "No one else tipped you off? Just the woman?"

The flesh under Wilcox's chin vibrated. "That's it. But this guy, Sam Roth . . . is that even his real name?"

Milo decided that the sheriff deserved something for his hospitality. "Manny, we're not sure *what* his name is. Each time he pops up on our radar, it's different. But his girlfriend might know something. Where's she now?"

The sheriff toyed with his damp glass, embarrassed. "Back at the motel. Had no cause to keep hold of her."

"I'll want her, too."

"Leslie can pick her up," Wilcox assured him. "But tell me—your chief said something about this—is that boy really called the Tiger?"

"If it's who we think it is, yes. That's what he's called."

Wilcox grunted his amusement. "Not much of a tiger

now. Pussycat, more like. He walks funny, too, kind of weak."

Milo finished his lemonade, and Wilcox offered more. He could see how the police got hooked on Mrs. Wilcox's homebrew. "Don't be fooled, Sheriff. Remember last year, in France?"

"Their president?"

"Foreign minister. And in Germany there was the head of an Islamist group."

"A terrorist?"

"Religious leader. His car exploded with him in it. And in London that businessman—"

"The one who bought the airline!" Wilcox shouted, happy to know at least this one. "Don't tell me this joker killed him, too. *Three* people?"

"Those are the three from last year we can definitely pin on him. He's been in business at least a decade." When the sheriff's brows rose, Milo knew he'd shared enough. No need to terrify the man. "But like I said, Sheriff, I need to talk to him to be sure."

Wilcox rapped his knuckles on his desk, hard enough to shake the computer monitor. "Well, then. Let's get you talking."

2

The sheriff had moved three drunks and two spousal abusers to the group cell, leaving Samuel Roth alone in a small cinder-block room with a steel door and no window. Milo peered through the door's barred hatch. A fluorescent tube burned from the ceiling, illuminating the thin cot and aluminum toilet.

To call his search for the Tiger obsessive would have been, according to Grainger, an understatement. In 2001, soon after he'd recovered from his bullet wounds and retired from Tourism, Milo decided that while his coworkers devoted themselves to finding the Most Famous Muslim in the World somewhere in Afghanistan, he would spend his time on terrorism's more surgical arms. Terrorist acts, by definition, were blunt and messy. But when someone like bin Laden or al-Zarqawi needed a specific person taken out, he, like the rest of the world, went to the professionals. In the assassination business, there were few better than the Tiger.

So over the last six years, from his twenty-second-floor cubicle in the Company office on the Avenue of the Americas, he'd tracked this one man through the cities of the world, but never close enough for an arrest.

Now, here he was, the man from that embarrassingly meager file Milo knew so well, sitting comfortably on a cot, his back to the wall and his orange-clad legs stretched out, crossed at the ankles. Samuel Roth, or Hamad al-Abari, or Fabio Lanzetti—or five other names they knew of. The assassin didn't check to see who was peering in at him; he left his arms knotted over his chest as Milo entered.

"Samuel," Milo said as a deputy locked the door behind him. He didn't approach, just waited for the man to look at him.

Even in this light, with its harsh shadows and the way it yellowed his skin, Roth's face recalled the three other photographs back at the office. One from Abu Dhabi, as al-Abari, his features half obscured by a white turban. A second from Milan, as Lanzetti, at a café along the Corso Sempione, talking with a red-bearded man they'd never been able to identify. The third was CCTV footage from outside a mosque in Frankfurt, where he'd planted a bomb under a black Mercedes-Benz. Each remembered image matched these heavy brows and gaunt cheeks, the pitch eyes and high, narrow forehead. Sometimes a mustache or beard hid aspects of the face, but now his only mask was a three-day beard that grew to the top of his cheekbones. His skin was splotchy in this light, peeling from an old sunburn.

Milo remained beside the door. "Samuel Roth—that's the name we'll use for now. It's easy to pronounce."

Roth only blinked in reply.

"You know why I'm here. It has nothing to do with your problems with women. I want to know why you're in the United States."

"Как вас зовут, мудаки?" said Roth.

Milo grimaced. He was going to have to go through the motions. At least a change of language would hide their talk from these Tennessee boys. In Russian, he answered, "I'm Milo Weaver, of the Central Intelligence Agency."

Samuel Roth looked as if that were the funniest name he had ever heard.

"What?"

"Sorry," Roth said in fluent English. He raised a hand. "Even after all this, I still didn't expect it to work." He had the flat, irregular accent of someone who'd absorbed too many.

"What didn't you expect to work?"

"I'm lucky I even remember you. I forget a lot of things these days."

"If you don't answer my questions, I'll hurt you. I am authorized."

The prisoner's eyes widened; they were bloodshot and tired.

"There's only one reason you'd risk entering the country. Who are you supposed to kill?"

Roth chewed the inside of his cheek, then spoke in a laconic tone: "Maybe you, Company man."

"We were tracking you since Barcelona—you know that? To Mexico, then Dallas, and that rented car to New Orleans where you picked up your girlfriend. Maybe you just wanted to know if she survived Katrina. You switched to your Italian passport—Fabio Lanzetti—before switching back in Mississippi. Changing names is a nice trick, but it's not foolproof."

Roth cocked his head. "You'd know that, wouldn't you?"

"Would I?"

Samuel Roth wiped his dry lips with his fingers, stifling a cough. When he spoke, he sounded congested. "I've heard a lot about you. Milo Weaver—a.k.a. many other names. Alexander." He pointed at Milo. "That's the name I know best. Charles Alexander."

"No idea what you're talking about," Milo said as nonchalantly as he could manage.

"You've got a long history," Roth continued. "An interesting one. You were a Tourist."

A shrug. "Everyone likes a vacation."

"Remember 2001? Before those Muslims ruined business. Amsterdam. Back then, I only worried about people like you, people who work for governments, ruining my business. These days . . ." He shook his head.

Milo remembered 2001 better than most years. "I've never been to Amsterdam," he lied.

"You're curious, Milo Weaver. I've seen files on lots of people, but you . . . there's no *center* to your history."

"Center?" Milo moved two steps closer, an arm's length from the prisoner.

Roth's lids drooped over his bloodshot eyes. "There's no *motivation* connecting the events of your past."

"Sure there is. Fast cars and girls. Isn't that your motivation?"

Samuel Roth seemed to like that. He wiped his mouth again to cover a large grin; above his sunburned cheeks his eyes looked very wet, sick. "Well, you're certainly not motivated by your own well-being, or else you'd be somewhere else. Moscow, perhaps, where they take care of their agents. At least, where agents know how to take care of themselves."

"Is that what you are? Russian?"

Roth ignored that. "Maybe you just want to be on the winning side. Some people, they like to bend with history. But history's tricky. Today's monolith is tomorrow's pile of rocks. No." He shook his head. "That's not it. I think you're loyal to your family now. That would make sense. Your wife and daughter. Tina and . . . Stephanie, is it?"

Involuntarily, Milo shot out a hand and gripped Roth's shirt at the buttons, lifting him from the cot. This close, he could see that his dry, peeling face was riddled with pink sores. This was not sunburn. With his other hand, he squeezed Roth's jaw to hold his face still. There was rot in the man's breath. "No need to bring them into this," Milo said, then let go. When Roth fell back onto the cot, his head knocked against the wall.

How had this man turned the interrogation around?

"Just trying to make conversation," said Roth, rubbing the back of his skull. "That's why I'm here, you know. To see you."

Instead of questioning that, Milo went for the door. He could at least squelch Roth's one voiced desire by removing himself from the room.

"Where are you going?"

Good—he sounded worried. Milo tapped the door, and one of the deputies started working the lock.

"Wait!" called Roth. "I have information!"

Milo jerked the door open as Roth again called, "*Wait!*" He didn't slow down. He left the room and kept moving as the deputy pushed the steel door shut.

3

The sultry noontime heat swallowed him as he fooled with the new Company-issue Nokia he was still learning to master, finally finding the number. Between a parked blue-and-white and the dead shrubs around the station, he watched as storm clouds began to fill the sky. Grainger answered with a sharp "What *is* it?"

Tom Grainger sounded the kind of irate people are when they've been abruptly woken, but it was nearly noon. "I'm verifying it, Tom. It's him."

"Good. I don't suppose he's talking, is he?"

"Not really. But he is trying to piss me off. He's seen a file on me. Knows about Tina and Stef."

"Jesus. How'd he get that?"

"There's a girlfriend. She might know something. They're bringing her in now." He paused. "But he's sick, Tom. Really sick. I'm not sure he could make a journey."

"What's he got?"

"Don't know yet."

When Grainger sighed, Milo imagined him kicking back in his Aeron chair, gazing out his window across the Manhattan skyline. Faced with the dusty pale-brick buildings along Blackdale's main street—half of them out of business but covered with Independence Day flags—Milo was suddenly jealous. Grainger said, "Just so you know—you've got one hour to make him talk."

"Don't tell me."

"I'm telling you. Some jackass at Langley sent an e-mail off the open server. I've spent the last half hour fending off Homeland with make-believe. If I hear the word 'jurisdiction' one more time, I'll have a fit."

Milo stepped back as a deputy got into the police car and started it up. He returned to the station's glass double doors. "My hopes are with the girlfriend. Whatever game he's playing, he won't play by my rules until I have something on him. Or if he's under duress."

"Can you put it to him there?"

Milo considered this as the police car left and another parked in its place. The sheriff might turn a blind eye to rough treatment, but he wasn't sure about the deputies. There was something wide-eyed about them. "I'll see once the girl's here."

"If Homeland hadn't been shouting at me all morning, I'd tell you to break him out and bundle him for shipment. But we don't have a choice."

"You don't think they'll share him?"

His chief grunted. "It's *me* who doesn't want to

share. Be a good boy and let them have him, but whatever he says to you is only for us. Okay?"

"Sure." Milo noticed that the mustached deputy getting out of the car was Leslie, the one who'd been sent to pick up Kathy Hendrickson. He was alone. "Call you back," Milo said and hung up. "Where's the girl?"

Leslie held his wide-brimmed hat in his hands, nervously rotating it. "Checked out, sir. Late last night, couple hours after we released her."

"I see, Deputy. Thanks."

On the way back inside, Milo called home, knowing that at this hour no one would be there to pick up. Tina would check the messages from work once she realized he was running late. He kept it short and concise. He was sorry to miss Stephanie's performance, but didn't overplay his guilt. Besides, next week they'd all be together in Disney World, and he'd have plenty of time to make it up to his daughter. He suggested she invite Stephanie's biological father, Patrick. "And videotape it, will you? I want to see."

He found Wilcox in the break room, having a fight with the soda machine. "I thought you kept to lemonade, Manny."

Wilcox cleared his throat. "I've had it up to here with lemons." He wagged a chunky finger. "You let that slip to my wife, and I'll have your ass on a platter."

"Let's make a deal." Milo came closer. "I'll keep your wife in the dark if you give me an hour alone with your prisoner."

Wilcox straightened, head back, and peered down at him. "You're talking *alone*-alone?"

"Yes, sir."

"And you think that's a good idea?"

"Why not?"

Sheriff Wilcox scratched the back of his flabby neck; his beige collar was brown from sweat. "Well, the papers are eating you guys up. Every day there's another yokel shouting about CIA corruption. I mean, I know how to keep *my* mouth shut, but a small town like this . . ."

"Don't worry. I know what I'm doing."

The sheriff pursed his lips, deforming his big nose. "Matter of national security, is it?"

"The most national, Manny. And the most secure."

4

When Milo returned to the cell, Samuel Roth sat up as if he'd been waiting for this chat, a sudden wellspring of energy at his disposal. "Hello again," he said once the door had locked.

"Who showed you my file?"

"A friend. An ex-friend." Roth paused. "Okay, my worst enemy. He's seriously bad news."

"Someone I know?"

"*I* don't even know him. I never met him. Just his intermediary."

"So he's a client."

Roth smiled, his dry lips cracking. "Exactly. He gave me some paperwork on you. A gift, he said, for some trouble he'd put me through. He said that you were the one who ruined the Amsterdam job. He also said you were running my case. That, of course, is why I'm here."

"You're *here*," Milo said, reaching the center of the cell, "because you beat up a woman and thought she wouldn't pay you back for it."

"Is that what you really think?"

Milo didn't answer—they both knew it was an unlikely scenario.

"I'm *here*," Roth said, waving at the concrete walls, "because I wanted to talk to Milo Weaver, once known as Charles Alexander. Only you. You're the only Company man who ever actually stopped me. You've got my respect."

"In Amsterdam."

"Yes."

"That's funny."

"Is it?"

"Six years ago in Amsterdam, I was high on amphetamines. Completely strung out. I didn't know half of what I was doing."

Roth stared at him, then blinked. "Really?"

"I was suicidal. I tried to walk into your line of fire, just to finish myself off."

"Well," said Roth, considering the news. "Either I was never as good as I thought, or you're so good you could beat me blind and drunk. So . . . it stands. You have even more of my respect now. And that's a rare and wonderful thing."

"You wanted to talk to me. Why not pick up a phone?"

The assassin rocked his head from side to side. "That, as you know, is unverifiable. I would've been handed to some clerk for an hour, answering questions.

If he didn't hang up on me, he would've called Tom—Tom Grainger, right?—and then the whole department would be involved. No. I only wanted you."

"Still, there are easier ways. Cheaper ways."

"Money doesn't mean anything anymore," Roth said patiently. "Besides, it was fun. I had to give one last chase. Not so difficult a chase that you'd lose me, but not so easy that the FBI or Homeland Security would stumble across me when I arrived in Dallas. No, I had to set up a trail outside the country that you—because you've been responsible for my case these last years—would be watching. Then I had to lead you around this enormous country. I'd hoped to make it all the way to Washington, or even to your home in Brooklyn, but it wasn't to be. A lot of things weren't to be. I wanted to go *further*. I wanted to really make you work."

"Why?"

"If I had the time," Roth explained, "I'd be elusive with you, because it's a known fact that no decent intelligence operative believes anything he's told. Each agent needs to beat it out of his subject, or, better yet, discover it on his own, without the subject ever realizing he's slipped up. But, sadly, there's no time. It has to be little Blackdale, and it has to be direct, because I won't be around by tomorrow."

"Going somewhere?"

Again, that smile.

Milo wasn't ready to believe this. It was pride, of course, balking against the idea that someone had for the last three days been leading him by the nose. "And Kathy Hendrickson?"

"She only knows that I paid her well for her performance. Yes—and for her bruises. She doesn't know why. Really, she knows nothing," he said, then gasped his way into a retching cough. Once it passed, he looked at his hand. "Oh." He showed his blood-speckled palm to Milo. "Faster than I'd hoped."

"What is?"

"My death."

Milo stared at the Tiger's face, at what he'd wanted to believe were the symptoms of a difficult run through the southern states. Bloodshot eyes, fatigue, and the skin itself. That yellow pallor wasn't from the fluorescents. "Diagnosis?"

"AIDS."

"I see."

The lack of sympathy didn't faze Roth. "I talked to some doctors in Switzerland—the Hirslanden Clinic, Zürich. You can check on that if you like. Look up Hamad al-Abari. Those mountain Germans are smart. Some new procedure they've got to examine the rate of growth through the T-cell count—something like that. They can figure out when the HIV virus got in me. Five months ago, it turns out. February. That places me in Milan."

"What were you doing in Milan?"

"I met my contact. The intermediary I mentioned before. He goes by the name Jan Klausner, but he can't speak decent German or Czech. From his accent, he might be Dutch. Midforties. His red beard is the only real thing about him."

Milo remembered that file photo of Fabio Lanzetti—

Milan, the Corso Sempione, with a bearded man. "We've got a picture of you two together."

"Good start."

"He gave you a job?"

"He's been feeding me jobs for years. Actually, the first one came six years ago, not long after Amsterdam. A surprise. I worried my failure there had made the rounds, that work would dry up. But then Jan showed up. The work was irregular—one or two a year—but it paid well. His last order was for January. A job in Khartoum. Mullah Salih Ahmad."

Milo thought back. The Sudan. January.

In January, a popular radical cleric known for inflammatory pro-al-Qaeda speeches, Mullah Salih Ahmad, had disappeared. Two days later, his garroted corpse was found in his own backyard. It had been international news for about five minutes, quickly overcome by the continuing civil war in the western Darfur region, but in the Sudan it stayed brutally current, and the blame was placed on the president, Omar al-Bashir, who seldom let critics remain in the limelight, or out of jail. Demonstrations followed, met by battle-gear police with guns. In the last month, more than forty had been killed in riots.

"Who hired you?"

The energy seemed to go out of Roth, and he stared, unfocused, past his interrogator. Milo didn't bother breaking the trance, though he imagined SUVs full of Homeland Security barreling down the dusty Tennessee roads toward them.

Finally, Roth shook his head. "Sorry. The doctors call it AIDS dementia. I lose track of stuff, forget things. Can hardly walk." With effort, he swallowed. "Where were we?"

"Mullah Salih Ahmad. Who hired you to kill him?"

"Ah, yes!" Through a twitch of pain, Roth seemed pleased that he could still find that memory. "Well, I didn't know, did I? I have this contact, Jan Klausner, maybe Dutch, a red beard," he said, unaware of his repetition. "He tells me nothing about who's hiring him. He just pays the money, and that's all right by me. But then there was the Ahmad job, and Jan's master cheated me on the money. Only paid two-thirds. Klausner says it's because I didn't follow the instructions, which were to *brand* the body with some Chinese pictograms."

"Chinese?" Milo cut in. "Why Chinese?"

"Good question, but no one tells me anything. Klausner just asks why I didn't do this. After all, I did have a metalworker make the brands. Sadly, though, the Sudan is not overflowing with expert machinists, and what I got turned out to be made of aluminum. Can you imagine? When I heated them up, the pictograms just melted." He coughed again, as if his body weren't built for so many words at a time. "No Chinese—that was Klausner's excuse for his master coming up short." Another cough.

Milo reached into his jacket and took out a small flask. "Vodka."

"Thanks." The assassin took a long swig, which only made him cough more blood across his prison oranges, but he didn't let go of the flask. He raised a finger until the coughs had trickled away, then said, "I better get it out quick, no?"

"What did the pictograms say?"

"Something like: *As promised, the end.* Weird, huh?"

Milo nodded.

"I could have let it go, and I considered that. But that's bad business. If people find out I let one customer cheat me, then . . ." He wiped his bloodstained lips. "You understand."

"Of course."

Roth coughed again, less wretched this time. "Anyway, I thought for obvious reasons that it was the Chinese. They've invested billions into that country for oil; they supply the government with guns. They'd want to protect their investment. But then . . . yes. I saw the newspapers. Everyone believed the president had it done. He'd been harassing Ahmad for years. So I had it, right? There was Jan Klausner's master, at least for this job." He blinked a few times, and Milo feared he'd drift off again, but then he was back. "I'm an impulsive worker. In other men that spells defeat, but somewhere along the way I made it work for me. Half-second decisions are part of the job, don't you think?"

Milo didn't dispute the point.

"President al-Bashir, it turned out, was on a diplomatic trip to Cairo. So, impulsively, I flew there. Fancy villa, all the security out. But I'm the Tiger, right? I figure a way in. All the way in. I find him in his bedroom— alone, luckily. And I put the question to him: *Omar, why are you stiffing me?* But listen to me, Milo Weaver. After we've gone through about twenty minutes' rigmarole, I realize he doesn't know anything about this. Did he want Ahmad dead? Sure. The man was a pain in his ass. But did he actually order the killing?" Roth shook his head. "Sadly, no. So, like the wind, I'm gone."

He took a sip of Milo's vodka, letting it sit on his tongue before easing it down his throat. He looked at the flask. "Russian?"

"Swedish."

"It's nice."

Again, Milo waited.

After another medicinal sip, Roth said, "I thought it through again and decided to search for Jan Klausner instead. I did some research—I know people, you see. People who can help. Turns out that Jan Klausner is registered in Paris, but under the name Herbert Williams, American. I went to his address, which is of course fake, but this, I believe, is where I took my wrong turn. I must have been spotted. A week later, Jan—or Herbert—he contacted me. It's February by then. He asked me to come to Milan again to collect the rest of my money. His master had realized the error of his ways."

"So you went," said Milo, interested despite himself.

"Money is money. Or, it used to be." That grin, weary now. "It went smoothly. We met in a café—February fourteenth—and he handed me a shopping bag full of euros. He also handed me, as an apology, a file on Milo Weaver, once known as Charles Alexander. *Your nemesis,* he tells me. *This man has been after you for half a decade.*" Roth frowned. "Why would he do that, Milo? Why would he give me your file? Any idea?"

"I have no idea."

Roth bobbed his eyebrows at this mystery. "Only

later, in Switzerland, once they told me the approximate time I got infected, did I remember what happened. You see, there were metal chairs at that café. Aluminum wire. Very pretty, but at some point during our coffee, I felt a little pinch from the chair. Here." He touched the underside of his right thigh. "Poked through my pants, right into my leg. I hopped up. There was blood. Klausner," he said, shaking his head at the memory, "he ran around and waved his hands. Told the waitress that his friend—meaning me—would sue them. I had to calm things down. Afterward, I checked the chair—there was no defect. Klausner had removed the needle."

Milo felt doubt slipping in. "Injection? That's a reach."

Roth shrugged with some effort. "I'm no scientist, but I've talked to some. At high concentrations it's theoretically possible to keep lab-grown HIV alive. With the right base, it could be done. Actually, it's the only possibility. You know from my file that I'm celibate and don't shoot drugs."

Milo considered not replying, but finally admitted, "The file on you is pretty thin."

"Oh!" That seemed to please the assassin.

All this time, Milo had remained standing in the center of the room. By now, the position felt awkward, so he settled on the foot of the cot, by Roth's feet. On the assassin's upper lip a thin trail of snot glimmered. "Who do you think Klausner's master is?"

Roth stared at him, thinking it over. "It's hard to

know. The jobs I got from him, they were inconsistent, just like your personal history. I'd always wondered this—does Mr. Klausner-Williams represent one group, or many groups? I've gone back and forth, finally deciding that he represents one group." He paused, perhaps for dramatic effect. "The global Islamic jihad."

Milo opened his mouth, then shut it. Then: "Does this bother you?"

"I'm an artisan, Milo. The only thing that concerns me is the feasibility of the job."

"So, terrorists paid you to get rid of Mullah Salih Ahmad, one of their own. That's what you're saying?"

Roth nodded. "Public killings and private killings serve different purposes. You of all people know that. You don't think al-Qaeda's only technique is to pack little boys with bombs and send them off to a heaven of virgins, do you? No. And the Sudan—at first, I couldn't see it either. Then I started watching. Who's winning now? Ignore Darfur for the moment. I'm talking about the capital. Khartoum. The Muslim extremist insurgency, that's who's winning. They have public support like never before. Ahmad's killing was about the best gift those bastards ever got, and with a Chinese brand on his body it would've been even better—blame it on the Chinese investors who prop up the president." He shook his head. "They'll have an Islamic paradise in no time, thanks to me."

Judging from his features, no one would have been able to tell how much this news excited Milo. He'd asked all his questions in the quiet way of the interrogator, as if no answer were more important than another. In that same way, he said, "There's something I don't understand, Roth. You learned that, five months ago, you caught HIV. You learned it in a Swiss clinic. Now, it's nearly killed you. Why aren't you on antiretrovirals? You could live well enough for decades."

It was Roth's turn to look passive as he studied Milo's face. "Milo, your file on me must be very small indeed." Finally, he explained: *"The Science of Christianity makes pure the fountain, in order to purify the stream."*

"Who said that?"

"Are you a man of faith, Milo? I mean, beyond the limits of your family."

"No."

Roth seemed to take that seriously, as if wondering whose path was better. "It's a tough thing. Faith talks you into doing things you might not want to do."

"Who were you quoting?"

"Mary Baker Eddy. I'm a Christian Scientist." He swallowed again, roughly.

"I'm surprised," Milo admitted.

"Sure you are, but why? How many Catholic gangsters are there? How many Muslim killers? How many Torah-loving angels of death? Please. I may not have lived up to the Church's tenets, but I'll certainly die by them. God has seen fit to strike me down—and why wouldn't He? If I were Him, I would've done it years ago." He paused. "Of course, those Swiss doctors, they thought I was nuts. Nearly forced me to take the treatments. They kept finding me outside, under a tree, on my knees, praying. The power of prayer—it didn't save my body, but it just might save my soul."

"What does Mary Baker Eddy say about revenge?" asked Milo, irritated by this sudden fit of moral poetry. He supposed it was what happened to killers like the Tiger, shut-ins who avoided even the intimacy of sex. There was no one to bounce your thoughts off of, no one to remind you that what came from your mouth wasn't necessarily wisdom. He pressed: "That's why you're here, right? You want me to take revenge on the person who's killing you."

Roth thought a moment, raised a finger (Milo noticed blood on his knuckle), and intoned: "*To suppose that sin, lust, hatred, envy, hypocrisy, revenge, have life abiding in them, is a terrible mistake. Life and Life's idea, Truth and Truth's idea, never make men sick, sinful, or mortal.*" He lowered his hand. "Revenge does not have a life of its own, but maybe justice does. You understand? I've given you all I have on him. It's not much, but you're a smart man. You've got resources. I think you can track him down."

"What about the money?" said Milo. "How did Klausner pass it on to you? Always in a shopping bag?"

"Oh, no," said Roth, pleased that Milo was asking. "Usually I'd be directed to a bank. Go in and empty an account. The banks changed, each account was opened under a different name, but I was always put down as a coholder. Under the Roth name."

Milo stared at the man. Given all the bodies Samuel Roth had collected over the years, there was something inappropriate about this last wish. "Maybe he's done me a service. He's closed a few of my cases by killing you. Maybe this Klausner is my friend."

"No." Roth was insistent. "*I* did that for you. I could've died in obscurity in Zürich. It was certainly more picturesque. This way, I help you out. Maybe you'll help me out. You're a Tourist. You can catch him."

"I'm not a Tourist anymore."

"That's like saying, *I'm not a murderer anymore.* You can change your name, change your job description—you can even become a bourgeois family man, Milo. But really, nothing changes."

Without realizing it, the Tiger had voiced one of Milo Weaver's greatest fears. Before his apprehension could show, he changed the subject. "Does it hurt?"

"Very much. Here." Roth touched his chest. "And here." He touched his groin. "It's like metal in the blood. You remember everything I've said?"

"Answer one question, will you?"

"If I can."

It was something Milo had wondered for the last six years, ever since he'd decided to focus his efforts on the assassin whose bullets he'd once tried to face. He'd learned a lot about the Tiger, even backtracking to find his first verified assassination in November 1997, Albania. Adrian Murrani, the thirty-year-old chairman of the Sineballaj commune. Everyone knew Murrani had been ordered killed by the ruling neo-communists—it was a year of many sudden deaths in Albania—but in this case the gunman had been hired from abroad. Despite the stacks of physical and eyewitness evidence collected from the assassinations that followed, Milo had never come close to answering the most basic mystery about this man: "Who are you, really? We never found a real name. We didn't even figure out your nationality."

The Tiger smiled again, flushing. "I suppose that's a kind of victory, isn't it?"

Milo admitted that it was impressive.

"The answer is in your files. Somewhere in that tower facing the Avenue of the Americas. See, the only difference between you and me is that we chose different ways of tendering our resignations."

Milo's thoughts stuttered briefly before he understood. "You were a Tourist."

"Brothers in arms," he said, his smile huge. "And later, you'll wish you'd asked another question. Know what it is?"

Milo, still spinning from the realization of Roth's Company past, had no idea what the question could be. Then it occurred to him, because it was simple, and the assassin's mood was so simple. "Why 'the Tiger?' "

"Precisely! However, the truth is a disappointment: I have no idea. Someone, somewhere, first used it. Maybe a journalist, I don't know. I guess that, after the Jackal, they needed an animal name." He shrugged—again, it looked painful. "I suppose I should be pleased they didn't choose a vulture, or a hedgehog. And no—before you think to ask, let me assure you I wasn't named after the Survivor song."

Despite everything, Milo smiled.

"Let me ask you something," Roth said. "What's your opinion on the Black Book?"

"The What Book?"

"Stop pretending, please."

Within the subculture of Tourism, the Black Book was the closest thing to the Holy Grail. It was the secret guide to survival, rumored to have been planted by a retired Tourist, twenty-one copies hidden in locations around the world. The stories of the Black Book were as old as Tourism itself. "It's bunk," said Milo.

"We're in agreement," Roth answered. "When I first went freelance, I thought it might be useful, so I spent a couple years looking for it. It's a figment of some overactive imaginations. Maybe Langley first spread it, maybe some bored Tourist. But it's a nice idea."

"You think so?"

"Sure. Something stable and direct in our befuddled world. A bible for living."

"Luckily for you, you have the Bible itself."

Roth nodded, and when he spoke again, his tone was earnest. "Please. You and me, we're enemies—I understand that. But trust me: The man who did this to me is much worse than I am. You'll at least look into it?"

"Okay," said Milo, not sure how long his promise would last.

"Good."

Samuel Roth hunched forward and lightly patted Milo's knee, then leaned back against the wall. Without ceremony, he clenched his teeth. Something crunched in his mouth, like a nut, and Milo smelled the almond bitterness in Roth's exhale. It was a smell he'd run into a few times in his life, from people either utterly devout or utterly frightened. The hard way out, or the easiest, depending on your philosophy.

The assassin's veined eyes widened, close enough that Milo could see his own reflection in them. Roth seized up three times in quick succession, and Milo caught him before he fell off the cot. The yellow-tinted head rolled back, lips white with froth. Milo was holding a corpse.

He dropped the body on the cot, wiped his hands against his pants, and backed up to the door. It had been years since he'd faced this, but even back then, when he saw death more often, he'd never gotten used to it. The sudden heft. The fast cooling. The fluids that leaked from the body (there—Roth's orange jumpsuit darkened at the groin). The quick cessation of consciousness, of everything that person—no matter how despicable or virtuous—had experienced. It didn't matter that minutes ago he'd wanted to ridicule this man's false piousness. That wasn't the point. The point was that, within this concrete cell, a whole world had suddenly ceased to exist. In a snap, right in front of him. That was death.

Milo came out of his daze when the door against his back shook. He stepped away so Sheriff Wilcox could come in, saying, "Listen, I got some folks here who—"

He stopped.

"*Christ,*" the sheriff muttered. Fear stalled in his face. "What the hell'd you *do* to him?"

"He did it to himself. Cyanide."

"But . . . but *why*?"

Milo shook his head and started for the door, wondering what Mary Baker Eddy said about suicide.

5

Special Agent Janet Simmons gazed at Milo across the scratched white table in the Blackdale interview room. Despite his size, her partner, Special Agent George Orbach, was clearly the inferior in their relationship. He kept getting up to leave the room, awkwardly returning with Styrofoam cups of water and coffee and lemonade.

Simmons had a fluid, engaging interview style, which Milo supposed was part of Homeland's new training. She leaned forward a lot, hands open except when she pulled a strand of dark hair behind her ear. Early thirties, Milo guessed. Sharp, attractive features marred only by a right eye that wandered. The ways she positioned her beauty were supposed to close the psychological distance between interviewer and interviewee, making it less adversarial. She even pretended not to notice his stink.

After sending George Orbach out again to find milk for her coffee, she turned to him. "Come on, Milo. We're on the same side here. Right?"

"Of course we are, Janet."

"Then tell me why the Company's working out of its jurisdiction on this one. Tell me why you're keeping secrets from us."

Mrs. Wilcox's delicious lemonade was starting to give Milo a sugar high. "I've explained it," he said. "We've been after Roth for years. We learned he'd crossed the border in Dallas, so I went to Dallas."

"And you never thought to call us?" She arched her brow. "We *do* have a Dallas office, you know."

Milo wondered how to put it. "I decided—"

"I? Tom Grainger no longer makes decisions in New York?"

"I *advised*," he corrected, "that if Homeland Security were brought in, you'd send in the cavalry. The Tiger would spot it in a second, and go underground. The only way to track him was with a single person."

"You."

"I've followed his case a long time. I know his modus operandi."

"And look how well that worked out." Simmons winked—*winked*. "Another successful day for Central Intelligence!"

He refused to meet her challenge. "I think I'm being very helpful, Janet. I've told you that he had a cap of cyanide in his mouth. He didn't like the idea of living in Gitmo, so he bit. You could blame Sheriff Wilcox for not giving him a cavity search, but I don't think that would be fair."

"He talked to you." Her tone became gentle; her wandering eye came back in line. "You had a conversation. That deputy with the girl's name—"

"Leslie."

"Right. He said you had twenty minutes alone with him."

"More like fifteen."

"So?"

"Yes?"

Admirably, Simmons didn't raise her voice. "So, what did you talk about?"

"A man like that, a superstar assassin—he needs more than fifteen minutes to start talking."

"So you just sat there? Staring at each other?"

"I asked him questions."

"Did you touch him?"

Milo cocked his head.

"Did you try to beat the information out of him, Milo?"

"Certainly not," he said. "That's against the law."

She looked as if she were going to smile at that, but changed her mind. "You know what I think? I think you and the whole Company—you're desperate. You've lost whatever shred of credibility you had left, and you'll do anything to keep hold of your pensions. You'll even kill for that."

"It sounds like you've put some real thought into this."

She let the smile appear this time; perhaps she thought he was joking. "Tell me what the Tiger had on you that was so damaging. Tom wasn't running him, was he? For your dirty little jobs? I don't know what you guys do in your tower, but I suspect it's pretty nasty."

Milo was surprised by her vehemence, but he was more surprised by her superiority. "I suppose Homeland doesn't have any secrets?"

"Sure, but we're not the ones on public trial. It's not our time yet."

George Orbach pushed his way into the room, clutching a handful of paper packets. "No milk. Just this powder."

Janet Simmons seemed disgusted by the news. "Doesn't matter," she said, crossing her arms. "Mr. Weaver is leaving now. He's in need of a good shower. I think we'll have to talk to Mr. Grainger instead."

Milo rapped the table with his knuckles and got up. "Please don't hesitate to get in touch."

"Fat lot of good that'll do me."

The morning storm had left as soon as it had arrived, leaving behind damp roads and moist, clean air. As he drove, Milo lit a Davidoff from the pack he'd broken down and bought when he filled up the tank. The smoke felt good, but then it didn't, and he coughed hard, but kept smoking. Anything to cut the edge off the stink of death.

He hadn't had his cell phone long enough to figure out how to change the ring tone, so when it woke up somewhere along Route 18 to Jackson, it played a stupid corporate melody. He checked to see if it was his wife, but it was Grainger. "Yeah?"

"Is what that bitch from Homeland says true? He's dead?"

"Yeah."

A pause. "Will I see you at the office today?"

"No."

"I'll catch you at the airport, then. We've got things to discuss."

Milo hung up and turned on the radio, flipping through staticky country stations until, inevitably, he gave up and pulled out his iPod, which he'd listened to half this trip. He slipped in the earbuds, clicked the French playlist, and skipped to track five.

His head was filled with the quick, swirling melody of *"Poupée de cire, poupée de son,"* sung by France Gall, Luxembourg's 1965 Eurovision winner, penned by Serge Gainsbourg. The very tune he'd taught Stephanie for her talent show, the performance he was missing.

He dialed Tina. Her voice mail picked up, and he listened to her story about not being in and the promise of a call if he left a message. He knew she was already at the show, next to an empty chair, watching their daughter sing Gainsbourg's phenomenal hit. He didn't leave a message. He'd just wanted to hear her voice.

6

Tina couldn't figure out what kind of idiot parents would think to dress their seven-year-old girl in pink tights and a tank top, tie a pair of pink angel's wings to her frail back, and then cover every inch with glistening sequins. You could hardly see the child from the spotlight's reflection as she pranced left and right on the stage to some dance beat with electric guitars, singing a warbling version of "I Decide," from (the principal had told everyone) "that hit Disney movie, *The Princess Diaries 2.*" It might have been a good song, but from her seat near the center of the Berkeley Carroll School's auditorium, Tina could only make out the thump of the bass drum and see a little glittering girl-shape shift around on that painfully bare stage.

But of course she clapped. They all did. Two stood and hooted—the idiot parents, Tina assumed. Beside her, in what should have been Milo's seat, Patrick struck his palms together and whispered, "In-fucking-credible! I'm getting my friends at CAA to sign up this one, ASAP."

Tina hadn't wanted to call Patrick, but with Milo pulling another no-show, Stef deserved as full an audience as possible. "Be nice," she said.

Milo had left another of his curt, unapologetic messages on their home phone, saying that there'd been a delay. As usual, he didn't call the delay by any name, just "delay."

Fine, she'd thought. *Miss your daughter's talent show, and I'll bring her real father.*

Then Milo himself had suggested calling Patrick. "For Stef. And videotape it, will you?"

That had taken some of the wind out of Tina's anger—that, and the fact that, for the last three days, Patrick had been trying to get her and Stephanie to come back to him. Milo, off on his vague, sudden business trip, had no idea.

Her reaction to Patrick's initial attempt had been to walk the phone to the kitchen so her daughter wouldn't hear her say, "Are you on *drugs,* Patrick?"

"Of course not," said her ex . . . *boy*friend sounded silly, but they'd never actually married. "How could you even think that? You know how I feel about drugs."

"I bet you've put away a few scotches."

"Listen," he said, trying to sound reasonable. "I look back now—I look back over all of it. I look back decades. What do I see? Two glowing years. The only two years I was really happy. With you. *That's* what I want to tell you. It was never better than that."

"I like Paula," she told him as she absently rubbed a sponge around the spotted aluminum sink. "She's a smart girl. Why she married you, I'll never know . . ."

"Ha *ha*," he said, and that's when she knew he really was drunk. She heard him take a drag off of one of his stinking cigarillos. "I'm the joke of the century. But think about it. Think about me. Remember how in love we were."

"Wait a minute. Where *is* Paula?"

Another long cigarillo-drag. "Your guess is as good as mine."

That, then, had clarified everything. "She's walked out on you. And after six years, you're running back to me? You *must* be seriously drunk, Pat. Or seriously stupid."

Onstage, a boy in a Superman outfit was delivering a monologue, a heavy lisp making the words hard to decipher. Patrick leaned close: "He's gonna fly soon. I can see the string attached to his belt."

"He's not going to fly."

"If he does, I'll buy him his first martini."

Patrick's long face and graying three-day beard earned him extra clients at Berg & DeBurgh. They thought that he, unlike his over-the-hill law partners, looked vital. These days, though, with the bruised shade to his weary eyes, he looked more desperate than vital. Paula Chabon, that Lebanese-French bombshell who sold her own line of jewelry at little boutique shops positioned in many world capitals, had moved to Berlin. An ex-lover had wooed her back. More than anything,

Patrick wanted to believe he could do the same thing, that he could woo Tina back. He really was pitiful.

Superboy ended his monologue by running around the stage in mock flight, but the cape hung sadly against his back, and Patrick was annoyed that his feet never left the ground. "Turn on the video," Tina told him after the obligatory applause.

Patrick tugged a small Sony video camera out of his pocket. When he turned it on, the two-inch screen glowed.

Without thinking, Tina squeezed his knee. "Here comes Little Miss!"

But the Berkeley Carroll principal came on first, squinting at the card in her hand. "Please welcome tonight's youngest, Stephanie Weaver, as she performs . . ." The woman frowned, trying to make out the words. "Poop-ee de sirk, poop-ee de son."

Titters rippled through the audience. Tina reddened. How could this bitch not have learned how to pronounce it first?

The principal snickered, too. "My French isn't what it used to be. But, in English, this is, 'Wax Doll, Sawdust Doll,' written by Serge Gainsbourg."

The crowd duly applauded, and as the principal left the stage Stephanie entered, walking flat but proud to the center. She was, without a doubt, the best dressed of the bunch. Milo had spent a whole weekend with Stephanie in the Village searching retro shops for the proper one-piece dress and tights. Then he'd scoured the Internet, discovering midsixties haircuts. Tina had found it all a bit much, and the idea of dressing their child in forty-year-old styles a little pompous—but now, seeing how the washed-out browns of the dress and the striped stockings glowed, just faintly, under the spotlights, and how her bobbed hair hung perfectly straight along the sides . . .

Beside her, watching their daughter, Patrick was speechless.

There was a click from the speakers, a CD spinning, and then an orchestral melody that grew into a wall of sound with a swift beat. Stephanie began to sing, those French words perfectly formed.

Je suis une poupée de cire,
Une poupée de son

When she couldn't get her daughter in focus, Tina realized she was crying. Milo had been right all along. It was beautiful. She glanced at Patrick gaping at that little screen, muttering, "Wow." Maybe this would finally convince him that Milo was A-OK, despite what he'd believed yesterday when he called her office, at Columbia's Avery Architectural and Fine Arts Library.

"I don't like him."

"What?" Tina had snapped back, already irritated. "What did you say?"

"Milo." She could tell he was slipping into an afternoon buzz, maybe one of his famous five-martini lunches. "I'm talking about Milo Weaver. I never trusted him, not with you, and certainly not with my daughter."

"You never even tried to like him."

"But what do you *know* about him? He's just some guy you met in Italy, right? Where's he *from*?"

"You know all this. His parents died. He's from—"

"North Carolina," Patrick cut in. "Yeah, yeah. How come he's got no southern accent?"

"He's traveled more than you know."

"Right. A traveler. And his orphanage—he told me it was the Saint Christopher Home for Boys. That place burned to the ground in 1989. Pretty convenient, don't you think?"

"I think it's pretty convenient you know this stuff, Pat. You've been snooping."

"I'm allowed to snoop when the welfare of my daughter's at stake."

Tina tried to purge that conversation from her head, but it kept banging at her as Stephanie sang, her voice carrying crystal-clear through the auditorium. Tina didn't even know what the song meant, but it was gorgeous.

"Look, Pat. I could bitch about how you left me when I was pregnant and needed you most, but I'm not angry about that anymore. The way things ended up . . . I'm *happy*. Milo treats us well; he loves Stephanie like his own. Do you understand what I'm saying?"

Stephanie's pitch rose, the music swirling around her. She nearly bellowed the last lines, then fell silent. A final few bars of music, as Stephanie rocked in the same nonchalant dance she'd seen France Gall do in that Eurovision performance Milo tracked down on YouTube. She looked so cool, so hipper-than-thou.

Patrick repeated, "Wow."

Tina whistled, standing and shouting, swinging her fist in the air, exhilarated. Some other parents stood and clapped, and Tina didn't care if they were just being polite. She felt giddy all over. Milo really would've loved this.

7

I t had been a lousy year and a half for the Company. No one could say exactly where the trail of bad luck had started, which meant that the blame leapfrogged up and down the hierarchy depending on the public mood, pausing to wreak havoc on this or that career. News cameras arrived to witness early retirements and awkward dismissals.

Before moving on, these humiliated unemployed dropped in on Sunday morning television roundtables to spread the blame further. It was the ex–assistant director, a soft-spoken career spook, now exceedingly bitter, who best summed up the general consensus.

"Iraq, of course. First, the president blames us for supplying bad information. He blames us for not killing Osama bin Laden before his big act of public relations. He blames us for uniting both of those failures into a disastrous, unending war, as if we pointed him to Iraq.

We defend ourselves with facts—*facts,* mind you—and suddenly the president's allies in Congress begin to pick us apart. What a coincidence! Special investigation committees. If you spend enough money and look hard enough, all organizations turn up dirty. That, too, is a fact."

Georgia Republican Harlan Pleasance was the one who really dropped the bomb, back in April 2006. He headed the second special investigation committee, which, based on the results of the first committee the previous month, focused on money trails. With access to the CIA budget (a secret since the 1949 Central Intelligence Agency Act), Senator Pleasance wondered aloud how the Company could fund, for example, the recently uncovered ten-million-dollar gift to the unlikely named 青年團, or Youth League, a militant Chinese democracy group based in the mountainous Guizhou province that had ironically named itself after the communist youth organization. It took less than three months for Senator Pleasance to report on CNN's *The Situation Room* that the Chinese militants' gift had come from part of the sale, in Frankfurt, of eighteen million euros' worth of Afghan heroin, which had been clandestinely harvested by Taliban prisoners under U.S. Army guard. "And no one told us a thing about it, Wolf."

It was an open secret within Langley that, while all this might be true, there was no human way to discover it from the existing paper trails. Another agency was feeding Senator Pleasance his information. Most believed it was Homeland, while others—and Milo was part of this group—believed it was the National Security Agency, which had a much older, historic beef with the CIA. It didn't matter, though, because the public didn't care where the information came from. The facts were just too enticing.

Whatever began the steady bloodletting, it was Pleasance's discovery that turned it into a public, and international, massacre. First, the embarrassed Germans rolled back their historic support and shut down many joint operations. Then it became a race. Fresh special committees demanded financial records as minor politicians took a stab at national recognition, while Langley began incinerating hard drives. Louise Walker, a typist, was arrested for this, and after a lengthy meeting with her lawyer became convinced that the only way out was to give a name. That name was Harold Underwood, a low-level bureaucrat. Harold was also assigned a convincing lawyer.

So it went. Eighteen months from beginning to end, resulting in thirty-two arrests: seventeen acquittals, twelve jail terms, two suicides, and one disappearance. The new CIA director, whose approval was rushed through the nomination hearings, was a tiny but vociferous Texan named Quentin Ascot. In front of the Senate, on elevated heels, he made his position clear. No more black money. No more operations that hadn't been approved by the Senate Committee on Homeland Security and Governmental Affairs. No more cowboy antics at Langley. "No more rogue departments. It's a new world. We serve at the pleasure of the American people, who pay our bills. We should be an open book."

The Company's collective groan could be heard around the world.

The four secret floors of offices on the Avenue of the Americas, stocked with Travel Agents who focused on the running of, and assimilation of information collected by, Tourists based in all the populated continents, was (behind closed doors) considered a prime target for the inevitable cuts. Director Ascot, it was rumored, wanted to relieve the world of Tourism altogether. He claimed that Tourists, with open-ended resources and no need to collect receipts, would bankrupt the Company. But since he didn't have enough internal support to erase the clandestine department, all he could do was slowly chew it up.

Milo learned of Ascot's first tentative steps when he arrived at LaGuardia from Tennessee and met Tom Grainger in the airport security office. The old man had sent away the "rent-a-cops," as he called most non-Company personnel, and through a two-way mirror they watched crowds jostling at the luggage carousel, the irregular flow of travelers along mass transit lines that had in recent years become national threat centers. Both men missed that almost-forgotten time when travel was about arriving someplace new, not about getting through the clunky measures of antiterrorist law.

"They're starting the postmassacre frenzy," Grainger said to the glass, a drawn look on his face.

Even by CIA standards, Tom Grainger was old—seventy-one years, most of his white hair lost to the shower drain, his cabinet full of prescription pills. He never appeared in public without a tie.

"The Grand Inquisitor has sent a memo through his underlings—through Terence Fitzhugh, to be precise. I'm to prepare for executions, he says. Ascot's predicting a war of attrition, and he's getting me to take out my own people. It's slow hara-kiri."

Milo had known Grainger since 1990, when he'd been invited to become part of the Company's clandestine world in London, and he knew the old man was always melodramatic when it came to Langley. His secret department in Manhattan was his private dominion, and it hurt him to be reminded that people in another state really pulled the strings. Maybe that was why he'd decided to appear at the airport, rather than wait for morning to talk in the office—no one here could listen to his bitching. "You've been through worse, Tom. We've all been through worse."

"Hardly," Grainger said dismissively. "One-quarter. That's how much we're losing. He's giving me the heads-up. Next year we'll work on one-quarter less funds, which'll barely cover operational costs. I'm supposed to decide which Travel Agents get pink slips, and which get transferred to more public departments."

"And the Tourists?"

"Aha! Too many. That's the gist of it. Twelve slots for the whole of Europe, working around the clock, and yet I'm supposed to get rid of three of them. *Bastard*. Who does he think he is?"

"Your boss."

"My *boss* wasn't there when the planes came, was he?" The old man rapped a knuckle on the glass. A boy standing nearby turned to frown at the noisy mirror. "I guess you weren't either, were you? You never did visit the old office . . . no." He was fully engaged in his memories now. "You were still a Tourist, just barely, and we were sitting at our desks, drinking Starbucks, as if the world wasn't preparing to explode."

Milo had heard all this before, Grainger's endless replay of September 11, when the former secret CIA office at 7 World Trade Center collapsed. It didn't happen immediately, because the nineteen young men who hijacked four planes that morning didn't realize that by hitting one of the smaller towers they could wipe out an entire Company department. Instead, they went for the glory of the enormous first and second towers, which gave Grainger and his staff time to flee in panic before the main targets crumbled, bringing number seven down with them.

"It was Beirut times fifty," said Grainger. "All of Dresden stuffed into a few minutes. It was the first wave of barbarians coming to sack Rome."

"It wasn't any of those things. Is this what you needed to talk to me about?"

Grainger turned from the glass and frowned. "You're sunburned."

Milo leaned against the LaGuardia security supervisor's messy desk and looked down. His left arm, which had hung out the driver's side window, was definitely a different tone. "You want to just wait for my report?"

"They've been calling like mad," said Grainger, ignoring the question. "Who's this Simmons bitch?"

"She's all right. Just angry. I would be, too."

Through the window, luggage clattered down a conveyor belt as Milo outlined his conversation with the Tiger. "He wanted me to track down the people who stuck him with HIV. Terrorists, he thinks. Sudan connections."

"Sudan. Great. But all he had for you was this one name. Herbert Williams. Or Jan Klausner. It's pretty sketchy."

"And the Hirslanden Clinic. He was there under the al-Abari alias."

"We'll look into it."

Milo chewed the inside of his cheek. "Send Tripplehorn. He's still in Nice, isn't he?"

"You're better than Tripplehorn," said Grainger.

"I'm not a Tourist. Besides, I'm due in Florida on Monday."

"Sure."

"Really," said Milo. "Me, the family, and Mickey Mouse."

"So you keep telling me."

They watched passengers press closer to the carousel, knocking into each other in an exhausted panic. To Milo's annoyance, his boss sighed loudly. He knew what that meant, and that knowledge told him why Grainger had taken the trouble to come out to LaGuardia—he wanted to railroad Milo into another trip. "No, Tom."

Grainger peered at the travelers, not bothering to reply. Milo would wait him out. He would stay silent, not even pass on the revelation that the Tiger had come from the ranks of their own Tourists. If it was true, Tom already knew it, and had kept this information from Milo for his own reasons.

Almost sadly, Grainger said, "Think you can head out tomorrow afternoon?"

"Absolutely not."

"Ask me where."

"Doesn't matter. Tina's on the warpath. I missed Stephanie's show."

"Not to worry. I called an hour ago with a personal apology for sending you out. I took the responsibility on my *own* shoulders."

"You're a real saint."

"Sure I am. I in*formed* her that you were saving the free world."

"She stopped believing that long ago."

"Librarians." Grainger sniffed at the travelers. "You should've listened to me. There are absolutely no odds in marrying smart women."

Truth was, Grainger actually had given him this advice a week before he and Tina married. It had always made him wonder about Terri, Grainger's now-deceased wife. "Might as well tell me about it," he said. "But no promises."

Grainger patted his back with a heavy hand. "See? That wasn't so hard."

8

It took them most of the sunset hour to reach Park Slope, the Brooklyn neighborhood Milo had grown to love over the last five years. When they were apartment hunting, Stephanie still just a baby, Tina had been immediately taken by the brownstones and upscale cafés, the cozy, soft-edged world of dot-com kids and successful novelists; it took Milo a while longer.

Family life was a different beast from what he'd known before—unlike Tourism, it actually was life. So he learned. First, to accept, and after acceptance came affection. Because the Slope wasn't about the nouveau riche torturing café workers with elaborate nonfat coffee specifications; Park Slope was about Milo Weaver's family.

The Tiger had called him a bourgeois family man. In that, at least, the assassin had been right on the mark.

At Garfield Place, he climbed out of Grainger's

Mercedes with a promise to talk the next morning in the office. But he knew, as he mounted the narrow interior stairs of their brownstone, that he had already made up his mind. Family man or not, he was going to Paris.

At the third floor, he heard a television. When he rang the bell Stephanie shouted, "Door! Mom, *door*!" Then Tina's quick footsteps and, "*Coming*." When she opened it, she was buttoning her shirt. Once she had him focused, she crossed her arms over her breasts and in a high whisper said, "*You missed her show*."

"Didn't Tom talk to you?"

He tried to come in, but she wouldn't step out of the way. "That man will say anything to cover for you."

It was true, so he didn't dispute it. He just waited for her to make up her mind. When she did, she grabbed his shirt, pulled him close, and kissed him fully on the lips. "You're still in the doghouse, mister."

"Can I come in?"

Tina wasn't truly angry. She came from a family where you didn't hide your anger, because by venting it you stole its power. That's how the Crowes had always done it in Austin, and what was good enough for Texas was good enough for anywhere.

He found Stephanie in the living room, splayed on the floor with a pile of dolls, while on television cartoon animals got into trouble. "Hey, girl," he told her. "Sorry I missed the show."

She didn't get up. "I'm used to it by now."

She sounded more like her mother every day. When he leaned over and kissed her head, she wrinkled her nose.

"Dad, you stink."

"I know, hon. Sorry."

Tina threw a tube of moisturizing cream at Milo. "For that sunburn. Want a beer?"

"Any vodka?"

"Let's get some food in you first."

Tina boiled ramen noodles—one of the five things, by her own admission, that she knew how to cook—and brought out the bowl. By then, Stephanie had warmed to Milo's presence and climbed up beside him on the sofa. She gave a rundown of the other performers at the talent show, their relative strengths and weaknesses, and the utter injustice of the winning performance— Sarah Lawton's rendition of "I Decide."

"But what about yours? We worked on it for weeks."

Stephanie tilted her head forward to glower at him. "It was a stupid idea."

"Why?"

"Be*cause*, Dad. No one understands French."

Milo rubbed his forehead. He'd thought it was a fine idea, his child performing a Serge Gainsbourg hit. It was unexpected. Innovative. "I thought you liked that song."

"Yeah."

Tina took the far end of the couch. "She was incredible, Milo. Just stunning."

"But I didn't win."

"Don't worry," he said. "One day you'll be running the New York Philharmonic, and Sarah Lawton will be serving up fries at Fuddruckers."

"*Milo*," warned Tina.

"I'm just saying."

A crooked smile filled Stephanie's face as she gazed into the distance. "*Yeah.*"

Milo dug into his noodles. "We've got it on video, right?"

"Father couldn't get it in focus. And I'm too small." That was how Stephanie differentiated the men in her life: Patrick was Father; Milo was Dad.

"He told you he was sorry," said Tina.

Stephanie, not in a forgiving mood, climbed to the floor to rejoin her dolls.

"So?" said Tina. "You going to tell me?"

"This is good," Milo said through a mouthful of noodles.

"Where?"

"Where what?"

"Tom's sending you off again. That's why he called—to soften me up. He's the least subtle CIA man I've ever met."

"Now, wait—"

"Also," she cut in, "I can see the guilt all over your face."

Milo peered over his bowl at the television. The Road Runner was defying gravity once again, as Wile E. Coyote suffered the fate of the rest of us, the ones chained to the laws of physics. Quietly, he said, "I need to go to Paris. But I'll be back by Saturday."

"You don't do that kind of work anymore."

He didn't answer. She was right, of course, but over the last year he'd disappeared on more and more "business trips," and Tina's worries had found voice. She knew enough about his life before they met to know that that man wasn't the kind of husband she'd signed up for. She'd signed on with the person who'd left all of that behind.

"Why's it so important you go to Paris? It's not like the Company doesn't have a whole army of goons to send."

He lowered his voice: "It's Angela Yates. She's got herself in some real trouble."

"Angela? From-our-wedding Angela?"

"They think she's selling information."

"Come on." She made a face. "Angela's the poster girl for Us-Against-Them. She's more patriotic than John Wayne."

"That's why I need to go," said Milo, looking up as Wile E. Coyote climbed out of a sooty hole after having plummeted a mile. "Those internal investigation guys—they won't take that into consideration."

"Okay. But you're back by Saturday. We *will* fly to Disney World without you. Isn't that right, Little Miss?"

"For *sure,*" Stephanie said to the television.

Milo held up his hands. "Promise."

Tina rubbed his knee, and he pulled her close, smelling her freshly washed hair as he gazed at the television. That's when he realized he'd been wrong: Wile E. Coyote wasn't subject to the same laws of physics as the rest of us. Against all odds, he always survived.

Tina sniffed, then pushed him away. "Jesus, Milo. You *stink.*"

9

To visit the tower at the intersection of West Thirty-first and the Avenue of the Americas, you first had to know that you were being tracked by cameras that covered every inch of sidewalk and road around the building. So by the time you entered, you were expected, and Gloria Martinez, the dour forty-year-old Company desk clerk, was ready with your ID. Milo made a sport of flirting with Gloria, and she in turn made a sport of rebuffing him. She knew his wife was, as she put it, half-Latina, and because of this she occasionally thought it important to remind him, "Watch out, and keep sharp things away from your bed."

Milo accepted this wisdom along with the breast-pocket ID, smiled for the camera attached to her terminal, and promised her, for the third time, "a secret vacation in Palm Springs." In reply, she drew a cutting finger across her neck.

At the next stage of entry, by the six-pack of elevators, stood three enormous football players they called door-men. These men held the keys that allowed access to the four secret floors, stretching from nineteen to twenty-two, that constituted Tom Grainger's domain. On this day, Lawrence, a tall, hairless black man, took him up. Even after five years of the same daily grind, Lawrence still waved a metal detector over Milo's body in the ele-vator. It bleeped around his hip, and, like every day, Milo pulled out his keys, phone, and loose change for examination.

They passed the nineteenth floor, that eerily sterile interview level of narrow corridors and numbered doors where, when necessary, the Geneva Convention became a joke. The twentieth was empty, set aside for future ex-pansion, and twenty-one contained the extensive library of printed Tourism files, a backup of the computer origi-nals. The doors finally opened on the twenty-second floor.

Were a visitor to accidentally reach the Department of Tourism, he would find nothing out of the ordinary. It was an enormous open-plan office, stuffed with low-walled cubicles where pale Travel Agents hunched over computers, digging through mountains of information in order to write up their biweekly reports—or, in the vernacular, Tour Guides—for Tom Grainger. It had the feel, Milo always thought, of a Dickensian accounting office.

Before 9/11 and the collapse of the previous office at 7 World Trade Center, the Department of Tourism had been divided along geographic lines. Six sections devoted to six continents. Afterward, as this new office was put together and all the intelligence agencies were being scrutinized, Tourism rearranged itself along thematic lines. At present, there were seven sections. Milo's section focused on terrorism and organized crime, and the many points at which they intersected.

Each section employed nine Travel Agents and one supervisor, giving the Avenue of the Americas (not counting an undisclosed number of Tourists spread around the globe) a staff of seventy-one, including its director, Tom Grainger.

One-quarter, Grainger had said. One-quarter of these people would have to go.

The old man was in a meeting with Terence Fitzhugh, Langley's assistant director of clandestine operations, who sometimes arrived unexpectedly to address aspects of Grainger's incompetence. While Milo waited outside the office, Harry Lynch, a twenty-something Travel Agent from Milo's section, frog-marched a bundle of laser-printed sheets down the hall, stopping when he noticed Milo. "How'd it go?"

Milo blinked at him. "How'd what go?"

"Tennessee. I caught the radio traffic late Tuesday, and I knew—I *knew*—that this was our guy. It took a while to verify, but I had a feeling in my spine."

Lynch felt a lot of things in his spine, a gift Milo was suspicious of. "Your backbone was right, Harry. Great job."

Lynch glowed with pleasure and ran back to his cubicle.

Grainger's door opened, and Fitzhugh stepped out. He towered over Grainger as he pointed at Milo with a manila envelope. "Weaver, right?" Milo admitted this was fact, and complimented his long memory—they hadn't spoken in half a year, and then only briefly. In a show of comradely affection, Fitzhugh slapped Milo's shoulder. "Too bad about the Tiger, but you just can't predict these things, can you?"

Grainger, behind him, was noticeably silent.

"But we're rid of one more terrorist," Fitzhugh continued, stroking the thick silver hair above his ear. "That scores one for the good guys."

Dutifully, Milo agreed with the sporting metaphor.

"So, what's on your plate now?"

"Just Paris."

"Paris?" Fitzhugh echoed, and Milo noticed a flicker of apprehension in his features. He turned to Grainger. "You got the budget to send this guy to Paris, Tom?"

"It's Yates," Grainger informed him.

"Yates?" Fitzhugh repeated again; perhaps he was hard of hearing.

"She's one of his oldest friends. It's the only sure way of pulling this off."

"Gotcha," Fitzhugh said, then patted Milo's arm and walked away, singing, "Oo-la-la!"

"Get in here," said Grainger.

The old man returned to his Aeron, settling against the bright backdrop of Manhattan, and placed an ankle on the corner of his broad desk. He did that a lot, as if to remind visitors whose office this really was.

"What did he want?" Milo asked as he took a seat.

"Like I told you, they're reaming me over the budget, and then you go and mention Paris."

"Sorry."

Grainger waved the problem away. "One thing before we get into this. Your new friend, Simmons, has apparently done a rush-job autopsy on the Tiger. She wants to prove you killed him. You didn't give her any reason to think that, did you?"

"I thought I was very cooperative. How did you hear about the autopsy?"

"Sal. Our friend at Homeland."

Grainger wasn't the only one with a friend in Homeland Security. Milo remembered the hubbub over the president's announcement, nine days after the Towers, that he was establishing a new intelligence agency. The Company, the Feds, and the NSA lined up to squeeze in as many of their own employees as possible. "Sal" was Tourism's plant, and periodically Grainger talked with him through an anonymous e-mail service called Nexcel. Milo had used it a few times himself.

"As you suspected," Grainger continued, "it was cyanide. Hollow tooth. According to Homeland's doctor, he only had a week or so left to him anyway. However, your prints are all over his face. Want to explain?"

"At the beginning of the interview, I attacked him."

"Why?"

"I told you before—he brought up Tina and Stef."

"You lost your cool."

"I was short on sleep."

"Okay." Grainger reached out to tap the oak desktop, referring Milo to an unmarked gray file in the center. "Here's the Angela thing. Go ahead."

Milo had to get out of his chair to retrieve the dull-looking folder that showed off the newest Company security technique: Top secret files were now left unmarked, to better avoid attracting interest. He left it closed in his lap. "What about the Swiss clinic?"

Grainger pursed his wide lips. "As he said. Registered under Hamad al-Abari."

"So you'll put Tripplehorn on it?"

"We've only got eleven Tourists in Europe right now. Elliot died last week near Bern. The rest, including Tripplehorn, are all occupied."

"Elliot? How?"

"Accident on the Autobahn. He'd been off the grid a week before we finally matched him up with the body."

Because of security, Milo didn't know any of the Tourists' real names, their ages, or even what they looked like—only Grainger and a few others, including Fitzhugh, had that level of clearance. The news of Elliot's death still bothered him. He scratched his ear, wondering about the man he only knew through a code name. How old was he? Did he have children? "You're sure it was accidental?"

"Even if I wasn't, I doubt we'd get the money for a proper investigation. *That's* the level of purgatory we've entered." When he saw the doubt in Milo's face, his tone softened. "No, Milo. It was an accident. Head-on, and the other driver was killed, too."

Milo finally opened the file. A couple of sheets of printed facts and a photograph—a mug shot of a fat

Chinese man in a People's Liberation Army colonel's uniform.

"The Brits discovered it," Grainger said. "Well, 'discover' is a strong word. They were lucky bastards. All routine, apparently. Six was keeping an eye on the opposition."

In Milo's experience, MI6 didn't have the manpower to keep an eye on each foreign diplomat in the country, even ones as important as the one in this photo—Colonel Yi Lien—but he didn't interrupt.

"The trip wasn't strange. The colonel took the ferry over to France every weekend."

"No Chunnel?"

"Fear of closed spaces—that's in his file. So he does the ferry, then drives on to a little cottage he's got in the Brittany countryside."

"Bought under his name?"

Grainger reached for his computer's mouse, but he was sitting too far back and had to drop his foot in order to reach it. "Of course not. Under a . . ." He clicked twice and squinted at the screen. "Yes. Renée Bernier. Twenty-six, from Paris."

"Mistress."

"Budding novelist, it says here." Another click. "She uses the place to write, I suppose."

"And meet with the colonel."

"Everybody's got to pay rent."

"Walk me through this," said Milo. "Colonel Yi Lien takes the ferry over to his French chalet. Spends the weekend with his girl. Then he boards the ferry. And drops dead?"

"Not dead. Heart attack."

"And MI6 is there to resuscitate him."

"Of course."

"And they go through his bag."

"What's with the attitude, Milo?"

"Sorry, Tom. Go on."

"Well, the colonel's a paranoid sort. Doesn't trust anyone in his own embassy, and for good reason. He's sixty-four, unmarried, with a declining career. He knows that pretty soon someone's going to suggest it's time to pack up for Beijing, and he doesn't want that. He likes London. He likes France."

"And why wouldn't he?"

"Right. But since he trusts no one, he keeps his laptop with him at all times. Big security risk. So our friends in MI6 took the opportunity, on the ferry, to copy his hard drive."

"Very resourceful."

"Aren't they?" Grainger clicked his mouse again, and his printer, buried in the bookshelf alongside a row of untouched antiquarian books, hummed as it spat out a page.

"And Colonel Lien? What happened to him?"

"Irony of ironies. He was recalled to Beijing not long after the heart attack."

Since Grainger wasn't going anywhere, Milo retrieved the printout.

It was an interoffice memo from the U.S. embassy in Paris, top secret. A relay from the ambassador to Frank Barnes, the head of the Diplomatic Security Service in France, concerning new guidelines in dealing with the

Chinese ambassador to France, who would temporarily be monitored by a three-man team.

"And Six just shared this with us for free?"

"They're our special friends," he said, smiling. "Actually, one of my personal special friends passed this on to me."

"Does your special friend think Angela passed this on to Lien? Is that what Six thinks?"

"Calm down, Milo. All they did was pass on the memo. The rest, we figured out on our own."

Like Tina, Milo still couldn't believe that Angela Yates, "poster girl for Us-Against-Them," would give away state secrets. "Has this been verified? The ferry; the heart attack?"

"Like I told you yesterday," Grainger said with theatrical patience, "Yi Lien's coronary made the British papers. It's public record."

Milo dropped the memo on Grainger's desk. "So what's the evidence?"

"That paper went through three sets of hands. The ambassador and Frank Barnes, of course. And the embassy's chief of security. That would be Angela Yates. We've cleared Barnes, and I hope you won't demand an exegesis of the ambassador."

He'd already listened to this overview yesterday in Grainger's car. But now, the physical reality of the memo was making him queasy.

"When was the last time you saw Yates?"

"About a year. But we've kept in touch."

"So you're still on good terms?"

Milo shrugged, then nodded.

"Good." Grainger looked at his mouse—it was a bulbous thing with a blue-lit scroll wheel. "Did you and she ever . . . ?"

"No."

"Oh." He sounded disappointed. "Doesn't matter. I want you to give her this." He opened a drawer and took out a black, thumb-sized flash drive, five hundred megabytes. It clattered on Milo's side of the desk.

"What's on it?"

"A mock-up report on Chinese oil concerns in Kazakhstan. The kind of thing they'll want to see."

"I don't know, Tom. You may have cleared Barnes, but you still haven't convinced me Angela's to blame."

"It's not your job to be convinced," Grainger told him. "You'll find out more from your contact. Trust me, there is evidence."

"But if Yi Lien's gone, then . . ."

"Networks always survive recalls, Milo. You know that. What we don't know is who's at the top of the food chain now."

Milo looked at Grainger's hairless scalp, thinking this over. It was a simple enough matter, and he was glad to be brought in; he could at least make sure they dealt fairly with Angela. But the Company didn't work like that—it didn't buy international air tickets because it felt like being fair. He was being brought in because Angela trusted him. "How long will it take?"

"Oh, not long," Grainger said, pleased the subject had changed. "You fly there, meet her, and hand over the drive. The story is that she'll hold it for a contact named Jim Harrington who'll arrive in Paris on Monday to pick it up. That'll give her"—he raised his hands— "if, of course, it *is* her—only two days to copy it."

"Is Harrington real?"

"He's flying to Paris from Beirut. He knows what to do, but he doesn't know why."

"I see."

"You'll get it done in no time. Hop an evening flight and be back home by Saturday morning."

"That's encouraging."

"Don't be sarcastic."

Milo knew why he was annoyed. It wasn't that he'd missed his coffee that morning, nor that he was feeling an acute desire for a cigarette. It wasn't even the miserable fact that he was preparing to set up a friend for treason—that only made him sick. He said, "When were you planning to tell me about the Tiger?"

Grainger, looking very innocent, said, "What about him?"

"That he was one of ours. That he was a Tourist."

The old man's expression lost its innocence. "You believe that?"

"I've spent the last six years tracking him. Don't you think this piece of information might have helped?"

Grainger stared at him for about ten seconds, then rapped his knuckles on the desk. "Let's talk when you get back. Okay? We don't have time for it now."

"The story's really that long?"

"It is. Your plane leaves at five, and you need to type up some explanation of the Blackdale fiasco that doesn't make us look like complete idiots. Also, put in all your receipts—I'm not paying for undocumented expenses anymore."

Milo grunted an affirmative.

"I'll tell James Einner to expect you. He's your liaison in Paris."

"Einner?" said Milo, suddenly awake. "You really think we need a Tourist for this?"

"Overkill never killed anyone," Grainger said. "Now go. Everything's been forwarded to your terminal."

"And the Tiger?"

"As I said. When you get back."

10

Milo had always felt comfortable in large airports. It wasn't that he loved to fly—that, particularly after the Towers, had become an increasingly unbearable experience with its various secure levels of undress. The only things he enjoyed forty thousand feet above sea level were the cleverly packaged airline meals and the day's music choices on his iPod.

Once he was on the ground again, though, in a properly designed airport, he always felt that he was wandering through a tiny city. Charles de Gaulle, for instance, was properly designed. Its striking sixties architecture— what designers in the sixties imagined a beautiful future would look like—made for a strangely nostalgic utopia of crowd control architecture and consumer pleasures, reinforced by the soft *ding* over loudspeakers followed by a lovely female voice listing the cities of the world.

Nostalgia was a good word for it, a false nostalgia for

a time he was too young to know. It was why he loved
Eurovision winners from 1965, the unreal Technicolor
of those midcareer Bing Crosby films, and (despite his
promises to the contrary) the perfect pair of a Davidoff
cigarette and a bracing vodka, served at an airport bar.

He hadn't wandered Charles de Gaulle in years, and
he soon realized things had changed. He passed a Mc-
Donald's and some bakeries, settling on the vaguely precious La Terrasse de Paris. There was no bar, instead a
cafeteria-style area where he searched in vain for vodka.
The only things available were small wines—red and
white. Frustrated, he settled on four deciliters of some
chilled mass-market Cabernet that cost nine euros. His
plastic cup, the cashier told him, was complimentary.

Milo found an empty table by the rear wall, bumping
into backs and luggage on the way, and settled down. Six
in the morning, and the place was packed. His cell phone
sang its irritating song, and it took him a moment to find
the thing in his inner pocket. PRIVATE NUMBER. "Yeah?"

"Milo Weaver?" said a thin, wiry voice.

"Uh huh."

"Einner. You landed all right?"

"Well, yes, I—"

"New York tells me you've got the package. Do you?"

"I hope so."

"Answer yes or no, please."

"Sure."

"The subject takes lunch every day at twelve thirty
precisely. I suggest you wait for her outside her place of
work."

Feeling more desperate for his nostalgic interlude,

Milo looked for an ashtray; there was none. He tapped out a Tennessee-bought Davidoff, deciding to ash into the cup and drink the wine from the bottle. "That'll give me time to nap. It was a long flight."

"Oh, right," said Einner. "I forgot how old you are."

Milo was too stunned to say what his mind muttered: *I'm only thirty-seven.*

"Don't worry, Weaver. We'll have you out of here in time for your vacation. I don't even know why they bothered flying you in."

"We done?"

"I understand the subject is an old friend of yours."

"Yes." Milo took a drag, losing his grip on his sense of humor, while someone nearby coughed loudly.

"Don't let that get in the way."

Milo suppressed the urge to shout a reply. Instead, he hung up as, a few seats away, a young man started a coughing fit into his hand, glaring at him.

Milo suddenly realized why. Round eyes watched him tap ash into his plastic cup, and he waited for the hammer to fall. It was swift—the cashier, having noticed the crime in action, called over a stock boy who had been crouched by the canned coffee mixtures, and he followed her pointed finger to Milo's corner. The boy, eighteen or so, wiped his hands on his orange apron as he weaved expertly between tables toward him. "Monsieur, ici vous ne pouvez pas fumer."

Milo considered standing his ground, then noticed the big sign with the symbol for no smoking on the wall, a few feet from him. He raised his hands, smiling, took one last drag, and dropped the cigarette into the plastic cup. He poured in some of the wretched wine to extinguish it. The stock boy, behind a bashful grin, was relieved not to have to throw this man out.

Grainger had booked him into the Hotel Bradford Elysées, one of those classical, overpriced monstrosities along the Rue Saint-Philippe du Roule that, were anyone to ever audit the books of the Department of Tourism, would be the first thing to go. He asked the front desk for a wake-up call at eleven thirty—about four hours from then—and picked up a *Herald Tribune*. In the ornate Bradford Elysées elevator, he read headlines. They weren't pretty.

More car bombs in Iraq, killing eight U.S. soldiers, and more riots in Khartoum, Sudan: a photo of a full square of angry men—thousands—waving placard photographs of the dead Mullah Salih Ahmad, a white-bearded holy man with a white taqiyah covering his bald scalp. Other signs in Arabic, the caption told him, called for the head of President Omar al-Bashir. On page eight, he found a single-paragraph story saying that Homeland Security had apprehended a suspected political assassin, whom they refused to name.

Yet the most important news was unwritten: Milo Weaver had arrived in Paris to set up one of his oldest friends.

Mawkishly, he remembered when both of them were young field agents in London. Lots of codes and clandestine meetings in out-of-the-way pubs and arguments with British intelligence about the mess their countries were just starting to make of the postcommunist world. Angela was smart and stable—a near-contradiction in their business—and she had a sense of humor. In intelligence, those three things together are so rare that when you find them, you don't let go. Given the amount of time they spent together, everyone assumed they were a couple. This served them both. It kept her homosexuality out of conversations, and saved Milo from diplomats' wives setting him up with their nieces.

For two months after the Venice fiasco, Angela couldn't speak to him—that's how much killing her boss, Frank Dawdle, had disturbed her. But the next year, when Milo became simultaneously a husband and a dad to a baby girl, Angela came to the wedding in Texas and showered happy praise on Tina. They had remained in touch, and when Angela came to town Tina always insisted they take her out to dinner.

He lay on the hotel bed without undressing and considered calling Tom. What to say? He'd already argued Angela's innocence. Should he report that James Einner was a dunce, unequipped to handle the operation? Tom didn't care what Milo thought of Einner.

The truth—and for a moment it disturbed him—was that, six years ago, as a Tourist, he never would have questioned any of this. The job would have been simple and clean. But he wasn't a Tourist anymore, and for that he had no regrets.

11

The American embassy was separated from the Champs-Elysécs by the long, rigorous Jardin des Champs-Elysées. He parked along Avenue Franklin D. Roosevelt and walked the length of the park, passing old Parisians on benches with bags of bread crumbs dangling between their knees, luring pigeons, while the midday sun burned hot and moist.

Paris in July is a bleak place to be. The locals have started to flee on their welfare-state vacations, and in their place Japanese, Dutch, Americans, Germans, and Brits stand in lines leading to ticket counters, their necks craned, waving brochures at perspiring cheeks, shouting at errant children. The elderly tourists move in packs, clutching walkers or fooling with wheelchairs, while the young stop periodically to bitch about the hard sidewalks and whisper, surprised, about how many black people there are in Paris.

Most of them, just before leaving home, watched Gene Kelly and Leslie Caron dance through white-bread streets and are shocked by today's rues and avenues. Instead of fat old men with mustaches offering slices of cheese with aperitifs, they're faced with white boys in dirty dreadlocks playing movie sound tracks on beat-up guitars, suspiciously pushy Africans selling miniature Eiffel Towers and models of the Louvre pyramid, and hordes of tourists like themselves, guided by stern elderly French women waving colored flags to keep them on track.

Of course, there was plenty of beauty in Paris, but, given his reason for being there, Milo could hardly see it.

He found a bench at the Place de la Concorde end of the park, facing tree-lined Avenue Gabriel and the embassy at number 2. He gave a smile to the old woman beside him on the bench, surrounded by pigeons. She returned his smile and tossed crumbs at the birds. It was only twelve ten, so he searched his pockets for cigarettes before guilt overwhelmed him and he let them be. He crossed his arms over his chest and stared at the white wedding-cake building with three uniformed marines in its yard wearing automatic rifles.

"Bonjour, monsieur," said the old woman.

Milo gave her a half-smile, no more than politeness. "Bonjour."

"Etes-vous un Touriste?"

A single tooth was missing from the front of her grin. She winked. He said, "Oui."

"Monsieur Einner voudrait savoir si vous avez le paquet." *Mr. Einner would like to know if you have the package*.

Milo looked around. There—parked along Avenue Gabriel was a white van advertising FLEURS. Smoke sputtered from its exhaust pipe, the only running motor in sight.

Flower delivery van. Einner had obviously spent his training period watching too many old spy movies.

He turned back and switched to English. "Tell him to come ask himself."

Her smile remained, but she didn't say anything. The wire she wore had already picked up his words. Across the park, the flower delivery van's rear door popped open, and a tall blond man crossed the grass toward them. James Einner's face was very red, his cherry lips sealed tight. Once he was in punching distance, Milo noticed that his red lips were peeling. He wondered if Einner had herpes, and made a mental note to update his file when he returned to New York.

"Hello, James," said Milo.

"Just answer the fucking question, Weaver. You're pissing all over our security."

Milo smiled; he couldn't help himself. "Yes, James. I have the package."

Einner saw nothing funny in any of this. "You're not in an office, Weaver. This is the real world."

Milo watched him storm back to the van. The old woman was stifling a laugh, biting her lip so that her giggles wouldn't be heard over the microphone.

Twelve thirty came and went, and Milo started to

worry. The black half-moon cameras along the edge of the embassy, and others attached to streetlamps, had no doubt been marking his progress. Some pale technicians in the embassy basement, sitting all day in front of monitors, had by now noticed his loitering and put him through the face-recognition software. Certainly they knew who he was. He didn't know whether they'd pass the information on to Angela Yates. If they did, might she choose to stay inside to avoid him? Maybe she suspected the embassy was watching her, and—regardless of her guilt or innocence—would choose to slip away from him entirely. Milo preferred that possibility.

Then, at twelve fifty-seven, she emerged from the embassy, nodding at the stiff marine who opened the door for her. She wore a light, colorful scarf that showed she was falling for French fashion. A thin mauve sweater was tight over her breasts, and her beige skirt stopped where her patent leather boots started, just below her knees. Five years in Paris had done an excellent job on Angela Yates, formerly of Madison, Wisconsin.

She left through the electrified gate, continued west on the sidewalk, then north to the Rue du Faubourg Saint-Honoré, and stopped to get euros from a Rothschild Banque ATM. Milo followed from his side of the street.

She was a brisk walker, and perhaps that was a sign she knew he was following. If so, she didn't bother looking back to check. Angela had never been a nervous agent. In London, she'd been the best.

The last time they'd seen each other, a year ago, had been at the Peter Luger Steak House with Tina and

Stephanie. In his memory there was a lot of laughter. Angela had come to town for some seminar, and over two-inch steaks and baked potatoes she imitated the various speakers' monotone voices. Even Stef had found the humor in it.

She turned up Rue Duras and stepped into a small, packed bistro with gilded windows. Milo crossed to her side of the street, galloping around a wild Renault, and stood by the framed menu, peering through the glass as she approached the bar. A fat man in an apron greeted her with big smiles. This was her regular. The manager put a hand on her shoulder and guided her between hunched backs, around harried waiters, to the far wall, and a small table for two. Perhaps, Milo thought as he entered, she was expecting company.

The manager, having finished with Angela, scuffled up to him with an expression of sympathetic pain. "Je suis désolé, monsieur. Comme vous pouvez voir, pas d'place."

"It's all right," he answered in English. "I'm joining the lady."

The manager gave a nod before running off to evict a young couple that had wandered in behind him—a tall, handsome man and a butch-looking woman with swollen eyes.

As he approached her table, Angela stared at an opaque sheet of paper with the day's specials written in calligraphy, black hair hanging over her face. When Milo reached the opposite chair, she looked up and, with an expression of shock in her lavender eyes, said, "Milo! Holy shit! What are you doing here?"

Yes, she'd seen him on the embassy cameras. And, yes, she'd expected company—him. He leaned down to kiss her flushed cheeks. "I was out on the street, looked up, and saw a beautiful lesbian walking in here."

"Sit down, you old fart. Tell me all about absolutely everything."

They ordered a carafe of house red and quickly fell into the rhythm of small talk they had both been trained to use to their advantage in spy school. But neither of them was trying, which was nice. It was good to see her again. Milo wanted to know what she'd been up to.

There hadn't been much, she admitted. A year ago, not long after their night at Peter Luger's, she'd had a falling-out with her girlfriend—some French aristocrat— and since then she'd focused entirely on her work. Never much of a social butterfly, Angela compensated for her heartbreak by rising in rank. She not only ran the embassy's CIA station but also oversaw the entire diplomatic network in France, covering consulates and American presence posts in Paris, Bordeaux, Lille, Lyon, Rennes, Strasbourg, Marseille, Nice, and Toulouse.

She was proud of her accomplishments—Milo could see this. She'd personally directed the uncovering of three leaks in the last nine months. The excitement in her face when she described—in abstracts, of course— the capture of the last one was classic Angela, the same excited face she'd used when Milo told her, six years ago, that he was getting married. She seemed much the same as she'd been back then and, notably, was still more of a patriot than Milo had ever been.

"It's infuriating," she told him. "You listen to the French rant about how we're a lumbering military giant, that we're making the world unsafe for everyone. None of them see our mistakes as honest mistakes. Know what I mean? Every time we do something they don't like, we're accused of trying to control the world's oil, or trying to nudge Europe off the world stage." She shook her head. "Don't they realize we're in an unprecedented situation? No country in history has ever had as much power and responsibility as we've got. We're the first truly global empire. Of course we're going to make mistakes!"

It was an interesting perspective, even if he didn't agree with it. Despite Grainger's love of that word, Milo no longer went for the easy label of "empire" to describe his country. Instead, he thought it was a vanity committed by Americans who wanted to see Rome in the mirror, who wanted to mythologize themselves. But all he said was, "Do the French give you trouble?"

"Behind the scenes, away from the public, they're very cooperative. In fact, they've been helping me on a pet project."

"Yes?"

She smiled, tight-lipped, her cheeks flushed. "It could be a major coup for my career. The big fish."

"You've got me interested."

Angela gave him a flirtatious wink. "An animal name."

"Animal?"

"*Grrowl,*" she breathed, a kitschy seduction.

He, too, was reddening. "The Tiger."

12

It hurt to see how proud she was as she leaned forward, whispering the story of an investigation she'd been running the last eight months. "Since November. After he took out Michel Bouchard, the foreign minister. Remember that?"

Milo did. Grainger had sent Tripplehorn to Marseille to look into the assassination, but the French had quickly tired of his questions. "We sent someone, but he was stonewalled."

She opened a hand in an expression of *c'est la vie*. "I had a friend, Paul, working the case. Knew him through the Marseille consulate. Unlike a lot of his coworkers, he didn't have a problem accepting my help. I knew it was the Tiger. I *knew* it."

"All I heard was that, after a few months, the French verified it was him."

"French, my ass. It was me. With Paul's help, of

course." She winked, drank more wine, and said, "Bouchard was with his mistress in the Sofitel. A little vacation away from the wife." She cleared her throat. "Very continental."

Milo smiled.

"Anyway, they'd been to some party—really, these people don't even *try* to hide their indiscretions—and came back roaring drunk. They got to the hotel, and his bodyguards walked him up to the room. It had been searched beforehand, of course, and they left him alone. The usual followed, and then, early the next morning, the girl woke up screaming." Angela reached for her wine again, looked at it, but didn't drink. "She hadn't heard a thing. The coroner said his throat was cut around three in the morning. The killer had gotten in through the balcony, done his job, and slipped out again. They found some marks on the roof, where he'd climbed down. Rope."

"And the girl?"

"Basket case. She and the bed were soaked in blood. Paul told me she'd had a dream about pissing herself. That was as close as she came to being aware of anything."

Milo topped off their glasses, emptying the carafe.

"There was no reason to think it was the Tiger. A man like Michel Bouchard has so many enemies. Hell, even *we* would've been happy to see him go. You heard his Armistice Day speech?"

Milo shook his head.

"He accused us of trying to take over Africa. The French think they're the guardians of that continent, and he's been lobbying us to release AIDS drugs willy-nilly to everyone."

"Something wrong with that?"

Angela looked at him, and he wasn't sure what the look meant. "Maybe, but like the rest of Europe he sees our refusal as a conspiracy to, I don't know, depopulate the continent so we can roll in and suck up its oil. Or something like that," she said and drank. "Anyway, he was killed ten days after that speech."

"You think we knocked him off?"

She let out a half-laugh. "Please. A French foreign minister? Give me someone important. No, it looked like the oldest reason—money. He was up to his neck in property speculation and had run up too many loans. He was going to dark places for his capital. The man invested millions in Uganda and the Congo while he was negotiating their development loans. If he'd survived, he'd be facing charges. Luckily for him, one of his lenders took care of the problem." Another shrug. "The man died a hero."

"And the Tiger?"

As she took a breath, Angela's eyes sparkled. This, then, was where she entered the story. "Luck, really. Like I said, I was convinced it was the Tiger. It didn't match his modus, but what other known assassin has the audacity to pull this off? Answer: No one. So I asked around, and it turned out that Tom Grainger—he's still your boss, right?"

Milo nodded.

"Well, Tom had three photos of him. From Milan, Frankfurt, and the Arab Emirates. Paul and I went through all the hotel security footage. Took forever, I can tell you, and we still came up empty. But I persisted. You know how persistent I can be—hey, what's that look?"

Milo didn't know he had a look, and said as much. In fact, he was wondering why Grainger hadn't told him about the photo request. Angela let it go.

"We went public. By then it was January, and it was the only thing to do. I printed up the Italian shot and sent it all around Marseille. Stores, banks, hotels. The works. Nothing. Came up completely dry. Weeks passed. I returned to Paris. Then, in February, Paul called. Some teller at the Union Bank of Switzerland said she recognized the face."

"How did her memory suddenly start working?"

"You forget how long French vacations are. She'd been skiing."

"Oh."

"Back to Marseille, then, and we went over the bank's footage. Bingo—there he was. November 18, three days before the assassination, emptying and closing an account of three hundred thousand dollars. Samuel Roth was listed as the account's cosigner—that's one of the Tiger's aliases. Of course, he had a passport to identify himself, and we got the copy they made. But more importantly, we had the account."

Milo's hands were on the table, on either side of his glass. "Yes?"

To stretch out the suspense, Angela took another sip. She was enjoying this. "Opened November 16 in Zürich under the name Rolf Vinterberg."

He leaned back, amazed that, in mere months, she had followed a trail farther than he had in the last six years. "So? Who's Rolf Vinterberg?"

"Hard to say. Address is just a door on a Zürich side street. He opened the account with cash. The Zürich branch camera catches a man with a hat. Tall. And the name's trash."

"How come I never heard any of this? Weren't you reporting to Langley?"

She looked uneasy, then she shook her head.

Admiration mixed with frustration. If she hadn't been so paranoid, they could have pooled their resources. But Angela didn't want to dilute the credit—this kind of catch really was a career-maker. He said, "I've been after him for years. Did you know that?"

There was no reason she would have known. She looked into her glass and shrugged. "Sorry." She wasn't sorry, though.

"I met with him on Wednesday. In the States."

"The Tiger?"

He nodded.

Her pink cheeks drained of color. "You're joking."

"He's dead, Angela. Took cyanide. Turned out one of his employers stuck him with HIV. Unlike us, his employer knew he was a Christian Scientist."

"Christian—*what*?" She didn't seem to understand. "He was what?"

"He wouldn't take drugs for it, so it was killing him."

She couldn't speak, could only drink her wine and stare at him. Angela had spent the last eight months building up an investigation—an impressive one, he had to admit—that would finally take her to the next level in her career, and with a few words, Milo had dashed those months of hope.

But Angela was also practical. She'd faced enough disappointment in her life not to wallow in it. She raised her glass to him. "Congratulations, Milo."

"Don't congratulate me," he said. "I was just running to the Tiger's directions. He laid a trail for me to follow, so I could hear his last wish."

"Which was?"

"To track down whoever had him killed." She didn't reply, so he added: "Which means you're still at the forefront of this. I'd like to know who decided to off him."

She sipped her wine. "Okay, Milo. Talk to me."

Over the next quarter hour, he filled her in on the details of the Tiger's story, watching her face run through a range of emotions as she slowly regained her hopefulness.

She cut in: "Salih Ahmad? In the Sudan? *He* did that?"

The news seemed to invigorate her, though he didn't know why. "That's what he admitted to," he said. "Why? You know something about it?"

"No," she answered, a little too quickly. "Go on."

When he told her about Jan Klausner, a.k.a. Herbert Williams, he remembered something. "You've got a shot of him. He's the one with the Tiger in Milan."

She frowned. "Your office must have cropped him out."

"I'll get you a full shot."

"Thanks."

By the time he finished, she was sitting straight again, biting her lower lip in anticipation. It pleased Milo that he could bring her back like that, but he got the sense—and there was nothing he could put his finger on as evidence—that she was holding something else back. Something she didn't trust him with. So he pressed his original point, to help her feel in control: "I can't follow this up from the States, so it has to be your game. I'll run to your directions. Sound good?"

"Aye aye, cap'n," she said, smiling, but followed with silence. Whatever she was holding back would stay with her, at least for now. She held up a slender hand. "Enough about work, okay? Talk family. Stephanie's what? Six?"

"Nearly," he said, reaching for the carafe, then remembering it was empty. "Mouth like a sailor's, but I'm not trading her in yet."

"Tina still ravishing?"

"More so. Probably best I didn't bring her."

"Watch out." She winked, then gave a misshapen smile that reminded him that Angela Yates was no fool. "So tell me what you want."

"Why do you think I want something?"

"Because you spent an hour outside the embassy waiting for me. You didn't bother calling ahead, because you didn't want a record of us meeting. And, like you said, you've got a family. I seriously doubt Tina would let you take a Paris vacation without her." She paused, her expression serious. "See where I'm going with this?"

The café was full of lunching French and very few, if any, Americans. Through the window, he noticed the tall, handsome man from earlier waiting on the street for a table—he wondered where his girlfriend, the one with swollen eyes, had fled to.

Milo folded his knuckles under his chin. "You're right: I need something. Small favor."

"Big trouble?"

"No trouble at all. Just an inconvenience. I need you to hold on to something until next week. On Monday, someone will ask you for it and you'll give it to him."

"Big? Small?"

"Very small. A flash drive."

She peered around the restaurant just as Milo had. She managed a whisper. "I'll need to know more."

"Fine."

"What's on it?"

"Just a report. I can't send it because all my contact's communications are compromised."

"He's in town?"

"Beirut, but he'll fly to Paris Monday morning and come to the embassy. Once he's got it, there's no more need for intrigue."

"So why the intrigue now?"

Angela, Milo believed, trusted him. At least, she trusted the London field agent she'd once known so well, but in the last years their relationship, despite periodic visits, had become more distant, and he didn't know if she'd buy the story. He sighed. "Truth is, I'm supposed to hand it over myself. But I can't stay in France."

"Why not?"

Milo scratched his nose, feigning embarrassment. "It's . . . well, it's my vacation. Tina's already reserved our hotel in Florida. Disney World. And she can't pull out of it. One of those cut-rate Internet deals." That part, at least, was true.

Angela laughed. "Don't tell me you're afraid of your wife!"

"I'd just like to spend my vacation *on* vacation. Not arguing."

"Not the man you used to be, are you?" She winked. "Why didn't you send someone from New York to deliver it?"

"There is no one else," he said. "I've been working up this report for the last month. I don't want anyone else looking at it."

"And then you remembered me."

"I remembered Angela Yates, my oldest friend."

"I'm assuming you didn't tell Tom about this."

"Look who's the sharpest knife in the drawer."

She glanced beyond Milo, scanning the crowd. "You going to tell me what's on it?"

Milo started to tell her what Grainger had ordered him to say, that it was an analysis of Chinese oil interests in Kazakhstan, but changed his mind. With Angela, curiosity was the killer. "Some Asian oil stuff. You don't need to know the details, do you?"

"I guess not." After a pause, she said, "Okay, Milo. For you, anything."

"You've saved my ass." A waiter slid past him, and he caught his arm, asking for a bottle of Moët. Then he leaned close to Angela. "Give me your hand."

She seemed unsure, but did as he asked. She had long fingers, and her nails were buffed but unpainted.

Milo took her dry hand in both of his, tenderly, as if they were lovers. Her eyes grew, just a little, as she felt the flash drive press into her palm. Lightly, he kissed her knuckles.

13

There were two messages waiting at the hotel. James Einner wanted to know if everything had gone as planned, though he worded it as "Has the money been transferred yet?" Milo crumpled that into his pocket. The other message, blank, was from Grainger, signed "Father." Despite already having a buzz from lunch, once in his room he poured a tiny vodka from his fridge into a glass. He opened the high French windows and leaned out to look down on the rush-hour gridlock of the Rue Saint-Philippe du Roule. He lit a cigarette before dialing.

Tina answered drowsily. "Yeah?"

"*Darling,* it's me."

"Which one?"

"The stupid one."

"Oh. Milo. Still in Paris?"

"Yeah. How're things?"

"I don't know. Just getting up. You sound—are you drunk?"

"Actually, a little."

"What time's it there?"

He checked his watch. "Nearly three."

"I guess that's all right."

"Listen, I might not get back until Sunday."

Silence, then the noise of sheets as she sat up straight. "Why?"

"Things are kind of complicated."

"How complicated?"

"Not dangerous."

"Okay," she said. "You know when our plane leaves, right?"

"Monday, ten in the morning."

"And if you're not here by then . . ."

"I'll be vacationing on my own."

"I'm glad that's understood," she said as he took a drag of his cigarette. "Hold it, mister."

"What?"

"You're *smoking*."

He tried to sound offended: "I'm *not*."

"You're in a whole heap of trouble," Tina said, then: "Hey, baby."

"Hey what?"

"Stef's here." Her voice muted slightly as she said, "Wanna talk to your daddy?"

"Why would I?" he heard Stephanie say.

"Be nice," said Tina, and after a moment Stephanie came on.

"This is Stephanie Weaver. To whom am I speaking?"

"You're speaking to Milo Weaver," he said.

"Very nice to speak to you."

"*Stop it!*" he screamed, and she started laughing. Once the fit had passed, she slipped back into her five years and babbled about every single event that had filled her Thursday. It was mesmerizing stuff.

"You called him what?"

"Sam Aston is a *jerk,* Dad. He called me prissy. So I called him a dirty rat. What do you expect?"

Once she'd run out of stories, Tina came back on and made veiled threats about what might happen if he didn't make it back in time. Milo made veiled whimpers. When he hung up, left with only the noise of the traffic, the world seemed a little deader. He called Grainger.

"What?" the old man shouted.

"It's me, Tom."

"Oh. Sorry, Milo."

"What was that about?"

"Nothing. Did everything work out? It's done?"

Below him, the traffic was getting loud, so he stepped back from the window. "Yeah."

"See what I told you? Fly home tonight and you won't miss a minute of your vacation."

"Is Einner running surveillance?"

"What surveillance?"

"You're not just waiting to see if that report turns up in Beijing, are you?"

"Oh. Of course not. Yes, he's running it."

"Then I'm going to float a little."

Grainger cleared his throat. "I don't know why you're making trouble over this."

"Because she's innocent."

"Has Einner shown you his evidence yet?"

"I don't need to see evidence, Tom. We spoke for nearly two hours. She's innocent."

"One hundred percent sure?"

"Let's say, ninety-seven."

"Three percent's enough to go on. You know that."

"But she's doing important work here," Milo persisted. "I'd hate to see that compromised."

"She's a security chief, Milo. It's not rocket science."

"She's trailing the Tiger."

Silence.

"Don't play stupid, Tom. You sent her photos of him months ago. Why didn't you tell me?"

"Milo," he said, his tone vaguely authoritative, "don't pretend to know everything that's going on here, okay? I made a decision that seemed correct at the time. And besides, she wanted to keep it quiet. I respected that."

"Sure."

"So, what's she got?"

"She has a lot more than I ever pulled together. She has him on video at the Marseille branch of the Union Bank of Switzerland, withdrawing his fee for killing Michel Bouchard. Three hundred grand. She followed the account to Zürich, set up by a Rolf Vinterberg."

"Vinterberg," Grainger said slowly, perhaps writing this down.

"Fact is, we should've had her working on the Tiger from the beginning. We would've caught him years ago. Compared to her, I'm a dunce."

"Consider that noted, Milo. But if she's trading secrets, I want to know."

"Okay."

"You're not going to make trouble for him, are you?"

"Who?"

"Einner."

"You know me, Tom. I'm just happy to be of help."

14

He returned to the park after four, having changed into something less obvious—a T-shirt and jeans, the earplugs of his iPod on view beneath a trilby hat he'd grabbed from a shop near the hotel. With sunglasses, it was enough of a disguise to avoid easy detection from the embassy's cameras, but wouldn't hold up to scrutiny. He didn't think he'd need that.

Einner's old woman had been replaced by an old man in a grimy Members Only jacket who leaned back on the bench, his face to the sun, a soiled plastic bag balled up beside him. Einner's flower van was still parked along Avenue Gabriel.

There wasn't much to do until five, so Milo let himself be taken away by the iPod mix—his French sixties was continuing, and he hoped it could raise his spirits. More France Gall, some pre-children's-music Chantal

Goya, Jane Birkin, Françoise Hardy, Anna Karina, and Brigitte Bardot with Gainsbourg, singing "Comic Strip":

SHEBAM! POW! BLOP! WIZZ!

By 5:10 P.M., the park was full of people heading home. Even the old man was sitting up, turning to look toward the embassy.

From his position, Milo couldn't see the embassy gate, so he started walking toward Avenue Gabriel, holding the iPod near his face, as if having trouble with it. But he stared ahead at the old man, who got slowly to his feet in an imitation of old bones, then crouched to fool with his shoelaces.

Milo, too, had to hide his face, because Angela had passed the FLEURS van and was walking in their direction, heading east through the park to the Place de la Concorde metro station. Milo, among the crowd, turned casually away from her. The old man followed Angela away.

Milo hurried toward Gabriel and reached the van as it was beginning to reverse out of its tight parallel parking situation. He rapped on the tinted rear window and waited.

Einner didn't answer immediately, probably looking out at Milo's face and wondering if he'd go away. Then he made up his mind and popped open the door. His lips were in terrible shape—it looked like he'd been chewing them. "What the hell are you doing here, Weaver?"

"Give me a lift?"

"Get out of here. Go home."

He started to pull the door shut again, but Milo put himself in the way. "Please, James. I need to come along."

"What you *need* to do is get home."

"Come on," Milo said, making friendly. "If you have to pick her up, it'll be easier with me. She won't run if I'm there."

Einner considered that.

"Honestly," Milo said. "I just want to help."

"Did you clear this with Tom?"

"Call him if you want."

Einner pushed the door open again and grinned to show that he wasn't such a bad sport. "You look like an over-the-hill teenager."

Milo didn't bother telling him what he looked like.

Einner's mobile control center was an elaborate affair consisting of two laptops, two flat-screen monitors connected to a mainframe, a generator, and a microphone and speakers. The seats had been moved flat against the right wall, facing the equipment. It made for a tight fit, particularly since the embassy lightweight behind the wheel drove by punching the pedals. The whole way to Angela's apartment in the Eleventh Arrondissement, Einner remained in radio contact with his shadows. They reported that Angela had boarded the metro, gotten out at Place de la Nation, and taken the long walk up tree-lined Avenue Philippe Auguste to her apartment on Rue Alexandre Dumas.

"Good thing you were on top of that," said Milo.

Einner was focused on a video feed of Angela's apartment building, taken from a wide-angle tie-pin job. They watched Angela push through the glass doors. He said, "If your role here is to offer sarcasm, we'll drop you off at the airport."

"Sorry, James."

They rode in silence and soon reached her neighborhood. Some members of the diplomatic crowd, which was big enough in Paris to constitute its own city, kept house in this eastern part of the eleventh district. The streets were lined with Beamers and Mercs.

From a speaker, they heard a click and a dial tone.

"You tapped her phone?" Milo said as a monitor displayed the number she'd dialed: 825.030.030.

"What did you think, Weaver? We're not amateurs."

"Neither is she. I'll bet your vacation time that she's on to you."

"Shh."

A woman's voice said, "Pizza Hut."

The computer's phone directory verified that this was true.

She proceeded to order a *Hawaïenne* pizza with a Greek salad and a six-pack of Stella Artois.

"Big eater," Einner said, then typed on a laptop. The second monitor, wedged against the inside of the roof, flickered and lit up on a high angle of Angela's living room. There she was, walking away from the phone to the couch, and yawning. Milo imagined the afternoon champagne had made the rest of her day a chore to get through. She found a remote among the cushions, flopped down, and turned on the television. They couldn't see the screen, but heard canned laughter as she unzipped her boots and set them beside the coffee table.

The van slowed, and the driver called back, "We're here."

"Thanks, Bill." Einner glanced at Milo before returning to the screen. "This could take days, you know. I'll call you when she does something."

"*If* she does something."

"Whatever."

"I'll keep you company."

After a half hour, the sun began to set at the end of the street, cutting though the rear windows. Pedestrians returned home, desperate to shed their suits. It was a pretty street, and reminded Milo a little of his home in Brooklyn, which he was beginning to miss. He still wasn't sure why he wasn't on a plane right now—what, really, could he do to help Angela? Einner might be arrogant, but he wasn't going to frame her. And if Milo turned out to be wrong, and she *was* selling secrets, then he couldn't help her anyway.

"How did all this come about?" he asked.

Einner leaned back, but kept watching Angela. She was smiling at something on the tube. "You know how it came about. Colonel Yi Lien's laptop."

"But why was MI6 looking at the colonel in the first place?"

He considered Angela a moment, then shrugged. "They'd been tracking him. Two-man team, routine stuff. Just keeping an eye on the opposition."

"*They* told you this?"

Einner looked at him as if he were a child. "You think they talk to Tourists? Please. Only Tom's ear is worthy of their secrets."

"Go on."

"Well, every other weekend, this colonel takes the ferry from Portsmouth to Caen. A little cottage north of Laval. One of those remodeled farmhouses."

"What about this girlfriend?"

"Renée Bernier. French."

"A budding novelist, I hear."

Einner scratched his cheek. "I've read a little of her opus. It's not bad." When Angela got up, he typed something, and the monitor switched to the bathroom as she entered, unbuttoning her skirt lazily.

"You're going to switch that off, aren't you?"

He gave Milo a sour look. "I don't get off on this, Weaver."

"What about Renée Bernier? Could she have accessed the memo?"

Einner shook his head at Milo's simplicity. "You really think we just sit on our hands here, don't you? We're all over her. She's a devoted communist, for sure. Her novel's one big anticapitalist rant."

"I thought you said it was good."

"We're not the unwashed masses. I can tell a good writer when I read her. Even if her politics are juvenile."

"That's very open-minded of you."

"Isn't it?" he growled, then changed cameras again as Angela flushed the toilet and returned to the couch, now wrapped in a plush white robe. "Anyway, you know the story. Colonel Lien boards the ferry from Caen after another of his lost weekends. Halfway across the Channel, he collapses. The two MI6 men resuscitate him, and take the opportunity to copy his hard drive."

"Why Angela?"

Einner blinked at him. "What?"

"Why is everyone convinced that she's the source? All this is so circumstantial."

"You don't know?"

Milo shook his head, and that provoked a blistery smile.

"*That's* why you're being so hardheaded about this." He tapped on the second laptop. A file marked SWAL-LOW popped up. Bird names, Milo noticed. Straight out of *The Ipcress File*. Michael Caine, 1965.

Einner began to go through his case.

What followed was hard to keep track of. He showed Milo surveillance photographs, copies of documents, audio files, and video clips taken over the previous two months, the result of a sustained surveillance effort run by the proud Tourist sitting next to him. Some reports placed Angela at Chinese embassy parties, but even Einner admitted that that in itself wasn't damning. He even noted that Angela was using sleeping pills most nights, as if that were a sign of a guilty conscience. Then he got to the important part.

"See this man?" he said, pointing at a red-bearded thirty-something in a fitted suit. He was standing at a street crossing by the Arc de Triomphe, just behind Angela, both waiting for the light to change. Milo's cheeks warmed—he knew this man. Einner said, "That was May 9. Here." He tapped the trackpad, and the same man was sitting behind the wheel of a taxi, no longer in a suit, while Angela was in the back. "That's May 14. This is the sixteenth." A tap, and there they both were again, in the bistro where Milo had entrapped her, sitting at separate, but nearby, tables. In this shot, however, she wasn't alone at her table. Sitting across from her was a young, earnest-looking black man, hands open, speaking insistent words at her. "June 20," Einner said, and showed Milo another street-crossing shot, again with the red-bearded man. "All we have on this man is—"

"Who's the kid?"

"What?" Einner said, annoyed at the interruption.

"Go back," Milo said, and when Einner had returned to the bistro shot he touched the screen. "This guy."

"Rahman Something . . ." He squeezed his eyes shut. "Garang. That's it. Rahman Garang. Suspected terrorist."

"Oh?"

"She reported it," Einner told him. "She was trying to get information from him."

"In a public place?"

"His idea, apparently. Not very professional, but she didn't argue."

"Did she get anything?"

Einner shook his head. "We think he fucked off back to the Sudan."

"Sudan," Milo breathed, trying to sound uninterested.

"And before you ask," Einner said, "no—we don't think she's helping out terrorists. She's not subhuman."

"I'm glad you know that."

Einner went back to the last photo, of Angela crossing the street with the red-bearded man. "Anyway, this man here—"

"Herbert Williams," said Milo.

"Shit, Weaver! Would you stop interrupting?"

"That's who it is, isn't it?"

"Well, yes," Einner muttered. "That's the name he used to register with the Police Nationale. How the hell did you know?"

"What else do you have on him?"

Einner wanted an answer first, but he could see from Milo's face that he wouldn't get one. "Well, he gave the police a Third Arrondissement address. We checked it out—a homeless shelter. So far as they know, he's never even knocked on the door. He claims to be from Kansas City. We had the Feds check on it, and Herbert Williams's records go back to 1991, when he applied for a passport."

"He had to use a social security number, right?"

"Classic scam. The number does belong to a Herbert Williams, a black male who died at the age of three in 1971."

"We've got nothing else?"

"The guy's slippery. We put some people on him after two of the June meetings, but he got away each time. He's a real pro. But look at this." Once again, he tapped the trackpad, and a countryside shot appeared. Milo's first reaction was aesthetic—it was a beautiful shot. Wide-open space, big sky, and a small cottage off to the left. Then he noticed a car near the center. Einner's cursor became a magnifying glass, and he zoomed in. Grainy, but clear enough—two men stood beside the car, talking. One was Herbert Williams, a.k.a. Jan Klausner. The other was a fat Chinese man, Colonel Yi Lien.

"Where did you get this?"

"It's old Company material, from last year. Tom tracked it down when he learned about the colonel."

Milo rubbed his lips; they were as dry as Einner's. He was starting to hate Tom Grainger's idea of security. "You've been following her for two months. Why did you start?"

"The French station's been full of holes for years. Langley wanted to look into it, but outside the usual channels, and we decided to start with Angela Yates."

"We?"

"Me and Tom."

It was a basic part of his job that Milo wasn't privy to all the operations his office ran, and he tried to remember if there had been any clues that Angela was under investigation. The best he could come up with was when, a month before, he had asked to use Einner, who was a surveillance expert, to bug a meeting between the Sicilian Mafia and suspected Islamic militants in Rome. Grainger had only said that Einner was indisposed, and gave him Lacey instead. "So," he said, "you think all this is enough to hang her?"

"Of course I don't, Weaver. That's why I'm sitting here with you, rather than arresting her and going home to my girlfriend." Einner cleared his throat. "Now you. Tell me how you know Mr. Williams."

"Motorcycle," said Bill, stiffening behind the wheel.

They leaned toward the window. The sun was mostly gone, and they could just make out the silhouette of a leather-clad cyclist heading toward them. Einner shifted, removing a small Beretta from his shoulder holster—a Beretta, of course. "Don't get all *Gunsmoke,* now," said Milo.

The motorcycle cut between two cars and leapt to the sidewalk. A red box on the rear said PIZZA HUT.

Once the deliveryman had roared past and up to Angela's door, Einner holstered the Beretta. "Come on. Out with it."

Milo told him about Klausner/Williams and the Tiger. The news seemed to throw Einner off his game. From the speakers, they heard the soft melody of Angela's doorbell. Einner's hands floundered in his lap. "I—well, the Tiger." Then: "This changes everything, doesn't it?"

"I don't think so."

Einner regained his focus. "If Angela's connected to someone who controls—or controlled—the movements of the Tiger, then we're not just talking about her selling some secrets to the Chinese. She's being run by someone with serious contacts. She could be freelance now. Open market."

"The plan's still the same," said Milo. "Identify her contact, then bring him in. Don't touch Angela until we have him."

"Yes," Einner admitted with a touch of distracted melancholy, "you're right."

Milo opened the back door and climbed down into the street. "I'm getting some dinner. Call if you change position, okay?"

"Sure," Einner said, then pulled the door shut. The Parisian air smelled of ham and warm pineapple.

15

Milo found a small, neon Turkish place on a side street near Place Léon Blum and ordered a gyro, eating it against a stand-up table. None of this felt right. Either Angela was innocent, which was what he wanted to believe, or she was guilty of selling secrets— but to the Chinese? It would be more in her line to sell them to a country she sympathized with. The Poles, for instance. She was a third-generation Polish American who had grown up hearing that hard language all around her. Her fluency was one reason the Company had originally brought her on. So was her idealism. Money, in itself, wasn't enough to make Angela betray anyone.

Einner, whether or not he was giving her a fair shake, had invested a lot of budget hours into his two-month surveillance operation, and backing off Angela would look like a waste of government resources—a risky move in the midst of cutbacks.

Besides, the evidence was there. Angela was connected to the Tiger's client, Herbert Williams, and that man was connected to the Chinese colonel. Did she know this man was connected to the Tiger, whom she was so desperate to catch?

Another question: Why was the Sudan coming up so much? Angela had been shocked to learn of the Tiger's job there, and had hidden something—probably Rahman Garang, the young Sudanese terrorist.

But why?

As he stuffed flakes of moist roasted lamb into his mouth, he began to feel like he had when he'd smoked in the airport. He was being watched. In the window's reflection, he saw the whole of the narrow place: the low counter with a cash register and a bored girl in a peaked yellow cap, the young couple just behind him, leaning close and whispering nonsensical love-talk, and the two Arab men at a table by the wall, drinking Fanta and saying nothing. He gave the men a longer examination, but no—no one seemed interested in him. Then he returned to the lovers.

Yes. A tall, handsome man and a butch woman with heavy, swollen eyes, who looked as if she'd been beaten. From the café where he'd met Angela.

He lengthened his focus back to the street. It was nearly nine thirty, and the neighborhood was quiet. He swallowed a few more bites of lamb, then, without cleaning anything up, left the restaurant.

He headed to the next intersection—a right would put him on the busy street leading back to Angela's. As he rounded the corner, he glanced back and saw, at the door, the couple exiting the restaurant, holding hands and walking casually in his direction.

Once out of sight, he broke into a run, flying past cars and couples of all ages out for a stroll. A coincidence was always possible, but Milo's carefully tended paranoia didn't buy it. Probably French intelligence—the Secrétariat Général de la Défense Nationale, or SGDN. They had a file on Milo, and certainly took notice of his arrival, sans family, and his visit with Angela. They would want to know what he was doing in their country. He, on the other hand, wanted to keep Angela's shaky situation as far from them as possible.

Instead of continuing straight at the next intersection, Milo took another right and waited behind the corner. He peered out in time to see the couple again. They emerged onto the street, kissed, and split up. The man walked to the left, away from Milo, and the woman walked straight, also away from him. He waited until they were gone, then phoned Einner.

"I'm being followed."

Einner hummed. "Well, the French are kind of nuts about their sovereignty."

"We can't let them know she's under investigation. They won't trust her."

"Then maybe you should go home, old man."

"Anything happen?"

"Just preparing for bed."

"She knows she's being watched."

"Clearly," Einner said. "And she knows it's best to wait for the surveillance men to tire. It's our job to not get tired."

Milo wanted to argue this, but there was nothing to debate. "I'll be at my hotel. Call me before you move in."

"If I must."

"You must."

He had made it halfway to the metro station when his phone rang. He frowned at the unknown French number, then stepped into a quiet alley and answered. "Hello?"

"Still in town?" It was Angela.

Milo hesitated, then: "My plane's in the morning. Nine o'clock."

"How about a drink at your hotel? I've got insomnia, and there's more you might be interested in."

"About what?"

"*Grrowl.*"

He laughed, trying to sound natural. "Don't tell me you were holding out on me."

"I would never tell you that."

"Why don't I come to you? I'll bring a bottle. Besides, I think the French've been watching me. No need for them to see us together in a public place."

"Like they could follow a man of your considerable skills."

"Ha," he said. "Just give me your address, will you?"

16

He picked up more Davidoffs and a bottle of Smirnoff from an all-night convenience store, then called Einner. Einner, of course, had already heard everything. "She tried to get to sleep. No luck. She was fooling with her sleeping pills, but I guess even a conversation with you was more appealing than those."

"Do me a favor and knock off the surveillance, will you? We're good friends, and the talk will get personal."

"If you want to fuck her, go ahead. Don't ask my permission."

"I will punch you, James. Don't think I won't."

"Can't wait, old man."

"We'll talk about things no one needs to know about. If she starts to bring up anything relevant, then I'll call you."

"What's the code?" said Einner, pleased to be back in his own territory of ciphers and pass-phrases.

"Hell, I don't know. You'll hear my voice."

"Call your wife," he said. "Say you told her you'd call, and you forgot."

"But they're friends. Angela will want to talk to her, too."

"She's in the middle of something and has to run."

It was good enough, so Milo agreed. "You'll turn off the surveillance as soon as I show up?"

"Yeah. Promise."

Milo doubted that, but if things became too confessional, he knew the approximate locations of the cameras and could obstruct them. The microphones, though, would be another matter. Head to her terrace, perhaps?

She buzzed him up, telling him to come to the fourth floor, and he used the rickety elevator. She was waiting in her doorway, in jeans and a T-shirt, a glass of white wine in her hand. "That was quick. Didn't wake you up, did I?"

"Please," he said, wagging the Smirnoff at her. "It's five in the afternoon for me." He kissed her cheeks and followed her in.

He soon got the impression that Angela had changed her mind. She'd made the call, but while waiting for him had realized her mistake. They put the vodka in the freezer for later and drank wine on the same sofa he'd seen through the video cameras.

To loosen her up, Milo started in with questions about her love life. Yes, there was the princess from a year ago, but what about since then? "You've never kept your hands to yourself for long."

That provoked a laugh, but the fact was that she hadn't

been to bed with anyone since that relationship ended. "It was hard. Remember how I was after Frank Dawdle turned bad? It was like that."

"A problem of trust."

"Pretty much." She sipped the wine. "You can smoke, you know."

Milo took out his Davidoffs and offered one, but Angela had quit. "I could've started smoking again when the relationship went south, but that would be admitting defeat."

He gave her a smile, then said, "What did you want to talk to me about?"

Instead of answering, she went to the kitchen, and Milo knew this was his chance. He could call Einner to switch everything on, if it wasn't already. But he didn't, and weeks later this mistake would become a nasty little detail in the history of Milo Weaver.

She returned with the wine bottle, topped off their glasses, and even returned to the kitchen again to put the bottle in the recycling bin. By the time she'd finished the ritual and settled on the sofa, she had decided on her tactic. "How much do you know about what's going on in the Sudan?"

"As much as anyone else, I guess. A long, nasty north-south civil war ended a couple years ago. We brokered that. But now, in the Darfur region you've got another civil war between the Sudanese Liberation Army and the government-supported Janjaweed militia. Last I heard, over two hundred thousand were dead and another two million displaced. In the east, in the capital, you've now got another civil war, triggered by the assassination of Mullah Salih Ahmad in January, which was blamed on the president—though we know better, don't we?" He smiled, but she didn't. "What else? Terrible economy, crude oil being its primary export." He squinted at her, remembering something: "But they don't sell us oil, do they? We've got an embargo on them. They sell it to China."

"Exactly," she said, unflustered by the name of that country. "Right now, they're supplying seven percent of China's oil. China supplies the Sudanese government with weapons to kill its own people—they'll do anything to keep the oil flowing." She touched her lower lip. "It's funny. China's been under a lot of pressure from the UN to encourage President al-Bashir to make peace in Darfur. Finally, last February, Hu Jintao—the Chinese president, no less—met with him to discuss this. At the same time, he announced the cancellation of Sudan's Chinese debt and promised to build him a presidential palace. How fucked up is that?"

"Very fucked up."

"But go back to Salih Ahmad. This afternoon, you told me the Tiger killed Ahmad, and he wasn't doing it for the Sudanese government."

"He might have been wrong. He never knew *who* he was working for. Muslim extremists was his best guess."

She frowned. "There's a kid I met with a few times back in May. Rahman Garang. Sudanese. He was part of Salih Ahmad's group."

"Terrorist?"

Angela tilted her head, then nodded. "I'm not sure what all Rahman actually did, but yes, I'd call him a terrorist—a budding one, at least. His family's been here for about five years, and when he came back to visit in May, the French picked him up. They'd connected him to some cell in Lyon. He was a real hardhead. Vitriolic. It turned out he wasn't actually connected to anything in France, but while he was held he kept blaming his interrogators for the death of his mullah. *You and the Americans,* he said. That's why I got a call from my ex—she's not actually a princess, though she acts like one. She's French intelligence. I think it was her way of making peace with me. I talked with Rahman once in jail, and he told me he wasn't afraid of me. I—meaning the United States and all its allies—had killed Mullah Salih Ahmad, and he fully expected to be killed next. The French let him go, due to lack of evidence.

"But I was curious. We'd all seen the news. It was in his interest to blame President al-Bashir. After all, overthrowing him is the whole point of that insurgency. I tracked down Rahman's family about a week later, then convinced him to talk to me again. We had lunch in the center—same place you found me today. Rahman's brother—Ali—insisted on coming along for protection. I agreed, but made him wait outside the restaurant while we talked."

May 16, Milo remembered from Einner's photos. As she gulped down her wine, he said, "Was he raving? Or did he actually know something?"

Angela set down the glass; it was empty. "A little bit of both. Rahman had been at the mullah's house in Khartoum the night his body reappeared. A lot of friends were there, a kind of vigil with the family. Rahman went to the bathroom. Through the window, he could see into the backyard. He saw a European—a white man—delivering the body. *That* was the crux of his argument."

"Did you show him the photos of the Tiger?"

She shook her head, possibly embarrassed. "Didn't occur to me. But I told him I would look into it. If I'd been a man, I don't think he would've believed me. But he seemed to like me. I drove him and Ali back to his house, and over the next several days started looking into it. Really, I had nothing to go on. I had no reason to think this one was also the Tiger. There are a lot of white faces in the world, and I assumed al-Bashir had just gone to the regional open market for his killers."

"Did you report this?" Milo asked. "That you were helping Rahman."

Again, she shook her head, but there was no shyness now. "You know what would've happened—no one cares about a potential suicide bomber's conspiracy theories. I just reported that I was working him as a possible source."

"I see."

"After five days, it still wasn't going anywhere, so I went to give Rahman the bad news. His family wouldn't let me in. His mother, father, sister—I was suddenly a leper. Ali finally came out. They didn't know where he was. The day after our lunch, he got a call. Told his mother he had an important meeting. That was the last they saw of him."

"He didn't head back to Khartoum?"

She shook her head. "He couldn't have. This kid had

no tradecraft. He wasn't using fake passports or anything like that." She paused. "Then, last week, his body was found in Gonesse, not far off the Charles de Gaulle flight path. Two bullets in the chest. Forensics says he's been dead a month and a half or so—just after I talked to him."

Now it was Milo who needed to move. He rubbed his knees, stood, and went to get the chilled vodka. He should have made that call to Einner a while ago, under the guise of calling Tina, but he assumed Einner was listening anyway. He poured the vodka into their empty wineglasses; Angela didn't argue. "Forensics give anything else?"

"Nine millimeter, PPK. Those are spread pretty evenly throughout the world."

"Sounds like his friends saw him talking to you."

"That's what Ali thinks."

"You talked to him?"

"He called me. As soon as the body was found. That's how I learned about it."

Over the next hour, working their way through the vodka, they mused over the connections that these revelations seemed to suggest. "Seemed" was the operative word.

"X," they agreed, had hired the Tiger to kill a radical mullah in the Sudan, and when the Tiger began investigating the identity of his employer, X had him killed.

"Anyone could have killed Rahman," she said, blinking to keep Milo in focus. "His terrorist friends see him talking to me, and they decide he's a double. Or, whoever had the mullah killed thought he was discussing X's identity with me, and so X had him killed for the same reason he killed the Tiger."

Milo had to hold his tongue, because what he wanted to say would have given away what he knew. X's agent, Herbert Williams, had been seen with Angela Yates. What if, instead of being her contact, Williams was spying on her? Williams had been there, in the restaurant, when Rahman was meeting with Angela.

Ignore the Chinese diplomat and his stolen secrets, and the picture became something else. Angela as victim, rather than security leak.

Yet the question the Tiger had posed on his deathbed remained: Who was X? Who would have hired the Tiger to kill both Mullah Salih Ahmad and the French foreign minister? Would some terrorist group want them both dead? While Ahmad's death in the end helped militant Islam's cause in the Sudan, the foreign minister's death would do nothing to help them.

What, further, would explain all the acts of assassination by the Tiger since 2001, when Herbert Williams became one of the Tiger's clients?

Maybe Herbert Williams *was* X. Perhaps he was just a broker of death for whatever powerful people needed someone vanquished. In which case, there was nothing to tie the various murders together.

"The Chinese," she said. "Branding Salid Ahmad's corpse looks a lot like a direct warning to the extremists— quit harassing our friend, or you'll end up like this man. But it's almost too obvious, isn't it?"

Milo nodded. "China's a lot of things, but it's not

shortsighted. The Central Committee doesn't want a fight with the Sudanese masses. China doesn't want to send its troops to Africa, or have the international community looking too closely—they're hosting the Olympics in a year. The brand was supposed to inflame anti-Chinese, anti-imperialist sentiment." He took a breath. "I'm with the Tiger on this—I think he was working for the jihadists."

"The only way to know is to find Herbert Williams," she said.

Despite the frustration of no solid answers, he was enjoying this. Sitting with Angela, going through the details and variables and working through possible solutions, reminded him of their friendship more than a decade before, when both were young, unattached, and wildly enthusiastic about their employer and their country.

Then the mood shifted. She rubbed her arms as if chilled by the morbid stories they were spinning. A little after one, she said, "I'll call a taxi. Don't want to be late for Disney."

After calling, she used the toilet and came out popping a pill from a prescription bottle.

"What's that?"

"For sleeping."

He raised a brow. "You really need those?"

"You're not my shrink, Milo."

"Remember when I tried to hook you on amphetamines?"

At first she didn't, then she did. Her laugh was natural. "Man, you were such a wreck."

He gave her a kiss on the way out, and she handed him the still two-thirds full Smirnoff bottle. "Let's stay in touch about this," he said. "You've done so much more than I ever could have."

She patted his ass to urge him out. "That's because I'm smarter than you are."

The taxi was waiting for him, and before getting inside he looked toward the flower van. From its passenger seat, Einner was staring at him, holding up a questioning thumbs-up sign. Milo gave him an answering thumbs-up, and the Tourist returned to the back of the van. To Milo's surprise, Einner had actually given him his privacy. Milo never would have been so generous.

17

He woke early Saturday morning with a hangover, his lungs suffering dry rot. The television shouted the weather in French. He tried to open his eyes, but the room was a blur, so he shut them again.

This was what happened when he was away from his family. There was no one around to remind him that it was a mistake to spend the night with a bottle of vodka and a pack of smokes, watching late-night French television. He hadn't been like this when he was a Tourist, but now, Milo-the-family-man traveled like an immature teenager just set free from home.

Something moved—a creak—and he opened his eyes again, smeared colors shifting. He pushed back, fist rising. From the chair beside his bed, Einner smiled at him.

"You with me?"

Milo tried to sit up against the headboard; it was

difficult. He remembered sinking into the vodka and, out of curiosity, a child-sized bottle of hotel brandy and another of ouzo. He coughed up some bitter phlegm, then swallowed it.

Einner held up the bottle for examination—only three or so shots remained. "At least you didn't down the whole thing."

Milo realized, not for the first time, that he was no good at living.

Einner set the bottle on the floor. "Awake enough to talk?"

"I'm still a little drunk."

"I'll order coffee."

"What time is it?"

"Six in the morning."

"Jesus." He'd slept two and a half hours, max.

Einner called down for coffee while Milo went to wash his face. Einner appeared in the bathroom doorway, grinning. "Not like when you were young, eh?"

Milo used the toothbrush to scrape stomach acid from the back of his tongue. He felt like he was going to be sick, but didn't want to do that in front of Einner. Not that.

By the time Milo came out again, he could get Einner in focus. Amazingly, the Tourist looked well rested as he flipped through stations, settling on CNN International. Milo wished he looked like that. A shower—that would help.

"You here for a reason, James?"

Einner raised the television's volume, his expression morose. "It's Angela."

"What about her?"

Einner started to speak, then looked around the room. From his jacket pocket he produced an oil-stained receipt and a pen. Leaning against the bedside table, he wrote one word and held it out for Milo to read:

Dead

Milo's legs tingled and threatened to give out. He moved to the bed, settled down, and rubbed his face. "What're you talking about?"

Again, Einner hesitated, lifted his pen, but decided he could tell this without giving much away. "You left last night. You gave me the thumbs-up, so I powered it all up again."

"Okay. And?"

"She was just climbing into bed. Out like a light."

"Sleeping pills," said Milo. "She took them when I was still there."

"Right. So there she goes. Off to sleep. After an hour, I left to get some food. Bill took over. I got back an hour after that. That's when I noticed—she hadn't moved. Not at all. She—" He paused, looking at the paper and pen, considering, but again changed his mind. He leaned to whisper in Milo's ear. "For something like an hour, she hadn't moved an inch. She didn't even snore. Another hour passed—same damned thing."

"Verified?" Milo whispered back.

"Forty minutes ago. I went in and checked her pulse. Nothing. I made sure to take the flash drive."

"But . . ." Milo began. "But *how*?"

"Bill thinks it was something in her pizza, but he's like that. I'm for those sleeping pills you mentioned."

Milo's stomach cramped. He had been right there, watching her commit unintended suicide. He regulated his breaths. "Did you tell the police?"

"Really, Weaver. You must be convinced I'm an idiot."

Milo didn't feel like disputing that. He didn't feel anything beyond an acute hollowness. He knew it was the shock before the storm. He took the remote from Einner and muted the television, where Palestinian children were jumping in a street, celebrating something. "I'm taking a shower."

Einner took the remote to the bed, flipped to MTV Europe, and raised the volume. The room filled with French rap.

Milo crossed to the window and lowered the blinds, feeling numb all over except for the phenomenally loud pulse in his head.

"What's that for?"

Milo didn't know. He'd closed the blinds on instinct.

"Paranoia," said Einner. "You've got a touch of paranoia. I saw that before, but I didn't know why—not until last night. I checked on it. You—" He returned to his whisper: "You used to be a Tourist."

"It was a long time ago."

"What was your legend?"

"I've forgotten."

"Come on."

"Last one was Charles Alexander."

The room went silent—Einner had muted the television. "You're jerking my chain."

"Why would I?"

"Because," Einner began, sitting up on the bed. He had a moment of thought, then raised the volume again. "They still talk about Charles Alexander."

"Do they?"

"Really." Einner nodded vigorously, and Milo was unnerved by this sudden flush of respect. "You left a few friends and a *lot* of enemies scattered across the continent. Berlin, Rome, Vienna, even Belgrade. They all remember you well."

"You keep delivering such good news, James."

Milo's phone rang—it was Tina. He took it to the bathroom to escape the thumping music. "Hi, hon."

"Milo? Are you at a club?"

"It's the TV," he said, pushing the bathroom door shut. "What's up?"

"When're you getting home?"

She didn't sound scared, just . . . "Are you drunk?"

She laughed—yes, she was. "Pat brought over a bottle of bubbly."

"What a prince." Milo wasn't jealous of Patrick; her ex was just a mildly annoying fact of life. "What's the problem?"

She hesitated. "Nothing, nothing. Pat's gone, Stef's in bed. Just wanted to hear your voice."

"Listen, I've got to run. There's been some bad news here."

"Angela?"

"Yeah."

"She isn't . . . I mean . . ." Tina trailed off. "She in any trouble?"

"It's worse than that."

He listened to her silence, as she tried to figure out what was worse than being caught for treason. Then, somehow, she got it. "Oh Christ." She began to hiccup, as she often did when drunk, or nervous.

An Italian man Milo once knew liked to say, "There's something banal about grief. All that kitsch just turns my stomach." The Italian was an assassin, so his philosophy served to protect him from the emotional impact of his jobs. As he showered, though, Milo found himself feeling the same way about Angela. It turned his stomach the way he kept evoking her features and her tone of voice, her bright, pretty face and the way she had taken to Parisian fashions. He remembered her funnily seductive *Grrowl*. Unlike the emptiness of shock, he now felt as if he were full to overflowing with the kitsch of death.

When he came out of the bathroom, the towel around his waist, Einner was drinking room-service coffee from a tray, staring at the television, where two hundred or more Arab protesters shouted, fists raised, pressing forward against a high steel fence.

"Where?" said Milo.

"Baghdad. Looks like Iran, 1979, doesn't it?"

Milo slipped into a striped shirt. Einner again raised the volume—a move that had by now grown into an omen of important subjects—but he just watched Milo dress; he seemed to be thinking. As Milo pulled on his slacks, Einner said in his stage whisper, "You ever come across the Black Book? Or is that just one of those Tourism myths?"

In the young man's face, Milo saw a moment of naïve expectation. For various reasons—in particular because he wanted Einner to quit second-guessing him—he decided to lie. The Tiger, strangely enough, had provoked honesty from him. "It's real enough," he said. "I tracked down a copy in the late nineties."

Einner leaned closer, blinking. "Now you're really jerking my chain."

"No, James. I'm not."

"Where, then? I've looked, but never got close."

"Then maybe you're not meant to find it."

"Give me a break."

Milo gave him the line he'd heard so many times when he was younger. It was the line that gave the Black Book of Tourism, whether or not it existed, more of an aura than it probably deserved. "The book finds you, James. If you're worthy, you'll find a way to put yourself in its path. The book doesn't waste time with amateurs."

Einner's cheeks flushed and his breathing became shallow. Then, perhaps remembering who he was, he smiled and lowered the television's volume to a bearable level. "Know what?"

"What?"

"You're a Class-A bullshitter, Milo Weaver."

"You've got me figured out."

Einner started to laugh, then changed his mind. He had no idea what to believe.

18

On Milo's suggestion, they left the hotel by the rear stairwell and slipped out through the service entrance. Einner insisted on driving, and as they sped along the A1 toward Charles de Gaulle, Milo filled him in on what Angela had told him the previous night.

"You were supposed to call me, Weaver. Wasn't that our deal?"

"I thought you'd at least leave the microphones on."

Einner shook his head, frustrated. "We made a deal. I stick to my deals."

"You cleared it with Tom, didn't you?"

A pause. "At first he said no, but he called back and told me to do as you asked. But still, Weaver. You should've called."

"Sorry, James." He continued with Angela's tale of the young Sudanese radical convinced his mullah had been killed by the West.

"So he saw a European face," said Einner. "What's that mean?"

"It means the Tiger wasn't lying. He *did* kill Salih Ahmad. And probably not for the president. If I believe Angela's story—and I do—then I don't think she was ever in contact with Herbert Williams. I think Williams was spying on her. Maybe he worried she was looking into his identity—who knows? If she was tracking Rolf Vinterberg in Zürich, and if Vinterberg is connected to Williams . . ." Anything, really, was possible. "All I know is that Angela started collecting evidence, then she ended up dead."

"What about Colonel Yi Lien?" Einner asked. "You can weave whatever complicated story you want, but the fact remains that he got hold of information that she had access to. This Williams character was photographed with Lien. You're not seeing this straight, Weaver."

"But it makes no sense," Milo insisted. "If Angela was leaking information, then why would her controller kill her? That only draws more attention."

"So she couldn't give up his identity," Einner said, as if this were obvious.

"No," Milo began, but he didn't have anything to follow it up with.

"Whatever the reason," said Einner, "killing Angela served *some* purpose. We just don't know what it is yet."

Einner was right, and he knew it. He noticed how the young Tourist's hands trembled on the wheel. Was that how he could be so bright-eyed this early in the morning? "Are you doing uppers?"

Einner gave him a sidelong glare as he took the air-port exit. "What?"

"Amphetamines, coke, whatever."

"You think I'm high?"

"I mean in general, James. For the job. To keep going."

A bouquet of road signs listed airlines. "Now and then, sure. When I need to."

"Watch out. They ruined me in the end. I was a real mess."

"I'll remember."

"I'm serious, James. You're a good Tourist. We don't want to lose you."

Einner shook his head to shake off the confusion. "Fine. Okay."

Together, they bought a ticket from a pretty Delta clerk who'd shaved her head bald, then settled in a cafeteria to wait for the plane. Since there was no hard liquor available, Einner took a small, leather-covered flask of bourbon from his jacket. He set it on the table and told Milo to drink. As it burned Milo's throat, the bourbon shook loose a thought. "Dead drop."

"What?"

"Something about this never felt right. If Angela was passing secrets to Herbert Williams, then why did she meet him in the flesh? That's not how you do it. You meet once, set up a dead drop, and never see each other again. That's Spying 101."

Einner considered this. "Some do meet face-to-face."

"Sure," said Milo. "If they're lovers, or associates, or friends. But Angela wasn't this man's lover. And she was too smart to risk exposure like that."

They both stared across the field of faces around them, running through this. Some faces stared back—children, old women, and: there. Milo straightened. The dirty-blond woman with the swollen eyes. She was some distance away, beside one of the curved bubble-windows, smiling distractedly, but not precisely, at him. The handsome man beside her wasn't smiling.

Milo wondered, stupidly, why they always showed up at restaurants.

"Wait here," he said and walked toward the couple. The woman's smile dissipated. She said something to her partner, who put a hand under the lapel of his jacket, as if he were packing heat. Perhaps he was.

Milo stopped several feet short so the man wouldn't feel the need to take his hand out of his jacket. To the woman, he said, "Did you assemble a good report? Want my flight plan?"

This close, he could see a light sprinkling of freckles on her cheeks. She spoke English well, but with a heavy accent, so he had to pay attention to each word. "We have plenty of information now, Mr. Weaver. Thank you. But perhaps you can tell me—who is your friend?"

All three of them turned to look at the cafeteria table, but Einner had already disappeared. "What friend?" Milo asked.

The woman cocked her head and blinked at him. She reached into her pocket and took out a leather identification booklet. A yellow card inside identified the woman as an SGDN officer attached to the DGSE, or the Direction Générale de la Sécurité Extérieure—external security. As he got to her name—Diane

Morel—she snapped the ID shut. "Mr. Weaver, the next time you come to France, I hope you'll get in touch with us."

He started to say something, but she was already turning and, with a nod at her partner to follow, heading down the corridor.

Milo walked back toward the table, worrying over this, then spotted Einner behind a family of Orthodox Jews. They met among the seats in between.

Einner stared at him, round-eyed. Milo held up a hand. "Yeah, I know. I'm losing it."

"But how do you know her?"

"She and her buddy were the ones following me."

"Why?"

"Just keeping an eye out for trouble."

Einner stared down the corridor at their dwindling forms. He turned to Milo. "Wait a minute. You don't know who that was, do you?"

"She's a DGSE agent. Diane Morel. The ID looked fine."

"DGSE?"

Milo finally placed a hand on Einner's shoulder and forced him into a plastic chair. "What's the big puzzle, James?"

Einner opened his mouth, closed it, then said, "But that's Renée Bernier."

"Colonel Yi Lien's girlfriend? The novelist?"

"Yeah. I've seen all the pictures."

Instinctively, Milo stood, but it was too late. The French agents were gone.

19

The eight-hour flight was without turbulence, and he was able to catch about three hours' sleep before landing at JFK a little after noon on Saturday. Once he'd endured the long line at passport control, he rolled his carry-on through tired crowds and out the front doors, then stopped. Leaning against a black Mercedes with tinted windows was Grainger, arms crossed over his chest, staring at him. "Need a lift?"

"I've got a car," Milo said, not moving.

"We'll take you to it."

"We?"

Grainger made a face. "Come on, Milo. Just get in the car."

The other half of "we" turned out to be Terence Fitzhugh from Langley, which explained Grainger's mood. The assistant director of clandestine operations was settled uncomfortably behind the driver's seat, his long legs just fitting in. After Milo had put his bag in the trunk, he was invited to join Fitzhugh. Grainger had been relegated to chauffeur, and Milo wondered if Fitzhugh was sitting behind him as protection against potential snipers.

"Tom tells me there was a problem in Paris," Fitzhugh said once they were under way.

"Not *a* problem. Many problems."

"More than Angela Yates getting killed?"

"Turns out your Chinese colonel, the one who had the memo, was being worked by the French." He peered up at Grainger, who was watching them in the rearview. "Lien's girlfriend, Bernier. She's DGSE. Real name, Diane Morel. Whatever she was doing with the colonel, French intelligence was getting its share of his hard drive."

"Is that some crude innuendo?" said Fitzhugh.

"You know what I mean."

"Tom? Why the hell didn't we know this?"

Grainger was focused on the traffic leading out to the parking lots. "Because the French didn't tell us."

"Did we tell them we were interested in the colonel?"

Silence.

Fitzhugh let it go and returned to Milo. "So. We shell out for airfare and an expensive hotel, and all you've got for us is bad intelligence and a dead employee?"

"More than that," Milo said. "Angela's supposed contact—Herbert Williams—he's the same cutout the Tiger dealt with. The same man who ended up killing the Tiger. Angela wasn't giving him anything; I think he was shadowing her."

"Better and better," Fitzhugh mused, tapping the back of Grainger's seat. "Any good news for me, Milo? I'm the one who has to go back to Langley and talk up Tourism. I'm the one who has to show them what kind of excellent work is done at the Avenue of the Americas. I could, of course, report that the office is full of idiots who don't know a DGSE agent when they see one and confuse a shadow with a contact, but I fear they'll decide it's time to cut the department entirely."

Milo rubbed his lips before answering. One of the virtues of Tourism is the individual agent's overall ignorance. All the Tourist need know is the content of his orders. Since leaving the field, though, Milo had grown weary of this continual self-justification to bureaucrats like Fitzhugh. "Listen," he said, "the problem's not with our operation. Without Einner's work, we wouldn't have extra photos of Herbert Williams. And without Angela's work, we wouldn't know that the Tiger was paid through a bank in Zürich by a man named Rolf Vinterberg."

"Vinterberg? Who the hell's Vinterberg?"

"It's an alias, but it does put us that much closer to whoever was paying the Tiger. Also, Angela came across a Sudanese radical who actually saw the Tiger delivering Mullah Salih Ahmad's corpse to his backyard."

"I see," said Fitzhugh, nodding. "So the president of the Sudan hired the Tiger. See? *That's* intel."

"We don't have anything on the president. In fact, I don't think it was him. Neither did the Tiger."

"Now I'm really fucking confused," said Fitzhugh.

"Think of it this way," Milo said in his most professorial voice. "We're looking for the person who killed the Tiger. I think that same person killed Angela *and* is responsible for killing Mullah Salih Ahmad."

Fitzhugh stared at him, unblinking, as he processed this.

Grainger turned into the Lefferts Boulevard B parking lot, neck craned. "Where's your car?"

"Let me out here."

Grainger parked between two rows of dusty cars, but the conversation wasn't over yet. Milo waited until Fitzhugh, having considered the matter carefully, said, "He's dead, Milo. The—look, I'm not going to call him the Tiger. That's just stupid. Give me one of his names."

"Samuel Roth."

"Okay. This Sam Roth—he's dead. Now, I can take this information to Langley, but to them it's a cold case—it's *Homeland's* cold case. Who paid him, who killed him—to Langley, that's all moot. It won't give the president a boner. To give the president a boner, they'll want something active to pass on. What they *want* is for us to stop the bad shit be*fore* it happens. The whole world thinks it knows who killed this mullah, so spending money to prove this wrong isn't exactly priority. Besides, the world's a better place without that fucking mullah. Got me?"

Milo did.

"What you need to do now is focus on the jihadis who are still alive. The ones who are still a threat to world peace and banking. That's the kind of live bait they want to hear about in Virginia."

"Yes, sir," said Milo.

"Good. I'm glad we see eye to eye." Fitzhugh stuck out a hand, and Milo took it.

Grainger helped him take his bag from the trunk, whispering, "Thanks."

"For what?"

"You know what. For not telling him the Tiger used to work for us. That would really mark the end of things."

"You promised to tell me about it."

"Tomorrow," Grainger said and patted Milo's shoulder. "Come by the office and I'll let you read the file. Deal?"

"Sure."

20

The conversation with Fitzhugh had done nothing to relieve his anxiety, had in fact exacerbated it, so after leaving the airport Milo popped the battery out of his phone, took some turns, and headed farther out on Long Island. He took an exit and parked among dilapidated clapboard houses. For ten minutes, he watched children hanging out on stoops until he was sure no one had followed him. He made a U-turn, then followed another path, looping toward the island's midpoint, where he parked again at a series of narrow storage rooms surrounded by a chain-link fence called Stinger Storage.

Milo had always been a many-key kind of man. He had a key to his car, his apartment, his desk in the office, Tina's parents' house in Austin, and one unmarked key that—were he asked—he would say led to his apartment building's shared basement. In truth, that key opened this storage space.

The key fit, but after so long the lock had clammed up, so it took a moment. Then he opened the door to the deep closet where he kept his secrets.

It was no bigger than a single-car garage, and over the years he'd filled it with items that might, at some point, prove useful. Money in various currencies, credit cards under different names, with driver's licenses to match. Pistols and ammunition. He had CIA-issued passports that he'd kept after jobs were done, claiming they'd been lost along the way.

In a separate combination safe in the rear of the room were two metal boxes. One was filled with family documents—documentation he'd collected over the years that tracked the life of his mother. His real mother, the ghost-mother he'd never told Tina, or even the Company, about. There were also copies of Company files about his biological father, another secret. For now he wasn't interested in this. He took out the second box.

Inside were documents that had nothing to do with the Company. He'd put them together years before, after reading of a family—husband, wife, and baby daughter—who had been killed in a road accident. He tracked down their Social Security numbers and slowly reintroduced them into society. Bank accounts, credit cards, some small property in New Jersey, and a post office box not far from that little house. Eventually, he ordered passports for all of them with his family's photographs. According to the official documents in that box, the Dolan family—Laura, Lionel, and little Kelley—was alive and healthy.

He slipped the three passports and two credit cards into his jacket pocket and locked everything up. Not until he was on the main road again, near where he had first changed direction, did he slip the battery back into his phone and power the thing up.

He couldn't say exactly why he'd taken this precaution. It was Fitzhugh, he supposed, biting at his heels. Or Angela being suddenly gone, and the unsettling feeling that her death meant a lot more than was visible to the naked eye. The ground had become just a little less secure. He got this feeling sometimes, either from real reasons or simple paranoia, and it calmed him to collect the Dolan papers and know that, at any moment, he and his family could disappear into the anonymous currents of human bureaucracy.

As before, he listened at the door. There was no television, but he could hear Stephanie quietly singing *"Poupée de cire, poupée de son."* He used his key and set his bag beside the coats, calling in a television-husband voice, "Honey, I'm home!"

Stephanie appeared from the living room and threw herself into his midsection, knocking the air out of him. Tina followed her out, but slowly, rubbing her disheveled hair and yawning a smile. "Glad you're back."

"Hangover?"

She shook her head and smiled.

Twenty minutes later, Milo was eating leftover stir-fry on the sofa; Tina was complaining about the stink—possibly of cigarettes, though she couldn't be sure—all over him; and Stephanie laid out her plans for Disney World before climbing off the sofa to go search for the television remote. Finally, Tina said, "You going to tell me about it?"

Milo swallowed a final bite of stir-fry. "Let me take a shower first."

21

Tina watched him groan as he got off the sofa, push past the coffee table, and leave the room. There was something surreal about this, the way that Milo had returned home from a trip where his oldest friend had died, and now everything was back to normal.

She'd met Milo in the most extreme of circumstances—not even her parents knew what had happened in Venice—and suddenly he was just *there*. No explanations, no apologies. It was as if he'd been waiting for years on that damp Venetian street for her to appear, waiting for someone to devote himself to.

"I'm a spy," he told her a week into their swiftly escalating affair. "Or I was, until the day we met."

She'd laughed at that, but it was no joke. The first time she'd seen him, he'd had a pistol in his hand. She'd assumed he was a cop of some sort, or a private investigator. Spy? No, that had never occurred to her. Well, why, then, did he quit that job after they met?

"Just too much, I guess. Way too much." When she pressed, he admitted something that she had to work a while to accept: "I came close to killing myself a few times. Not pleas for attention, because in that life an attempted suicide doesn't get you any attention. It just gets you retired. No, I wanted to die, just so I could stop having to live. The effort was driving me nuts."

That threw her. Did she want a potentially suicidal man in her life? More importantly, did she want one in Stephanie's life?

"I grew up in North Carolina. Around Raleigh. When I was fifteen, my parents died in a car accident."

At that, her face had stiffened, and maybe it was this tragedy that made her suddenly feel a rush of love for this man who was still, essentially, a stranger. Who, after that, wouldn't be touched now and then by a terrible melancholy, even toy with thoughts of suicide? Before she could put her emotions, and the obligatory apology, into words, he'd gone on, as if he needed to quickly relieve himself of the whole story.

"It was a small family. My father's side had all passed away, and my mother's folks died not long after I was born."

"So what did you do?"

"I didn't have much choice, did I? I was fifteen, and the state put me in an orphanage. In Oxford. North Carolina, not England." He shrugged. "Not so bad as it sounds. In fact, my grades went up, and I got a scholarship. Lock

Haven University. Small school in Pennsylvania. During a student exchange to England, some embassy goons visited me. Brought me to see Tom, who was in London then. They thought I might want to serve my country."

There was nothing inherently wrong with the story, and Tina had never had a reason to disbelieve it. Even if he fudged details here and there, was that really the point?

She had no legitimate complaints about Milo Weaver. He was a secretive man, but that was an inevitable symptom of his job. She knew this when they married. The important thing was that, unlike many men, he made no secret of his love for her and Stephanie. Even when he was away, she knew that he was thinking of them. Though he drank, he wasn't a drunk, and if he snuck a cigarette now and then, who was she to complain? And depression? No—though he sometimes returned from the office sulking from things he couldn't discuss, he made sure it never crossed into their lives. With her and Stephanie, at least, he just wasn't that kind of man.

Now . . . now, someone they'd both known was dead. Stephanie was on the floor, watching a movie about gnomes, and Milo had fed himself and escaped her on the pretense of washing. She felt utterly alone.

Once she heard the shower running, she unzipped the bag Milo had left by the door.

A set of dirty clothes, with extra socks and underwear. His iPod. A pair of running shoes. ChapStick, a bag of Q-tips, deodorant, sixty-strength sunblock, a toothbrush, toothpaste, and floss. Pocket tissues. A bottle of multi-vitamins. Motion sickness wristbands. Soap. A ziplock bag held assorted medical stuff—drugs, a hypodermic needle and syringe, bandages, suture and needle, zinc oxide tape, and latex gloves. There were more drugs claiming to be doxycycline, Zithromax, Imodium, Benadryl, Advil Cold and Sinus, Prilosec OTC, Ex-Lax, Pepto-Bismol tablets, Tylenol.

At the bottom, she found a pair of no-prescription glasses, a four-ounce bottle of blond hair dye, and twenty-five crisp twenty-dollar bills. And duct tape. For some reason, that bothered her more than the syringe.

She repacked everything, zipped up the bag, and went into the steamy bathroom. Behind the opaque shower door, Milo washed loudly, humming some song she didn't know.

"Who's that?" he said.

"Me." She settled on the toilet. The steam was loosening her sinuses, and she used toilet paper to wipe her nose.

"Christ," she heard him say.

"What?"

"It's really good to be home."

"Hmm," she hummed.

After a moment, he shut off the water, opened the door, and reached a long arm for the towel on the wall hook. She passed it to him. "Thanks," he said reflexively.

She watched him towel off as all husbands do, maritally unaware of his nakedness. She looked at those two spots on the right side of his chest, the scars he'd earned the moment they met. Six years ago, Milo's body had been one of his many alluring traits. He wasn't much of a communicator, but he was a looker, and had a few skills in bed. When they were living together briefly in Boston, Margaret had called him "hot."

But six years in one city with a family had given him a gut, loosened his once-firm ass, and replaced his pectorals, which had once stood out, with a layer of fat. He'd become a chubby deskman.

Not that he wasn't still attractive, she thought guiltily. He was—but he'd lost that *edge* that is the property of people who take very watchful care of themselves.

He was dry now, staring down at her with a smile. "See something you like?"

"Sorry. I'm spacing out."

Unfazed, he wrapped the towel around himself.

Tina watched him squeeze toothpaste onto his toothbrush. With a hand, he wiped a clear spot into the mirror's condensation. She wondered why he needed to see himself to brush his teeth. She said, "Tell me about Angela."

The toothbrush halted in Milo's mouth. He pulled it out. "You don't want to know."

"She's dead?"

"Yes."

"How?"

"You know I can't tell you that. But I'm looking into it."

He went back to his teeth, as if that settled the issue,

and though she hardly knew why, this time his decisiveness pissed her off. "I feel like I don't know who you are, Milo."

Milo spat again and shut off the water. He turned to her. "What's this about?"

She exhaled. "It's all the *secrecy*. Over the last year, you've been coming back from more and more trips with bruises, or sulking, and I'm not trusted to know what's been damaging my husband."

"It's not about trust—"

"I *know*," she said, irritated. "You're protecting us. But that's a lot of legal hairsplitting. It doesn't help me. It doesn't help Stef."

"Some wives and husbands don't know anything. You know that, right? Some think they're married to insurance salesmen or war correspondents or financial consultants. You know more than they know."

"But they know about the lives before the Company."

With what felt like coldness, he said, "I've told you my entire life story. I'm sorry if it's not interesting enough."

"Forget it," she said and stood. "You want to tell me stuff, fine. But don't make me poke around searching. It's humiliating."

Milo caught her by the shoulders and looked into her face. "You want to know what happened in Paris? I'll tell you. Angela Yates was poisoned. I don't know who did it, but that's how she died."

Tina was suddenly able to draw a clear picture of the

lovely, lavender-eyed woman who'd eaten steak with them and kept them laughing for a whole evening. "I see." She swallowed.

"You don't," he said. "Because I think she died because the Company was dealing in bad information. Which means that *I* was dealing in bad information when I was investigating her. Which makes *me* responsible for her death."

Tina couldn't manage another "I see," so she just stared back.

Milo let go of her shoulders and gave her one of his famous half-smiles that was more sadness than anything else.

He said, "When I flew to Dallas, I was following the Tiger."

"The Tiger?" she said. "You mean that famous . . ."

"Assassin, yes. I ended up in a little town in Tennessee, where I watched him die in front of me. Suicide. It was horrible. I think his death is connected to Angela's."

"But . . . *how*?"

He didn't answer that; he only muddied the waters more: "I'm stupid, Tina. I don't know half of what I should know, and it's upsetting. It's also getting me in trouble. The hounds from Langley are barking at me, and there's a woman from Homeland Security who believes I killed the Tiger—she found my fingerprints on his face. My prints were on him because I attacked him. I attacked him because he brought up your name— yours and Stef's. I attacked him because I was afraid for you."

Tina opened her mouth to speak, but she couldn't get any air. There was too much moisture; it was like breathing water. Milo took her by the shoulders again and half-carried her through the hall to the bedroom. He sat her on the bed and squatted in front of her. His towel had fallen off somewhere; he was naked again.

Finally, she managed: "Well, you've got to do something, right? Prove you didn't kill that guy."

"I'll figure it out," he said, and for a moment she believed him. "Okay?"

She nodded, because she'd gotten some of the truth she'd asked for, but couldn't take it. She should've known this before, that there was a good reason Milo kept things from her. She was just a goddamned librarian, after all. There was a good reason he left her and all the other simple, law-abiding people in the dark.

She lay on the bed, Milo helping get her feet up, and stared at the ceiling. She whispered, "Poor Angela."

"Who?" said a high voice.

She raised her head to see, beyond Milo's penis, Stephanie standing in the doorway, gaping at her naked father. She was holding the towel he'd dropped.

"Shouldn't you *shut* the door?" said Stephanie.

Milo laughed—an unbelievably natural laugh—and said, "Give me my towel, will you?"

She did, but didn't leave.

"And *scram,* kid! Let me get dressed, and we'll figure out what all to do at Disney World."

That convinced her, and she left them alone. Tina said, "You sure we should still go?"

He latched the towel around himself. "I'm taking

my family on vacation, and no one's going to stop me. No one will get that pleasure."

It was the kind of answer she would have wanted to hear only an hour ago. But now, knowing what she knew and hearing his hard, almost brutal tone, she didn't know what she should want.

22

Sunday morning was like most Sunday mornings family men grow accustomed to, and then start to depend on. The smell of coffee, eggs, and toast, sometimes bacon, the rustle of newspaper and discarded advertising supplements, and everyone moving slowly in loose-fitting robes. Milo read a *New York Times* editorial on the administration's failure to leave Afghanistan with a stable government, six years after its post-9/11 invasion. It was depressing stuff. Then, on the facing page, he noticed a letter to the editor from Dr. Marwan L. Khambule, Columbia University, concerning the U.S.-supported embargo on Sudan. Were it not for Angela, he probably would have skipped it.

Though its aims—specifically, to force a peaceful settlement in Darfur—are commendable, the practical results are abysmal. Buoyed by Chinese oil investments, President al-Bashir has no need of Western funds. His present situation supplies him not only with the money, but also the arms, to continue his fight in Darfur and defend his rule against extremists in Khartoum.

By contrast, the trade embargo cuts off the sole potential income for the beleaguered citizens of the Darfur region, who receive no benefits from Chinese holdings in the country.

Dr. Khambule went on to explain that a more appropriate means of bringing al-Bashir to the peace table would be to offer U.S. help quelling the jihad ravaging the capital. "The carrot, so to speak, instead of the stick."

A little after ten, Tom Grainger appeared. He stood in the doorway facing Tina, carrying a plastic bag weighed down with a thick newspaper. "Hope I'm not interrupting."

Stephanie called her godfather "Uncle Tom," which was something they hadn't been able to unlearn her. She shouted it and threw herself at him. He caught her smoothly, bag rustling, and raised her with surprising strength to his hip.

"How's the prettiest girl in the United States?"

"I don't know. Sarah Lawton lives on the other side of town."

"I'm talking about you, young lady."

"Bring something?"

From his jacket pocket, Grainger produced a Hershey bar. Stephanie grappled at it, but he passed it over to Tina. "Your mom decides when you get that."

"Thanks anyway," Stephanie said.

Grainger sat across from Milo at the kitchen table. Tina delivered a cup of coffee, and he gave her a sad smile of thanks as she went to join Stephanie in the living room, closing the door behind herself. "Something wrong with her?"

Milo frowned. "Don't think so."

"Want to step out?"

"Have you bugged my place?"

"Anything's possible, Milo."

Toting his newspaper bag, Grainger gave his farewells, and Milo promised to pick up milk on his way home. Stephanie explained to Grainger that she preferred hazelnuts in her chocolate, and the old man promised to make a note of this. They took the steps down to Garfield in silence, then walked up Seventh Avenue, which was full of baby carriages and families of many shades.

They ended up at a Starbucks clone that called itself a patisserie, serving fresh French pastries and coffee. They took their cups to the sidewalk tables, the sun warming them gently, and watched families stroll by.

"Talk to me," said Milo.

Grainger seemed apprehensive. He lifted his bag and placed the thick *Times* on the table. That's when Milo noticed it was only the thin front section. Inside were papers in a manila folder. "It's a photocopy," he said.

"Tiger?"

The old man nodded. "Benjamin Harris. In 1989, he left BU with a graduate degree in journalism. By 1990, he was on the CIA payroll, sent to Beijing, and stayed there until 1993, when he died in a car accident."

"Died, huh?"

"Obviously not."

"How long?"

"Three years. November '96—that's when he disappeared." Grainger paused, glancing with approval at a pair of women in short skirts, then looked back. "Among others, Lacey, Decker, and another Tourist named Bramble went after him. Catch or kill. Lacey and Decker came up empty. Bramble was found dead in Lisbon. I thought about sending you, but you had that thing in Vienna, the old commie spy."

"I did that job with Frank Dawdle's help," Milo said.

"Dawdle," Grainger repeated. "What a surprise he turned out to be. A friend. That's how I thought of him. Naïve, I guess." He looked at his hands, which were pressed together between his knees. "I figured it out eventually, you know. Why he suddenly broke. I'd let too much slip. We were preparing to retire the guy, and I told him that this—meaning the Portorož hand-off— would be a nice finale to his career." He paused again. "If I'd just played it a little closer to the chest, he might be alive today."

Milo wasn't interested in Grainger's conscience. He pulled the heavy newspaper into his lap. "Harris disappears in '96 and goes solo. He has a fine career in liquidation until one of his clients knocks him out with HIV. All that time, you pretend you have no idea who he is. And you *know* I'm running around with my head cut off, looking for him."

"Read the file," Grainger said wearily. "You'll get it."

"Why were you protecting him?"

Grainger didn't like to be pestered. He could take it from superiors, but not from subordinates. He leaned over the table, closer to Milo, and said, "Look on page three of the file. His original case officer, the one who brought him into the Company, vetted him, and pulled him into Tourism."

"You?"

"Pah!" said Grainger, waving a hand. "I'm a little more perceptive than that."

Milo finally understood. "Fitzhugh."

"Exactly." He saw Milo's expression. "It's not just about protecting that old bastard's career, of course. With the climate the way it is, how do you think CNN would spin this?"

"We trained the mujahideen," said Milo. "This isn't anything new."

"Tourists aren't shocked by anything."

They sat in silence, watching families under the hot sun. Grainger was drenched in sweat, his blue short-sleeve blackened around the armpits. "What about this?" said Milo, lifting the newspaper-covered file.

"What about it?"

"Why'd you break security and copy it? I was going to come into the office."

Grainger wiped off his forehead. "You think I want a record of you looking at that file? You think *you* want a record of it?"

"Fitzhugh would check the library lists?"

"You can bet he would."

A frantic golden retriever puppy sniffed at Grainger's foot, pulling at a long lead held by one half of a mixed gay couple. The black man scolded, "Ginger! Get off him!"

"Sorry," said his Asian partner, smiling. "I keep saying he needs training."

"He needs nothing of the sort," the first snapped.

"It's all right," Grainger said, looking very much like an old, confused man.

Milo suddenly wished they were having this conversation in the office, not here among all these families.

"Listen," said Grainger, watching the couple disappear. "About your vacation."

"Don't start."

"This is about the worst time for you to run off to Florida."

Milo shook his head. "Like Fitzhugh says, it's a cold case. Vinterberg's not coming back to the Union Bank of Switzerland, because there's no Tiger left to pay. Angela won't be passing any secrets to the Chinese, because she's dead, and the French can investigate her killer on their own. They can tell us what's going on. I'll look into it again when I get back."

"What about Janet Simmons?" said Grainger.

"What about her? If she thinks I killed the Tiger, tell her to bring on the evidence."

Grainger shifted his feet on the concrete, staring at his loafers. "She's scheduled a meeting with Fitzhugh for tomorrow. She says it's about you."

"Listen, Tom. Simmons has nothing. She's just angry she didn't get to run an interrogation. She'll get over it."

Grainger shrugged, as if everything Milo said were, by definition, up for debate. "Just keep that file safe."

23

That evening, after Stephanie had gone to bed, Milo took the newspaper-covered file from his sock drawer, where he'd slipped it as soon as he got home. Tina, taking the milk from him, had said, "How many papers do you need?" Now, as she undressed, she said, "You're not staying up, are you?"

"Just some reading."

"Not too late. We'll have to be in the car by six. You know how long it takes to get through security."

"Sure."

"Don't 'sure' me, mister," she said, crawling leisurely onto the bed, naked. "Give me a kiss."

He did so.

"Now come to bed."

A half hour later, as she drifted to sleep, he put on his underwear and took the file into the living room, yawning. He poured a vodka, tried to stop thinking of cigarettes, and began to read the file on Benjamin Harris, ex-Company, ex-Tourist, ex-Tiger. Ex–human being.

Benjamin Michael Harris was born on February 6, 1965, to Adele and David Harris of Somerville, Massachusetts. While his parents were noted as members of the Church of Christ, Scientist, Benjamin's religion was marked as "none." This was no surprise. If he truly wanted to become a field agent, he would exclude anything that might get him placed behind a desk.

The approach was made in January 1990 by Terence A. Fitzhugh, an Asia specialist who had just taken a new position in the Directorate of Operations (which, in 2005, was absorbed into the National Clandestine Service). Harris had graduated from Boston University the previous year in journalism, with a minor in Asian languages, but the approach was made in New York, where Harris was freelancing for the *New York Post*. Fitzhugh's initial report on Harris noted "an unexpected ability to gain confidence, which in this reviewer's considered opinion should be the hallmark of field agents. We have in the past depended too much on technical prowess, and as a result operations have left too many players psychologically devastated. This is best remedied by field agents who can work the psyche as well as the body. Cooperation, not coercion."

Despite his feelings about Fitzhugh, Milo agreed. It was one of Tourism's flaws, he'd once told Grainger, that Tourists were trained as hammers rather than feathers. Grainger had found the metaphor flimsy, so Milo tried again: "Tourists should be mobile propaganda machines. Personal and political propaganda." Unconvincingly, Grainger had said that he would make a note of this.

After an extended training period at the Farm, Harris was sent to Beijing to apprentice under the then-famous Jack Quinn, who, according to Company lore, had carried much of Asia's cold war on his own shoulders, moving people and information in and out of Vietnam, Cambodia, Hong Kong, China, and Malaysia. The only country where he'd stumbled was Japan, where, from 1985 until his death from cancer in 1999, he was persona non grata.

Quinn's early reports on his young recruit were enthusiastic, citing Harris's ability to absorb information quickly, his near-native fluency in spoken Mandarin, and a highly developed sense of tradecraft. Harris had, in the four months from August through November 1991, developed a network of twelve agents from the clerking sections of the Chinese government, which produced information that, when backtracked, led to an average of three monthly reports on the tensions and machinations within the Chinese Central Committee.

By 1992, however, discord had appeared in the Beijing station. Comparing memos written by both Quinn and Harris, the problem was clear. Harris, the rising star, was attempting to gain control of the station, while Quinn, by now past his prime; was doing everything he could to hold on to his position. Langley's opinion, inferred from additional memos, was that Quinn's position should be inviolable, and they approved disciplinary action against Harris. A three-month forced leave followed, which he spent in Boston with his family.

Here, Fitzhugh reappeared, visiting Boston and making assessment reports on his young discovery. Though he noted Harris's anger about his shoddy treatment, Fitzhugh also pointed out that his protégé "has developed far beyond his years in all areas of tradecraft and mental aptitude. His continued employment should be assured." Fitzhugh's report ended abruptly at that point, the rest of the text blacked out.

When Harris returned to Beijing in February 1993, there was a monthlong honeymoon before trouble reappeared. Quinn complained of a renewed attack on his position, and Langley unhesitatingly suggested disciplinary action, but insisted that under no circumstances was Quinn to send him back. Harris was demoted, his networks taken over by Quinn; according to some hastily scribbled memos, Quinn worried that he'd overdone the discipline. Harris had taken to drinking, appearing late at the embassy, and sleeping with a variety of shopgirls from all around the capital. Twice the Beijing police picked him up for public displays, and once a friendly official in China's Ministry of Foreign Affairs suggested to Quinn that the young troublemaker be sent to a country "where such activity is considered more the norm."

That suggestion was dated July 12, 1993, and followed by a copy and translation of a police report, five days later, of an automobile accident in Guizhou province, along the Guiyang-Bije highway. The diplomatic car, signed out to Harris, plummeted 305 meters off the Liuguanghe Bridge. Upon hearing of this, Quinn demanded that an American team be sent to sift through the wreckage of the car. China generously acquiesced. The team cleared away the mess, and Harris's remains were transferred to a family plot in Somerville.

The file did not contain Harris's rebirth as a Tourist, nor a list of his works or the Tour Guides resulting from his travels. Such a breach of security was more than even Grainger could have managed. What he included was a report on Harris's 1996 disappearance, though in the report he was referred to by his Tourism name, Ingersoll.

Last known location: Berlin, an apartment on Frobenstrasse. After a week of trying to get in touch about a new operation, Grainger (who had by then been running the Department of Tourism only two years) sent Lacey to track him down. The apartment had been cleaned from top to bottom. Grainger wrote a memo to Fitzhugh, asking if he'd had any word; he hadn't. Lacey, then, was assigned to track Ingersoll/Harris.

It took nearly a week of meetings with Harris's known associates for Lacey to come up with a Trabant stolen by Harris and driven east, all the way to Prague, where it was abandoned. Grainger requisitioned Czech police reports to find that another car—a Mercedes—had been stolen two streets from where the Trabant had been deposited. This took them west again, into Austria, where Decker joined Lacey, and both found the Mercedes ditched in Salzburg. In each case, the abandoned car had been wiped entirely clean of fingerprints, which became its own kind of fingerprint—that level of cleanliness was probably a sign of Tourism.

The trail petered out in Milan, where the frequency of stolen cars made following leads impossible.

They picked up the trail again by pure luck, three months later in Tunisia, where Decker had just finished a job and was vacationing at the Hotel Bastia in L'Ariana, on the Gulf of Tunis. While working with Laccy, he'd studied a photograph of Ingersoll/Harris, and he saw that same face in the Hotel Bastia restaurant. The man with Harris's face was eating soup and staring out at the water. Decker got up, went to his room, and collected his pistol. When he returned to the restaurant, however, Harris was gone. Four minutes later, he broke into Harris's room, which was empty.

Decker called Tunis, directing the embassy to watch the train stations, harbors, and airport. One young man, just graduated from Banking Section to Security, called in that he had spotted Harris at Carthage Airport. When Decker arrived, he found a cluster of police around the men's bathroom, examining the young man's corpse. He'd been strangled.

Decker called in a list of possible destinations—if, in fact, Harris had stuck to flying—which included Lisbon, Marseille, Bilbao, Rome, and Tripoli. Grainger contacted Tourists in each of those areas, ordering them to abandon whatever they were doing and station themselves at the airports. Only by the next day, with the discovery of Bramble's corpse at Portela Airport, did they realize that Harris had flown to Lisbon.

It was nearly one when Milo finished reading. It

frustrated him to know he would be a wreck in the morning, while his reason for staying up hadn't given him any fresh answers.

He stretched, filled a tall glass with vodka, and dropped a lighter into his pocket. He slipped on sandals and took the file and vodka into the stairwell, then climbed to the rooftop-access door. Once outside, looking over the Park Slope roofs leading to the hazily lit Prospect Park, he drank some of the alcohol, but just a sip. He put the file on the concrete roof and doused it with the vodka, opening the file to get the center wet as well.

He lit his little funeral pyre and stared for a long time at the flames and ash that caught on the breeze and flew away, thinking of where he'd been during the saga of Harris's move to the open market. Vienna, with Frank Dawdle, then–Vienna station chief, planning the execution of a retired Eastern Bloc lieutenant general named Brano Sev. Dawdle had been nervous, he remembered—an old man who'd spent the seventies in the field, but the eighties and nineties behind a desk—yet at the same time excited that, once again, if only as support, he was in on the action. It had been Dawdle's job to watch the house and give the signal when, as usual on a Saturday, Sev's wife left the house to go into town for shopping with their daughter. Sev always remained at home on Saturdays. According to sources, he was working on a memoir. Grainger later told him that this job was a favor to some Eastern European friends who thought it best that the old man's memories die with him. The U.S. government, Grainger suggested, had just as much to lose from this man's stories.

It went smoothly. Dawdle gave his signal, and Milo climbed into the house through a first-floor window. On the stairs, he stepped along the wall-edge to avoid creaks, and when he found the elderly cold warrior in his office, pen to paper, he was surprised by how small and meek the man looked. Milo removed his pistol, and the old man, hearing the noise, turned. There was surprise in his face, but the shocking thing was that it passed so quickly. Brano Sev's eyes, magnified by thick glasses, relaxed, and he shook his head. In German, he said: "You certainly took your time." Those were his last words.

Milo kicked at the embers, poured the last of the vodka, and lit the remaining pieces. It took a while, but finally everything turned to ash.

24

She had booked them into a long, red-roofed atrocity called Disney's Caribbean Beach Resort, where even the lobby was set up with stanchions and padded ropes to arrange the crowds into orderly lines, as if this were another ride. Restaurants of no recognizable real-world cuisine threaded through the complex, and after each long day of chasing Stephanie to the various attractions they collapsed in these places, ordering nachos or spaghetti, and then wandered out to the crowded "beach" that bordered the man-made lake.

Despite an initial onrush of sarcasm, by the second day Tina was much less annoyed by Disney Reality. There was something narcotic about the easy predictability and the soft, cushioned safety that surrounded them at every moment. Ignoring the sudden outbursts of children, there was no chaos here, no unpredictable variable. There was nothing even remotely connected to the miserable stories of the planet's shadow side, that parallel world in which her husband worked.

Tuesday night, after a long phone conversation with Grainger that had interrupted their dinner, Milo even said that it might be time to quit the Company completely. "I don't want this anymore," he said. He seemed surprised when she didn't get up and start cheering him.

"What else would you do?"

"Anything."

"But your skill-set, Milo. Really. And what kind of résumé would you have?"

After considering this, he said, "Consulting. Security consulting for big business."

"Aha," she said. "From the military to the industrial. Very complex."

He laughed, which pleased her, then they made love, which pleased her more.

It was a moment, one of those rare things that when you're old enough you know to appreciate, because the truth is you might never feel it again. Happiness. Despite the machinations in Milo's world, here in the fictitious land of Disney they had a little oasis.

Like anything that good, though, it was short-lived, crumbling by the third day.

"Space *Mountain*," Stephanie shouted over the hubbub around them.

She was just ahead, Milo gripping her hand. He looked down with a confused expression. "Yeah. There it is." He pointed. "Space Fountain."

"Not *fountain*. Mountain!"

He turned back to eyeball Tina. "Can you understand a word this kid's saying?"

With impressive precision, Stephanie landed a quick kick on Milo's shin. He gripped it, hopping on one leg. "Oh! *Mountain*!"

Tina hurried to catch up.

They registered themselves for the ride using the Fastpass that allowed them to wander for most of the forty-five minutes' expected wait, listen to Stephanie's one-sided conversation with Minnie Mouse, then go find some snacks that required another twenty-minute line.

Stephanie was unimpressed by the oranges Milo bought, so he explained that the vitamins were necessary for their upcoming space flight. "Astronauts have to eat barrels of fruit before they're allowed anywhere near the space shuttle."

She believed that for approximately five seconds then glared up at him with a half-smile and sliced through his logic: "That makes no sense, Dad."

"Doesn't it?"

An exasperated sigh. "They take vitamin pills. Not oranges."

"When was the last time you went into space, Little Miss?"

"Come *on*."

Among the stanchions that forced Space Mountain guests into a line that folded back on itself ten times, Stephanie rechecked her height with the forty-four-inch marker as Milo's phone sang. He turned away when he took it, so Tina couldn't hear the conversation. It lasted about a minute before he hung up, turned around with a smile, and said, "You two sit together, okay?"

"And you?" said Tina. "You're not going?"

"Of course he's going," said Stephanie.

"I'll sit near the back. You guys get in front. Turns out there's an old friend here. I'm going to sit with him."

"Who's this old friend?"

"She's a Lebanese dancer," Milo said, then broke into a grin when he saw the expression on her face. "I'm *kidding*. An old friend. He might have something for me."

Tina didn't like this, but Milo had warned her before they left that, given the way work was going, they might have to make a concession now and then. Still, a secretive meeting at Space Mountain? "You'll introduce us on the other side?"

Milo's lower lip shivered briefly. "Yeah, of course. If he has time."

Stephanie turned up her hands. "Who *doesn't* have time at Disney World?"

Right on, Little Miss.

They reached the front, where two empty trains sat at the platform. Each train consisted of two narrow cars, each with three seats, one behind the other. Milo kissed his girls and told them he'd take the next train, right behind them. A uniformed teenager led them to the front, but Milo whispered something to the boy, showed his Company badge, and took the second-to-last seat on the second train. Tina sat behind Stephanie, then turned to look back at Milo, but couldn't see him because of the other passengers. When she leaned out of the car to peer around them, another uniformed teen-ager, a girl, said, "Ma'am, please stay inside. It's for your safety."

Tina thanked her for her concern.

"You think so?" said Stephanie.

"What, hon? I didn't hear you."

"I *said,* do you think we're really going into space?"

"Maybe," Tina answered as she again tried to get a look at Milo. The train lurched and clicked slowly forward into the dark tunnel ahead.

Briefly, she forgot about the mystery of her husband's secret visitor. She was too distracted by the corny space-age music and the dated-looking asteroids and space-ships and light shows inside the huge dome. For once, Stephanie had no sarcastic quips, only happy squeals as they rose and plummeted wildly.

By the time they lurched to a stop and climbed out, Stephanie had regained her voice. "Let's do it again!"

"Let me get my breath first."

They waited by a steel fence for Milo to arrive.

"Why didn't he take our train?" said Stephanie.

"Maybe his friend was running late."

She pressed her chin against the railing, thinking about that, then raised her head. "There he is!"

Some family in bright orange shirts filled the first four seats, and in the fifth seat Milo was expressionless, in front of an old man who was probably in his seventies. Tina watched closely as they got out, noting the old man's softly wrinkled, wide-jawed face. He had deep-set, heavy eyes, not unlike Milo, and his thin white hair had been shaved down to a flattop, like her own father wore back in the seventies.

Despite his frail appearance, he needed no help climbing out of the train, and when he stood he was tall and imposing. Both men smiled as they came over, and the older man swiped at his cheek, as if scaring away a fly. Before Milo could say anything, he had stuck out the same hand and spoken in a voice flavored with a heavy Russian accent. "Very pleased to meet you, Mrs. Weaver."

He took her dry hand and kissed her knuckles.

"Yevgeny Primakov," Milo told her. "Yevgeny, that's Tina, and this one here," he said, picking up Stephanie, "is the finest chanson singer since Edith Piaf. Meet Stephanie."

Primakov's smile was huge as he kissed the hand she presented him, and he laughed when Stephanie wiped the kiss off on her pants.

"You're right to do that," said the Russian. "Very perceptive."

"You're an old friend of Milo's?" asked Tina.

"You could say that." A smile. "I've been trying for years to get him to work for me, but the man's stubborn. A patriot, I think."

"Want a drink?" Milo cut in. "I'm parched."

Yevgeny Primakov shook his head. "I wish I could, but I need to find my own family. You go on. Maybe we'll find you later." He turned to Tina. "Everything Milo ever said about your beauty was absolute modesty."

"Thank you," she muttered.

"Take care, Yevgeny," Milo said and took his family down the exit ramp.

It was a curious incident, and when pressed, Milo would only admit that Yevgeny was an old agent, retired, and that "he was one of the very best, in his day. He taught me a few tricks."

"A Russian agent taught you things?"

"Tradecraft knows no national borders, Tina. Besides, he's not a Russian agent anymore. He moved to the United Nations."

"What does a spy do at the UN?"

"He finds ways of making himself useful."

In the spaces between his words, she could tell the meeting had troubled him. Whatever they had discussed had thrown a wrench into his jolly mood. "Were you talking about Angela?"

"Mostly." He paused. "He knew her, wanted to find out what's going on."

"Did you have much to tell him?"

"Not enough," he said, then turned fully away from her and said to Stephanie, "Who's hungry?"

They dined in one of those characterless restaurants in the Caribbean Beach Resort, and Milo managed some light, happy chatter as Stephanie expounded on the relative merits of Space Mountain. They returned to the apartment by nine thirty. Everyone was exhausted, so they cleaned up, put Stephanie to bed, and went to bed themselves. Sex would have required too much energy, so they lay together looking out the glass terrace doors at the moon bouncing off the man-made lake.

"Having a good time?" Milo asked.

She nodded into his chest. "It's nice to be away from the library."

"Next year, let's see Switzerland. You've never been."

"If we can afford it."

"I'll knock over a bank."

She gave a polite, close-mouthed laugh "Milo?"

"Yeah?"

She sat up so he'd know this was important. "I don't want you to get angry."

He sat up, too, the sheet falling from his chest. "Well, don't make me angry."

That wasn't the answer she'd hoped for. "Listen. I've got a bad feeling."

"You're sick?"

She shook her head. "Something's not right here. That much I know for sure. Then some old Russian pops up, and I don't believe anything you're telling me about him."

"You don't trust me," he said—a statement, not a question.

"It's not that."

"It's that exactly," said Milo, but he didn't get up or make any move to walk out, as he sometimes did during arguments. Instead, he looked past her at the windows.

"For example. How did you learn such good Russian?"

"What?"

"You're completely fluent. Tom says you speak it like a native."

"I studied. You know that. I'm good at languages. Even when I'm no good at anything else."

In Tina's exhale was a cluster of involuntary nonsense words. No reply made any sense to her. How could she put into words something that was only a gnawing anxiety in her bones?

They both jerked when Milo's phone lit up and vibrated a trail across the bedside table. His eyes, wide now, remained on her as he picked it up. "Yeah?" Still staring at her, his features stiffened as he said, "And Adam's." Then: "*Now?* But I'm with—" She watched his face dissolve into some indefinable expression. "Okay."

Milo put the phone down but continued to stare at her. That's when she realized he hadn't been staring at her at all. He'd been staring *through* her, to somewhere else. Now, he got up, naked, and went to the terrace doors. He looked out, then turned to the drawers and began to dress as if the building were on fire.

"Milo?"

He put on his shirt. "Look, I can't explain everything. Not now. There's no time. If I had time, I'd explain everything. Absolutely everything." He moved to the closet, ripped open the door, and took out his suitcase. Squatting beside it, he turned to her. "You're right. I'm too secretive. I'm sorry. I really am. But right now, I have to leave."

She got out of bed, also naked. "I'm coming."

"*No.*"

Milo seldom spoke with such force. It was enough to push her back into bed, pulling up a sheet to cover herself.

He came to the edge of the bed. "Please. You have to stay here. In a little while, people will come looking for me. You answer their questions completely. Don't hold anything back. They'll know."

"Know *what*?" said Tina. "What have you done?"

Again, he went blank. Then a vague smile appeared. "Truth is, I haven't done anything—nothing really wrong, at least. But listen to me. Are you listening? I want you to go to Austin. Stay with your parents a few days. A week, even."

"Why?"

"You'll want to rest up. That's it. Okay?"

Stunned, she nodded.

"Good." He went back to the suitcase, removed a small, pressed-flat knapsack, and filled it with little items he packed every time they went on a trip. To this, he added his iPod, then a wire clothes hanger from the closet. She wondered why. The packing took only a minute and a half, then he zipped up the knapsack, took his phone, slipped into his sneakers, and sat beside her on the bed. When he raised his hand, she flinched involuntarily. The dismay in his eyes made her feel terrible.

"Come here," she said and kissed him on the mouth.

He whispered into her ear: "I don't want to do this. But it's necessary."

"I'm completely confused."

"I know."

"You're going to do what you used to do?" she whispered.

"I think it's the only thing I can do."

He kissed her again, went to the door, then looked back. "Give Stef my love. Tell her it's business." He grunted. "She's used to it."

Then he was gone.

She didn't know how long it took, though it couldn't have been more than seven or eight minutes, her staring at the empty bedroom doorway, numbed by everything she didn't understand. She heard noises outside—faint footfalls on the unnaturally green Disney grass—then silence. She slipped into her robe. Then the sharp sound of a fist on the front door. She ran to get it before Stephanie woke. A woman stared back at her—sort of, because one eye seemed focused elsewhere—and held out an unfolded ID. "Where is he?" the woman asked.

With remarkable fortitude, Tina grabbed the corner of the woman's ID so she could read DEPARTMENT OF HOMELAND SECURITY and the name SIMMONS, JANET beside her photograph. She started to say something about how they better have some kind of a warrant, but it was too late. Janet Simmons and a large man who'd shown no papers at all were already in the apartment, opening doors.

That's when she heard Stephanie, sounding stone-cold awake: "Cut it out! I'm trying to sleep!"

25

He kissed his wife again, went to the door, then turned back. She looked tiny in that big Disney bed. "Give Stef my love. Tell her it's business." He realized how often he said this kind of thing. "She's used to it."

He galloped down the outdoor stairs, heading for the parking lot. Through the cricket songs he heard them in the cool night air— two engines, approaching.

He hit the ground leaning low and padded over tended grass toward the parked cars. Headlights splayed across the resort. It was after ten by now, the vacationers either at nearby family-friendly clubs or dozing off the fatigue of standing in hot lines all day. Nothing would wake them up.

Squeezing between a Subaru from Texas and a Florida Mazda, he heard the cars park, doors flung open, and voices. A woman's voice, familiar. He looked through the driver's side window of the Subaru and watched them cross the grass. Special Agent Janet Simmons, in one of her blue Homeland Security suits, took the lead, followed by three men clutching Homeland-issue SIG Sauers. Simmons mounted the steps, George Orbach right behind her, while the other two men remained on the ground, spreading out to check escape paths.

Riverrun, past Eve.

And Adam's.

Go, Milo.

Now? *But I'm with—*

Simmons is coming to get you. She's nearly there. Go.

Milo looked up the height of the resort and spotted his bedroom terrace, where Tina had left the light on. As he watched, he took out his cell phone, popped out the battery, and removed the SIM card, then pocketed everything, thinking through his next steps.

The window to the right of their terrace brightened. That was the living room. Simmons had decided to knock first, which he appreciated. On the grass before him, one of the agents stepped back to get a better look at the terrace, to be sure no one was climbing out. Through the window, Milo saw silhouettes—Tina, Janet Simmons, and George Orbach. He waited, listening for any sign that his daughter had woken. All he caught was crickets, and the indistinct murmur of adult voices. Then the silhouettes moved through the apartment.

Still crouching, he padded farther away, weaving through cars until he had reached the edge of the lot. He unzipped his knapsack and unraveled the wire hanger as the figures on the grass moved, finally convinced he wasn't up in the apartment. With the hanger straightened, he formed a small hook at the end, then searched for an older-model car. It was difficult—this was the midrange resort, full of middle-class families who changed their cars every four years—but he finally spotted the one eyesore: a rusted late-eighties Toyota Tercel. He began to wedge the hanger down between the window and the door.

Fifteen minutes later, he was heading southwest on I-4. If Janet Simmons was on the ball, she'd send men to nearby Orlando International to search for him, so he would instead leave from Tampa. He still didn't know where he was going, but he needed to get out of Florida. This state would not give him answers.

He pulled to the side of the road by a closed barbecue restaurant and put the phone together again. SIM card, battery, then he pressed the power button. It gave him a Nokia welcome, then started to ring—PRIVATE NUMBER. He knew who that was. Milo pressed the hangup button; then, before Simmons could dial again, he typed 411. He asked an operator for the American Airlines desk at Orlando International. As she connected him, his phone beeped, signifying another incoming call. He ignored it, then asked the woman at the airport for their next flight to Dallas. "That leaves at 6:00 A.M., sir."

"I'd like to reserve a seat."

"Do you have a credit card?"

He tugged out his wallet. "The name is Milo Weaver, and I'll be putting this on my MasterCard."

Five minutes later, he'd settled the reservation, and

Simmons had tried three more times to get in touch. He disassembled the phone again and continued southwest, away from Orlando.

Outside Polk City, he found a mall with a few cars in the lot. It took two minutes for him to break into an annoying-looking Ford Tempo, then another two minutes to use a shirt from his knapsack to wipe down the Tercel.

He stopped again after Lakeland, took three hundred dollars from an ATM using the Dolan card, then used that money to fill up the tank at an all-night station. In the convenience mart, he bought cigarettes, a padded envelope, a book of stamps, a spiral notebook, and a black marker. Back in the car, he scribbled in the notebook:

Miguel & Hanna—Please Burn this Note
and Hold these for T&S in Safe Place.
<u>Very Important</u>
<u>No One Should Know.</u>
Thanks for your Trust. —M

He folded the page into the envelope, then went through his knapsack, coming up with three passports. He slipped Laura Dolan and Kelley Dolan into the envelope and put the Lionel Dolan passport into his own pocket. He sealed the envelope and addressed it to Tina's parents in Austin, Texas, pasting on more stamps than necessary.

Nearly two hours had passed by the time he reached Tampa International. Milo parked in the short-term lot a little after midnight, wiped down the steering wheel, and took his knapsack with him into the north entrance.

Once he'd passed the sliding glass doors, he grabbed a complimentary airport map and settled on a bench. There was a mail drop one floor up on the transfer level. From his seat, he read the monitors listing departure cities and times. It turned out that the "International" in the airport's name was a little misleading, since the best they could manage was a single London flight each day and a couple of Canadian destinations. Not that it mattered; he wasn't planning on leaving the country just yet.

There—Delta could take him to JFK at 7:31 A.M., an hour and a half after Simmons would realize he wasn't on the Orlando flight. He hoped that would give him time.

At the Delta counter, three other people stood in front of him—a father, mother, and teenaged son, also heading to New York.

That's when it caught up with him, and he felt dizzy, thinking of Janet Simmons back in that apartment, interrogating his family. He should have stayed. He'd spent six years shielding Tina from his job, and in a matter of days all that work had been undone. He'd told her too much about Angela's murder, and now she was in the middle of something she had no way of understanding, because Milo didn't understand it either. Why did he have to run?

He had to run because the old go-code had been used, and even after six years it was still hardwired to his feet. Grainger would only have used it if there was no other way.

"Sir?" said the Delta clerk. "You wanted to go somewhere?"

His 747 touched down at JFK just after 10:00 A.M.—the pilot apologized to everyone for being nine minutes late. The large woman who'd been squeezing Milo tight against the window turned out to be afraid of flying, and told him in a manic southern accent that she didn't care how late they were, just as long as she could walk on solid earth again. He said he could see her point. Her name was Sharon; he said his was Lionel. She asked if he was from the city, and, sticking to the original Dolan's particulars, he told her he was from Newark, and that his wife and daughter were still in Florida; he'd had to fly back unexpectedly for work. His answer seemed to disappoint her.

He took stock of his possessions. He'd had to dump the clothes hanger in Florida to avoid awkward questions from Tampa airport security, but he knew seven other ways to pick up a car if necessary. He had his Dolan passport and Dolan credit cards, but didn't want to use the cards more than he had to. Best to work with cash, and in his wallet he still had two hundred and sixty dollars, which wouldn't take him far in New York.

He spent twenty-five dollars on a shuttle service into town, reaching Grand Central by one. He got out in the shadow of the MetLife Building, then went to the Grand Hyatt, grabbing a tourist map and taking a seat in the huge, mirrored lobby, next to a marble fountain.

It took five minutes to settle on his path. The Avenue of the Americas was out of the question. Even if he

called to set up a meeting with Grainger elsewhere, he
had no idea what his position was with the Company. All
Grainger had said was "Go." After the risk of last night's
call, Milo didn't want to sink him into deeper trouble.

He descended into the subway and spent seven dollars
on a day pass, then took the train north to Fifty-third
Street and the Museum of Modern Art. He skipped the
milling crowds waiting to enter the galleries and went to
the gift store. He'd visited a month ago with Tina and
Stephanie during the thousandth Van Gogh exhibition.
They'd come for Stephanie's benefit, but other than a few
comments on his choice of colors, she didn't have much
use for the one-eared Dutchman. It was in the gift shop
that she'd come alive. Milo, too, had enjoyed the store
and puzzled for a long time over an interesting piece of
jewelry he hoped was still there. He came around to the
glass cases and found it: the magnetic bracelet collection, designed by Terrence Kelleman.

"Can I help you?" said a teenaged boy in a MoMA
shirt on the other side of the case.

"That, please."

It was remarkable in its simplicity. A series of a hundred or so quarter-inch-long nickel-plated rods clinging
together solely by magnetism. He snapped it open to test
the strength, then put it back together. He tried another
link—yes, it might work.

"I'll take it," he told the boy.

"Gift wrap?"

"I think I'll wear it now."

Forty-five dollars lighter, it took another twenty minutes to get south again, to the Lord & Taylor on Fifth and

West Thirty-eighth. He browsed by the entrance, on the edge of the expansive cosmetics department, examining the security. It was a simple two-pillar alarm-detector with shielded power cables leading to the wall. It didn't matter, but was good to know.

He took the stairs up to the third floor, where a field of men's clothes was on display. For the next half hour he looked at suits, finally settling on a midpriced Kenneth Cole three-button job. It was a bit long in the arms, covering his new bracelet, but otherwise fit perfectly, and was neither ostentatious nor cheap. It would do—that is, it would satisfy one of Tourism's many important rules, which is to always look like a businessman.

Still in the dressing room, he popped off the bracelet and rubbed the end against each of the store's magnetized alarm strips. He knew that in theory this should work, but wasn't convinced until, after rubbing for a full minute, he heard the soft snap of the strip unlocking. He removed it carefully. Once the shirt, slacks, and shoes were also free, he transferred his wallet and keys to his new clothes.

When he came out, one of the younger salesmen was watching. Milo looked around conspicuously, rising to see over racks of clothes. "Janet?" he called, then walked over to the salesman. "Hey, did you see a short woman, yea high, with a nose ring?"

The salesman helpfully looked around with him. "Maybe she's downstairs in the women's section."

"She can't stay still." Milo pointed at the stairs. "Can I run down and show this off?"

The salesman shrugged. "Sure."

"Cool. Thanks." Milo went back to the dressing room and took his knapsack.

"You can leave that," the salesman informed him.

"You think I don't watch *Cops*? I'll keep it on me. That all right?"

"Sure. You just bring that suit back."

"Like I said, I've seen *Cops*. Think I want to end up on a police car's hood?"

The salesman laughed; Milo winked.

By three, dressed in Kenneth Cole, he was at a pay phone on Ninth Avenue, just around the corner from Penn Station and across the street from a shamrock-motif bar called the Blarney Stone. He slipped in a coin and dialed Grainger's private mobile number. After three rings, he heard the old man's voice: "Uh, yes?"

Milo spoke in an imitation of Sharon's southern drawl. "Yeah, this Thomas Grainger?"

"Yes."

"Well, look, I'm Gerry Ellis from Ellis Dry Cleaning. Yesterday, you dropped your shirts off here. Someone went and lost the receipt, but we know it's a home delivery. Right?"

Grainger paused, and in that brief space Milo feared he wasn't going to understand. But he did: "Yes. That's right."

"Well, listen. We've got your address, but we don't have the delivery time. When were we supposed to drop it off this evening?"

A pause. "Make it six o'clock. Is that all right?"

"No problem, Mr. Grainger. We'll be there."

Milo went into the Blarney Stone. It was a dark,

dismal-looking place with photographs of famous Irish people from literary, cinematic, and musical history. He took a stool at the bar, across from Bono and two down from a thin, unshaven man who looked very much like a regular. The bartender—an over-the-hill redhead—sounded more Jersey than Dublin. "What'll you have?"

"Vodka. Smirnoff."

"We've got Absolut."

"Then I'll have Absolut."

As she measured out a shot, he turned so he had a clear view through the window to the pay phone across the street. He took out a Davidoff. The bartender delivered his shot. "You know you can't, right?"

"What?"

"That." She pointed at the cigarette between his lips.

"Right. Sorry."

For the next half hour, Milo kept his post at the bar. It was enough time to learn that no one had traced his call and come to collect forensic evidence, and enough time for the bartender to offer some conversation, him to reject it, and the regular to question his manners. Milo considered taking out his frustration on the drunk, but feared it would end in murder, so he paid his bill and left quietly.

He took the 1 train north to West Eighty-sixth, where he found an inconspicuous French café with fresh bread and very small coffees among the tall old–New York apartment towers. He sat at an outdoor table so he could smoke.

There was nothing in the papers. If Simmons had

something incontrovertible on him, she might get Homeland to post his photograph in the major newspapers with some vague terrorist attributes. Then again, she might not. Homeland seldom posted terrorists' photos, because they didn't want them escaping to fight another day.

Without more information—without knowing what, exactly, had triggered his attempted arrest—it was impossible to predict what Simmons would do next.

What he needed was a theory of everything, but each piece didn't quite line up with the others. The Tiger, for instance. That he had led Milo on a chase in order to gain vengeance on the client who had killed him—he could believe that. But how, he wondered, had that client gained access to Milo's file? All the Tiger had said was that he'd seen a "file." Company or foreign?

Then Angela. She hadn't been selling secrets to the Chinese, but someone had—how else had they gotten that memo? He returned to the Chinese. Had the People's Republic's intelligence service, the Guoanbu, known that she was under investigation? Or did they know she was looking into their precious oil source, the Sudan? Had she gotten too close to something without knowing?

His head spun. *Anyone* could have switched her sleeping pills. The French? They had probably realized, soon into Einner's flower-van surveillance, that Angela was being watched. But again: Why? She was on good terms with French intelligence.

The answer—if, indeed, he ever found one—would

come via Herbert Williams, a.k.a. Jan Klausner, the Tiger's client. A man with a face but no identity, serving the interests of X.

Too many variables; too much unknown. He clutched at his cigarette and inhaled deeply. Then, remembering, he took out his iPod and asked France Gall to sing away his anxiety . . . but she just couldn't pull it off.

26

Tom Grainger's enormous apartment at 424 West End Avenue, at Eighty-first Street, had been purchased by his wife, Terri, two years before she succumbed to breast cancer. The West River House was a magnificent place for any Company man to live in, and occasionally people grumbled suspicions about how he could live so well. But other than the penthouse and a little lakeside home in New Jersey, Grainger owned nothing. Fiscal responsibility had never been his strong point.

For twenty minutes, as the sun moved behind the towers, Milo watched from the shadows of the glass-shelled Calhoun School across the street. Other residents returned from jobs, the perky doorman chatting with each one, and a few deliverymen from FedEx, Hu Sung Chinese, and Pizza Hut arrived. He walked around to the underground parking lot on Eighty-first

and followed a Jag down the incline. He took a circu-
itous path around the edge of the lot, avoiding security
cameras.

It was a path he'd charted out before, on other occasions when he'd wanted to meet the old man undetected
and discuss things neither was supposed to know. The
only trick was the entrance to the stairwell, which was
watched by a camera lodged in the ceiling. There wasn't
anything to do about that other than to cross into its
field of vision facing away from the camera, so that all it
picked up was a man of average height heading inside.

He climbed the whole way up to the eighteenth floor
and rested in the stairwell, waiting in the silence for six
o'clock to arrive. When it came, he tugged open the
door and peered into the soft-lit corridor, then jerked
back. In a chair at the end of the corridor sat one of the
FedEx deliverymen, a box leaned against his chair, fooling with an iPod.

Milo squatted by the cracked door and closed his
eyes, waiting for the sound of him making his delivery,
or the pleasant *ding* of the elevator arriving to take him
back to the lobby, but after five more minutes he still
heard nothing. That's when he knew. Again, he peered
out, and this time the man's eyes were shut, the iPod
plugged into one ear. From the other, Milo noticed a
flesh-colored wire that led down to his collar.

Softly, he let the door fall shut. It was the call. The
Company had either traced Grainger's warning call
from last night, or—and he now realized his mistake—
using the phone logs, they had traced the call from Gerry
Ellis Cleaners to a pay phone.

There was nothing, then, to do. Milo returned to the bottom of the stairwell, removed his jacket and held it in a ball to his stomach, then entered the parking lot backward. To the camera, he looked like someone carrying a box. He left the building.

Tom Grainger was no fool. He'd been in the field during half the cold war and certainly knew what was going on. So Milo returned to the shadow of the Calhoun School, sat on a ledge, and waited. After an hour, a passing hippie bummed a cigarette, and in answer to the man's question, Milo said he was waiting on his girlfriend. "Women these days, eh?" said the hippie.

"Yeah."

Milo's patience paid off. A little after seven, the city now lit by its own artificial illumination, the doorman let Grainger out. Milo watched him turn the corner onto Eighty-first, heading toward Central Park. Grainger didn't look around. A minute later, the doorman appeared again, opening the door for another man—in a suit, not a FedEx uniform—who stepped out onto the sidewalk and, talking on his cell phone, also walked down Eighty-first.

He knew that second man—Reynolds, a forty-five-year-old ex–field agent who'd recently ended his embassy tenure. Milo followed, a half block back.

All three men crossed Broadway and turned left on Amsterdam, where Grainger went into the Land Thai Kitchen at number 450. The shadow took a position across the street by a Mexican restaurant, Burritoville, while Milo waited at a southern corner of the block, groups of young diners swarming past him.

The old man was inside less than ten minutes, emerging with a plastic bag full of takeout boxes. Milo withdrew into the shadows. Grainger appeared at the corner, the bag high so he could peer inside. Beside a trashcan, he stopped.

He could also see Reynolds, a few doors back, watching Grainger take out a box, sniff, open it up, and put it back in. Then he took out a much smaller box, sniffed, made a face, then opened it. He shook his head in disgust, tossed the box into the trashcan, and continued back up Eighty-first, toward home. Reynolds followed, but Milo didn't.

The whole walk here, Milo had watched out for a second or third shadow. Three-man teams were the norm for intensive surveillance work, but it had struck him that Fitzhugh—and Fitzhugh had to be the one behind this—had assigned Reynolds to the job; Reynolds, who was off active duty. Fitzhugh wanted to keep this quiet and had decided on a skeleton crew: Reynolds and the FedEx man Milo didn't know.

Once they were out of sight, Milo jogged up to the trashcan, snatched the light, nearly empty takeout box, and kept moving swiftly up Amsterdam, then east on Eighty-second until he reached Central Park. Along the way, he'd opened the box, taken out the single slip of paper, and dropped the box into another trashcan.

Near a streetlamp, he paused among some Japanese tourists discussing the details of a map. He unfolded the small square of notepaper and cursed Grainger for his brevity. He'd given no answers, only the tools to find them. Perhaps, though, the old man was just as in the dark as he was.

After a scribbled international cell phone number, he read:

> E in Frankfurt:
> The Last Camel / Collapsed at Noon

and a single word:

> Luck

27

While waiting for his ten o'clock Singapore Airlines flight in JFK's recently reopened Terminal 1, pushing back his desire to fly instead to Florida and collect his family, he rechecked his belongings and added a few things from the gift shops: an extra T-shirt, underwear, a digital wristwatch, and a roll of duct tape.

Then, after passing from the United States into that stateless netherworld of the duty-free international terminal, he joined other travelers at the Brooklyn Beer Garden. He found a lonely Dutch businessman who kept his cell phone on the table. The Dutchman, he learned, was heading to Istanbul, trading in pharmaceuticals. Milo bought the man another beer and told him he sold advertising airtime for NBC. The Dutchman was intrigued enough by Milo's off-the-cuff story to get up and buy two more beers in return. While he was at the bar,

Milo took the man's cell phone, popped it open under the table, removed the SIM card and replaced it with the one from his phone, then put it back on the table.

Before boarding, he turned on his phone and used the Dutchman's SIM card to call Tina. She answered on the third ring with a wary "Yes . . . ?"

"It's me, hon."

"Oh," she said. "Hi."

The silence was unnerving, so he broke it. "Look, I'm sorry about—"

"What are you *saying?*" she said, edgy. "This isn't the kind of thing you just say sorry to. It doesn't work that way, Milo. I need *more*."

A light, girlish voice in the background said, "Daddy?"

The blood rushed to Milo's head, mixing with the beers and his overall lack of food. "I don't know much. All I know is those agents are after me for something I didn't do."

"For Angela's murder," she said.

"Let me talk to Daddy!" said Stephanie.

Now he knew—Simmons believed he had killed Angela. "I have to figure this out."

Again, silence, punctuated only by Stephanie's plea: "I want to talk to Daddy!"

Explain, she'd said, so he tried: "Listen, Tina. Whatever those people from Homeland said, it's not true. I didn't kill Angela. I didn't kill anyone. But I just don't know enough to say more than that."

"I see." Her voice was flat. "Special Agent Janet Simmons seemed to think she was pretty justified in her suspicions."

"I'm sure she thinks so. But whatever she's calling evidence . . . I don't even know what it is. Did she tell you?"

"No."

He wished she knew something. "The only thing I can think of is someone's setting me up."

"But *why*?" she insisted. "Why on earth—"

"I don't *know*," he repeated. "If I knew why, I would know who. If I knew who, I could figure out why. You follow me? And in the meantime, Homeland Security thinks I'm either a killer or, I don't know, a traitor."

Again, silence.

He tried again: "I don't know what that woman's been telling you, but I've got nothing to be ashamed of."

"And how are you going to prove that?"

He wanted to ask if the proof was for them or for her. "Are you going to Austin?"

"Tomorrow, probably. But where are you?"

"Good. I'll be in touch. I love—"

"Daddy?"

He jerked physically; she'd handed over the phone without telling him. "Hey, Little Miss. How are you?"

"I'm tired. Your friends woke me up."

"Sorry about that. They're jerks, aren't they?"

"When're you coming back?"

"As soon as my work's done."

"Okay," she said, again sounding so much like her mother that Milo's stomach started to cramp. When they finished, Stephanie claimed not to know where her mother was, so they hung up.

Milo stared across the rows of chairs at families,

some excited and others bored by their prospective trips. A fresh cramp hit him. He got up, stiff, and half-jogged down the carpeted terminal, past electric walkways, until he reached the bathroom. He shut himself into a stall and was sick, getting rid of all the beer his body hadn't yet absorbed.

He wiped his mouth, gargled water, and returned to the corridor. The sickness had gotten rid of a mental block he hadn't even known was there, fogging up his vision of what to do next. He didn't want to use the Dutchman's phone card after boarding the plane—calling Tina had compromised it—so he put it to use now, dialing +33 1 12. A female operator informed him in French that he had reached France Telecom directory assistance. He asked for the number for a Diane Morel in Paris. There was only one listing, and he asked her to put him through. It was five in the morning there, so the old woman who answered sounded vaguely terrified. Yes, she was Diane Morel, but she sounded at least sixty. He hung up.

It was a wash, but at least he knew he couldn't simply call up Diane Morel and have a leisurely conversation about Angela Yates and Colonel Yi Lien. If he called the DGSE and asked to be passed on to her desk, or her home, his location would be tracked in minutes and relayed to the Company, and their conversation would be rushed. Milo needed time with Mme. Morel. He popped the battery out of his phone and tossed the SIM card in a wastebasket.

Eight hours later, at one on Friday afternoon, a stolid, graying German behind Plexiglas compared his passport photo to the well-attired but exhausted-looking businessman in front of him. "Mr. Lionel Dolan?"

"Yes?" said Milo, smiling broadly.

"Are you here for business?"

"Happily, no. Tourism."

Just saying it again brought back unwanted memories. Milo remembered all those other airports, border guards, customs officials, and carry-on bags. He remembered plainclothes policemen and agents clutching newspapers and the times when he, too, held those newspapers, sitting for hours in airports, waiting for contacts who sometimes didn't arrive. Frankfurt Airport, one of Europe's great, ugly hubs, had hosted him many times.

The border guard was holding out his passport, so he took it. "Have a good vacation," the man told him.

Steady, but not hurried. He carried his knapsack past the customs officials, who—like most of Europe's customs officials—weren't going to bother a man in a tie. He continued through the crowded baggage claim, heading directly out to the noisy, car-choked curb, where he smoked a Davidoff. It didn't taste as good as it should have after the long flight, but he finished it anyway as he walked to a pay phone near the taxi stand. He dialed the number he'd memorized somewhere over the Atlantic.

It rang three times. "Ja?"

"The last camel," said Milo.

A pause, then: "Collapsed at noon?"

"It's me, James."

"Milo?"

"Can we meet?"

Einner didn't sound overjoyed by the call. "Well, I *am* in the middle of something."

"Right now?"

"Uh, yeah," he said, then Milo's throat closed up as he heard a muffled voice in the background trying to scream. He knew that sound. The noise of someone who'd been gagged.

"When'll you be free?"

"Give me . . . I don't know. Forty minutes?"

"Where?"

"I'm in the Deutsche Bank right now, so—"

"The twin towers?"

"Yeah."

Milo imagined him in an office in one of the upper floors of those famous mirrored towers in the center of the financial district, some unfortunate CEO bound and gagged under his desk, while Einner casually made a date on the phone. He'd forgotten how rough Tourism could be.

"Listen, you know the Frankfurt Opera? Let's meet in front of there around two. I'll have another chance to prove we're not uncultured hacks."

"Should you be saying all that aloud, James?"

Einner grunted. "This guy? In ten minutes, he won't be able to say a thing."

The man's muted howls rose in pitch.

28

He took a clean, sparse train to Frankfurt Hauptbahnhof, where he hooked his knapsack over his shoulder and went on foot past afternoon gridlock toward the Friedensbrücke. Instead of crossing the bridge, he turned left up the dock running alongside the Main River. All the well-dressed businessmen and teenagers and pensioners reminded him of Paris. Only a week ago.

He grabbed a schnitzel sandwich from a street vendor and walked back inland to the long park at Willy-Brandt-Platz, where he took a bench and gazed at the glassy modern face of the Oper Frankfurt. Despite Einner's confidence that he could speak openly in front of his captive, Milo kept an eye on passersby. It was a habit he'd lost in the last six years, a habit he needed to regain if he wanted to stay a free man.

All Tourists know the importance of awareness.

When you enter a room or a park, you chart the escapes immediately. You take in the potential weapons around you—a chair, ballpoint pen, letter opener, or even the loose, low-hanging branch on the tree behind Milo's bench. At the same time, you consider the faces. Are they aware of you? Or are they feigning a forced ignorance that is the hallmark of other Tourists? Because Tourists are seldom proactive; the best ones bring you to them.

Here in the sunny park, he noticed a woman at the curb having trouble starting her car. That was a typical setup. Feign exasperation until the target makes his own decision to come and help. Then you have him.

Two children—twelve or so—played along the base of a huge, lit-up euro sign that dominated the park. Another potential trap, because Tourists are not above using children for their ends. One child falls and pretends injury; you go to help; a "parent" approaches. Simple.

And over there, by the eastern edge of the park, a university student took vertical photos of the European Central Bank skyscraper that looked down on everything. Casual photographers were everywhere in a city like this, and they could shoot you from all directions.

"Hands up, cowboy!"

Milo almost fell off the bench as he jumped and twisted, finding Einner with a finger pistol pointed at him, grinning madly. "Jesus."

"Little rusty," Einner said as he safely pocketed his hand. "Keep going like this, old man, you'll be dead by sundown."

Milo recovered his breath, ignored the dangerous

sound of his heart. They shook hands. "Tell me what you know."

Einner nodded in the direction of the opera house. "Let's walk."

They moved together, neither in a hurry.

"It's not what you think," said Einner. "They haven't called in Tourists—you're not that important yet. Tom told me to expect you."

If it was true, Milo was relieved. He was starting to believe that having Einner on his trail would be a serious problem. "Did Tom tell you why you should expect me?"

"I got that elsewhere. Had breakfast with a friend at the consulate. She's not . . ." He paused as they reached the street, wondering how to put it. "She's not quite a security risk, but she's no security saint either. She told me about a wire that came in, for all embassies and consulates, to look out for Milo Weaver."

"Company wire?"

"State Department."

"Are they looking?"

"Well, you don't get these all-embassy alerts often. They're looking. Last I heard, a lead went cold in Istanbul."

As they crossed the street, Milo felt a tug of regret for the Dutchman, whose phone had been a beacon for all the Company agents in Turkey. The feeling passed, though, when he realized that, by backtracking the Dutchman and his SIM card, they certainly knew that Milo had flown out of JFK and, within a few hours, when. "How about Frankfurt?" he asked when they reached the Opera doors. "Are you done here?"

The Tourist checked his watch. "Been off the clock eighteen minutes. I'm all yours."

Milo held open the door for him. "And you've got a car?"

"I can always get a car."

"Good." They entered the broad, modern lobby, and when Einner veered toward the opera café Milo tugged his arm and guided him through a side corridor leading past the bathrooms.

"You know a better place for a drink?"

"I know another exit. Come on."

"Jesus, Milo. You really are paranoid."

While Milo could only jimmy the doors of old-model cars, Einner had a more advanced tool at his disposal—a small remote control for power-door locks. He pointed it at a Mercedes C-Class saloon, pressed a small red button on the quarter-sized mechanism, and waited while it automatically went through possible code combinations. After forty seconds, they heard the car alarm bleep its disarming, then the doors unlocked with a quiet pop. It took just over a minute for Einner to start the car. They were soon heading out of town, and Einner said, "Where to?"

"Paris."

The destination didn't faze him. "We'll have to watch out for a couple hours, until we reach France. In case the owner reports this thing missing."

"Then drive fast."

Einner obliged, roaring out of town and crossing to the A3, which took them to Wiesbaden, where they switched roads and, after an hour, merged onto the broad, smooth A6 that would take them to France.

"You going to share?" Einner asked.

Milo gazed out the window at a highway landscape; he could have been in upstate New York and not known the difference. "I want to talk to Diane Morel, a.k.a. Renée Bernier."

"The communist novelist?"

"The very same."

"And what do you expect from her?"

"A little clarity. The Chinese colonel was the reason we came after Angela."

Einner let this sit before pressing. "And?"

"And what?"

"And is there a reason you need my help? Really, Milo. You expect people to take everything on faith." Milo didn't answer, so he said, "You know why I'm good at my job?"

"Because you're so pretty?"

"It's because I think as little as possible. I maintain no pretensions about understanding anything. Tom calls me, and that's all I need to know. Tom is God when he's on that line. But you, my friend. You're not Tom."

He was right, so Milo told him an abbreviated version of what had come before, including the quick end of his vacation and Grainger's secreted message to contact him. "Everything here, in Europe, really started with this colonel and Renée Bernier. I need to get my facts straight before pushing on."

"Okay," said the Tourist. "What happens after Diane Morel enlightens you?"

"I decide on the next step."

Though Grainger had told Einner to help Milo out, all Tourists know their orders last only until the next orders arrive. For all Einner knew, in the morning he'd receive a call to kill his passenger, but for the moment he seemed satisfied by temporary certainties.

Milo noticed that the owner of the Mercedes had fitted an adapter to use with an iPod. He went through his bag until he'd found his own and plugged it in. Soon the car was filled with France Gall.

"What's this?" Einner sounded irritated.

"The best music in the world."

It was after four thirty when they crossed the European Unionized nonborder into France, having seen three police cars but receiving no grief from any of them. The sun hung low in the windshield, sometimes obscured by a gray smudge of cloud in the direction of Paris. "We'll keep the car until tomorrow," Einner told him. "We'll find a Renault, I think. I'm trying to sample all of Europe's brands before I finally buy one myself."

"Tom wouldn't let you do that, would he? All the registration involved?"

Einner's shrug suggested this was a concern for lesser Tourists. "I've built up a legend for a rainy day. It's good to get a few purchases on it."

Milo thought of the Dolan legend he'd spent years building up. "Apartment?"

"Little one. In the south."

He supposed all Tourists did the same thing. The

smart ones, at least. "So what was the trouble in Frankfurt? Were you teaching manners to bankers?"

Einner chewed his peeling lower lip, wondering how much to share. "It's a dirty business, banking. But the job was straightforward enough. Get some answers, then get rid of the evidence."

"Successful?"

"I always am," said Einner.

"Sure you are."

"You don't believe me!"

After a moment, Milo said, "To the Tourist, success and failure are handed out in equal measure. To the Tourist, successes and failures are the same things—jobs completed."

"Jesus. You're not quoting the Book again, are you?"

"You really should get hold of it, Einner. Makes the life a lot easier to take."

Einner's drawn expression gave Milo a measure of satisfaction. He remembered his own Tourism days, the irregular biorhythms that would one day make him suicidal, and the next lead him to feelings of invincibility. He saw too much of that latter feeling in Einner, which would lead to a sudden death. If the only way to make him listen was to lie about the source of his lessons, then so be it.

"Where'd you find it?" he finally asked, staring hard at the darkening road.

"Bologna." Milo grunted amusement to make himself more believable. "In a bookshop, if you can believe it."

"You're kidding."

"A dusty old place with racks up to the ceiling."

"And how did you get there?"

"I followed the clues. I won't bore you with all the steps, but the final piece was in a Spanish mosque. Wedged in the spine of the imam's Qu'ran. Can you believe it?"

"Wow," said Einner. "What was the final piece?"

"The address of the bookstore, and the location in the shelves. On the top, of course, so no one would pick it up by accident."

"Big?"

Milo shook his head. "Not much more than a pamphlet."

"And how long did it take?"

"To find the Book?"

"From the beginning. From when you first made an effort to look for it."

Milo wanted to assure him that the search wasn't easy, but also give him hope. "Six, seven months. Once you get on the trail, the search builds momentum. Whoever set up the clues knew what he was doing."

"He? Why not a she?"

"Find the Book," said Milo. "You'll figure it out yourself."

29

A half hour before Paris, the low summer sun disappeared behind slate clouds, and rain dropped from the sky. Einner turned on the wipers, cursing the storm. "So, where to?"

Milo checked his watch—it was 7:00 P.M. He'd hoped to track down Diane Morel, but he doubted she'd be in the office this late on a Friday. "Angela's. I'll spend the night there."

"And me?"

"I figured you had a girlfriend to visit."

Einner rocked his head from side to side. "Not sure if she's available."

Milo wondered if there really was a girlfriend after all.

Einner drove along Angela's street, slowly, to look for DGSE watchers. They spotted no one, saw no vans on the street, so Einner dropped him off two blocks away, and Milo jogged in the hard rain to the apartment. In the doorway, he wiped water off his face and searched the buzzers. At the bottom of the second column the name M. GAGNE was highlighted with a scribbled star. He pressed the buzzer.

It took about two minutes for M. Gagne—a woman, it turned out—to speak through the intercom. A wary "Oui?"

"Uh, excuse me," he said in English, too loudly, "I'm here about Angela Yates. She's my sister."

The woman let out an audible gasp, then the front door buzzed. Milo pushed through.

Madame Gagne was a widow in her late sixties. Her husband, the previous superintendent, had died in 2000, and the job fell inevitably to her. She told him this in her claustrophobic salon after having decided that Milo truly was the brother of Angela Yates, even though Angela had never said a thing about siblings. "But she was the quiet one, was she not?" the woman asked in her thin, airy English.

Milo agreed that Angela was indeed the quiet one.

He said that he had come to collect some family heirlooms before the rest was taken away by L'Armée du Salut—the Paris branch of the Salvation Army—next week. He apologetically told her he spoke no French. He gave his name as Lionel, in case she asked to see his papers, but she didn't. Once she'd ushered him in for a small glass of wine, it became clear that Madame Gagne was lonely.

"You know how I did learn my English?" she asked.

"How?"

"At the end of the war, you know, I was only but a small child. A baby, really. My father was kill by the Germans, and my mother—Marie was her name—my mother was alone with me and my brother, Jean. He is dead now. She found American soldier—a black man, you understand? Big Negro from Alabama. He stayed—he love my mother very much, and he was good to Jean and me. It did not last—these things, good things, they do not—but he lived with us to when I was ten, and he teached me English and jazz." She laughed aloud at the memory. "He took us when he had the money. Do you know that I saw Billie Holiday?"

"Did you?" Milo asked, smiling.

She waved a hand to temper his enthusiasm. "Of course I was only but a child, I understand nothing. She was too sad for me. For me, was Charlie Parker and Dizzy Gillespie. Yes," she said, nodding. "That was music for me. For a child. *Salt peanuts, salt peanuts*," she sang. "You know that song?"

"It's a wonderful song."

As their conversation reached the forty-minute point, he tried not to let his anxiety show. He felt he must have missed a watcher, or maybe police cameras were being used, and he waited for Diane Morel and her handsome partner to break down the door and put him in shackles. But this, as Einner would have said, was just paranoia. Angela had been dead a week, and the DGSE didn't have the funds to pay anyone to sit in a car for that long.

Besides, he liked Madame Gagne's stories. They touched on his particular nostalgia for that time when

Europe was rebuilding itself, and beginning anew. The short-lived Franco-American honeymoon. The French had loved these American jazz musicians, the Hollywood films shipped over by the boatload, and the English pop music they imitated with the *yé-yé* girls that filled Milo's iPod. He brought up France Gall, and to his surprise Madame Gagne immediately launched into a brief rendition of "*Poupée de cire, poupée de son.*" His eyes glazed over, his cheeks warm.

Madame Gagne leaned closer and used her loose-fleshed fingers to squeeze his hand. "You are thinking of your sister? Things like this—suicide, I mean. You must know there is nothing you can do. Life, it goes on. It *must.*"

She said this with the conviction of someone who knew, and he wondered how her husband had died. "Listen," he said. "I haven't reserved a hotel room yet. Do you think that I . . ."

"Please," she interrupted, squeezing again. "It is paid through the month. You stay as long as you like."

She let him in with a long key, handed it over, then expressed surprise that the place was such a mess. "It was the police," she said in a bitter tone, then remembered her English: "*Pigs*. Tell me if they steal something. I will make the complaint."

"I'm sure that won't be necessary," he said and thanked her for her help. Then, almost as an afterthought, he said, "Before my sister died, did she have any unexpected visitors? Some friends you hadn't seen before, or workmen?"

Madam Gagne's eyelids fell, and she rubbed his arm. "You live in the hope, I see that. You don't want to believe what she did."

"It's not that," he began, but she held up a hand.

"The pigs, they ask this, too. But in the day, I work with my sister. Her flower shop. I see no one."

Once she was gone, he took a bottle of Chardonnay from the refrigerator, filled a glass, then drank and refilled it. He sat on the couch to think over how to do this.

Do not sleep. Do not dream of Tina and Stef.

It was a simple one-bedroom, but unlike most French apartments the rooms were large. Diane Morel's people had been through it, a blunt search that left the kind of chaos that police all over the world never feel it's their duty to set right, and he knew he would have to focus on areas they would have missed.

Angela's search for the Tiger had been her pet project. She hadn't requested funding allowances, and she hadn't reported her progress to the embassy. So she probably hadn't stored her case notes in the embassy. They would have to be here—unless, of course, she had committed everything to memory. He hoped she hadn't been that brilliant.

He began with the kitchen. Kitchens offer the most options for concealment. There were water and gas pipes, appliances, and cabinets full of containers. To cover his movements, he tuned her stereo to a classic rock station that ran the gamut from sixties chanson to seventies progressive. He removed all the dishes and glasses from the cabinets and pulled back the cabinet papers. He checked the pipes for loose joints. He fingered the undersides of the drawers and the table, then went through everything in the refrigerator, dipping his fingers into marmalade, soft cheeses, and ground meat that had gone bad. He checked the seams of the refrigerator and pulled it out to look over the tubes gridded across its rear. Finding a screwdriver in a drawer, he disassembled the microwave, telephone, and food processor. After two hours, as the stereo played "Heroin" by the Velvet Underground, he admitted defeat and proceeded to put everything back together.

He didn't need to do this, but he remembered how clean her apartment had been last week. Despite being exhausted and dirty, he didn't have the heart to leave the place in chaos. So he took his time—he had all night, after all—and worked until the kitchen was clean again.

Einner buzzed while he was taking apart the bathroom, and when he let him in the young Tourist handed over a greasy bag with a gyro and fries. He'd eaten his own dinner in a doorway up the street, watching for shadows. "Not a peep. We should be fine, at least until morning."

Because Milo didn't want to spend too long at the scene of Angela's death, he gave Einner the bedroom. He wasn't sure how much longer he could keep at this—he was bleary from fatigue—but he pushed on, settling beside the toilet and shaking the pipes leading to the water heater, then drawing his hand along the pipes' length. There. His finger caught the corner of a small aluminum box, the size of two thumbs side by side, magnetically attached to the pipe.

On the outside of the box was one of those

reproductions of old French alcohol ads that Europhile New Yorkers buy in poster prints to cover their living rooms. A bobbed brunette in a red Victorian dress clasped her hands together in excitement, staring at a tray of glasses and a bottle of Marie Brizard mixer. A slogan read, PLAISIR D'ETÉ, PLEASURE OF SUMMER.

It was a magnetic key holder, and that's what it held. A single door key with a three-leaf-clover grip. There were no identifying features. He pocketed it and replaced the holder behind the pipe.

He didn't tell Einner about the key. There was no point in doing so until they had the next piece of the puzzle, but nothing else turned up. What they were faced with, in the end, was a clean apartment.

30

Einner took the deathbed, and Milo slept on the sofa. Unconsciousness came swiftly, and in the late morning he woke with the sheet knotted around his sweaty body and the key pinching the inside of his fist. He didn't remember taking it out of his pants.

They didn't leave until after noon. Madame Gagne appeared at the foot of the steps to greet them. Milo introduced his friend, Richard, and the old woman smiled sadly at Einner, as if he, too, had lost a sister.

It was raining again. As they ran to the car, Einner declared that he knew the finest place in all of Paris for a proper American breakfast. Milo, however, wanted to get moving. "Twentieth District."

Einner considered his wet windshield a moment. "You're kidding. The DGSE headquarters?"

"She does work there, you know."

"Yeah. And if our government's blaming you for

Angela's murder, then the DGSE will happily hand you over."

"Which is why I need your help. You have a gun?"

Einner reached beneath his seat and pulled out a small Pistolet Makarova. It disturbed him that he hadn't noticed Einner put it there. "It's my backup. The one from yesterday's in the Main River."

They took a lengthy route, heading out to Boulevard Adolphe Pinard, which circled the city. They drove south and took the exit for Boulevard Périphérique. After a roundabout, they continued down another lane until they had reached Boulevard Mortier. They rolled past the unassuming, rain-streaked DGSE building at number 141, then drove two more blocks to where, on the corner, Milo spotted a glassed-in phone booth. "Pull over here and turn the car around."

The rain drenched him again before he could reach the booth. The phone book had been stolen, so he dialed 12, information, and asked for the phone number to the DGSE's central office.

He was first put through an endless menu. It took five minutes before a male operator picked up. Milo said, "Pourrais-je parler à Diane Morel?"

"Ne quittez pas," said the operator, and after a moment of on-hold Muzak, he returned and said, "La ligne est occupée."

She was there, but on another line. Milo said, "Je la rappellerai," and hung up. He held up a finger for Einner's patience, waited another minute, then called again. The same operator picked up.

Deepening his voice, Milo said, "Il y a une bombe dans vos bureaux. Elle explosera dans dix minutes." There is a bomb in your offices. It will explode in ten minutes.

He hung up and ran back to the car. "Go."

They drove back those two blocks and stopped at the intersection before the DGSE headquarters.

"Keep the engine running," Milo said as, through the noise of the rain, they heard a faint two-toned alarm. "You'll either drive forward or backward. I'll tell you."

"The hell did you do?" Einner said as people began to emerge from the building. Not running, but not strolling either.

"Shh."

A few had umbrellas they popped open, but most had fled too quickly. Since it was the weekend, there were only twenty or so to evacuate, and then he saw them. They crossed the road together and found shelter under a café awning.

"Ahead," said Milo.

"What?"

"Now!"

Einner sped forward in first gear, splashing through puddles as they reached the awning. Morel and her partner weren't alone; others had just lit cigarettes and were hugging themselves. They all stared at the Mercedes. Milo rolled down his window and caught Morel's eye. "Get in."

Both she and her partner stepped forward. Milo raised a finger. "Just you."

"I'm not going anywhere without him," she said.

Milo glanced at Einner, who shrugged. "Okay," said Milo. "Hurry."

They got in the back through separate doors, the man first. Before Morel's door was shut, Einner was already moving.

"Was that you?" she said. "The bomb?" She sounded out of breath.

"Sorry. I just need to chat."

The man beside her shook his head. "You have a funny way of talking."

Milo gave him a smile, then stuck out his hand. "First, though, please give me your phones."

"No," said Morel.

Milo finally produced Einner's pistol. "Pretty please."

31

After several evasive maneuvers, including a dangerous U-turn in a tunnel, they left Paris proper and stopped at a near-empty bar outside Les Lilas, in the suburbs. Following some negotiation, Milo and Morel took a table in the back, while Einner and Adrien Lambert, her partner, began a staring contest at the bar. The bartender, a heavy man in a soiled smock, brought over espressos as Morel said, "So glad you've returned to our country, Mr. Weaver."

Milo thanked the bartender and watched him leave.

"You wanted to talk to me?"

"I have some questions."

"What luck!" she said, tapping the table. "I have questions, too. For example, we heard from our American friends that you were on the loose, but we have no record of your entry into Europe. Please. What name are you traveling under?"

"I'm sorry," Milo told her. "That's one question I can't answer."

"Then maybe you can tell me why you murdered Angela Yates."

"I don't know who killed her. I'm trying to find that out."

Diane Morel crossed her arms under her breasts, watching him across the table. "Then maybe you can tell me why you care about a little civil servant like myself."

"You have a friend with a place in Brittany," Milo told her. "When he was still working out of London, you visited him on the weekends and in the meantime worked on what I hear is an excellent socialist-themed novel. He's Chinese, and I assume he made the trip across the Channel from London just to meet with you. Am I right?"

Diane Morel opened her mouth, then shut it. She stretched back in her chair. "That's interesting. Who told you that?"

"A friend."

"The CIA knows a lot of things, Mr. Weaver." She grinned. "To tell the truth, we're often jealous. We have a paltry staff, and every year the socialists attack our budget. They came close to scrapping us completely in the seventies." She shook her head. "No, I'm not the type of woman to write a new Communist Manifesto."

"Then I'm misinformed."

"Not entirely."

"No?"

Diane Morel noticed his interest. "I'll tell you everything, Mr. Weaver. Just be patient."

Milo tried to exemplify patience.

She rubbed the spot between her brows. "Last week, Friday, you were seen lunching with Ms. Angela Yates. That same night, you were with Mr. Einner, watching Angela Yates's apartment. You left early, yes, but then you returned and visited Ms. Yates. Some hours later she died of poisoning. A barbiturate, the doctors tell me. They say all her regular sleeping pills were replaced with this drug."

"Yes," said Milo.

"Mr. Einner and another associate entered the building at 5:16 A.M., Saturday. Then, Mr. Einner went to your hotel. Soon after, both of you fled through the rear entrance." She cleared her throat, sounding like a heavy smoker. "We found both of you at the airport, fleeing. Remember?"

"Einner wasn't leaving," said Milo. "And we left through the back of the hotel because I was in a hurry."

"To get home."

He nodded.

"In actuality, Mr. Einner did flee, but not by airplane. He got in his car and left the airport. Unfortunately, we lost him. He disappeared."

"I suppose he had someplace to be."

"Had I known in the airport that Angela Yates was dead, you wouldn't have left the country. Sadly, I didn't learn this until that afternoon." She pursed her lips, considering him. "You see where I'm going with this, don't you? It looks a lot like premeditation."

"Does it really?"

Diane Morel stared at him. Unlike Janet Simmons,

she had no lightness in her face. With her swollen eyes, she looked as if the motif of her life had been suffering. "Also, you tell me you know nothing about Angela Yates's murder, but the story I've just described suggests something different. It suggests that you came to Paris and worked with Mr. Einner until your job was completed. As soon as Angela was dead, you left." She paused. "If I'm missing something, please let me know."

"Angela was a friend of mine," he said after a moment. "I didn't kill her, and neither did Einner. If I believed he did, I'd hand him to you right now."

"A question," she said, raising a finger. "Who, exactly, is Mr. James Einner? He seems to have been working with embassy personnel, but there's no public record of his employment there. In fact, he only arrived in Paris three months ago. Before that, he was in Germany for three weeks; before that, Italy for two months . . . before *that,* he was in France again, Portugal, and Spain. And before Spain—he arrived there a year and a half ago—there's no record at all of him in Europe. Who *is* Mr. Einner?"

That was the one question Milo wished she hadn't asked. Diane Morel had done her homework. "I don't know," he said. "That's the truth. But I will tell you something that I hope we can keep private."

"Go on."

"Angela Yates was under suspicion of treason. Selling secrets."

"To whom?"

"To China."

Morel blinked again, rapidly. It wasn't the kind of thing the Company would ever admit to, and he hoped it would push the question of James Einner out of her head. Finally, she said, "That's curious."

"Is it?"

"I now ask the same of you, Mr. Weaver. Some privacy."

Milo nodded.

"Until about a year ago, Ms. Yates and I were also close friends—which, I imagine, is why I haven't just shot you and handed your body to the Americans. I, too, would like to know the truth."

"I'm glad."

"My point is that I tried to get her to do the same thing. Sell secrets." She shook her head, biting her lip. "I find it very surprising that Angela would sell them to the Chinese. In fact, I'm sure she wouldn't."

"I agree," he said, then stopped. A year ago . . . "Oh."

Morel sat up. "What?"

This was the woman Angela had dated, who had left her with a broken heart. Morel had broken her heart by showing that their affair had simply been a way to turn her. "Nothing. Go on."

She let it go. "Angela wouldn't sell to us, but she did work with someone else. We spotted her having meetings with a man."

"A red beard," Milo said.

Morel frowned, then shook her head. "No. Why do you say that?"

"Just a hunch. Go on."

"The man she met with was clean shaven. An old man. Turns out our friend Angela *was* a double agent of sorts."

Milo stared back. "Who for?"

"For the United Nations."

He wanted to laugh, but it was too ludicrous even for that. "You mean Interpol. That would make sense."

"No. I mean she worked for the United Nations."

"Really," he said, finally smiling nervously. "The United Nations has no intelligence agency. Maybe she was getting information from them."

Morel rocked her head from side to side. "That's what we thought at first. She met with someone from the UNESCO office here in Paris. His name is Yevgeny Primakov."

"Primakov?" Milo said dumbly.

"You know him?"

He shook his head to cover the sudden feeling of panic. Not Yevgeny. "Go on."

"We did some background checks. Primakov used to work for the KGB. He reached a colonel's rank and kept it when the KGB became the FSB. Then he quit in 2000 to work for the UN out of Geneva. There's not much on him, but in 2002 he worked with some representatives from Germany, trying to institute an independent intelligence organ. Their argument was that the Security Council could only make educated decisions with an independent agency giving them information. Of course, it didn't even reach a vote. China, Russia, and your own country made it clear that they would veto it."

"There you go, then," said Milo. "There is no UN intelligence agency for Angela to work for."

Morel nodded, as if Milo had finally put her suspicions to rest, but said, "In early 2003, Mr. Primakov vanished for approximately six months. He reappeared in July of that year in the Military Staff Committee of the Security Council, working out of the financial section. He's kept his position despite changeovers of all the other staff. I find it all highly suspicious."

"Are you telling me that this man, Yevgeny Primakov, is running a secret agency within the United Nations? Impossible."

"Why is it impossible?"

"If there was an agency within the UN, we would know about it."

"You mean *you* would know about it."

"Listen." Milo felt himself reddening. "For the last six years I've been running a desk that deals solely with Europe. If there was a new intelligence agency working the same beat, I'd figure it out pretty quickly. You can't hide that kind of stuff. Inexplicable events start to build up, little black holes that need filling. After a year or two, it becomes simple to put together, and there you have a new organization."

"But don't be so sure," said Morel, smiling. "Back in the seventies, this Primakov was running successful operations for the Soviets in Germany. He helped a network of Baader-Meinhof terrorists. He knows how to keep things quiet."

"Okay," said Milo, still not believing, but for reasons

he couldn't share with Diane Morel. The same reasons he'd never shared with the Company, nor even with his wife. "Please. Tell me about Colonel Yi Lien."

"You seem to know everything already, Mr. Weaver. Why don't you tell me?"

So Milo did. "You met with him on weekends at his cottage. But you were working *on* him, weren't you? You might have slept with him—I suppose that was unavoidable—but he brought his laptop, so you could take what you liked from it. Am I right so far?"

Diane Morel didn't answer. She waited.

"We know all this because MI6 was watching the colonel. They're the ones who helped him when he had his heart attack; they also copied his laptop. That's how we learned he had some of our embassy documents, which he received at the cottage from a man named Herbert Williams, or Jan Klausner. We suspected that Williams received the documents from Angela, which is why we were watching her."

"Is that why Mr. Einner killed her?"

He shook his head. "You don't understand. Einner didn't kill her. He didn't want to kill her. We needed to see who she passed the information on to."

Morel's face had turned a deep shade of red as Milo talked. She appeared livid, but didn't shout. Quietly, she said, "Do you have a cigarette? I left mine in the office."

Milo tapped out two Davidoffs and lit hers for her. She took a long drag, exhaled smoke, then looked at the cigarette. "They're not very good."

"Sorry." Through his own smoke, he said, "Did you

talk to Angela's neighbors? She took sleeping pills regularly, so they were probably switched on Friday, during the day. A neighbor could have seen the murderer come into the building."

"She took pills *every* night?"

"Maybe. I don't know."

"That's not very smart," she said, then glared at the surface of the table, perhaps at the ashtray. "Was Angela depressed?"

"She didn't seem so."

Morel took another drag. "We talked to the neighbors. A few descriptions, but in a town the size of Paris workmen and deliverymen show up all the time."

"Anyone suspicious?"

She shook her head. "They say she didn't get many visitors."

"Did you ever talk to her? In the last year, I mean."

"Sometimes. We were in the same business, after all. We remained friends of a sort."

"She came asking for information?"

"Sometimes I asked as well."

"Did she ever ask about Rolf Vinterberg?"

She blinked. "Once, yes. She wanted to know if we had anything on him."

"Did you?"

"No."

"What about Rahman Garang?"

A look flashed across Morel's face—whatever trust she'd felt was evaporating fast. "That was a mistake. We have them sometimes, just like the CIA."

He understood. "I don't care about that. But Angela

was working with him, trying to figure out who killed Mullah Salih Ahmad. Did you help with that?"

Again, she shook her head. "The last time we talked was two weeks ago. A week before . . ." She shifted in her chair. "She was upset about that little terrorist's death. She wanted to know if we'd killed him."

"What did you tell her?"

"The truth. We didn't know anything about it."

Milo didn't doubt this. Two weeks ago, upon learning of Rahman Garang's murder, Angela's suspicions must have run in all directions, and like any good investigator she'd followed up on anything she'd had the ability to follow up on.

Morel looked into her empty espresso cup. "You were talking about Yi Lien earlier."

"Yes."

"And his laptop computer."

"Right."

She scratched the back of her neck. "Mr. Weaver, Lien never brought his laptop to the cottage. He never even took it out of the London embassy. It would have been an unforgivable security risk."

"Perhaps you didn't see it."

"I saw everything he brought with him."

"But that's . . ." He trailed off. He'd wanted to say "impossible," but it wasn't, not really. All it meant was that someone, somewhere between the ferry where Lien had his heart attack and Grainger's office in New York, was lying.

Morel watched the changing expressions on his face.

She leaned forward to get a better look. "This is news to you, isn't it?"

There was no sense lying to her, so he didn't.

"I think you should find out why you're getting such bad information."

"I think you're right," he said, and when she didn't answer, he added with a grin: "I hear the novel's pretty good."

"What?"

"The novel you're supposed to be writing."

"Oh, that," she said, leaning back again. "Some years ago a computer programmer in the Foreign Ministry committed suicide. Nothing suspicious about it, but for a long time she passed information to a Cuban boyfriend. Very devout Marxist, it turned out—you see, in France, Marx is not yet dead. When we went through her belongings, we came across the novel she'd written. She hadn't shown it to anyone. I imagine she thought it would be discovered and published posthumously." She paused. "Instead, I used it to convince the colonel that I'm not only beautiful, but a literary genius. Sometimes I feel sorry for the girl."

Morel got a long-focused, melancholy look in her eyes, so Milo said, "She loved you, you know."

"What?" The word seemed to terrify her.

"Angela. In the café, she told me she'd been dumped by a French aristocrat. That was you."

Morel tugged at the hem of the soiled tablecloth. Then: "Aristocrat?"

"Consider it a compliment."

She nodded.

Gently, Milo said, "Where did you and she meet?"

"What do you mean?"

"Angela was a private person. Any relationship she had, she'd want to keep secret. Particularly if her lover was a DGSE agent."

Diane Morel raised her shoulders, looking squarely at him, but didn't answer.

"You wouldn't meet in her place, because people would know. You wouldn't meet in your place for the same reason. It would have to be somewhere else."

"Of course. Security is always a consideration."

"Where did you go? Did she have another apartment?"

Morel smiled. "So you've been to her apartment, and you've searched it. And you're hoping there will be another place where she hid the evidence that will prove your innocence. Is that right?"

"In a nutshell."

"Well, you're out of luck. It was a friend's apartment, in the Nineteenth Arrondissement. You won't find anything there. We went there two, three times. After that, we only used hotels. Understand?"

"The address," he said. "Please."

"Rue David d'Angers, number 37, apartment seven. Near the Danube metro stop." He committed it to memory by repeating it back to her; then she said: "Tell me about the man with the red beard."

He blinked at her, and she smiled.

"Let's not play games. Just tell me."

"It's the man Angela was seen with during the surveillance on her. Herbert Williams. The one we thought was her contact to the Chinese."

Morel nodded.

"Why?"

"Because one of the neighbors reported that, on that Friday afternoon, around four, she'd let in a man with a red beard and a funny accent. He said he was a civil engineer, checking on the foundation of the building."

"Was she with him the whole time?"

"She was just heading out."

"I think that was Angela's murderer."

"I do, too," Morel said, then looked past the bar, where Einner and Lambert were talking animatedly. "The rain's stopped. Are we done?"

"I guess so. What are you going to do about this?"

"About what?"

"This. When you go back to the office."

She pursed her lips in an expression of consideration. "I'll have to report the meeting. There were witnesses, after all."

Milo nodded.

"But it doesn't have to be immediate. And once I've typed up the report, it'll certainly take a while to reach your embassy. A day or two."

"Try to make it two, will you?"

"I'll try."

He just about believed her. "Thank you. For being so open."

Morel leaned closer. "When you do finally talk to them, please tell your masters that if anyone else in Paris ends up dead because of their misinformation, your government can forget about having so much flexibility in the French Republic. You understand?"

"I'll pass it along," Milo said.

He felt poor, as if he owed her something for all her cooperation, but had nothing to give. Then he realized that, small as it was, he did have something.

"You know, Angela dealt with the end of your relationship by throwing herself into her work. She told me that. But that's not why she had to take sleeping pills. It's not your fault she died."

Morel began to nod, then changed her mind, remembering who she was, and who he was. "Of course it wasn't my fault. It was yours."

She stood up, crossed to the bar, and tugged at Lambert's sleeve. Milo, from his seat, nodded at Einner's questioning glance, and the Tourist handed back their cell phones. Then they watched the French intelligence agents walk out into the cool, damp afternoon. Both men stared at the empty doorway a few seconds more.

32

Rue David d'Angers was one of six major streets that grew like irregular flower petals out of Place de Rhin et Danube's ovule. It was decided—that is, Milo decided—that Einner should stay in the car, parked along the street as lookout, while Milo and his knapsack went inside. He trusted Diane Morel to a certain extent, though her partner, Lambert, might do anything. "Need the gun again?" Einner asked.

"If I do, that means I'm doing something wrong."

Number 37 lay at the beginning of the street, its corner facing the Danube metro stop in the middle of the square. The one key Milo had from Angela's apartment didn't fit it, so he looked at the board of buzzers. Rather than listing apartment numbers, there were only names. There—one of them was a business: Electricien de Danube. He pressed it.

"Nous sommes fermés," came the answer, a man. We are closed.

"S'il vous plait," said Milo. "C'est une urgence." It's an emergency.

"Oui?"

"Mon ordinateur." My computer.

The man didn't answer at first, but he could hear him sighing. The door buzzed as he said, "Quatrième étage." Fourth floor.

"Merci."

Milo pushed inside, then moved under the stairwell, where five soiled trashcans were lined up. He hid, squatting behind them, suffering the stink of old cabbage and bad meat.

First he heard the sound, four floors up, of a door opening. Then: "Hello?" Then feet stomping as someone came down the stairs, muttering to himself. The old man came all the way to the ground floor and peered out the front door, finally saying, "Merde," and slowly ascending the stairs again. Once his door slammed shut, Milo emerged from the claustrophobic stink and mounted the stairs.

Luckily, apartment seven was on the third floor, so he didn't have to pass the electrician's door. The name beside the doorbell was Marie Dupont—essentially, a French version of Jane Smith.

On the off chance a friend named Dupont actually did live there, he rang the bell, but got no answer. He heard a television (Formula One racing) from the next apartment, number six, but nothing from seven.

It was a typical old-Europe heavy door with two

small opaque windows that opened from the inside so that fearful pensioners could have entire conversations without ever opening their doors. And, he noticed, there were two locks.

His heart sank, because he knew before he verified it what would happen. His key fit the lock in the center of the door, which worked a loud double dead bolt—but it didn't fit in the second lock, just below the handle. He had no idea where that second key could be. It wasn't under the doormat.

Damned Angela and her overdone security. Like the door itself, the frame was heavy and old, reinforced on the outside by steel. Very effective, just like Angela Yates.

Milo quietly returned to the ground floor and went back into the courtyard, looking up. On this side, terraces rose up, beginning with the second floor. Each terrace was accessed by a sliding glass door, and in the five-foot space between the terraces was a small, high window, probably from the bathroom.

A drainpipe along the corner grew to the building's height, but, after tugging at it, he knew it wouldn't hold. So he returned to the third floor and rang the bell for number six.

After a minute, the inset window opened an inch and a young man stared back at him. "Qui est là?"

"Uh," Milo began, trying to sound flustered. "You speak English?"

The man shrugged. "A little."

"Oh, wow. That's super. Listen, can I use your bathroom? I've been waiting for my girlfriend, Marie, all day. She just called and it looks like I've got another half hour. You mind?"

The young man rose slightly so he could see down the length of Milo's body, perhaps checking for a gun.

Milo showed off his empty hands and flashed the unzipped knapsack at him. "A change of clothes," he explained. "Really. I've just got to take a dump."

Convinced, he unlocked the door, and Milo kept up the act, pointing and asking, "This way?"

"Yes."

"Swell."

Once inside, he closed and locked the bathroom door, turned on the noisy fan, then listened until he heard the man walk back to his television.

The small window sat at head height above the tub. Its deep frame was grimy from old showers and dust, but a flip of the latch popped it open. He reached into his knapsack and took out the duct tape, then filled it with his jacket, tie, and dress shirt. He put the knapsack on the floor beside the toilet. In his undershirt, he held the duct tape roll in his teeth, climbed on the edge of the tub, and pulled himself up so he could slip his head through the window. Two and a half feet to his right, and down, was the guardrail of Marie Dupont's terrace. Five feet to the left of it was this apartment's terrace. Directly below, a long drop led to the hard courtyard floor.

It was a narrow window, but by turning himself sideways he could get his shoulders through. It was difficult holding his body aloft, his legs inside the bathroom swinging until they caught the shower curtain rod.

Eventually, gasping through clenched teeth holding the tape, and sweating, he got out to his waist, and for a moment, to an outside observer, it looked as if the apartment had grown a human torso, one arm propped against the outside wall to keep it perpendicular. His center of gravity was off now, and if he let go of the wall he'd tumble to his death. He used his free hand to take the duct tape from his mouth and toss it onto the Dupont terrace, where it rolled until it hit the railing.

It had been a long time since Milo had put himself through this kind of thing, and he was suddenly sure he didn't have it in him anymore. As Tina had pointed out to him a few times, he'd gotten fat. As Einner liked to point out, he'd gotten old. Why was he hanging out of a window three floors above Paris?

Stop it.

He pushed farther, until his hips had passed through the frame and he could lean forward, his knees now bent along the inside of the wall to keep him up. He stretched out his hands—briefly hanging unsupported along the wall—and caught the Dupont guardrail. He squeezed harder than he needed to, terrified that now, as he unhooked his aching legs from the window, he'd plummet. But he didn't. Instead, gripping the rail, he straightened his legs, and when they slid out the window and his body dropped, his tightened stomach hit the concrete edge of the terrace floor, making him nauseous. Yet his hands held, and so did the railing. He breathed through pursed lips, trying to get his strength back, then slowly pulled himself up.

His burning arms almost didn't make it, but he threw a leg over the corner of the terrace floor, which helped. All his extremities now worked painfully for one purpose, and soon he was crouched on the outside edge of the terrace, the pain all over him, shocked that he was still alive. He climbed over the rail and squatted, staring at his red, numb, shaking hands.

He didn't have time for this. He grabbed the duct tape and tore off ten two-foot-long strips, plastering them on the glass door until he'd made a square of tape. He punched his elbow into the center of it. Glass shattered, but quietly, and remained attached to the tape. He peeled off the tape, exposing a jagged hole in the glass, stuck his arm through, and unlocked the door from the inside.

Without bothering to take in the apartment, he walked directly to the front door and, using a key hanging from a wall hook, unlocked it. He went to number six again and rang the bell. Formula One lowered in volume, then the little window opened. The young man gaped at him.

"Sorry again," said Milo, "but I left my knapsack in your bathroom."

The man, stunned, started to reply, then changed his mind and disappeared. After thirty seconds the door opened and he handed over the knapsack. "How did you get out?"

"I was going to thank you, but I didn't want to interrupt your show. And I hope the bathroom doesn't stink—I opened the window to air it out."

The man frowned at Milo's grimy undershirt and slacks. "What happened?"

Milo looked down at himself, then pointed a thumb toward the open door of number seven. "Marie got back, and . . . really, man. You don't want to know."

33

He'd only just started on the living room, with its broken terrace door, emptying a small desk and riffling through an extensive DVD collection full of Angela's taste—*The Misfits, North by Northwest, Chinatown, Some Like It Hot*—when the door buzzer rang. He slipped off his shoes and padded to the foyer, wishing he'd brought the pistol, but it was only Einner. He was holding out his telephone. "It's for you."

Milo took it back to the living room, and the first thing Grainger said was "You alone?"

Einner had wandered into the kitchen; he heard the refrigerator open. "Yeah."

"I've been sacked, Milo."

"What?"

"Fitzhugh calls it vacation, but it's not that at all. He's furious I tipped you off about Homeland, and he's not happy I showed you Benjamin Harris's file."

"How did he find out?"

"I think one of the clerks told him, but it doesn't matter. I'm packing for a week in New Jersey. I've had enough of the city."

Guilt trickled into his bloodstream—the Company was the only thing the old widower had left in his life, and because of Milo it was now gone.

"What have you got?" asked Grainger. "Einner says you talked to the DGSE."

"Listen, Tom. I'm not even sure I should be running. I might just turn myself in."

"You should stay away," Grainger assured him. "I told you Simmons was meeting with Fitzhugh. She knew you were in Paris and demanded the report on Angela. I didn't show it to her, but I guess Fitzhugh got scared; he'd given in by Tuesday." He paused. "It's all about that blank spot in the surveillance, Milo. You shouldn't have asked Einner to turn off the cameras."

"You're the one who approved it."

"Which is something I'll have to live with. Now tell me what you've got."

Milo explained the most important facts. First, that the whole investigation into Angela Yates had been a ruse. "Yi Lien never brought his laptop out of the embassy. Diane Morel verifies this. That means someone was lying to you. Maybe your MI6 contact. You should get in touch with him."

"Not possible. Fitzhugh has informed Six of the end of my tenure. They know not to share information with me."

"Okay. I'm in a safe house Angela set up. I'm hoping she'll have some records around here."

"Whatever you learn won't mean a thing if you don't have physical evidence. Remember that. What happens if the apartment comes up dry?"

"I'm not sure."

"If you run into a wall, call me in New Jersey. I might be able to come up with something. You have the number?"

"Remind me, will you?"

Milo took a pen and paper from the desk and scribbled the 973 number of Grainger's lakeside house.

"One more thing," said Grainger. "With me gone, Fitzhugh is officially running Tourism. He has no idea where you are, but if he does learn that you're with Einner, you know what'll happen."

Einner appeared, chewing a Snickers bar he'd found, gazing up at the pen-and-ink nudes Angela had decorated the place with. "I think I do."

Grainger wasn't going to depend on Milo's predictive powers: "He'll call Einner—he has his go-code—and order him to bring you in. Catch or kill. So I suggest you lose Mr. Einner as soon as possible."

"Understood," he said as Einner gave up on the nudes and smiled at him. "And Tom?"

"Yes?"

"If Tina gets in touch, can you find a way to tell her I'm all right? That I'll be back as soon as I can?"

"Sure. But you know that woman. She never believes a word I say."

Milo hung up, gave the phone back to Einner, and asked him to look through the bedroom.

"I thought you wanted me to watch the street."

"This is more important," he said, though in truth he wanted Einner in earshot, just in case Fitzhugh made his call.

In the end, they only needed twenty minutes. Believing the Rue David d'Angers apartment to be safe, Angela had merely slipped her growing case file on the Tiger into a folder attached to the underside of the IKEA sofa that faced the small television. A stack of maybe two hundred documents, photographs, and handwritten thoughts ripped from notebooks. She'd organized them with paper clips so that anything she found on, for example, Rahman Garang could be added to a paper-clipped section with his photo and basic information on top. Milo was in awe of the lengths to which she'd gone, collecting phone records and occasional photos she'd shot herself.

He took the stack to the bedroom and found Einner in front of the open wardrobe, breaking the heels off of Angela's shoes, looking for hollow spaces. "Come on," said Milo. "Let's get out of here."

They took the papers to a brasserie in Montmartre, and over grilled racks of lamb began to sort through the information.

"You're telling me she did all this on her own?" Einner asked.

"That's what I'm telling you."

"She was better than I thought."

"Better than any of us thought."

Starting from the point she had told Milo about, Angela had focused on bank records for Rolf Vinterberg in Zürich. Using her connections, she had accessed the records of three other banks in town, two of which also showed a Rolf Vinterberg opening accounts that were closed soon after by Samuel Roth. She'd written on one page:

RV—Resident of Zürich.
Alone?
No.
What Company?

Behind that note-to-self was a twenty-page single-spaced list of Zürich companies, divided by main activity. He had no idea why these particular ones had interested her, or what criteria she'd used. Four pages in, she had circled Ugritech SA with a black marker. How she'd come upon this particular company in the haystack of possibilities wasn't shown here, but he had to believe that Angela had her reasons, which could be hidden in any of the other pages, half of which Einner was reading through.

The name rang a bell, but he wasn't able to put a finger on it until he turned to the next page, which was a printout from the Web site of Ugritech, a company focused on spreading technology through Africa. Then he saw it—first, the photograph. A handsome man with wavy hair and a seductive smile. "DIRECTOR: Roman Ugrimov."

Milo exhaled loudly enough that Einner stopped reading. "Find something?"

"See anything about Ugritech there? It's a company."

Einner shook his head, then went back to his pages as Milo closed his eyes, remembering 10:27 A.M., September 11, 2001, the moment when thirteen-year-old Ingrid Kohl landed hard against Venice cobblestones. Roman Ugrimov's *"And her I love, you bastard!"*

There were not many people Milo could say he hated. Hatred doesn't last long in the Company, because with the amount of information you have access to, it becomes too easy to see the perspectives of those who commit heinous acts. But even knowing a fair amount about what had happened, Milo had never found a way to explain the murder of Ingrid Kohl to his satisfaction.

On September 13, after he'd made sure the pregnant woman, Tina Crowe, was out of danger, he snuck out of the hospital and marched into Ugrimov's palazzo. The visit was a futile act that he couldn't even back up with aggression because of the holes in his chest, but it was enough to make him despise Roman Ugrimov. The Russian had too much faith in his own invincibility—it didn't matter how many crimes he committed; all he had to do was write a few checks. In Italy, the police only questioned him once about the death of the girl in his charge, and soon afterward the official record reflected the story they'd chosen, or been paid, to believe: The poor girl had committed suicide.

"Here it is," Einner said.

Milo blinked at the sheet being held out for him to read. "What?"

"Ugritech. Here."

It was a photocopy of a *Le Temps* article, in French, dated November 4, 2006, that told of Sudanese minister of energy and mining Awad al-Jazz's diplomatic visit to Europe, listing the countries on his agenda. He was seeking investors for a new electrical infrastructure, to replace the one that had been decimated by civil war. In the second column, with a blue ballpoint pen, Angela had circled a meeting between Ugritech director Roman Ugrimov and the energy minister, at Ugrimov's home in Geneva. Present at the meeting were "various American investors." No address given.

There, then, was the connection Angela had found. She was phenomenal.

Milo in turn shared Angela's suspicion that the money used to pay the Tiger had come through Ugritech. Luck, he realized, had played into her calculations—had it not been for that terrible day in 2001, she wouldn't have given Ugritech a second look.

Why, he wondered, hadn't she shared this with him? Was it possible she hadn't trusted him?

"So where does this take us now?" asked Einner.

"Me," said Milo. "I've taken too much from you already."

"You've got me interested now. We've got Sudanese assassinations, tech companies buying them, and disappearing Chinese laptops. What else could a Tourist ask for?"

Milo tempered his arguments so that Einner wouldn't suspect that he was doing this for his own self-preservation, but nothing could convince him.

Einner had started, in his words, "a job," and damned if he wasn't going to see it through.

"So, where?"

Milo wondered again if this was all a mistake. Not just bringing Einner along, but this whole chase. It occurred to him that, had he let himself be taken in Disney World, it all might have been wrapped up by now. Grainger's call had left him no time for reflection. He might, at this very moment, have been sitting in his living room, eating ramen noodles and listening to Stephanie's particular take on the world.

But a Tourist soon learns that might-have-beens are a luxury for others. Tourism allows no time for regret, and in fact regret is a plague to the Tourist. So he put his regrets aside and said, "We're going to Geneva. Is the car filled up?"

Einner rocked his head from side to side. "Wait here. I think it's time for a new set of wheels."

34

Tina sometimes had the feeling that she didn't appreciate things enough. She remembered how she'd been in Venice, of all places, hating the heat and dirt and packs of tourists and—yes—the oppressively heavy baby in her stomach. As if all those constituted the worst the world could dish out. Then she'd met Frank Dawdle and learned that things could get much worse.

She'd let those opening Venice days go by utterly unappreciated. She was a genius at missing what was in front of her, and she wondered if, somehow, she was doing it again here in Austin on a Saturday afternoon.

There were some parallels. Her significant other was gone in a puff of smoke, and she found herself sweating too much on her parents' back porch. Austin heat is not unlike Venice heat in that it's wet, sapping your whole body when you leave the protection of air-conditioned houses. And, as in Venice, she was alone, just her and her daughter.

"Lemonade?" asked her mother, sticking her head out the sliding glass door and reminding her she wasn't really alone. Not technically.

"Sure, Mom. Thanks."

"Be right back."

Hanna Crowe closed the door to keep in the artificial cool, and Tina gazed at the brown crabgrass and two dying poplars recently planted by the privacy fence. This was nothing like Venice. In these suburbs north of Austin, water was a precious commodity, and land spread wide and empty. People lived separated by high fences. This was a completely different world.

Hanna brought an enormous plastic cup full of iced lemonade and sat beside her daughter on the lawn chair. For a while, they just stared at the dead grass. Hanna looked younger than her fifty-six years, her skin permanently pink from the Texas sun. She often wished aloud that she'd been born with her husband Miguel's south-of-the-border tan, but just as often praised her daughter's olive complexion for carrying the best of both worlds. Finally, Hanna said, "Haven't heard from him, have you?"

"He won't call again."

"Sure he will."

Tina was annoyed that her mother couldn't, or wouldn't, get her head around this. "He can't, Mom. The Company thinks he's done something wrong, and he needs to show them he's innocent before he can get in touch."

"But just one call—"

"No, Mom. One call, and they trace his location like that," she said with a snap of her fingers. "He can't risk it yet."

Her mother smiled sadly. "You know what it sounds like, don't you?"

"Yeah, I know. Paranoia."

Hanna nodded.

"But it's not. You've seen the sedan parked over in front of the Sheffields', right? I pointed it out to you."

"Friends of the Sheffields, I'm sure."

"Then why don't they get out of the car, Mom?"

Ever since arriving two nights ago, Tina had been unable to impress her mother with these details. Her father got it, so why couldn't she?

"Well," said Hanna, "it's nice to have you here. We haven't seen Stephanie in months."

Tina closed her eyes. How, really, could she expect her mother to understand? Both her parents knew Milo worked for the CIA, but they believed he was an analyst of some type, dealing with classified information that precluded him ever discussing his job over family dinners. They certainly never learned the true story behind their first meeting, never knew that he had been the kind of Company employee who sometimes carried a gun and even had clearance to use it.

The men who shared time in the sedan by the Sheffields' worked for the woman who had abruptly ended their vacation. Special Agent Janet Simmons. Though her initial impression had been that Simmons was probably the biggest bitch she'd ever met, now, with a few days' distance, she could recall how Simmons had been trying to show Tina how reasonable she was. "Yes, I think he murdered Angela Yates and another person. That's why I want to bring him in. But why would he run, Tina? Can you tell me that?"

"No, I can't."

"Exactly, Tina. If he's innocent, I'm all for hearing his version. But I need him in front of me." She shook her head, and her wandering eye fixed on the far wall. "This sudden escape doesn't look good at all. Maybe you know something you're not telling me? Maybe you know where he's gone?"

Tina, with all honesty, admitted she knew nothing, and over the past days she'd wondered just how little she knew at all. Even petty Patrick had his suspicions. Was that because he was such a miserable, self-pitying man, or was it because he could see what she was blind to?

Her mother was saying something that ended with ". . . fresh tortillas right off the grill."

"What was that?"

Hanna Crowe smiled and rubbed her daughter's forearm. "That new restaurant off I-35. I was thinking we'd go tonight. What do you think?"

"Sure, Mom. That sounds good."

Miguel Crowe had been considered a big man from the time he turned nineteen and won a scholarship to the University of Texas to study engineering. Once he'd arrived in Austin from Guadalajara, he began planning for his future, making contacts with the oil company recruiters who visited twice a year. By the time he graduated, he had negotiated a position with Exxon Mobil in the Alaskan fields, bringing along his new wife, Hanna, who quit her comparative literature studies to follow her husband north. Tina was born in Nome, but by the time she was six, they had moved back to the corporate head-quarters in Irving, a suburb of Dallas. He was the only Mexican national ever to have joined the board of direc-tors when he took early retirement in 2000, amid a wave of national hatred for oil conglomerates.

Upon retiring, he bought an Austin bicycle shop fallen on hard times. He expanded the store, rebranded it, and took out ads in the *Chronicle* for what was criti-cally referred to by locals as "the Wal-Mart of cycle stores." There was irony all over his new business ven-ture, and Tina sometimes asked how many local stores he'd put out of business.

"Christ, Tina. I thought you'd be happy I was help-ing the environment."

Despite his business ethics, Tina adored her father. Nearing sixty, he was broad and dark-skinned and from certain angles looked like a Mexican wrestler. When he was with Stephanie, though, all the business went out of him, and he wanted nothing more than to stay on the floor at her level, discussing whatever the girl directed the conversation toward.

That morning, he'd insisted on taking Stephanie to see the store, but by the time they got back at two they'd also visited Chuck E. Cheese's and gotten some Baskin-Robbins for dessert, which had spread a dark stain on Stephanie's lime overalls. Hanna stripped them off and went to work on the stain while Stephanie searched for some replacement clothes. Miguel also disappeared briefly, taking the day's mail to his office, then wandered back into the living room, one of the envelopes stuck in his pocket. Unconsciously, he flipped on their widescreen television. CNN informed them of stock prices.

"How was she, Dad?"

"She can charm anyone, that kid. I should use her for my negotiations."

"Didn't feed her too much, did you?"

Her father ignored that, but sat up on the couch, glancing at the empty doorway. He took the padded envelope from his pocket and tossed it onto the space between them. "Take a look at that."

She lifted it and quickly read the scrawled address—her parents'—on the cover. She knew that handwriting. No return address. Inside were two crisp passports and a slip of spiral paper asking her parents to please hold the passports for T and S, Tina and Stephanie.

"My God," she muttered as she looked at her own photograph beside the name Laura Dolan. And there was Stephanie, but now named Kelley.

When her mother walked in, she stuffed the passports back into the envelope, as if this were a secret between her and her father, which perhaps it was, but her mother was only walking through to the bathroom for extra detergent.

"What do you think?" Miguel asked once his wife was gone again.

"I don't know what to think."

"An escape plan, maybe?"

"Maybe."

Miguel switched to MSNBC's financial news as Hanna blew back through the room, saying, "I hope you didn't ruin her appetite, Mig."

"Just the ice cream, hon. We played games at Chuck E.'s."

She answered with a doubtful *hmm* and was gone.

He sighed. "I don't know what all's going on, Tina, but if he's looking to pack you and my granddaughter off to some other country, then he's going to get some serious shit from me. I'll not have it."

"He wouldn't do that."

"Then why the passports, Tina?" When she didn't answer, he started to channel-surf, muttering, "Some serious shit, indeed."

35

Because of its historical aloofness, Switzerland had never joined the European Union, but in a June 2005 vote its citizens chose to become part of the Schengen Agreement, opening its borders to the larger passport-free European zone. This made the trip in the Renault Clio hatchback Einner had picked up south of Paris that much easier, and they reached Switzerland in four and a half hours, Milo taking over the wheel after the third dark hour.

While still in the passenger seat, Milo continued going through Angela's papers, using Einner's penlight. Much of it was peripheral—Rahman Garang's credit card records, articles on Ugritech's installation of computer systems in the Democratic Republic of Congo, Kenya, and Sudan, and, for no apparent reason, a daily summary from the United Nations Web site:

HIGHLIGHTS OF THE NOON BRIEFING
U.N. Headquarters, New York
Wednesday, June 20, 2007

U.N. Mission in Sudan Discusses Ways
to Further Assistance to the Implementation
of Peace Agreement

- The UN Mission in Sudan, in today's briefing, notes that, over the weekend, the acting Special Representative for Sudan, Taye Brook Zerihoun, met with the State Minister to the Presidency, Idris Abdel Gadir.
- Their discussion focused on a proposal to hold high-level consultations between the UN Mission in Sudan and the Government of National Unity to make the Mission's assistance to the implementation of the Comprehensive Peace Agreement more focused and effective.
- Meanwhile, the UN Mission reported that yesterday, an international NGO-hired vehicle traveling in South Darfur was shot at by an unknown armed man.
- On that same day in West Darfur, an international NGO convoy of two vehicles with five staff members was stopped by two unknown armed men, and the staff was robbed of personal effects and communication equipment.

Following this was an article from, of all things, the Chinese *People's Daily*, dated September 25, 2004: SUDANESE GOVERNMENT FOILS COUP PLOT.

> Sudan foiled a plot by Islamists to overthrow the government on Friday afternoon, the Interior Ministry said in a statement.
>
> Elements of the Popular Congress (PC) headed by jailed Islamist leader Hassan al-Turabi planned to carry out the plot in Khartoum at 2 p.m. (1100 GMT) right after the Friday prayers, said the statement . . .

That was three years ago; now, with the murder of Mullah Salih Ahmad, the rebellion was in the streets.

It was hard to concentrate. The rumble of the transmission gave him an ache in his lower spine. He was still sore from his acrobatics and short on sleep. He wanted to call Tina, to hear her voice and Stephanie's. He wanted to know exactly where they were.

Later, as he drove, Milo rubbed his face, staring into the midnight highway darkness. His mind wandered. He thought that in spy films or television shows, there was always a clear objective. A tape of a conversation that proved some important fact. A man who had the answers to a specific question. These stories were enjoyable for their very simplicity. The truth was that intelligence work seldom, if ever, ran in straight lines. Facts accumulated, many of them useless, some connecting and then disconnecting. It took a patient, trained eye to figure out which to hold on to and which to lay aside. Angela had had that kind of eye. He didn't know if he had it.

"Whoa!" said Einner, rising from sleep.

Milo blinked, then swerved the car back onto the highway.

"You suicidal or something?"

"Sorry."

"Let me take over." Einner sat up; he licked his teeth. "Where are we?"

"Just crossed over. Here." Ahead was a sign:

EXIT 1
GENÈVE-CENTRE
LA PRAILLE
CAROUGE
PERLY

They argued over which hotel to check into. Milo wanted something small and inconspicuous, like De Genève. "*That* flea pit?" said Einner. "Jesus, Milo. You want to kill us before we've had a chance to fight?" De Genève was not a flea pit, but Einner had made it a habit on his unlimited Tourism expense accounts to stay in the finest lodgings a city had to offer. In Geneva, this meant the Hotel Beau-Rivage, overlooking Lake Geneva's harbor full of yachts.

"They track this car," said Milo, "and that's the first place they'll look."

"But they won't find the car. You really do worry too much."

"That's because I'm on the run."

"Come on. Trust me."

As he steered down Rue de la Servette, which led directly to the water, Milo almost laughed at that. Part of it was the fatigue, but more, it was a basic truth of Tourism that you trusted no one. Yet if you had to trust anyone, it had better not be another Tourist.

They left the car behind the hotel. It was nearly one in the morning, but the harbor was alive with music and people. The activity seemed to wake Einner, who snapped his fingers to the rhythm of a samba emanating from a party boat in the middle of the lake.

Einner decided to put their rooms on one of the five credit cards he had in his wallet, under the name Jack Messerstein. Once they'd gotten the keys to their adjoining rooms on the fourth floor, Einner whispered to him, "You go on up. I'll ditch the car."

"Now?"

"I know a guy who knows a guy. And he never sleeps."

"Can I use your phone?"

Einner didn't seem sure about that.

"Don't worry," he said. "I'm not calling home."

It was true. He was merely ensuring that Einner didn't receive new orders just yet.

Before going upstairs, he checked the lobby phone book—no listing for Ugrimov. With a Dolan card, he withdrew a stack of Swiss francs from an ATM and asked a desk clerk about Roman Ugrimov, an old friend living nearby. Yes, he knew Ugrimov—a man with that much flagrant wealth couldn't go unnoticed. Did he know where Roman lived? The clerk, eyeing the money, shook his head sadly, but in exchange for a few bills directed Milo to a stunning-looking prostitute sipping white wine in the hotel bar. Thinking Milo a potential customer, she touched his arm often. Once he said what he wanted, she pulled back. "You're a cop?"

"Old friend."

"My customers pay for my discretion, Mr. Old Friend."

"Then let me pay for it, too."

Roman Ugrimov, it turned out, wasn't one of her customers, but the circle of Geneva prostitutes in her class was small, and she knew a girl—"Very young, you know. He likes them young"—who had been to his place a few times. For two hundred and fifty francs, around two hundred dollars, she made the call and scribbled Ugrimov's address on a Löwenbräu beer coaster.

The room was called "deluxe," and indeed it bore no resemblance to the hundreds of mid- to low-priced rooms he'd lived in during his life as a Tourist. The large bed had a headboard of romantic drapes; there was a sitting area with love seats; the whole room had an elegant old-world feel. The marble bathtub was built for two. The window overlooked the lake and pleasure boats and lights of the city. What a waste, he thought, being here without his family.

36

They skipped breakfast, and once they were under way Einner explained that he'd delivered the stolen Renault to a friend who ran a chop shop on the outskirts of Geneva. In return, the friend gave him a Daewoo that had been stolen in Spain, repainted, and registered under a new name with Swiss papers. For a cheap car, it gave a smooth ride, even along the mountainous northern coastline of Lake Geneva.

"You look better this morning," Einner said as he drove. "Any fresh perspectives?"

"Just that sleep is a good idea," Milo said, because that was true. It was more than simply being rested, though. It was this, reentering his old life so suddenly. He'd woken this morning sore, but feeling like he was a Tourist, and his brain had reverted to its old methods of boxing up his anxiety. It was a temporary measure, he knew, but a necessary one. It could only last so long before the anxiety burst out and broke him completely, as it had six years ago, nearly killing him. He said, "And maybe I'm starting to feel hopeful."

"I'll bet the Book has something to say about hope," said Einner. He glanced over to see if Milo would share the Black Book's knowledge on this point, which Milo was happy to do.

"It tells you to not get hooked on it."

They reached Ugrimov's estate by eleven thirty via winding mountain roads that brought them past obscured mansions to a high electrified gate clotted with video cameras and a squawk box. Milo got out of the car, crunching over gravel, and pressed the speaker button. A heavy Russian voice said, "Oui?"

Milo answered in Russian: "Please tell Roman that Charles Alexander is here to see him."

Silence followed, and he glanced back to see Einner, in the car, staring expectantly at him. The speaker clicked, and Roman Ugrimov spoke through it. "Mr. Alexander-Weaver? It's been a long time."

Milo looked into one of the video cameras, smiled, and waved. "Half hour at most, Roman. I just want to talk."

"And your friend?"

"He doesn't need to come in."

"Then he can wait there."

Milo went over to the car and told Einner to stay where he was. After a few minutes, a black Mercedes appeared on the other side of the gate, rolling slowly through the trees. Two men got out, one of them famil-

iar from their last meeting six years ago. "Nikolai," said
Milo.

Nikolai pretended not to remember him. His associate opened a door in the gate, and when Milo stepped
through they frisked him, then locked the door again.
They walked him to the car, put him in the rear, and
reversed out of sight.

Milo had imagined that Ugrimov's house at the end
of the long, winding driveway would be akin to a man-
sion, but he was wrong. The Russian, surprisingly, had
more humble tastes. The Mercedes stopped in front of
a low but very wide stone house that curved like a U,
the bottom facing forward and the inside hiding a stone
courtyard and swimming pool. That's where Ugrimov
was waiting for him, sitting on an aluminum lounge
chair sipping something pink and frothy. He got up with
a grunting noise, set his drink on a glass table, and
came over to shake Milo's hand. The last six years had
turned his thick gray hair white. "It's been a long time,"
Ugrimov told him in Russian.

Milo agreed, then sat in a matching lounge chair
that Roman Ugrimov offered.

"Something to drink? Nikolai blends a tasty grapefruit daiquiri."

"No thanks."

"As you like," he said, settling back into his own
chair.

The warm noontime sun made the bright stones hard
to look at. "I need some information, Roman."

"Information, I can handle. Information is my

business. But you're not going to threaten me again, are you?" Ugrimov asked with a smile. "I found your last threats distasteful."

"You killed that girl. I watched you."

"You weren't even looking at the terrace, Mr. Weaver. No one was. Not when she jumped." He shook his head in an imitation of grief. All this man's emotions, Milo thought, were imitations. "It was a sad enough day without you pointing fingers."

"I'm not here about her. I'm here about your company, Ugritech."

"Oh, good. I'd been hoping for some fresh investors."

"Who's Rolf Vinterberg?"

Ugrimov pursed his lips, then shook his head. "No idea."

"How about the three hundred thousand dollars placed by Rolf Vinterberg into the Union Bank of Switzerland, in an account later emptied by Samuel Roth? Or the meeting that took place here, late last year, with the Sudanese energy minister?"

The Russian considered him over the edge of his glass as he loudly slurped the last of his daiquiri. He set the glass on the table. "Do you have any idea what we at Ugritech do, Milo?"

"I don't really care."

"You should," he said, wagging a finger. "We do good things. We bring the twenty-first century to the black masses. Others look to China for the next big thing, but me, I'm an optimist. I see our future in our past, in the dark continent from which we all crawled. Africa has potential. Natural resources—minerals, oil, open terrain. It should be dictating its own terms. But it's not. Why do you think that is?"

Milo wasn't sure if Ugrimov was being serious. "Corrupt governments?"

"True, yes. But that's not the cause; it's an effect. At the root of Africa's problems lies a single word: ignorance."

Milo rubbed his nose and sat up straighter. "Roman, I'm not interested in your racist views."

The Russian laughed loudly at that, then quickly settled down. "Don't turn politically correct on me. Of course they're not stupid. Ignorance is the lack of objective knowledge, which is an African curse. Why do villagers believe condoms will not prevent the spread of AIDS?"

"Because Catholic priests tell them so."

"Very good. In that case, the Catholic Church encourages African ignorance. And why do some believe that sex with a virgin will kill the HIV virus?"

"I get your point, Roman."

"I see you do. Ugritech—and, please, I do know the egomania the name suggests—is one effort to break the gridlock of African ignorance. We start with computers, hooked into the Internet. Last year, we installed two *thousand* computers in Nairobi schools and community centers."

"How many in Khartoum?"

"About the same amount. I don't remember."

"Is that why the energy minister visited you here?"

Ugrimov looked at his empty daiquiri glass.

"Nikolai!" he called, and the bald man appeared. "Do you mind?"

Apparently, Nikolai didn't. He took the glass and went back inside.

"Well?" said Milo.

Roman Ugrimov put his palms together in front of his lips. "You, Milo Weaver—there are stories going around now that you're on the run. Is that right?"

A pause. "Yes."

"A man on the run from his own people suddenly shows up on my doorstep. It's strange, isn't it?"

"Are you going to answer my questions, or not?"

"Please. You're in such a rush. You really should try a daiquiri."

"Thank you, but no."

"Did you kill someone?"

"No."

"But of course I shouldn't believe you, should I? You never believed that I didn't kill my dear Ingrid, even though I told you that she took her own life."

"Fair enough."

A sudden smile flashed across Ugrimov's face. "Remember when we last talked? You were upset, of course. I mean, you'd been shot, hadn't you? Anyone would be upset."

"I was upset because you wouldn't answer my questions," Milo remembered aloud. "You wouldn't tell me why Frank Dawdle had visited you. You might as well tell me now."

"You ask a lot."

Milo shrugged.

"It was simple, Mr. Weaver. Franklin Dawdle wanted a new identity. South African. He knew I had contacts who could make this happen quickly."

"That's why he was there, to ask for it?"

"He asked for it several days before. The day you people killed him, he was coming to pick it up. I suppose you found the passport on his body. Yes?"

Milo had been too out of it back then, and no one had told him a thing. "How did Ingrid come into it?"

Ugrimov's expression changed. "Ingrid Kohl. She was a beautiful girl—you never met her, but . . . you saw her pictures?"

"I saw her on the terrace—the night before."

The Russian swallowed loudly. "Your Frank Dawdle was a cretin. I expect that of CIA men, but not to this level. He came with a simple business transaction—yes, he was paying for the passport. But he had to sully it with a threat. He had evidence that I was more than just a guardian to my beloved Ingrid. Photographic evidence, apparently."

"She was very young, Roman."

"Thirteen," Ugrimov admitted, then chewed his lower lip a moment, gazing past Milo at the glass doors, perhaps at his own reflection. "Pregnant, too. With my . . . our . . ." He closed his eyes, cleared his throat, and finally looked directly at Milo: "It would've been bad for business if that got out. No one cares about the circumstances or the nature of your love. They only see numbers."

Milo, thinking of Stephanie, wanted to point out that thirteen-year-old girls could be manipulated into believing anything, even love. He quickly cut the connection. "You killed her to show him he had no control over you anymore."

"She jumped," he whispered.

Milo wondered if, over the years, Ugrimov had convinced himself of that lie.

"Anyway, that was a tragedy. A tragedy compounded perhaps by Dawdle's death seconds later—then overshadowed by what happened soon after in New York City." A sudden smile. "And happiness! You met your wife in the midst of tragedy, didn't you?"

It disturbed Milo how much this man knew, but he didn't show it. He needed Roman Ugrimov. "Yes, and we're still together."

"I heard."

"From who?"

Another smile.

Milo said, "Do you remember Angela Yates? She was with me in Venice."

"Indeed I do. She's the pretty one who took care of the cretin Dawdle. I read that she committed suicide recently. Then I heard you were wanted in connection with her murder. Which, then, is true?"

"She was killed, but not by me."

"No?"

"No."

The Russian pursed his lips. "These questions you're asking, about my Africa company—do they have to do with her murder?"

"Yes."

"I see." He smacked his lips together. "Mil

The same day pretty Angela Yates killed that cretin, the world we knew suddenly stopped, didn't it? Now, people who couldn't even spell it before have actually read the Qu'ran. Or," he said, smiling, "they at least claim to know its message."

"And you've changed with the world?"

Ugrimov rocked his head from side to side. "You could say that. My priorities have evolved. My friends are now many shades."

"Are you supplying computers to terrorists?"

"No, no. Not that. Never that."

"How about China?"

A puzzled frown; a shake of the head.

Milo was getting tired of beating around the bush, which was de rigueur when talking to Russians. "Tell me."

"What'll you give me in return?"

Milo wasn't sure he had anything a man of Ugrimov's reach and influence could want. "How about information?"

"About what?"

"Anything you want, Roman. If I know it, I'll answer the question."

Nikolai returned with a fresh grapefruit daiquiri and placed it beside Ugrimov. The Russian smiled. "I like your style, Milo Weaver."

Silence followed, as they waited for Nikolai to leave.

37

You want to know about two things. Some person named Rolf Vinterberg who puts money into a bank, and my relationship with the government of the Sudan. Correct?"

"Yes."

"As it so happens, these two things are not entirely unconnected. In fact, I'd call them very connected. You know, of course, that I'm a powerful man. But like many powerful men, I sit on a bubble. At any moment, it can burst. One example was your Franklin Dawdle, the cretin. In that case, it was my personal tastes that threatened to pop the bubble. These days, I'm established enough that it couldn't hurt me. But six years ago, I was still negotiating contracts in the public eye. I was just beginning to insinuate myself into the European economy." He shrugged. "I was vulnerable."

"Which is why you killed Ingrid. You didn't want to be vulnerable anymore."

Ugrimov dismissed this with a wave of his hand. "Let's not stir up old dust. What I want to talk about is after that sad day. Three months, to be precise. December 2001. I was approached, via some American friends, by a young man who had a similar proposition. Yes, he, too, was blackmailing me! I thought: *What have I done that God keeps cursing me?* Who knows? And this time it wasn't about girls—no, it was something more sinister."

"What was it?"

A swift shake of the head. "If I told you, then it wouldn't be my secret, would it? Suffice it to say, it was financial in nature. This young man would not only remain quiet about his knowledge of it, but would also make sure that no one else learned of it. He would be my protector, so to speak."

"What was his name?"

"He introduced himself as Stephen Lewis, and that's what I've always called him."

"American?"

"I doubted his name, but never his American character. Pushy, you know. Like the whole world belongs to him."

"What did he want you to do?"

Ugrimov drank more of his daiquiri, then got up and closed the terrace doors. As he wandered back, he stared hard at the open end of the courtyard, which led into forest. He sat down and lowered his voice. "You've already seen what he asked me to do. To take cash—different amounts each time—and deliver them to a variety of Zürich banks, opening accounts under two names: my man's name and Samuel Roth. What could I do? Yes? What would you do? I did as he asked, of course. Not often—two or three times a year. And what's illegal about it? Nothing. I send one of my employees with some false papers—Rolf Vinterberg is the one we've used the last two years—and he opens the account."

There it was. Milo felt unexpectedly thrilled. The simple money-laundering scheme used to pay the Tiger for his jobs; Angela had only been a hair's breadth away. Then he wondered aloud, but without hope, "Did he have a beard?"

"What?"

"Stephen Lewis. Does he have a red beard?"

Ugrimov brightened. "You know him! Red on top, red in the face, red in the beard. You know this man!"

There, again. Connections. He shook his head. "Not yet I don't, but I hope to meet him soon. Go on. Please."

"Well, there's not much more on that point. It was always as he promised. My fiscal secrets never came to light, and every now and then I'd be approached by Mr. Lewis. He'd give me the cash—euros—with the bank instructions, and I'd have my Mr. Vinterberg follow those instructions. In fact, after a few years the agreement benefited me even more. Some other problems arose, and some bureaucrats in Germany started demanding Switzerland send me to them. Truly, I was scared. I told Lewis, and Lewis—don't ask me how—made sure Switzerland would leave me in peace." He nodded reverently. "And that they did. Until recently, at least."

"What happened?"

"I got a note on Monday from the Swiss Foreign Ministry. Guess what? The new administration has decided I might not be an ideal citizen anymore, because of the angry Huns in Berlin."

"So you contacted Lewis."

"How could I? He never left me a phone number—we didn't work like that. But—coincidence of coincidences!—four days ago, I got my final visit from Mr. Stephen Lewis. I considered this fortuitous, as I could ask for his help. However, he hadn't shown up with a bundle of euros and banking instructions. He'd shown up empty-handed. He told me our arrangement had reached its conclusion. He thanked me for my cooperation and assured me that his people would never reveal our little secret, just as long as I didn't reveal it either. As for the new German problem plaguing me, he admitted he couldn't do anything about it anymore. That time had passed."

It was an incredible piece of luck. The Swiss Foreign Ministry letter had been Milo's ticket, converting Roman Ugrimov's anger into a desire for revenge. Otherwise, they might have sat here in silence, Ugrimov betraying nothing of his long-standing arrangement with Stephen Lewis, a.k.a. Jan Klausner, a.k.a. Herbert Williams. How many names did the bastard have?

Ugrimov cleared his throat, then sipped the daiquiri. "I don't know what game you're playing, Milo Weaver. I hope it's not aimed at me."

"I don't think it is," Milo said truthfully. "Tell me about the Sudan."

"Oh! Well, you'll like this. The connection between the events I've just described and the Sudan is, of course, the elusive Mr. Lewis."

Hands on his knees, Milo said, "Tell me."

"Well, this is back in late October, when we were still friends. Lewis came to me—to here, in fact—and asked a favor. Could I invite the energy minister, Mr. al-Jazz, to my house? Some friends of his would like to invest in electricity. I knew the minister, of course. Not my favorite—I still have a nasty feeling he's dismantling our computers as fast as we can install them. Anyway, Lewis made it clear that our continued cooperation hinged on this, so I said okay. I sent out the invitation, the minister accepted, and on November 4 I welcomed him into my home. There was Lewis, of course, with four mute American businessmen. And before you ask," he said, raising a hand, "no. They didn't give their names. In fact, they were rude. At Lewis's request, I withdrew to the parlor, and didn't come out again until I heard the energy minister shouting and storming down the hall to the front door, his security men right behind him. I went out to wish him a safe drive home. To my glee, he was livid. Know what he said?"

Milo indicated that he didn't.

"He said, *We'll sell to whoever we goddamned want to!* Yes, he did say that. Then: *Threaten my president, I'll bury yours!*" Ugrimov nodded vigorously. "It was a very lively evening."

"You have no idea what they discussed?"

Ugrimov shook his head. "Some of Lewis's people swept for bugs first. Afterward, they all left without a word, and I drank myself to sleep. One of those moments when you no longer feel master of your own domain. Know what I mean?"

"Yes. I do."

That was all Milo could say as, staring at the Russian, he made more connections. Herbert Williams represented a group of American businessmen. They used the Tiger to murder a Muslim extremist after—and this was crucial—a failed talk with the Sudanese energy minister. *Threaten my president . . .* It was as the Tiger had suspected. The murder was supposed to enrage the population, to make an unstable government that much less stable. Not for the terrorists, though, but for some businessmen. Why? *We'll sell to whoever we goddamned want to!*

Sell what?

The only thing the Sudan had that was of value to anyone in America was oil.

Who did Sudan sell its oil to? The Chinese; U.S. companies bought none, because of the embargo.

The sun was too hot to deal with. Milo got up and walked to the glass doors, where the extended roof protected him. He regulated his breaths.

"You all right, Milo Weaver?"

"I'm fine. Is that all?"

Ugrimov stretched out in his chair and brought the now-melted daiquiri to his lips. "That's the whole thing. And now, it's time for reciprocation. I ask you any question I like?"

"If I know the answer, I'll tell you."

"Fair enough," said the Russian. His face turned bleakly serious: "Where do you suggest I go?"

"What?"

"I'm going to have to leave Switzerland soon. Where to? Someplace with a good climate, of course, but someplace where I won't be hounded by German bankers. I thought about your country, but I'm not very positive about Americans these days."

"How about the Sudan?"

"Ha!" Ugrimov seemed to find that funny, and Milo realized that there was nothing this man needed from him. He'd shared the story out of spite, nothing more.

"What about Lewis?" Milo asked. "I imagine you tried to find out who he was, didn't you?"

"Of course I did. Years ago."

"And?"

"And what? Guys like that, they cover their tracks. We came up with a couple names. Herbert Williams, for one, in Paris."

"Was the other name Jan Klausner?" Milo asked.

Ugrimov frowned, then shook his head. "No. It was Kevin Tripplehorn."

"Tripplehorn?"

The Russian nodded. "There's no telling how many aliases this guy has."

Tripplehorn, Milo thought, and kept repeating it in his head. That's when he knew. Not everything, not yet, but enough. Kevin Tripplehorn, the Tourist. Tripplehorn, who was also Jan Klausner, Herbert Williams, Stephen Lewis. Tripplehorn, who had posed with Colonel Yi

Lien in a photo and floated around Angela Yates in order to spy on her, or incriminate her. Tripplehorn.

He woke without knowing he'd passed out. Ugrimov, above him, was slapping his cheeks, then tried to feed him some daiquiri. It was too bitter. The back of his head throbbed.

"You need to take care of yourself, Milo. You can't depend on others to do it for you. My advice? Depend on your family, no one else." Ugrimov stood and called, "Nikolai!"

Nikolai kept a suspicious eye on Milo as he drove the sick man back to the gate. Milo, in the late stages of shock, kept thinking about Ugrimov's last words. *Depend on your family, no one else.* It was a curious thing to say.

Einner, at the gate, stood smoking one of Milo's Davidoffs, and dropped it to the ground when he saw the Mercedes approaching. When Milo got out, his legs stronger now, Nikolai also got out and pointed at Einner. "You," he said in stiff, angry English. "Don't you litter!"

38

On the drive back into town, Einner told him that Geneva was one of his favorite cities. "Have you kept your eyes open? The girls here. I'm in a permanent state of erotic excitement."

"Uh huh," Milo said to passing trees.

"I'll show you. Unless you've got us housebreaking. You don't, do you?"

Milo shook his head.

"Fine. We'll get some nightlife, then." The trees gave way to houses as they neared the lake. "You know, you can tell me what happened back there. I'm working with you, after all."

But Milo didn't speak. It was Tourism, which taught him to measure the number of facts he let loose, and the fact that Tourism had become the root of everything. He still hadn't reached that next level of understanding. So he lied, because that, too, was Tourism. "Ugrimov was a dead end. Had to expect a few."

"And Ugritech?"

"If someone's using his company to move money, he doesn't know about it."

Einner frowned over this failure. "But at least we're in Geneva, am I right? And you've got the best guide you could hope for. We on for tonight?"

"Sure," said Milo. "I'll need to catch a nap first."

"Well, you're not a young man anymore."

They reached the Beau-Rivage by four. Einner said that while Milo slept, he would get his own kind of rest at a whorehouse he never missed when visiting town. "Very classy place. Clean. They treat you right. Sure you don't want a pop?"

Milo wished him happiness, picked up a complimentary *Herald Tribune,* and headed to the elevator. As he rose toward his room, he noticed at the bottom of the front page a photograph of a gentle-looking old man with a white comb-over and a soft smile. Datelined Frankfurt, it told of Herr Eduard Stillmann, ten-year board member of Deutsche Bank, found bludgeoned to death in his twenty-eighth-floor office. Police had no leads as of yet. Milo knew, as he set the paper on his bed and began to undress, that they never would have any.

During his Tourism days, sleep sometimes happened this way. He'd run into a wall of information, and it would exhaust him physically and mentally. Not even Tourists can make so many connections in a snap. It takes time and reflection, like art. Milo was no better

than the average Tourist, and when he woke and showered and dressed that evening, his mind was still ruptured by too much knowledge.

He wasn't even suspicious when Einner said, "I've
got to head out in the morning."

"Oh?"

"Call came. New pastures for this one. Think you
can handle it on your own?"

"I'll give it an honest try."

He only lasted an hour at Platinum Glam Club, a
throbbing pulse of slick nightclub on the Quai du Seujet,
facing the Rhône where it flowed from Lake Geneva.
Fifteen minutes in, he'd gone deaf from the techno
music and the rich Swiss youth packed in around him,
screaming to be heard. Lights flashed, lasers scribbled
on the walls, and he soon lost track of Einner in the
crowd that led to the dance floor. His entry fee entitled
him to a free drink, but it was too much work trying to
fight his way to the bar, where toned young men in spiky
bleached hairdos flipped bottles to the agonizing rhythm
of the music, as delivered by a certain DJ Jazzy Schwartz.
He backed away, knocking into pretty girls with tall,
multicolored drinks and short skirts who pretended he
wasn't there, and tried to make it to the couches that
lined the room. By the time he reached them, though,
they were filled. He had no idea why he was here, so he
worked his way to the entrance again.

With the door in sight, a girl with black, straight
bangs and a silver lamé one-piece blocked his path,
holding a tall mojito between her breasts. She had a big
smile as she shouted something he couldn't hear. He

fooled with his ear to show the problem, so she took his neck with her free hand and brought his ear to her mouth. "Want to dance?"

He touched her bare, moist shoulder to show she shouldn't be offended, but he didn't want to dance.

"Your friend says you do!" she growled, as if catching him in a lie.

In answer to his expression, she pointed behind him. Over a field of well-coiffed heads, he saw Einner with another young girl—a blonde as tall as him—bouncing on the dance floor, waving a thumbs-up at Milo.

"He paid already!" the girl shouted.

It took Milo a moment too long to get it—he was slow, after all—and he leaned down, gave her a kiss on the cheek, and said, "Another night."

She caught him as he started to leave. "What about the money?"

"Keep it."

He broke loose and fought an incoming pack of young men in gray suits and ties and finally climbed the stairs to the cool street facing the Rhône. His ears hummed. The crowd out here was nearly as thick, a riot of revelers the four burly doormen had deemed unacceptable. Some, however, were content with the street, and they shared wine and beers and cigarettes on the curb. A drunk girl spun in the street as her girlfriends, clutching cans of Red Bull, laughed. A passing Mercedes honked at her until she happily jumped out of the way, and Milo began walking back to the hotel.

He'd forgotten how empty all this made him feel. Einner was still young. For him, the cities of Europe were a wonderland of music, violence, and casual sex. It had been that way for Milo as well . . . until it wasn't. Until he realized that the cities of Europe were like one city, a city with plenty of potential, but without variety. He never stayed long enough to discover the nuances that made a place particular. For him, cities were all part of the bright lights of a Platonic "city"; the *where* made no difference.

He rubbed his eyes and, at the lake now, crossed to the shoreline, the water black and almost invisible. It was all clear now, the fact he'd been unwilling to accept. Tripplehorn was one of Grainger's Tourists. Grainger had been controlling everything from the beginning.

He picked up a bottle of Absolut from a convenience store, got his key from reception, and took the elevator again—he was getting sick of its elegant, mirrored interior—and undressed in his room. He considered finding a hotel computer to draft some kind of message to Tina. Just a word to say he was all right. But by now, he knew, the Company—or at least Janet Simmons— was watching both her e-mail accounts. So instead he poured a shot of vodka and drank it down.

There was a slow, steady throb at the base of his neck that reminded him that his primary emotion was despair. You put a man on the run, take him from his family, and then show him that the one person he trusts has been using him, and the man starts to crumble—or the woman, as Angela proved back in 2001. The betrayal makes him desperate for something stable in all this, and the only thing that comes to him is his wife and daughter, who he cannot see, touch, or talk to. And without that family, it might as well be 2001 again, him standing on the edge of a Venetian canal contemplating suicide. Without his family, there was no reason not to jump.

Despite these dismal thoughts, Milo only drank that one shot. He remembered Einner's change in orders and knew what he had to do next.

James Einner didn't get back to the hotel until three. By then, Milo had jimmied the door between his room and Einner's, packed his knapsack and stuck it in the closet, checked on flight times using the hotel phone, and lay on his bed, but didn't sleep. He heard the Tourist come into the adjoining room, heard him stumble against something and curse, then head for the toilet. Milo slipped into the room with his roll of duct tape held behind his back. "Get laid?" he called.

"What?" came Einner's surprised voice through the cracked bathroom door. "Oh. No. I thought you'd be asleep by now."

"No," said Milo, settling casually on the foot of Einner's bed. He could do it now, while the man was on the toilet, but he liked Einner, and didn't want to humiliate him.

"Hey," said the Tourist.

"What?"

"How'd you get in my room?"

Shit.

Milo walked swiftly to the door, pushed it open, then kicked at Einner's hand as it swung the little Makarova toward him. It went off—a loud crash in the small space, a bullet burying itself into the tiles above the tub—and as Einner began to stand, his pants still looped around his ankles, Milo brought his elbow down, hard, against the younger man's shoulder. It knocked him back onto the toilet. Milo raked the heel of his other hand up against Einner's chin, knocking the back of his head against the wall. The Makarova clattered to the floor.

Milo knocked his head against the wall a second time, and Einner's red-veined eyes bulged as he opened his mouth, trying to speak, but Milo used his elbow again, once, against his trachea. Einner couldn't say a thing. Milo picked up the pistol.

He knew he was hurting the Tourist, but he needed him stunned for a few minutes. He ripped the shower curtain down, rings popping off the rod, and spread it on the bedroom floor.

When he returned, Einner was again struggling to get to his feet, gasping sickly.

"Don't," Milo told him and showed off the gun. Einner seemed to calm down, knowing that he'd be dead already if that was the plan, but panicked again when Milo grabbed the pants crumpled around his feet and pulled him, with a thud, off the toilet and dragged him out of the bathroom. His arms flailed; he moaned; his shirt rolled up to his chest; and a putrid streak of brown marked his path.

That, Milo thought with regret, is the most humiliating part. He pulled off a length of duct tape and bound Einner's wrists together in front of his stomach, then his feet.

Heaving, he dragged Einner onto the shower curtain.

"What," Einner managed.

"Don't worry," Milo said calmly. He folded one side of the curtain over the front of Einner's body, one end covering his face.

"*What!*"

Milo folded back the corner, uncovering the face. Einner was completely red now. It was a primal reaction to the idea of being suffocated in plastic. "You're going to be fine," he said, looking for some way to reassure him as he folded the opposite side of the curtain over his body, so that he was wrapped up. He tore off a length of duct tape with his teeth. "Listen to me, James. I have to leave. But I have to make sure you're not on my tail. Because you're a good Tourist. I don't think I'd be able to shake you. So I have to incapacitate you for a while so I can run. Understand?"

Einner, regulating his breaths, spoke through his damaged larynx. "I get it."

"Good. I don't want to do this—you can believe it or not, whatever you want—but I can't afford to have you follow me."

"What did Ugrimov tell you?" Einner managed.

Milo almost told him, then realized he couldn't. "No, James. I don't want you reporting back to Fitzhugh. Not yet, at least."

Einner blinked wet eyes at him.

Milo placed the short length of tape over Einner's mouth. He got to his feet and used the rest of the roll around the outside of the curtain, from the shoulders to the feet, so that there would be nothing for Einner to pick at with his fingers. As he did this, he had to roll

Einner's body a couple of times and lift his feet and shoulders. He tried to be gentle, but he knew there was nothing gentle about plastic and duct tape. And there was nothing gentle about the fact that he'd left the Tourist's pants down, the last of his shit staining the inside of the curtain and his thighs. Einner certainly wanted nothing better than to kill him.

When he was finished, he rolled Einner beside the bed. The Tourist's eyes had cleared up, and above the gray tape they glared at him. Milo showed him the Makarova and put it in a dresser drawer, then pulled the mattress off the bed and set it at an angle, covering Einner and leaving him in a heavy darkness that would muffle any sounds he tried to make as he waited for the cleaning lady to arrive.

In Einner's wallet, he found six hundred dollars' worth of Swiss francs, which he pocketed; he considered taking the keys to the car, but changed his mind. He shut the door without saying anything more, grabbed his knapsack, and left.

At Geneva International, after watching his back through two taxi rides but finding no sign of shadows, he looked over the departures. He was just in time for the 7:30 A.M. Air France Flight 1243, which he bought with the Dolan credit card for nearly three thousand dollars. He jogged to the gate. During the hour-long layover in Charles de Gaulle he felt himself panicking again, looking out for swollen eyes. But Diane Morel wasn't waiting for him.

Once on the next plane, he remembered one of Einner's aphorisms: "Tom calls me, and that's all I need to know. Tom is God when he's on that line."

Tourists never question the *why* of their orders. God told Tripplehorn to follow Angela Yates around Paris, while Einner innocently took photographs of her. God told Tripplehorn to meet Colonel Yi Lien—for all Milo knew, he'd just asked the colonel for a cigarette. God told Tripplehorn to make a deal with an insidious Russian businessman and deliver monies for passage to various bank accounts; God told him to run a famous assassin and direct him at various people of interest. God told him to replace Angela's sleeping pills with barbiturates. God had even told Tripplehorn to set up a hidden needle in a Milan café chair, so that the Tiger, comforted by his faith in Christian Science, would slowly fade away instead of uncovering Tripplehorn's identity.

Tripplehorn was not to blame for any of this. He was simply Job to Grainger's God, and God was the originator of everything.

39

He landed at JFK Monday afternoon all eyes. But after waiting in the interminable passport line that snaked around stanchions, reminding him of Disney World, Lionel Dolan crossed the border into the United States of America without trouble. He rented a Hertz Chevy from a stiff young man with pimples, and on the curb spun the car keys on a finger and watched travelers lean on oversized bags and discuss prices with New York–harried bus drivers. Taxis came and went. Police officers loaded down with radios and other equipment lurked in the corners. But no one, so far as he could tell, gave a damn about the twitchy man in his late thirties who kept rubbing his jaw and looking around. He went to find his Chevy.

Milo wanted to collect his things from Stinger Storage. That little garage held money, extra credit cards, old IDs, and a variety of useful weapons, just waiting for him. Instead, he drove north to I-95, out of Long Island toward New Rochelle, then headed west toward Paterson. While that garage was full of promise, he had to assume it had been compromised. He was a fool, he now knew, and he'd probably made plenty of mistakes over the years. Now, no doubt, a few broad-shouldered Company men were there, one behind the payment counter, a few others sitting in black SUVs with the air conditioners running full blast.

He drove quickly, but not in any visibly panicked way, knowing by the time he turned south again, parallel to Manhattan but inside New Jersey, that he only had an hour until Lake Hopatcong. Did Tom know he was coming? He probably suspected. Had Tom requested Company backup? At this point, Milo could admit to knowing nothing. All he could do was drive in such a way that the radar-toting Jersey cops wouldn't pull him over.

Soon, mountains straddled the highway. It had always been a strange feeling, when he and Tina and Stephanie would head out for occasional weekends with the Graingers, to realize how much nature was so close to Manhattan. In the city, it seemed as if the entire world were made of concrete, steel, and glass. The sight of forests was a perpetual surprise. As he had six years ago, driving to Portorož on the first stage of a journey that ended with Tina and Stephanie, he thought that maybe this was the only place to really know balance, in the mountains.

No, he was too old to believe in the promise of new terrains. What he, as a Tourist, could not have known was that people are geography. Only people give character to nature. Wherever his family was, that was where he belonged.

He and Tina and Stephanie used to drive this road to see both Tom and Terri, when she was still alive. Terri Grainger had been a schizophrenic entertainer, wanting one moment to invite the world into her house for feasts, drink, and good company, and other times wanting only solitude out here, solitude even from her husband. But when she was "on," she was one of the great hostesses, making Tina feel that, in their lakeside house, she could find a subtle replacement for the family in Texas she missed.

All those *T*'s—Tom, Terri, Tina, and Texas. He grinned, remembering something Tina had once said about Patrick and Paula in Paris.

For a long time, Tina accompanied Terri to her chemo sessions. She became the older woman's confidante. Then, when the cancer worsened, and even the most optimistic knew this was going to be a losing battle, Terri shifted gears. She withdrew and ended phone calls in midsentence. She didn't want Tina to suffer through the end with her.

Milo parked under the pines along Brady Drive, not far from the shore, but a good half mile from Grainger's house, hooked his knapsack over his shoulder, and began to walk. Pickup trucks and Fords rolled past, and sometimes a driver gave a toot on the horn and a wave. Milo smiled and waved back. Once he was close enough, he climbed off the road and worked his way through the foliage toward the lake.

Grainger had picked it up in the seventies from an

estate sale. It was from the thirties, built in a Teddy Roosevelt–inspired cabin style. According to Grainger, during the Depression the industrialist who owned it had moved here from Manhattan, with his wife and servants, in order to save money.

The Graingers had let the servants' quarters collect spiders and hedgehogs—the two floors and three bedrooms of the main house were enough to keep up.

He spent forty more minutes in the woods, circling the house to see it from various angles and check the trees for surveillance. Once he was convinced the woods were empty, he approached the house. On the far side, where the living room windows looked out on Grainger's parked Mercedes and the small pier, he saw that Grainger's rowboat was gone.

The house was unlocked, so Milo went inside and looked around. It was empty. He climbed the stairs by the door, passing the bedroom and heading for Grainger's office. It was a small room, with a single large window that looked over Lake Hopatcong.

It was the time of day photographers call the magic hour, when the light of the setting sun refracts just so, and faces seem to glow in the way pregnant women are said to glow. The lake glowed, and so did the small form in its midpoint: Tom Grainger, fishing.

He went through desk drawers until he reached the locked one at the bottom, which he had to force open with a screwdriver from another drawer. During those old weekends, he'd seen the contents of this drawer: the German Luger Grainger claimed had been taken from a German soldier during the Battle of the Bulge, and a box of 9mm ammunition. He checked the breech, then loaded the magazine.

If Grainger was surprised to see him, he hid it well. He was tying the boat to the pilings when Milo stepped out from behind a tree, the pistol hanging by his hip. "Catch anything?"

Grainger, breathing heavily, didn't bother looking up from the rope. "Never do. Not in the last years, at least. I've got a suspicion some jackass dumped something in the lake and killed them all." He straightened, finally looking at Milo. "On the other hand, I've caught nothing since Terri died. So maybe it's just me." He noticed the Luger and frowned. "You didn't break my desk to get to that, did you?"

"Afraid so."

Grainger shook his head. "The key was in the top drawer."

"Sorry."

"Oh well." He started to take the fishing pole and lures from the boat, then looked up at the clear sky. "I'll leave them. It's not going to rain."

"Good idea." Milo waved the gun. "Let's go."

Protest—that's what was missing here. Grainger wasn't protesting anything beyond the destruction of his desk. He had known that Milo would come. In fact, Milo suspected the old man had been waiting for him, day after day, fishing to fill his absent hours.

They found places in the living room. First, Grainger went to the liquor cabinet, which was stocked with a dozen bottles, and picked out a ten-year-old scotch. He poured it into a collins glass, replaced the bottle, and filled another with Finlandia vodka. He gave the vodka to Milo, then took the narrow, leather-padded chair, while Milo sat on the cushioned sofa. Between them was a low coffee table, and against the wall sat an antique radio, from the days when the house was first built. Grainger said, "So. I see you made it back in one piece."

"I did."

"And you came to see me. Am I your first stop?"

"You are."

"Good." Grainger sipped his scotch. "Tell me. What evidence have you collected?"

Milo took a breath. He knew the answers lay with this man, but the whole trip here he hadn't actually formulated how he was going to extract them. He had no method at his disposal, because the methods he knew didn't take into account godfathers and old friends and Company men who knew all the methods by heart. He said, "I've figured out that I didn't need to collect anything for my defense, Tom. You tricked me into running."

"I just tried to help you out."

Milo felt the urge to shout—nothing in particular, just whatever nonsense touched his lips when his mouth opened. It wasn't only that Grainger was his friend and the closest thing to family Milo had in his daily life; it was *this*: the comfortable chairs, the living room stocked with old-world knickknacks, and the two of them nursing drinks from crystal glasses.

Milo put his vodka on the coffee table and went to the kitchen.

"The evidence," Grainger called.

346 | Olen Steinhauer

Instead of answering, Milo returned with a thick roll of duct tape.

Grainger's smile faded. "For Christ's sake, Milo. Can't we just have a conversation?"

Milo pulled off a length with a loud grinding sound. "No, Tom. We can't."

Grainger knew better than to fight back as Milo attached the end to the back of his chair, then pulled the roll around his body five times, securing the old man to the chair from his shoulders to his elbows. He ripped off the end with his teeth and pressed it flat against the back of the chair. Then he stepped back, checking his handiwork, and returned to the sofa.

"You're going to have to feed me my scotch," said Grainger.

"I know."

"Stick and carrot?"

"Bait and switch," Milo suggested, then blinked. He could hardly make out Grainger's face. It was the sun. When he wasn't looking, the sun had disappeared behind the mountains.

"So tell me," Grainger said as Milo turned on a floor lamp, "what evidence have you collected? Not suppositions, mind you. Not hearsay. Evidence."

Milo returned to the sofa. "You set me up, Tom. You had me flee from Disney World when I didn't have to run. I was under suspicion, but that was all. Right?"

Grainger, trying without success to shift under his bonds, nodded.

"It was you all along. You passed money to Roman Ugrimov, who then passed it to the Tiger. You controlled Tripplehorn, who ran the Tiger. That was why you hid the Tiger's Tourism file from me for so long. It had nothing to do with Fitzhugh recruiting him."

"Yes," Grainger admitted after a moment. "I hid the file from you for those reasons, but I showed it to you later *because* Terence Fitzhugh recruited him."

"Let's not get off track. You ran the Tiger. Angela, like me, was hunting for the Tiger. So you had her killed. That was another Tripplehorn job."

"Yes."

"Colonel Yi Lien had nothing to do with anything. You just placed Tripplehorn in a few strategic spots and let the cameras do the work."

Almost reluctantly, Grainger said, "MI6 —well, I made that up, didn't I?"

"So, it follows that you ordered the assassination of Mullah Salih Ahmad in the Sudan."

"Yes." Since Milo didn't seem to want to follow it up immediately, he repeated the word he'd used earlier: "Evidence? You *do* have some evidence behind all this, don't you?"

Milo wasn't sure if he should answer. To admit there was no real physical evidence might make the man clam up. Still, Grainger was adept enough to see through his lie, and would want to know precisely what the evidence was.

But his silence was enough. Grainger shook his head morosely. "Shit, Milo. You don't have any, do you?"

"No."

"What have you been doing these last days? Boozing?"

Milo stood up, as if to remind him who was running this conversation, then grabbed the glass of scotch and brought it to Grainger's lips. Once he'd gotten a good sip, Milo put the glass back down and said, "Please, Tom. Just tell me what the hell's going on."

Grainger considered that, then nodded. "If you can't figure it out yourself, then okay. It's the oldest reason in the book. It's why we can't keep our hands to ourselves anymore."

"Oil," said Milo.

Grainger tried to shrug, but the duct tape limited his movement. "Sort of, yes. On the surface. But the answer that gets the gold star is empire. And you get bonus points if you mention China."

40

Once he'd started talking, Grainger couldn't stop. The duct tape kept him in place, but his head tilted and shifted freely as he explained details of a story that (it seemed to Milo) he had been wanting to get out for a long time.

"Listen, Milo—and try not to be childish about this. You've got a continent wet with oil, as well as some of the most corrupt governments this world has ever seen. You think the Sudan's a land of peace and love? They were tearing out each other's throats before we ever decided on our little intervention. And we tried to do it peacefully. You know that. Our people met with the energy minister at Ugrimov's house. We put it to him: Stop selling crude to the Chinese, and sell it to us instead. We'll lift the embargo. Hell, we even offered to pay more. You hear me? The president gets more money to build his palaces and statues to his own glory. But he's a proud man. Politicians who murder their own people usually are. The energy minister gave him a call, and he refused us outright. So we cajoled. We threatened. We finally told him that if he didn't take our deal we'd make his life, and his country, more of a hell than it already was."

"So it was just about oil. Is that really what you're saying?"

"Milo, you sound like one of those protesters who still bring up the *Exxon Valdez* eighteen years after the fact. It's about the big picture. That's all it's ever about. We don't mind losing a little oil here and there. A country doesn't want to sell to us? We're not going to get our feathers ruffled. This is not about oil; it's about the century that's upon us. It's about China. They get seven percent of their crude oil from the Sudan. Each year, China uses more oil—it *requires* more to grow its economy. Losing seven percent won't decimate China now, but what about next year? Ten years from now? China needs all the oil it can get its hands on. One-third of its imported oil is African. They can't afford to lose it."

"But you keep saying the same thing, Tom. Oil."

Below the strips of duct tape, his hand on the arm of the chair shifted, and he raised a finger. "Wait. That's just the beginning. Because what will China have to do to make sure they get their oil? They need a stable Africa, don't they? They go to the United Nations. They ask for intervention in the Sudan. And for as long as is conscionable, the United States will veto these resolutions. That's the beauty of being a permanent member of the Security Council. You can veto whatever you like. Keep vetoing until China is pushed into a corner. Until—and this is the important part—*they're forced to intervene on their own.* Send in thousands of their own People's Army. We've got our Iraq, and it's draining us silly. If we can't pull out, we can at least pull some old enemies down. It's time to give China a few Iraqs. See how they manage."

Milo kept his hands folded in his lap, staring at the old man. He was full of life, as if letting these secrets loose had given him a transfusion. "You agree with this tactic?"

Grainger made as much of a shrug as the tape would allow. "It's insidious, I'll give it that. And there is a certain beautiful logic to it. Little strikes, a single assassination, and you can collapse an entire country. Governments have a great way of fostering the belief that they're immutable. It's seldom true."

"You haven't answered my question."

"I believed in it for a long time, Milo. For years. But it got messy, didn't it? If you just knock out a terrorist sympathizer, like the mullah, then who can really complain? You're doing the world a service. When chaos follows, you can call it a surprise. Well, it was seldom that simple. There were witnesses who had to be gotten rid of. Angela's friend Rahman, for example."

"Then Angela herself."

"Yes," said Grainger. "We tried to get rid of her with libel. You know that. When she called me looking for photos of the Tiger, I knew she'd gotten close. So we set her up for treason. Either make her retire or, at worst, put her in jail a while—not long, just long enough for the trail to go cold. But by then the cracks were apparent, even to an idiot like me. Too many dead witnesses. So when it came time to put the final screws on Angela, I decided to put you in there. After all, you'd gotten closer than anyone else—you'd actually met the Tiger. So I thought that you could be the one. You were an old friend of Angela's. Like those assassinations, I could do one small thing, then let chaos take over, and pretend to my masters that I didn't know it would end up this way."

"You wanted me to unravel it."

"Yes. Then you made that call to me. You remember? After your lunch with Angela." He sighed. "You signed her death warrant with that call."

Milo tried to remember what he'd said, but that conversation, after all that had happened in the last two weeks, was just a blip.

Grainger explained: "You told me that Angela had followed the trail to Rolf Vinterberg. One step away from Ugrimov, another step away from us. Who do you think was in the office with me when you called?"

"Fitzhugh."

"Exactly. He had me call Tripplehorn immediately, while he was sitting there, and give the order to take out Angela as soon as possible."

"But—" Milo began, then found himself without words. Was he really responsible for Angela's murder? "You could've rescinded the order once he left the office."

"Perhaps." Grainger again tried to shrug. "Maybe I was too scared by then."

Milo walked over to the liquor cabinet and refilled his vodka. "You want more?"

"Thank you. Yes."

He poured vodka into Grainger's glass and pressed the rim to Grainger's lips. The sip made the old man cough.

"Where's my scotch?"

Milo didn't answer. He set the glass aside and took a sip from his own. "This doesn't feel right. It feels like an elaborate story to cover your own ass."

Grainger licked his pale lips. "I see what you mean. Spying, and in particular Tourism, is all about story-telling. After a while you collect too many layers. It's hard to discern story from truth. But what I'm telling you now really is the truth. Ask me what you like."

"Your call for me to leave Disney World."

"You know the answer. Twofold. Keep you out of custody, so you could continue your investigation. Also, put you on the run, turn the screws. You'd frustrated me by going on vacation, and I needed you back on the job. It was the only way to convince you."

"The same thing with the Tiger's file," said Milo. "You gave that to me so I wouldn't trust Fitzhugh, in case he took over and called me."

Grainger nodded. "Connecting the Tiger with Fitzhugh—I was just pushing you toward the real state of affairs. You wouldn't have connected them on your own. Don't get me wrong—him recruiting the Tiger means nothing. He doesn't want anyone to know about that, but it's not damning. I wanted you to start down

the path of damnation. Collect real, physical evidence."
He shook his head. "I guess I overestimated you, Milo.
You've got nothing."

"I've got a trail that leads directly to you."

"Yes, a trail. But where's your bag of tricks? I thought
that by the time you made it here you'd have videotapes
and fingerprints and bank records. You can't even prove
I was part of this, unless you're recording our conversation. You're not, are you?"

Milo shook his head.

"Very shoddy. Not that a confession in this situation
would hold up in court." He paused. "If you can't even
prove my guilt, how are you ever going to prove
Fitzhugh's masterminding it? You think he's an amateur? His involvement was always verbal, and he never
got anywhere near the action. He's never even met Roman Ugrimov—they wouldn't recognize each other if
they were in the same room. How are you going to collect evidence against a man like that?"

It was a remarkable moment, Milo thought. Grainger
had been forcibly retired, he was duct-taped to his chair
and faced with the barrel of his own pistol, yet he still
spoke as if he were in his Avenue of the Americas office, running a whole world of Tourists. "You're not
giving the orders anymore, Tom."

Perhaps he, too, realized the ludicrousness of his
position, because he sighed. "It's probably best I'm not
in charge. See what a mess I've made already?"

Milo didn't answer.

"You know when it started, don't you? This thing
with the Tiger. Just after you left Tourism. You'd just

finished protecting that fascist Tweede Kamer representative from him. You'd stopped him, yes, but we all knew the man was good at his job, so this information was filed away for future use. Next thing we know—next *day*, really—you're in Venice, and in New York we get hit by terrorists. We gather the military and prepare to hit back in Afghanistan, but Fitzhugh and a few others—they knew where the wind would start blowing. They discussed options. Fitzhugh visited me right here, in this house. They were rebuilding our offices, and it was the one clean place to meet. He asked if we could use Tourists as part of our tactic. Sneak them into the Middle East and take out this Saudi or that Iranian. I told him we didn't train Tourists for that kind of assassination, and it would be best to go private and use someone like the Tiger." Grainger nodded. "Yes. I was the first one to say his name. Fitzhugh came back a week later with a counterproposal. Use a Tourist to track the Tiger and approach him as a client."

"Tripplehorn."

"Of course."

Milo imagined six years' worth of surgical strikes, killings he'd charted and been at pains to find a common thread among. A moderate Islamic figure in Germany, a French foreign minister, a British businessman. What, he'd always asked himself, unites these killings? He'd been stumped, falling back on the theory that nothing united them; they were simply jobs for different people. Sometimes, perhaps, they were, but whenever Tripplehorn, a.k.a. Herbert Williams, a.k.a. Jan Klausner, a.k.a. Stephen Lewis, approached the Tiger with a job, the underlying thread was always American foreign policy.

He imagined not only six years of assassinations, but also six years at his computer in the office, the efforts of all his Travel Agents, and the years of feigned help from this man in front of him. Six years of tracking a man that no one, in the end, wanted caught.

"But he came to me," Milo said suddenly. "The Tiger came to me because he had my file. That was you as well?"

"I passed it to Tripplehorn to hand over. The orders to inject him with HIV had come from above. There was no way around that. The only thing I could do was add a piece of information to the Tiger's knowledge. Fitzhugh didn't think the Tiger would know where he'd picked up the disease. I knew he was underestimating the guy. I knew—or at least I suspected—that a celibate, religious man would put it together. I hoped he would look for you, if only because your file was the last piece of information handed over by his killers."

"Everything went according to plan," Milo said, marveling at the way the old man's brain worked.

"Not everything, Milo. You. You were supposed to go on the run, but return with the evidence. I even gave you Einner for help. Where is he now?"

Milo cleared his throat. "I had to incapacitate him."

"Probably for the best. But you see what I'm getting at, right? I gave you all I could, but I guess I had too much faith in you."

"You should've been open with Angela, and with me. You didn't give anywhere near what you could have."

Grainger pursed his lips to stifle a yawn. "Maybe you're right. But if I'd told you everything from the beginning, what would you have done? I know you: You're not as patient as you used to be. You would have taken it straight to Fitzhugh; you would have strong-armed him. You wouldn't have tried to track down the evidence. You would have acted like a Tourist, cornered Fitzhugh and his band, and put them down. You wouldn't have taken the time to collect what's needed to put a stop to the whole operation. In short, you would have acted like the thug you are."

"But it's over," said Milo. "Your assassin is dead."

"You think they won't find another? Despite everything, the fact is that the technique works more often than it fails. There's a Cambodian boy based in Sri Lanka. He doesn't have a silly name yet, which is preferable. Jackson's down there as we speak, tracking him."

Milo finished his vodka, then got the bottle to refill both their glasses. "So what are you trying to convince me to do?"

"Really, Milo. You're smarter than this. With no evidence, what have you got? Just my word. And if they know where you are now, then they'll make sure I'm not able to tell you a thing."

"They don't know where I am."

"You better be sure of that. Because after they get rid of me, they'll make sure you can't tell anyone what I've told you."

A nerve in Milo's cheek began to spasm, so he rubbed it. It was anxiety, the realization that Grainger was right. Then another thought came to him: Grainger was lying. The old man was cornered. He knew that Milo would take him back to the Avenue of the Americas. Grainger had perhaps even planned for this eventuality. As he had said, the intelligence game is all about story-telling. Grainger presented no real evidence either, just stories to fill the gaps between actual events.

Milo realized he hadn't been breathing. He inhaled. It was a hell of a story, the kind that only a veteran like Grainger could dream up. A part of him even still believed it—that's how good it was. He tipped Grainger's vodka into the waiting lips, then sat across from him.

Before he could speak, the telephone on the far table began to ring. Milo stared at Grainger. "Expecting someone?"

"What time is it?"

"Eleven."

"I haven't mixed with the villagers in a long time. Maybe Fitzhugh, checking on us."

Milo got up, the alcohol rushing to his head but not debilitating him, and turned off the lamp. In the darkness, the phone continued to ring—seven, now—and he stood beside the heavy drapes, peering into the night-time darkness, toward the lake. He saw trees and the gravel road in the moonlight before a cloud slipped a little farther and obscured the scene. On the ninth ring the telephone quieted. Milo didn't know what he believed. "We're going."

"Please," Grainger said. "I'm exhausted. Fishing all day takes it out of you."

He turned back and saw Grainger's dark form slump,

chin against the duct tape across his chest, breathing loudly. "You all right?"

The head raised. "Just tired. But really, if there's someone out there, it's the Company. I'd rather be executed in bed, out here, than be grilled for months in Manhattan, then shot in some dirty safe house."

Milo returned to the window. Lake, moonlight, and silence. If he hadn't been tracked here, there really was no hurry. Just his desperation to have all this finished. He let the curtains drop. "We'll leave in the morning. Early. Same bed, though."

"You always were sweet on me."

"And you've had enough to drink."

"I've just started," said Grainger. "Can you take off this tape so I can get to my scotch? This vodka is hell on my stomach."

41

They slept in the upstairs bedroom, tied together at the wrists with a length of rope Milo had found in a kitchen drawer. Overall, it was a steady sleep, broken only once when Grainger sat up and started speaking. "At first, I didn't like the idea. I want you to know that. That's why I lied and said our Tourists wouldn't be any good for assassinations."

"It's all right," Milo said. "Go back to sleep."

"If I'd known how it would end up, I would've found a way to nip it in the bud. Really. Maybe if I'd let our Tourists do the killings, we could've kept control to ourselves."

"Go back to sleep," Milo repeated, and Grainger dropped to his pillow and began to snore, as if his words had been part of a dream.

They woke and shaved and showered, never far apart, and Milo cooked scrambled eggs and toast. Grainger let half the breakfast go by in silence, then began again. He seemed desperate for Milo to believe him. "Really, I thought you'd get the answers. It might have been stupid, but it made sense at the time." He paused, watching Milo chew. "You don't believe me, do you?"

Milo swallowed his eggs. "No," he said, if only to stop Grainger's chatter. "I don't believe you. Even if I did, I'd still take you back. I can't live like this, and you're the only one who can set things right for me. And Tina."

"Ah!" said Grainger, smiling wanly. "It's all about your family, of course." He swallowed. "You're probably right. You're too young to ruin your career for this. They'll trump up something to prove I was behind everything, me alone. They can pack me away and begin again with this Cambodian boy."

Milo felt cold toward the old man, because all he cared about now was his immediate future. He would drive Grainger straight back to Manhattan, help supervise the initial interrogation, and then collect his family from Texas. Simple.

When Grainger finished his breakfast, Milo rinsed off the plates. "It's time to go."

As if reading his mind, Grainger said, "Time to get your life back?"

Milo put on his jacket and found a blazer for Grainger, checking its pockets before handing it over.

"You know," Grainger said, "a part of me still believes. A part of me believes that by talking to you I'm betraying the empire. Isn't that funny? We've been marking our territory like an imperial dog since the end of the last big war. Since 9/11, we no longer have to go about it sweetly. We can bomb and maim and torture to our heart's content, because only the terrorists are willing to stand up to us, and their opinion doesn't matter. You know what the real problem is?"

"Put on your jacket."

"The problem is people like me," Grainger continued. "An empire needs men with iron guts. I'm not tough enough; I still need to make excuses about spreading democracy. The younger guys, though—even Fitzhugh—they're the kind of men we need if we want to keep moving forward. They're tough in a way my generation never was."

"The jacket," Milo repeated, and Grainger gave him a sour look before stretching an arm into his blazer.

They stepped out into the cool, tree-shaded morning, and Milo locked the front door while Grainger stood, hands on hips, staring at the house. "I'm going to miss this."

"Don't be mawkish."

"Just being honest, Milo. You should know that's all I've been with you. In this house, at least."

Milo grabbed his elbow and led him down the steps to the leaf-covered walkway. "We'll have to walk to my car. I don't want to take yours."

"I think I can manage," Grainger said and smiled.

Something buzzed around Milo's ear, like a mosquito, then Grainger vibrated. He felt the vibration through Grainger's elbow, and though the smile didn't leave the old man's face, his head was tilted back and his forehead looked different. A small shadow of a hole lay against his forehead. Milo heard a second buzz, and Grainger's right shoulder popped back, spewing blood. He let go. The old man dropped onto his side, and in the back of his head Milo saw a large, gory hole, leaking blood and brain matter into the dirt.

For what seemed like a long time, Milo stared at the body. In reality, it wasn't more than a quarter of a second, but time is a relative thing, and, looking down at Grainger's corpse, time stretched long enough for him to realize with a shock as strong as a sniper's bullet that he'd been wrong. Grainger had told the truth. The old man knew that after speaking to Milo, he would be a dead man. So, too, would Milo.

As another bullet buzzed past, he threw himself back, dropped, and rolled behind the three concrete steps leading from the front door. He took out the Luger and breathed loudly through his lips, thinking: *Three bullets. Suppressor. Suppressors decrease accuracy range, so the shooter is not far away.*

Question: Would the shooter come to him, or would he wait?

Answer: It was Tuesday, which meant mail. He seemed to remember morning deliveries at, say, nine thirtyish. The shooter would know this, too. It was now nine o'clock.

He couldn't leave his position, because the shooter would be trained on these three lousy steps, waiting. At some point in the next half hour, though, he would have to approach. Milo closed his eyes and listened.

He tried to hold back all the thoughts that buzzed inside him now, but it was impossible. Grainger had

been telling the truth. The truth. It was the only explanation. Get rid of the old man before he could spill the
truth in one of those camera-ridden cells on the nineteenth floor of the Avenue of the Americas. Get rid of
Milo before he could pass on any messages. Everything,
Fitzhugh had decided, would end here, by a quiet lake.

And what of Tina and Stephanie? They would be in
Austin, under surveillance. That, he knew. But by
whom? By the Company, or Homeland? He surprised
himself by hoping that Janet Simmons was keeping an
eye on them.

If he got out of here alive—

No, *when* he got out of here alive. That was another
Tourism rule. Never doubt your ability to survive. With
doubts come mistakes.

When he got out of here alive, he—

Stop. One thing at a time. Listen. Nothing exists except sound. When a man walks, he cannot aim.

There: crunch *crunch.*

Milo rose, Luger at arm's length, elbow bent slightly,
and pivoted as he walked backward. Two hundred yards
away, maybe, out of range, a figure in hunting camou-
flage stopped and raised his rifle. Milo disappeared behind the house.

He needed close quarters, so he ran down the lake
side of the house until he found the window to the dining room. He used an elbow to break it, the sound of
shattering glass echoing across the lake. As he climbed
inside, he heard feet running across dry earth.

He dropped to the carpet, lost track of his pistol,

then found it under one of the chairs. He went to the living room windows that faced the front of the house. Standing a few feet back, Milo peered out in time to catch sight of the shooter, the long-barreled rifle hanging from his back and a SIG Sauer in his gloved hand, working his way around the house. Before he disappeared, Milo saw that he was a tall man, nose thick and bent from old breaks; the bottom half of his face, below the hunter's cap, was covered in a thick red beard.

Milo returned to the doorway to the dining room, looped an arm around the frame, and aimed at the broken window. He watched and waited until, from the opposite side of the house —guest bedroom, if his internal floor plan was right—another window shattered. He hurried to the closed door, popped it open, and aimed. But the broken window was empty.

There —another window breaking, the living room. He hurried back, again finding nothing.

Tripplehorn had given himself three possible entrances in three different rooms. Milo climbed the stairs and waited on the landing, squatting to make a smaller target.

From his position, he could hear the Tourist climb into the house, but wasn't sure which window he was using. It didn't matter. However he'd entered the house, he would have to use the stairs to reach Milo.

For three minutes, he only heard footsteps and doors opening suddenly. No one appeared at the bottom of the steps. Tripplehorn was searching the first floor before continuing to the next. Finally, he heard a high voice with an indeterminable accent say, "You'd better come down here."

"Why should I, Tripplehorn?"

A pause. "That's a funny name. Wish I knew who it was."

"It's me. Milo Weaver. I run the European desk."

"Don't know who you're talking about."

"I used to go by Charles Alexander."

Another pause, then a whisper that might have been *Shit*. Tourists had no qualms about killing other Tourists—this, in fact, was always a possibility—but Einner had been kind enough to point out that the name Charles Alexander had made the rounds.

"Who sent you?" asked Milo, the hand on his pistol sweaty now.

"You know who runs me."

"It used to be that man in the front yard."

"Grainger?" said the Tourist. "He's given few orders recently."

Milo's eyes were damp, so when Tripplehorn threw himself past the stairs, firing upward, his reaction was delayed. The Tourist shot blindly, loud bullets drilling into the upper steps, and Milo shot back twice, but too late. Tripplehorn disappeared on the other side of the stairs.

"You've got no position," Milo called. "Just get out of here."

"I'm patient."

Milo took a breath and stood slowly. "You've got ten minutes until the mailman comes. You can't be patient." As he spoke, he took two steps down, feet by the wall to avoid creaks.

"I'll kill the postman, too," said Tripplehorn.

Milo was five steps down; ten more to go. "How's Fitzhugh going to explain that away? I doubt you're supposed to kill civilians."

Another pause. Milo stopped. Tripplehorn said, "If I did leave, you know I'd still be waiting out there."

Milo couldn't keep moving and speaking at the same time; Tripplehorn would hear his voice nearing. He said, "And what would you do? Shoot me while the cops are here, looking at the body? Come on, Tripplehorn. It's over. You know it."

"If you are who you say you are, then you know I can pull it off."

As he said those words, Milo descended two quick steps. He didn't answer.

"If you are Alexander, you know that failure isn't an option."

Two more steps. Now he was six from the bottom. That would do.

"Alexander? You still with me?"

With his arm extended, the pistol was only three steps from the corner. Behind it, Tripplehorn said, "Well, maybe you're right. Maybe I should just go with half the job done," and then launched himself out into the open, his gun raised high so he wouldn't again shoot too low.

By the time he got off his second, wild shot, Milo had put a bullet in his chest, knocking him backward.

He dropped and slid against the front door, leaving a smear of blood. His arm was still out, clutching his pistol, and he was blinking up at Milo.

"Shit," he whispered, gurgling. "You got me."

"You should've worn a vest."

Tripplehorn's hunting jacket was drenched now, making the dark-and-light-green design a little more monochrome. Milo kicked the pistol from his hand; it slid into the living room. He squatted close to Tripplehorn's head, remembering that face from the Corso Sempione, sitting across from the Tiger, giving the assassin a bag of money and a shot of HIV. "Tell me who's running you," said Milo.

Tripplehorn coughed blood onto the hardwood floor. He shook his head.

Milo didn't have the heart to force it out of the man. He knew, or he believed he knew, that Terence Fitzhugh was running him. There was nothing else to say. He shot Tripplehorn in the forehead. He searched the corpse, taking his cell phone and the little automobile unlocker that he had so admired when Einner used it in Europe.

He left by the front door, continuing past Grainger's corpse and into the woods. There, he was sick. As he crouched in the leaves, he realized it wasn't the normal sickness that overcomes a person at the sight of death. It was the sickness of too much adrenaline and too little to eat. That troubled him even more than the deaths, that he was no longer reacting like a real human being.

He stared at his vomit in the grass. He was thinking and feeling like a Tourist now. Unbalanced.

Despairing over this, his Tourist side calculated the

next step. He didn't even cringe from it. He wiped his mouth with the back of his hand and returned to the house.

Five minutes later, from behind the shattered living room window, he clutched Grainger's car keys and watched the little mail truck bounce over ruts in the driveway until it had a direct view of Grainger's body. It stopped, and a fat man in a white uniform climbed out. He approached, halving the distance to the corpse, then turned and ran. He got into his truck, turned it around in a cloud of dust, and roared off.

Ten minutes, max.

Milo opened the front door and heaved Tripplehorn's body, now wrapped in Hefty bags, down the front steps, past the corpse, and to Grainger's Mercedes. He put Tripplehorn into the trunk, then got behind the wheel. He drove fast to the main road, then turned right, toward the mountains, as the low whine of police sirens grew somewhere behind him.

He'd found a good dropping point in the upper reaches of Route 23 when Tripplehorn's phone buzzed silently on the passenger seat. PRIVATE NUMBER. On the fourth ring, he picked up but said nothing.

Fitzhugh said, "The American handed Leamas."

Milo paused, knowing it but unsure. With an accent-less voice, he whispered, "Another cup of coffee."

"Is it done?"

"Yes."

"Both?"

"Yes."

"No trouble?"

"None."

A sigh. "Good. Take some time off. I'll be in touch."

Milo hung up, remembering what that go-code had come from. *The Spy Who Came in from the Cold:*

> The American handed Leamas another cup of coffee and said, "Why don't you go back and sleep?"

> *If only I could,* he thought.

42

There were three of them. They took shifts. The heavy one on the night-to-early-morning shift wore a mustache as if he hadn't heard the seventies were long past—this one, she christened George. Jake watched the house from around 6:00 A.M. to 2:00 P.M.— he was a gangly fellow with no hair on top and a thick novel always pressed open against the steering wheel. The one out there now was Will—or he was until Monday afternoon, when she walked out to the red sedan with a huge cup of lemonade and learned his real name.

He watched through his impenetrable aviator sunglasses and straightened when he realized her destination. He jerked a pair of earphones from his head, reminding her of Milo and his iPod, and rolled down his window as she approached.

"Afternoon," she said. "Thought you might be thirsty."

She'd flustered him. "I'm, uh . . . I'm all right."

"Don't be a stiffy," she said, winking. "And take off those glasses so I can see your eyes. Can't trust someone without eyes."

He did so, blinking in the bright light. "Really, I don't think I should—"

"Please." She forced the cup through the window so that his choices were either to take it or let it spill in his lap.

He peered around, as if afraid of witnesses. "Thanks."

She straightened. "You have a name?"

"Rodger."

"Rodger," she repeated. "Of course, you know my name already."

Embarrassed, he nodded.

"Just bring us the cup when you're done."

"I'll do that."

When she got inside, Miguel, stretched on the sofa watching the History Channel, asked why she was looking so pleased with herself.

It was something Milo had once said about enemies. Though he seldom spoke of his history as a field agent, aphorisms sometimes slipped from his lips. They'd been watching an old movie on television where two enemy agents, who'd spent the first half of the film shooting at one another, sat at a café and talked quietly about all that had come before. "I don't get it," she'd said. "Why doesn't he shoot him?"

"Because it does no good now," he'd answered. "Killing him serves no purpose. When they don't have to be at each other's throats, spies chat if they can. You learn things that might be useful later on."

Less than an hour later, Rodger knocked on the door. Hanna answered it, blinked as he took off his glasses, and said, "Is that my cup?"

He admitted it was and handed it over as Tina appeared, calling, "Might as well come in, Rodger."

"I don't think that's such a—"

"You're supposed to make sure I don't run off, right?"

He cleared his throat. "Well, it's not exactly that. We're just watching out for you."

Hanna said, "What?"

"That's rich," Tina said, then smiled. "I'm *joking,* Rodger. Please. It's hot out there."

This was how they began to talk. Tina poured him another lemonade, and they sat at the kitchen table while her parents left them alone. It wasn't an interrogation, really. She just admitted she knew nothing about what was going on, and deserved to know something. It wasn't Rodger's place to share anything, though, and he remained hesitant, even as he accepted his third lemonade.

"I know what she thinks," Tina told him. "Your boss, Janet Simmons. She told me my husband is a killer. I mean, does that make any sense to you? Why would he kill one of his oldest friends?" She shook her head. "It makes no sense to you either, does it?"

He shrugged, as if it were all too complicated for a simple man like him. "Listen," he said finally. "This doesn't have to be some big conflict. Special Agent Simmons is good at her job; she's got years of experience.

From the way she tells it, the evidence is strong. And then he fled." He raised his hands, palms out. "That's all I know, okay?"

That really was all he knew—she could see it in his naïve face. She felt as if she were in Starbucks, angry with the cashier, but needing to yell at some absent manager.

What, really, could she do? Simply wait in the hope that Milo would call again? She'd been unfair during the last call, and had spent the whole week regretting it. Where was he? Was he even alive? Christ, she knew nothing.

Then, Tuesday night, it had happened. The message. It came to her Columbia account, a bulk-e-mail sent to twenty other names to hide the fact that it was only for her. She knew this because the other addresses had each been misspelled, just slightly. The return address was janestuk@yahoo.com. It read:

FW: Texas BBQ Party!
Dear Friends,
    To celebrate Drew's 19th birthday you're all invited to enjoy some REAL Texas BBQ in Loretta's back yard at 6 PM on Thursday, July 19. It's gonna be a blast!

—Jane & Stu Kowalski

She and Milo knew the Kowalskis from Stephanie's school, but their son, Drew, was only seven. She clicked REPLY and said she was sorry, but she couldn't make it, she was in Austin for a few days. She'd bring back some *"Real* Texas BBQ sauce" as a present.

Now, it was five o'clock on Thursday. Time to go. Stephanie was with Hanna, playing Chutes and Ladders, while Miguel was again in front of the television, watching financial news. She gathered his keys and shook them. "Can I take the Lincoln? Want to get some ice cream."

He took his eyes off the television and frowned. "Want company?"

She shook her head, gave him a peck on the cheek, then told Stephanie to be good; she'd be back in a sec. Stephanie was winning her game, and had no desire to leave it. On her way out, Tina left her cell phone on the table beside the front door—she'd seen enough television to know satellites could track her that way in a matter of seconds. Then she took two jackets from the wall hook and folded them so they looked like laundry.

The heat blasted her when she stepped outside, and she paused, clutching the jackets. She crossed to the paved driveway and the Lincoln Town Car her father replaced each year with a fresh one. As she fooled with the lock, she noticed the red sedan in front of the Sheffields' bilevel. Rodger pretended not to be looking at her, but she noticed him leaning forward to start up his car.

Damn.

She stayed calm. She put the jackets on the passenger seat, then drove slowly down the lane, up the next right, and out to the highway that led into town, the red sedan always in her rearview.

She pulled into a plaza off the highway and parked in

front of a coin-operated Laundromat. The sedan parked two rows back. She went inside, where the warmth of the machines fought the limpid air-conditioning, and put the jackets in a washer but didn't insert any coins. The few other Thursday afternoon customers didn't seem to notice. She took an empty seat not far from the front windows and watched the parking lot.

It took him a while, but she knew he would have to do something. He couldn't see inside, and with the heat he had to be getting thirsty. Or maybe he just had to pee. It took forty minutes. He got out of his car in his dark sunglasses and trotted over to the 7-Eleven beside the Laundromat.

Go.

She ran out, leaving the jackets behind, ignoring the sweltering heat, dove into the Town Car, and screeched out of the parking space, nearly hitting a bicyclist. Instead of heading to the highway, she turned right onto a back road and parked behind the plaza. Then she got out, pulse racing, and ran around the high, graffitied wall to stand at the corner and watch the lot.

The Laundromat and 7-Eleven were on the far side of the plaza, but she could still spot Rodger in his sunglasses, clutching a red-and-white Big Gulp as he stepped outside. He stopped, looked around (she pulled her head back), and ran to his car. He didn't drive away immediately, and she suspected he was calling in his failure and asking for orders. That's how these people were. They always wanted orders.

Then the sedan took the same path as Tina had, but

turned left onto the highway. He crossed the median and headed back toward her parents' house.

She was overcome by exhilaration. Tina Weaver had thwarted the Department of Homeland Security. Not many people could say that.

She started the car, but waited until her shaking hands had calmed. The exhilaration didn't disappear, but it mixed with a resurgence of fear. What if they decided to do something to her parents? Or Stephanie? That was ludicrous, of course, because she only wanted to lose them for a short time. But maybe they'd figured out that e-mail; maybe they knew exactly what she was doing, and would kidnap her family to manipulate her.

Did they even do that? Television was no help on this point.

She continued down the back roads, past small, ramshackle houses lacking even brown grass. It had been a dry summer here, and some of these chain-linked yards looked like miniature dust bowls. She emerged onto a paved road and drove north on 183 toward Briggs.

At a bend in the highway, in a bare dirt clearing, sat a broad, screened-in building below the sign LORETTA'S KITCHEN. She had come here as a child, and when she married she brought Milo. "Real Texas barbecue," she'd told him. They'd sometimes sneak out here, away from her parents, to eat brisket and biscuits with gravy and talk over their life plans. It was the location of many of their fantasies, where they felt they could know with reasonable certainly what university Stephanie would go to, where they would retire to when they won the lottery, and, before a doctor gave them the difficult news that Milo was sterile, the name and character of their next child, a boy.

The clientele of Loretta's was evidenced by the pickup trucks and big rigs gathering heat around it. She parked between two rigs, waited until six, and walked through the hot dust and into the restaurant.

He wasn't among the crowd of construction workers and truckers getting their hands dirty on the picnic tables, so she went to the window and ordered a brisket plate, biscuits and gravy, and ribs from a pink-cheeked girl who, after taking her money, gave her a number. She found a free table among the chatter and laughter of the sweaty, sunburned men, ignoring their intense but friendly stares.

She watched the highway and the dusty parking lot through the screened walls, waiting, but didn't see him. Then he was right behind her, saying, "It's me," and touching her shoulder. His cheek was suddenly beside hers. She grabbed his face and kissed him. The tears, too, had crept upon her unawares, and for a moment they only hugged; then she pushed him back to get a look at him. He looked tired, baggy-eyed, pale. "I worried you were dead, Milo."

He gave her another kiss. "Not yet." He glanced out at the lot. "I didn't see anyone following you. How did you get away?"

She laughed and stroked his rough cheek. "I've got a few tricks up my sleeve."

"Twenty-seven!" the girl at the window called.

"That's us," said Tina.

"Stay here." He went to the window and returned with a tray overflowing with food.

"Where've you been?" she asked when he'd settled beside her.

"Too many places. Tom's dead."

"What?" Her hand on his arm squeezed tight. "Tom?"

He nodded, lowering his voice: "Someone killed him."

"Someone . . . who?"

"Doesn't matter."

"Of *course* it does! Did you arrest him?" she asked, then wondered if that was a stupid thing to ask. Despite the years she'd spent with a Company man, she really knew nothing about his work.

"Not really. The guy who pulled the trigger—I had to kill him."

She closed her eyes as the stink of vinegary barbecue sauce overwhelmed her. She thought she might be sick. "Was he trying to kill you? This guy?"

"Yes."

Tina opened her eyes and stared at her husband. Then, overcome again, she grabbed him and squeezed. He was here, finally, and she felt the kind of consuming love that fills you with the desire to eat your loved one, a feeling she hadn't felt since their courtship. Her teeth grazed his stubbly cheek, which was wet from tears she could taste. His? No—he wasn't crying.

He said, "The point is, everyone will think I killed Grainger. I'm on the run now, but once they've made up their minds, there won't be a safe place in the country for me."

She got control of herself and pulled back, her hands still on him; his hands were on her. "So, what now?"

"I've spent days thinking about that," he said, strangely matter-of-fact. "Every way I turn it, I can't figure out how to solve the problem. The Company wants me dead."

"What? Dead? Why?"

"It doesn't matter," he said, but before she could protest, he added, "Just know that if I show my face again, I'm dead."

She nodded, trying to mirror his logical composure. "But you were collecting evidence before. Did you get it?"

"Not really."

Again, she nodded, as if these things really were part of her world, things she could actually grasp. "So what's the answer, Milo?"

He took a raspy breath through his nose and looked at the untouched food. To it, he said, "Disappear. Me, you, Stephanie." He held up a hand. "Before you answer, it's not as hard as it sounds. I've got money hidden away. We've got new identities—you got the passports, right?"

"Yes."

"We can go to Europe. I know people in Berlin and Switzerland. I can make a good life for us. Trust me on this. Of course, it won't be easy. Your parents, for instance. It'll be hard to visit them. They'll have to come to us. But it can be done."

Despite his slow speech, Tina wasn't sure she had heard him right. An hour ago, the worst news she could imagine was that Milo had been injured. She'd nearly collapsed, imagining that. Now, he was telling her that, as a family, they should disappear from the face of the earth. Had she really heard him right? Yes, she had—she could tell from his face. Her answer came out before her brain had a chance to process it: "No, Milo."

43

He'd been crying since Sweetwater, a half hour back. For the first hours of driving, there had been no tears, just red, stinging eyes. He wasn't sure what had finally triggered them. Perhaps the billboard advertising life insurance, with the Midwestern family smiling back at him—happy, insured. Maybe that was it. It didn't matter.

What really struck him as the sun set up ahead, turning to flame against the flat, arid West Texas landscape, was that he hadn't actually been prepared for what happened. Tourists survive by foreseeing unexpected eventualities and preparing for them. Maybe his oversight meant he'd never been much of a Tourist in the first place, because he never even considered the possibility that his wife would refuse to vanish with him.

He went through her excuses. At first, they didn't have anything to do with herself; it was all about Stephanie. *You can't just tell a five-year-old her name's something else and she's going to lose all her friends, Milo!* Though he hadn't posed the question, he should have asked if it was worse or better than having her dad disappear. He hadn't asked it because he was afraid of the answer: Well, she does still have Patrick, doesn't she?

Finally, she admitted that it had to do with herself as well. *What would I do in Europe? I don't even speak Spanish well!*

She loved him, yes. When she saw how her refusal was killing him, she kept grabbing his face and kissing his flushed cheeks and telling him just how much she loved him. That, she insisted, wasn't the issue, wasn't even a question. She loved Milo completely, but that didn't mean she would ruin their daughter's life in order to follow him across the world, spending years looking over their shoulders for some hit man. *What kind of life is that, Milo? Think about it from our perspective.*

Well, he had, hadn't he? He'd imagined them with Stephanie at Euro Disney, finishing their aborted vacation with laughs and candy and no more interruptions from the cell phone. The only difference was that they used different names. Lionel, Laura, and Kelley.

Now he knew why the tears had finally reached him: It was the realization that she was right. Grainger's death had rattled him, turned him into a desperate dreamer, imagining that the soft-edged world of Disney could be theirs.

Milo had been too in love with his fantasies to realize how childish they were.

And now, where was he? In the desert. It went out in

all directions—flat, two-toned, empty. His family gone, his one real ally in the Company dead, killed by his stupidity. There was only one ally left to him in the world, someone he never wanted to call, whose calls he always dreaded.

At Hobbs, just over the New Mexico border, he stopped at a generic gas station/convenience store with peeling white walls and no air-conditioning. The fat, sweating woman behind the counter sold him quarters and directed him to a pay phone in the rear, by the canned soups. He dialed the number he'd memorized back at Disney World, then put in all his quarters.

"Da?" said that familiar old voice.

"It's me."

"Mikhail?"

"I need your help, Yevgeny."

Part Two

TOURISM IS STORYTELLING

**WEDNESDAY, JULY 25 TO
MONDAY, JULY 30, 2007**

1

Terence Albert Fitzhugh stood in what had once been Tom Grainger's twenty-second-floor office. No longer. Through the ceiling-high windows behind the desk lay a vista of skyscrapers, the canopy of the urban jungle. Beyond the blinds on the opposite wall lay a field of cubicles and activity where all the young, pale Travel Agents made sense of Tourist chatter, culling it into slim Tour Guides that eventually made it to Langley, where other analysts produced their own policy-ready reports for the politicians.

Each of those Travel Agents, he knew, hated him.

It wasn't him in particular they hated, but Terence Albert Fitzhugh as a concept. He'd seen it in Company offices throughout the world. A kind of love develops between department heads and their employees. When a department head is ousted, or killed, departmental emotions grow volatile. When that department is, like

Tourism, invisible to the outside world, the staff depends on its chief that much more.

He would deal with their hatred later. Now, he shut the blinds and went to Grainger's computer. Even a week after his death, it was still a mess, because Tom Grainger had been a mess—one of those old cold warriors who'd spent too much time depending on pretty secretaries to keep order. When faced with their own computers, these old men ended up with the most cluttered desktops on the planet. He had made everything else into a mess as well.

At first, of course, Fitzhugh thought he had cleaned up Grainger's mess. Tripplehorn had received his orders, and when Fitzhugh called back, the Tourist confirmed in a strangely flat voice that the job was done. Fine.

Then, at the scene, he'd noticed the blood inside the house. Why had Tripplehorn taken away Weaver's body? There was no need for that. The next day, forensics almost gave him a coronary—the blood wasn't Weaver's. They didn't know whose it was, but he did.

Tripplehorn had not answered his phone; Milo Weaver had.

Then, after a frantic week of scouring the country, a miracle.

Fitzhugh accessed the network server, typed in his code, and replayed the video of that morning. A surveillance technician had done a quick edit of footage from various cameras. It began outside the building, among the throng of midtown commuters jostling wearily to their jobs. A time code ticked at the bottom of the screen: 9:38. Among the crowd was a head that the technician had marked with a roving arrow. It started on the other side of the Avenue of the Americas, paused, and jogged through a gridlock of yellow taxis to their side.

Cut to: a second camera, on their sidewalk. By then he'd been identified, and in the lobby the doormen were taking positions. On the street, though, Weaver seemed to reconsider. He stopped, letting people bump into him, as if suddenly confused by north and south. Then he continued to the front door.

A high lobby camera, looking down. From here, he could see where the doormen had positioned themselves. The big black guy, Lawrence, was at the door, while another waited by the palm tree. Two more hid in the elevator corridor, just out of sight.

Lawrence waited for him to enter, then stepped up to him. There was a moment when everything seemed all right. Agreeably, they chatted in low tones as the other three doormen approached. Then Weaver noticed them approaching, and panicked. That's the only explanation Fitzhugh could come up with, because Milo Weaver turned on his heel, swiftly, but Lawrence was ready for that; he'd already grabbed Weaver's shoulder. Weaver punched Lawrence in the face, but the other three doormen had arrived, and they piled on him.

It was a remarkably quiet scene, just a little scuffling and the gasp of the pretty desk clerk—Gloria Martinez—just out of sight. When they all got to their feet, Weaver was cuffed behind his back, and three doormen led him to the elevators.

Strangely, Weaver smiled as he passed the front desk, even winked at Gloria. He said something that the camera didn't pick up. The doormen heard it, though, and so did Gloria: "I think I lost my tour group." What a card.

He lost his sense of humor once he reached his cell on the nineteenth floor.

"Why did you kill him?" was Fitzhugh's opening gambit. Whatever Weaver said now would tell Fitzhugh what to do next.

Milo blinked at him, hands chained behind his back. "Who?"

"Tom, for Christ's sake! Tom Grainger!"

A pause, and in that moment of silence, Fitzhugh didn't know what the man would say. Finally, Weaver shrugged. "Tom had Angela Yates killed. That's why. He set her up to look like a traitor, then killed her. He lied to you and me. He lied to the Company." Then he pushed it further: "Because I loved that man, and he used me."

Had Milo killed Tripplehorn, and then, for his own reasons, shot Tom Grainger? If so, it was a burst of cool, fresh air in Fitzhugh's muggy life. He said, "I don't give a shit what you thought about him. He was a CIA veteran and your direct superior. You *killed* him, Weaver. What am I supposed to think? I'm your superior now—should I worry that if you smell something you don't like I'll be next on the slab?"

It hadn't been time for questions yet, though, so he made a show of frustration, claiming he had meetings to attend. "Reorganization. Restructuring. Cleaning up your goddamned mess."

On the way out, he'd whispered to Lawrence, "Strip him to his birthday suit and give him the black hole."

Lawrence, with his bloodshot eye, betrayed a moment of disgust. "Yes, sir."

The black hole was simple. Strip a man naked, give him a little while to become comfortable with his nakedness, and, after an hour or so, turn off the lights.

Blackness in itself was disorienting, but on its own it had no impact. It was just blackness. The "hole" came sometime later—hours, maybe minutes, when the doormen, wearing infrared goggles, returned two at a time and beat the hell out of him. No light, just disembodied fists.

Take away time, light, and physical security, and a man quickly wants nothing more than to sit in a well-lit room and tell you everything he knows. Weaver would remain in the hole until tomorrow morning, by which time he would welcome even Fitzhugh's presence.

Back in the office, he read through Einner's report, delivered after their travels to Paris and Geneva. Despite Milo's attack on him, Einner insisted that Milo could not have been responsible for Angela's death. "He had the opportunity to switch her sleeping pills, but not the motive. It became obvious that he wanted to find her killer more than I did."

In a blue font, Fitzhugh added his own assessment—"Rampant Speculation"—to Einner's report, then typed his initials and the date.

A little after four, someone knocked. "Yes? Come in."

Special Agent Janet Simmons opened the door.

He tried not to let his irritation show. Instead, he thought the same thing he'd thought during their first meeting—that she might have been an attractive young woman if she hadn't put so much effort into appearing otherwise. Dark hair pulled severely back, some navy suit with too-loose slacks. Lesbian slacks, Fitzhugh secretly called them.

"Thought you were still in D.C.," he said.

"You got Weaver," she answered, gripping her hands behind her back.

Fitzhugh leaned back in the Aeron, wondering how she'd learned that. "He came to us. Just walked his ass through the front door."

"Where's he now?"

"Couple floors down. We're giving him the silent treatment. But he's already admitted to killing Tom."

"Any reasons?"

"Fit of anger. Thought Grainger had used him. Betrayed him."

She reached the available chair, touched it, but didn't sit. "I'll want to talk to him, you know."

"Of course."

"Soon."

Fitzhugh rocked his head from side to side to show that he was a man of multiple minds—not schizophrenic, but complicated. "Soon as possible. Be sure of that. But not today. Today there's no talking. And tomorrow, I'll need a full day alone with him. Security, you know."

Simmons finally sat in the chair, her wandering eye gazing over Manhattan while her good eye locked on to him. "I'll pull jurisdiction if I have to. You know that, right? He killed Tom Grainger on American soil."

"Grainger was one of our employees. Not yours."

"Beside the point."

Fitzhugh eased back in the chair. "You act as if Weaver's your nemesis, Janet. He's just a corrupt Company man."

"Three murders in a month—the Tiger, Yates, and Grainger. That's a bit much, even for a corrupt Company man."

"You can't seriously think he killed all of them."

"I'll have a better idea once I've spoken to him."

Fitzhugh ran his tongue over his teeth. "Tell you what, Janet. Give us another day alone with him. Day after tomorrow—Friday—I'll let you sit in on the conversation." He held up three stiff fingers. "Scout's honor."

Simmons considered that, as if she had a choice. "Day after tomorrow, then. But I want something now."

"Like what?"

"Milo's file. Not the open one—that's useless. I want yours."

"That'll take a little—"

"*Now,* Terence. I'm not giving you time to misplace it, or take out all the juicy stuff. If I'm waiting to talk to him, then I better have some interesting reading."

He pursed his lips. "There's no need to be aggressive about this. We both want the same thing. Someone kills one of my people, and I want him scratching concrete for the rest of his life."

"Glad we're agreed," she said, though gladness left no mark on her face. "I still want that file."

"Can you at least wait ten minutes?"

"I can do that."

"Wait in the lobby. I'll send it down."

"What about the wife?" she asked as she stood. "Tina. Have you questioned her?"

"Briefly in Austin, after Weaver made contact, but she knows nothing. We're not bothering her anymore; she's been through enough."

"I see." Without offering a handshake, she walked out, leaving Fitzhugh to watch her march in her lesbian slacks through the maze of cubicles.

He lifted the desk phone and typed 49, and after a doorman's military opening gambit—"Yes, *sir*"—he cut in: "Name."

"Steven Norris, sir."

"Listen carefully, Steven Norris. Are you listening?"

"Uh, yes. Sir."

"If you ever send a goddamned Homelander upstairs again without clearing it with me first, you're out of here. You'll be guarding the front gate of the U.S. embassy in Baghdad wearing a George Bush T-shirt instead of body armor. Got it?"

2

She'd taken a room on the twenty-third floor of the Grand Hyatt, atop Grand Central Station. Like any room Janet Simmons worked in, it quickly became a mess. She despised hotel blankets, stripping them off immediately to make a pile at the bottom of the bed. To this, she added the extra pillows (one was more than enough for her), room service menus, the alphabetical book of guest services, and all the sundry extras that overflowed the bedside tables. Only then, finally cleared of distractions, could she sit on the bed, open her laptop, and start a new Word document to transcribe her thoughts.

Simmons didn't like Terence Fitzhugh. There was the irritating way his eyes measured her bustline, but that wasn't it. What she hated was his sympathetic frowns, as if everything she said was a piece of revelatory, disappointing news. It was pure Beltway theater. When she stormed his D.C. office after the murder of Angela Yates, he gave her that same kind of treatment, with an "I'm going to get right on top of this, Janet. Be assured."

She'd expected nothing, and so it was a shock when an envelope arrived the next afternoon at her office at 245 Murray Lane. A highly censored, anonymous surveillance report on Angela Yates. And there it was. At 11:38 P.M. Milo Weaver entered her apartment. Surveillance was paused (no reason given—in fact, there was no reason listed for the surveillance at all). By the time the cameras were on again, Weaver was gone. An estimated half hour later, Angela Yates died from barbiturates. A single window of opportunity, and there was Milo Weaver.

Later, at Disney World, she'd found a frightened but stubborn wife and a cute, sleepy kid, both puzzled by the sight of Simmons, Orbach, and the other two men waving pistols. But no Milo Weaver. Grainger, it turned out, had warned him off.

Then, a week ago, Tom Grainger came up dead in New Jersey. It was a strange scene. The outline of Grainger's corpse in the front yard was straightforward enough, but what about the three windows that had been broken from the outside? What about the unidentified blood at the foot of the stairs, just inside the front door? What about the seven bullets lodged in the stairs themselves—9mm, SIG Sauer? No one offered an explanation, though it was clear enough that a third person had been on the scene. Fitzhugh pretended to be baffled by the whole thing.

In Austin, Tina Weaver disappeared for three hours.

When Rodger Samson questioned her, she admitted that Milo had wanted her and Stephanie to leave the country with him. She'd refused. He'd vanished again, and Janet had believed that she would never see Milo Weaver again. Then, that morning, she'd received the enlightening call from Matthew, Homeland's plant in what the CIA considered its ultra-secret Department of Tourism.

Why had Milo turned himself in?

She opened the manila envelope that Gloria Martinez had handed her, and began to read.

Born June 21, 1970, in Raleigh, North Carolina. Parents: Wilma and Theodore (Theo) Weaver. In October 1985, a *Raleigh News & Observer* clipping told her, "an accident occurred on I-40 near the Morrisville exit when a drunk driver ran head on into another car." The driver, David Paulson, was killed, as were the occupants of the second car, Wilma and Theodore Weaver of Cary. "They are survived by their son, Milo."

She typed the requisite facts into her Word document.

Though no documentary evidence backed it up, a report explained that Milo Weaver, at fifteen, moved into the St. Christopher Home for Boys in Oxford, North Carolina. The lack of documentation was excused by another newspaper clipping, circa 1989, reporting that a fire had destroyed the St. Christopher complex and all its records, one year after Milo left North Carolina behind.

By then, a scholarship had taken him to Lock Haven University, a tiny school in a sleepy Pennsylvania mountain town. A few pages charted an irregular student who, while never arrested, was suspected by local police as being "involved with drug-users and spends much time in the old house at the corner of West Church and Fourth where marijuana parties are a regular occurrence." He'd arrived at the school majoring in "undecided" but by the end of his first year had settled on international relations.

Despite its size, Lock Haven boasted the largest student exchange program on the East Coast. During his third year, in the fall of 1990, Milo arrived in Plymouth, England, to study at Marjon, the College of St. Mark and St. John. According to these early CIA reports, Milo Weaver quickly found a circle of friends, most from Brighton, who were involved in socialist politics. While calling themselves Labour, their true beliefs led more down the path of "ecoanarchism"—a term, Simmons noted, that wouldn't come into popular use for nearly another decade. An MI5 plant inside the group, working in cooperation with the CIA, reported that Weaver was ideal for an approach. "The ideals of the group are not his, but his desire to take part in something larger than himself predicates most of his endeavors. He has fluent Russian and excellent French."

The approach occurred during a weekend trip to London in late December, a month before Weaver was scheduled to return to Pennsylvania. The MI5 plant— "Abigail"—brought him to the Marquee Club on Charing Cross, where, slipping into a rented back room, he was introduced to the London head of station, who in the reports was referred to as "Stan."

The conversation must have been favorable, because a second meeting was arranged for three days later in Plymouth. Milo then dropped out of school and, lacking a UK visa, went underground with his environmental anarchist friends.

It was a strikingly fast recruitment, which Simmons also noted in her Word document, but of that first job there was nothing else, and the file referred the researcher to File WT-2569-A91. Still, she knew Milo's role in the operation lasted only until March, because that was when he was put onto the CIA payroll and sent to Perquimans County, North Carolina, where, along the Albemarle Sound, he trained for four months at the Point, a Company school less well known than the Farm but just as accredited.

Milo was sent to London, where he worked (twice, if the file was to be believed) with Angela Yates, another wanderer brought into the Company family. One report suggested they were lovers; another report insisted that Yates was a lesbian.

Milo Weaver began to settle into the Russian expatriate community, and though the actual case files lay elsewhere, Simmons could chart a career of insinuation. He mixed with all levels of Russian expats, from diplomats to petty crooks. His focus was twofold: shed light on the burgeoning mafia gaining a foothold in the London underworld, and uncover the occasional spies sent from Moscow while the Soviet Empire suffered its death throes. Though he did well with the criminal element—in the first year his information led to two major arrests—he excelled at spycatching. He had at his disposal three major sources within the Russian intelligence apparat: DENIS, FRANKA, and TADEUS. In two

years, he uncovered fifteen undercover agents and convinced a stunning eleven to work as doubles.

Then, in January 1994, the reports changed tone, noting Milo's slow decline into alcoholism, his trenchant
womanizing (not, apparently, with Angela Yates), and
the suspicion that Milo himself had been turned into
a double by one of his sources, TADEUS. Within six
months, Milo was fired, his visa was revoked, and he
was given a plane ticket home.

Thus ended the first stage of Milo Weaver's career.
The second documented stage began seven years later,
in 2001, a month after the Twin Towers fell, when he
was rehired, now as a "supervisor" in Thomas Grainger's
department, the details of which were vague. Of the in-
tervening years from 1994 to 2001, the file said nothing.

She knew what that meant, of course. Weaver's dis-
solution in 1994 had been an act, and for the next seven
years Milo Weaver had been working black ops. Since
he was part of Grainger's ultra-secret department,
Weaver had been a "Tourist."

It was a nice sketch of a successful career. Field agent
to ghost-agent to administration. Those lost seven years
might have held the answers she sought, but they would
have to remain a mystery. If she admitted to Fitzhugh
what she knew of Tourism, Matthew would be compromised.

Something occurred to her. She flipped back through
the sheets until she'd returned to the report on Milo
Weaver's childhood. Raleigh, North Carolina. Orphanage in Oxford. Then two years at a small liberal arts
college before arriving in England. She compared these

facts to "Abigail's" report: "He has fluent Russian and excellent French."

She used her cell phone, and after a moment heard George Orbach's deep but groggy voice say, "What *is* it?" That's when she realized it was nearly eleven.

"You home?"

A broad yawn. "Office. Guess I passed out."

"I've got something for you."

"Other than sleep?"

"Take this down." She read off the particulars of Milo Weaver's childhood. "Find out if anyone in the Weaver clan is still alive. Says here they're dead, but if you can find even a distant second cousin, then I want to talk to them."

"We dig deep, but isn't this a bit much?"

"Five years after his parents' death, he was fluent in Russian. Tell me, George—how does an orphan from North Carolina do that?"

"He takes a course. Studies hard."

"Just look into it, will you? And find out if anyone's still around from the St. Christopher Home for Boys."

"Will do."

"Thanks," Simmons said and hung up, then dialed another number.

Despite the hour, Tina Weaver sounded awake. In the background, a television sitcom played. "What?"

"Hello, Mrs. Weaver. This is Janet Simmons."

A pause. Tina said, "Special agent, even."

"Listen, I know we didn't get off on the right foot before."

"You don't think so?"

"I know Rodger interviewed you in Austin—was he all right? I told him not to press too much."

"Rodger was a real sweetheart."

"I'd like to talk with you about a few things. Tomorrow all right?"

Another pause. "You want me to help you track down my husband?"

She doesn't know, Simmons thought. "I want you to help me get to the truth, Tina. That's all."

"What kinds of questions?"

"Well," Simmons said, "you're pretty familiar with Milo's past, right?"

A hesitant "Yeah."

"Any surviving relatives?"

"None that he knows of," she said, then made a wordless sound, like choking.

"Tina? You all right?"

"I just," she gasped. "I get hiccups sometimes."

"Get yourself some water. We'll talk tomorrow. Morning okay? Like, ten, ten thirty?"

"Yeah," Tina agreed, then the line went dead.

3

I n the morning, a Company driver picked Fitzhugh up from the Mansfield Hotel on West Fourty-fourth and dropped him off at the Avenue of the Americas building by nine thirty. Once behind the desk, he picked up the phone and dialed a number. "John?"

"Yes, sir," said a flat voice.

"Can you go to Room 5 and give the treatment until I get down there? No more than an hour."

"Face?"

"No, not the face."

"Yes, sir."

He hung up, checked his e-mail, then connected to Nexcel, signing in with Grainger's username and password. One message from Sal, that occasional oracle in Homeland:

```
J Simmons has gone to DT HQ unexpect-
edly.
```

"Thank *you*," he said to the computer. The message might have been of use had it come before Simmons ambushed him here at "DT HQ" yesterday. He wondered if Sal was really earning his Christmas bonuses.

There was a stack of real mail on the desk, and among the interdepartmental memos he found a buff envelope, postmarked Denver, addressed to Grainger. Security had placed CLEARED stamps all over it, so he ripped it open. Inside was a brick-colored passport, issued by the Russian Federation.

With a fingernail, he opened it to find a recent photograph of Milo Weaver with his heavy, accusing eyes and long jowl, looking in some ways like a gulag survivor. But the name beside the picture was Михаил Евгéнович Властов, Mikhail Yevgenovich Vlastov.

"Oh, fuck me," he whispered.

He went to the door and pointed through the cubicles at one of the Travel Agents, using a finger to beckon him. Once the door was closed again, Fitzhugh snapped his fingers, as if the name were on the tip of his tongue, which it wasn't.

"Harold Lynch," the analyst said. He couldn't have been more than twenty-five; a sweat-heavy lock of blond hair curled over his smooth, high forehead.

"Right. Harry, listen. There's a new lead to follow. Milo Weaver as Russian mole."

The disbelief was all over Lynch's face, but Fitzhugh pressed the issue.

"Opportunities. Find when he had access to information, and, soon afterward or even simultaneously, access to the FSB. Line that up with known Russian intel. Take this." He handed over the passport and envelope. "Have someone run it through whatever we've got. I want to know who sent it, how tall they are, and what their favorite food is."

Lynch stared at the passport, overwhelmed by this sudden shift in gear.

"Get along, now."

No matter who sent it, the passport was an unexpected gift. Even before the interrogation had begun, Fitzhugh had been handed a serious weapon. Murder and treason—Weaver might talk his way out of one charge, but two?

He decided to share the good news with Janet Simmons. His secretary, a heavyset woman in pink, tracked down and dialed her number. On the second ring, he heard, "Simmons."

"You'll never guess what appeared today."

"I probably won't."

"Russian passport for Milo Weaver."

She paused, and in the background he heard the hum of an engine—she was driving. "What does that make him?" she said. "A dual citizen?"

He'd expected a little more joy from her. "It just might make him a double agent, Janet. It's not one of ours."

"Under his name?"

"No. Mikhail Yevgenovich Vlastov."

A pause. "Where'd it come from?"

"Anonymous. We're looking into that now."

"Thanks for telling me, Terence. Give Milo my best."

At ten thirty, Fitzhugh used his keycard in the elevator to access the nineteenth floor, where instead of cubicles there were corridors of windowless walls marked by pairs of doors. One led to a cell, the other to the control room for each cell, full of monitors and recording equipment. He entered the control room to cell five, carrying a plain gray folder.

Nate, a hard-drinking ex-agent with the stomach of a goat, sat crunching Ruffles in front of monitors where Milo Weaver, on a floor, naked, screamed from electric shocks delivered to his exposed body parts. The sound echoed sickly in the small room.

A small, thin man in a blood-spattered white smock did his work silently—that was John. One of the doormen held Weaver's shoulders down with rubber gloves, while the other doorman, the big black one, stood by a wall, wiping his mouth and staring.

"What the hell's he doing?" Fitzhugh asked.

Reaching for another potato chip, Nate said, "Just evacuated his breakfast. It's right there by his feet."

"Christ. Get him out of there."

"Now?"

"Yes, now!"

Nate slipped on a wireless headset, tapped on the keyboard, and said, "Lawrence."

The black man stiffened and put a finger to his ear.

"Get out. Now."

While Weaver screamed, Lawrence walked slowly to the door. Fitzhugh met him in the corridor and, despite the fact that the doorman was a head taller, shoved a stiff finger into his chest. "If I ever see that again, you'll be out of here. Got it?"

Lawrence nodded, eyes moist.

"Get back to the lobby and send up someone with balls."

Another nod, and the big man walked off to the elevators.

Nate had told John to prepare for his entrance, so when Fitzhugh opened the door, Milo Weaver was crouched, leaning against the wall, blood seeping from spots across his chest and legs and groin. The remaining doorman stood at attention by the opposite wall while John packed up his electrodes. Weaver began to cry.

"It's a shame," said Fitzhugh, arms crossed over his chest, tapping the folder against his elbow. "A whole career flushed down the toilet because of a sudden desire for vengeance. It doesn't make sense to me. It doesn't make sense here," he said, tapping his temple, "nor here"—his heart. He squatted so he was level with Weaver's red eyes and opened the folder. "This is what happens when Milo Weaver defends his dignity?" He snapped the folder around to reveal page-sized color photos of Tom Grainger, crumpled in front of his New Jersey house on Lake Hopatcong. Fitzhugh went through them one at a time for Milo's inspection. Panoramic shots, showing the position of the body—five yards from those concrete steps. Close-ups: the hole through the shoulder, the other through the forehead. Two soft dumdum bullets that widened after entry, taking out a massive chunk as they left, leaving a mutilated shell of Thomas Grainger.

Milo's crying intensified, and he lost his balance, falling to the floor.

"We've got a weeper," Fitzhugh observed, standing.

Everyone in that small white room waited. Milo took loud breaths until the tears were under control, wiped his wet eyes and runny nose, then worked himself into a hunched standing position.

"You're going to tell me everything," said Fitzhugh.

"I know," said Milo.

4

Across the East River, Special Agent Janet Simmons worked her way through slow Brooklyn traffic, stopping abruptly for pedestrians and children leaping across Seventh Avenue. She cursed each one of them. People were like that—they blundered through their little lives as if nothing would ever cross their paths. Nothing, not automobiles, crossfire, stalkers, or even the unknown machinations of the world's security services, who could easily confuse you with someone else and drag you to a cell, or simply put a misplaced bullet in your head.

Instinctively, she parked on Seventh, near where it crossed Garfield, so that she wouldn't be seen from the window.

She'd made a lot of noise with Terence Fitzhugh, but the truth was that she had no real jurisdictional authority concerning Milo Weaver. He'd killed Tom Grainger on American soil, but both were CIA employees, which left it to the Company's discretion.

Why, then, was she so insistent? Not even she knew for sure. The murder of Angela Yates—perhaps that was it. A successful woman who had made it so far in this most masculine of professions had been killed in her prime by the man Simmons had let go in Tennessee. Did that make her responsible for Yates's death? Maybe not. She felt responsible nonetheless.

This baroque sense of responsibility had plagued her much of her life, though her Homeland therapist, a skinny, pale girl who had the nervous, awkward movements of a virgin, always turned the equation around. It wasn't that Janet Simmons was responsible for all the people in her life; it was that Janet Simmons believed she *could* be responsible for them. "Control," the virgin told her. "You think you can control everything. That's a serious error of perception."

"You're saying I have control issues?" Simmons taunted, but the virgin was tougher than she looked.

"No, Janet. I'm saying you're a megalomaniac. Good news is, you chose the right profession."

So, her urge to right Milo Weaver's wrongs had nothing to do with justice, empathy, philanthropy, or even equal rights for women. That didn't mean that her actions, in themselves, were not virtuous—even the virgin would admit that.

Yet for weeks her desires had been stumped by a simple lack of real evidence. She could place Weaver at the deaths of the victims, but she wanted more. She wanted reasons.

The Weavers' brownstone lay on a street of brown-stones, though theirs was noticeably more run-down. The front door was unlocked, so she climbed the stairs without buzzing anyone. On the third floor, she rang the bell.

It took a moment, but finally she heard the soft pad of bare feet on wood leading up to the door; the spy hole darkened.

"Tina?" She produced her Homeland ID and held it out. "It's Janet. Just need a few minutes of your time."

The shift of the chain being undone. The door opened, and Tina Weaver stared back at her, barefoot, in pajama bottoms and a T-shirt. No bra. She looked the same as at their last meeting in Disney World, only more tired.

"Did I come at the wrong time?"

Tina Weaver's body shrank slightly at the sight of Simmons. "I'm not sure I should speak to you. You hounded him."

"I think Milo killed two people. Maybe three. You expect me to let that go?"

She shrugged.

"Did you know he's back?"

Tina didn't ask where or when; she just blinked.

"He turned himself in. He's at the Manhattan office."

"He's all right?"

"He's in trouble, but he's fine. Can I come in?"

Milo Weaver's wife wasn't listening anymore. She was walking down the corridor toward the living room, leaving the door open. Simmons followed her to a low-ceilinged room with a big flat-screen television but old, cheap-looking furniture. Tina dropped onto the sofa, knees up to her chin, and watched Simmons take a seat.

"Stephanie's at school?"

"It's summer vacation, Special Agent. She's with the sitter."

"They're not missing you at work?"

"Yes, well." Tina wiped something off her arm. "The library's flexible when you're the director."

"The Avery Architectural and Fine Arts Library, at Columbia. Very impressive."

Tina's expression doubted anyone would be impressed by that. "You going to ask your questions, or what? I'm pretty good at answering. I've had plenty of practice."

"Recently?"

"The Company sent some goons two days ago, right in this room."

"I didn't know."

"You guys aren't very good at communicating, are you?"

Simmons rocked her head. "The different agencies cooperate like an estranged couple. But we're in counseling," she said, smiling to cover her annoyance: Fitzhugh had lied about interrogating Tina. "Fact is, we're now investigating your husband on multiple levels, with the hope of understanding how the levels connect."

Tina blinked again. "What multiple levels?"

"Well, murder, as I said. Two suspected murders and one verified murder."

"Verified? Verified how?"

"Milo confessed to killing Thomas Grainger."

Simmons braced herself for an explosion, but got

none. Wet, red-rimmed eyes, yes, and tears. Then, a quiet sobbing that shook Tina's whole body, her elevated knees swaying.

"Look, I'm sorry, but—"

"*Tom?*" she spat out. "Tom Fucking Grainger? No . . ." She shook her head. "Why would he kill Tom? He's Stef's *god*father!"

Tina cried for a few seconds, face down, then raised her head, cheeks damp.

"What does he say?"

"What?"

"Milo. You said he confessed. What's his goddamned excuse?"

Simmons wondered how to put it. "Milo claims that Tom used him, and in a fit of anger he killed the man."

Tina wiped at her eyes. With eerie calmness, she said, "Fit of anger?"

"Yes."

"No. Milo, he—he doesn't *have* fits of anger. He's not that kind of person."

"It's hard to know what people are really like."

A smile filled Tina's face, but it didn't match her voice: "Don't be condescending, Special Agent. After six years, day-in-day-out, with the stress of raising a child, you get a pretty good idea what someone's like."

"Okay," said Simmons. "I take it back. You tell me, then—why would Milo kill Tom Grainger?"

It didn't take long for Tina to reach a conclusion: "Only two reasons I can think of. If he was ordered to do it by the Company."

"That's one. The other?"

"If he needed to protect his family."

"He's protective?"

"Not freakishly so, but yes. If he thought we were in serious danger, Milo would take whatever steps necessary to remove that danger."

"I see," Simmons said, as if committing this to memory. "A week ago, he visited you. In Texas. You were at your parents' house, right?"

"He wanted to talk to me."

"About what, exactly?"

She chewed the inside of her mouth thoughtfully. "You know this already. Rodger told you."

"I try not to depend on the reports. What did Milo want to talk to you about?"

"About leaving."

"Leaving Texas?"

"Our lives."

"I don't know what that means," Simmons lied.

"It *means*, Special Agent, that he was in trouble. *You,* for instance, were after him for some murders he didn't do. He told me Tom was dead, but all he said was someone had killed him, and he had killed that man."

"Who's this other man?"

Tina shook her head. "He didn't share details. Unfortunately, that's the kind of man he—" She paused. "He always avoided details that might upset me. He just said that the only way to stay alive was to disappear. The Company would kill him, because they would *think* he killed Grainger. He wanted us—me and Stef—to disappear with him." She swallowed heavily, remembering. "He had these passports all ready. One for each of us, with other names Dolan. That was the family name. He wanted us to disappear, maybe to Europe, and start life again as the Dolans." She went back to chewing her cheek.

"And you said?"

"We're not sitting in Europe, are we?"

"You said no. Any reason?"

Tina stared hard at Janet Simmons, as if shocked by her lack of intuition. "All the reasons in the *world,* Special Agent. How the hell do you rip a five-year-old girl out of her life, give her a new name, and not leave scars? How am I supposed to earn a living in Europe, where I can't even speak any languages? And what kind of a life is it when you're looking over your shoulder every day? Well?"

Simmons knew it from the way the series of rhetorical questions burst out, so smoothly, as if it were a speech Tina Weaver had been practicing ever since that moment, a week ago, when she refused her husband's last request: They were reasons after the fact, the ones she used to justify her abandonment. They had nothing to do with why she'd said no in the first place.

"Milo's not Stephanie's biological father, right?"

Tina shook her head, exhausted.

"That would be . . ." Simmons pretended to be trying to remember, but she knew all this by heart. "Patrick, right? Patrick Hardemann."

"Yes."

"How much of Stephanie's childhood was he around for? I mean, before Milo."

"None of it. We split up while I was pregnant."

"And you met Milo . . ."

"On the day I gave birth."

Simmons raised her brows; her surprise was honest. "Now, *that's* serendipity."

"You could say so."

"You met in . . ."

"Is this really necessary?"

"Yes, Tina. I'm afraid it is."

"Venice."

"Venice?"

"Where we met. Vacation. I was eight months pregnant, alone, and I ended up spending time with the wrong guy. Or the right guy. Depending on your perspective."

"The right guy," Simmons said helpfully, "because you met Milo."

"Yes."

"Can you tell me about this? Really, everything does help."

"Help you put my husband behind bars?"

"I told you before. I want you to help me get to the truth."

Tina put her feet on the floor and sat up so she could face Simmons head-on. "Okay. If you really want to know."

"I do."

5

Tina couldn't get over how hot it was. Even here, at an open-air café along the Grand Canal, just short of the arched stone monstrosity of the Rialto Bridge, it was unbearable.

Venice, surrounded by and veined with water, should have cooled off some, but all the water did was raise the humidity, the way the river did in Austin. But in Austin she hadn't carried an eight-month heater in her bloated belly that swelled her feet and played havoc with her lower back.

It might have been more bearable, were it not for the crowds. The entire world's population of sweaty tourists seemed to have come to Italy at the same time. They made it impossible for a pregnant woman to move comfortably along the narrow, bumpy passages and avoid the African vendors selling Louis Vuitton knockoffs, ten hanging from each arm.

She sipped her orange juice, then forced herself to gaze at, and appreciate, a passing vaporetto overflowing with camera-toting tourists. Then she returned to the paperback she'd opened on the table—*What to Expect When You're Expecting.* She was on the page in chapter twelve that dealt with "stress incontinence." Great.

Stop it, Tina.

She was being remarkably unappreciative. What would Margaret, Jackie, and Trevor think? They had pooled their meager resources and bought her this final splash-out five-day/four-night Venetian holiday before the baby arrived to put the last nail in the coffin of her social life. "And to remind yourself that that prick isn't the only example of manhood out there," Trevor had said.

No, philandering Patrick wasn't the only example of manhood out there, but the examples she'd come across here weren't encouraging. Lazy-eyed Italians whistled and hissed and muttered invitations at any piece of ass that walked by. Not her, though—no. Pregnant women reminded them too much of their own blessed mothers— those women who hadn't beaten their sons anywhere near enough.

Her belly not only protected her from the men, but encouraged them to open doors for her. She received smiles from complete strangers, and a few times old men pointed at high facades and gave her history lessons she couldn't understand. She started to think things were looking up, at least until last night. The e-mail.

Patrick, it turned out, was in Paris with Paula. All those *P*'s confused her. He wanted to know if she could "swing through town" so she and Paula could finally meet. "She really wants to," he'd written.

Tina had crossed an ocean to get away from her problems, and then—

"Excuse me."

On the other side of her table stood an American, somewhere in his fifties, bald on top, grinning down at her. He pointed at the free chair. "May I?"

When the waiter came, he ordered a vodka tonic, then watched another vaporetto glide past. Perhaps bored with the water, he started watching her face as she read. He finally spoke: "Can I buy you a drink?"

"Oh," she said. "No, thanks." She gave him a smile, just enough to be polite. Then she took off her sunglasses.

"Sorry," he stuttered. "Just that I'm here alone, and it looks like you are, too. You'd get a free drink out of it."

Maybe he was all right. "Why not? Thanks . . ." She raised her brows.

"Frank."

"Thanks, Frank. I'm Tina."

She stuck out her hand, and they shook with stiff formality. "Champagne?"

"You didn't see." She grabbed the arms of her chair and scooted it back a foot. She touched her large, rounded belly. "Eight months now."

Frank gaped.

"Never seen one of these before?"

"I just . . ." He scratched his hairless scalp. "That explains it. Your glow."

Not again, she wanted to say but cut herself short. She could at least be pleasant.

When the waiter arrived with his vodka tonic, he ordered her another orange juice, and she pointed out that a simple orange juice was outrageously expensive here. "And look how much they give you," she said, holding up her tiny glass. "Outrageous."

She wondered if she was being too negative again, but Frank pushed it further (complaining about the Vuitton knockoffs she'd seen before) until they were both complaining pleasantly about the idiocies of tourism.

In answer to his questions, she told him she was a librarian at MIT's art and architecture library in Boston, and she let out just enough casual, sarcastic asides to make it clear that the father of her baby had left in a particularly poor fashion. "You've got my whole life already. What are you, a journalist?"

"Real estate. I work out of Vienna, but we've got properties all over the place. I'm settling a deal on a palazzo not far away."

"Really?"

"Sold it to a Russian bigwig. So much money, you wouldn't believe."

"I probably wouldn't."

"The papers have to be signed in the next forty-eight hours, but in the meantime I'm entirely free." He considered his next words carefully. "Can I take you out to the theater?"

Tina slipped on the sunglasses again. Despite herself, she remembered Margaret's most insistent advice five months ago when Patrick first walked out: *He's a boy, Tina. A child. What you need is an older man. Someone with a sense of responsibility.* Tina wasn't seriously considering anything like that, but there was always a certain logic to Margaret's unasked-for wisdom.

Frank turned out to be a pleasant surprise. He left her alone until five, when he arrived in a tailored suit, carrying a pair of Teatro Malibran tickets and a single orange lily that smelled hallucinogenic.

She knew little about opera and had never considered herself a fan. Frank, despite having feigned ignorance, turned out to be something of an expert. He'd somehow gotten seats in the platea, the stalls on the floor of the opera, so they had an unencumbered view of the Prince, the King of Clubs, and Truffaldino in *The Love for Three Oranges*. He sometimes leaned in to whisper a plot point she might have missed—it was performed in French—but the plot hardly mattered. It was an absurdist opera about a cursed prince forced to go on a quest for three oranges, in each of which slept a princess. The audience laughed more often than Tina did, but the jokes she got she enjoyed.

Afterward, Frank treated her to dinner at a marginal trattoria and told her stories about his long years living in Europe. She found his description of the expatriate lifestyle particularly enticing. Then he insisted on buying her breakfast, which she first took as a rudely hopeful suggestion. She'd misjudged, though, and all he did was walk her back to the hotel, kiss her cheeks in the

European manner, and wish her a good night. A real gentleman, unlike those Italian men lurking on every corner.

She woke early on Tuesday and, after a quick wash, began to pack her things for the next morning's flight home. It was a shame—now that she had finally recovered from her jet lag and met an interesting, cultured man, it was time to leave. She thought her last day might best be used taking a boat trip out to Murano to see the glassblowers.

She brought it up to Frank after he picked her up and they had reached the huge, pigeon-infested glory of St. Mark's Square. "This time it's my treat," she told him. "There's a boat leaving in an hour."

"I wish," he said earnestly, guiding her to an open-air café. "It's the damned job. The Ruskie can call for me at any moment, and if I'm not available it'll fall through."

It was during their continental breakfast that Frank went silent, staring past her shoulder, tense.

"What is it?" She followed his gaze, spotting a bald, thick-necked man in a black suit cutting through the crowds toward them.

"The palazzo." He bit his lower lip. "I hope they don't want to meet now."

"It's fine. We'll hook up later."

The tough-looking bald man reached the edge of their table. His head was shiny with sweat. "You," he said, his Russian accent thick. "It's ready."

Frank patted his lips with a napkin. "Can't it wait until we're finished eating?"

"No."

Frank glanced, embarrassed, at Tina. He put the napkin on the table with shaking hands. Was that fear? Or just excitement over a huge commission? Then he smiled at her. "You want to see the place? It's really fabulous."

She looked at the remnants of her breakfast, then at the Russian. "Maybe I shouldn't—"

"Nonsense," Frank cut in. To the Russian, he said, "Of course it's no problem, right?"

The man looked confused.

"Exactly." Frank helped Tina to her feet. "Not too fast," he told the Russian. "She's not built like you."

As soon as they passed the palazzo's front door and faced the steep, narrow steps leading up into the gloom, Tina regretted having come along. She should have known better. The bald Russian looked like the kind of Slavic thug that always populated action movies those days, and the steady walk from St. Mark's all the way up here had mauled her feet. Now, she was faced with this mountain to climb.

"Maybe I should wait down here," she said.

Frank's expression was almost horrified. "I know it looks tough, but you won't regret it. Trust me."

"But my—"

"*Come,*" the Russian said, already halfway up the first flight.

Frank reached out a hand. "Let me help."

So she let him help. He had, after all, been a perfect gentleman so far. She used the memory of the previous night—the opera and the dinner—to distract her from the ache in her heels as Frank helped her up to the oak door at the top of the steps. She looked back, but only saw that bleak, indeterminate gloom of ancient buildings. Then the gloom disappeared as the Russian opened the door.

When she stepped inside, she realized Frank had been right. It really was worth it.

He took her across the hardwood floor to a modernist wooden sofa. The Russian went into another room. "You weren't kidding," she said, twisting to take everything in.

"What did I tell you?" He stared at the door that had been left open an inch. "Listen, let me go take care of the papers in private, then I'll see about a little tour."

"Really?" She felt much like a surprised child, cheeks flushed. "That'd be great."

"I'll be quick." He touched her shoulder, which was warm and damp from the effort of getting up here, and followed the Russian into the next room.

At MIT, she'd learned so much about overdesigned pieces of furniture from magazines—*Abitare, I.D., Wallpaper*—but had never seen them in reality. In the corner sat a Kilin lounge chair made of black leather and imbuia wood, designed by Sergio Rodrigues. A Straessle International chariot chaise, circa 1972, faced it. Tina herself was supported by a slatted rosewood couch designed by Joaquim Tenreiro. Banally, she wondered how much this room had cost.

She heard a sound and looked up to see a gorgeous girl—early teens—step in from the terrace. She had straight brown hair to her waist, pearly skin, and bright eyes. She wore a pink summer dress that showed off the pubescence of her silhouetted body.

"Hi," said Tina, smiling.

The girl's eyes alighted on Tina's stomach. She said some excited German words and joined her on the couch. Hesitantly, she held a small hand over Tina's belly. "I can?"

Tina nodded, and the girl stroked her. It was soothing, and brought color to the girl's cheeks. Then she tapped her own stomach. "I have. Too."

Tina's smile faded. "You're pregnant?"

The girl frowned, unsure, then nodded excitedly. "Ja. I have baby. *Will* have baby."

"Oh." Tina wondered how the girl's parents were reacting.

"Ingrid."

Tina took the small, dry hand. "I'm Tina. You live here?"

Ingrid didn't seem to understand, but then the inner door opened and a tall older man with wavy gray hair and an immaculate suit stepped through, smiling, followed by a meek-looking Frank.

Ingrid clapped her hands over Tina's belly. "Schau mal, Roman!"

Roman walked over, and Tina let him take her hand and kiss her knuckles. "Nothing more beautiful than an expectant woman. Pleased to meet you, Miss . . . ?"

"Crowe. Tina Crowe. Are you Ingrid's father?"

"A proud uncle. Roman Ugrimov."

"Well, Mr. Ugrimov, your place is really beautiful. Just amazing."

Ugrimov nodded his thanks, then said, "Ingrid, meet Mr. Frank Dawdle."

The girl stood and politely shook Frank's hand. Ugrimov, behind her, placed his hands on her shoulders and, looking directly at Frank, said, "Ingrid here is everything to me, you see? She is my entire world."

Ingrid smiled bashfully. Ugrimov had said this with a little too much conviction.

Frank said, "Tina, I think we should be going."

She was disappointed—she actually had wanted to see the rest of the palazzo—but there was an unsettling tone in Frank's voice that made her think it might be better to leave. Besides, the collision of Ingrid's pregnancy and her uncle's attentions left her feeling uneasy.

So she got up—a little wobbly, and Ingrid came to steady her—then took Frank's arm. He mouthed, *Sorry*—probably for the tour. It didn't matter.

The bald thug walked them back down, which was so much easier than coming up, and at the halfway point they heard Ingrid's voice from behind them—she was laughing, a loud, nasal *hee-haw,* like a mule.

By the time the bald man opened the door to the square, she realized that something about this wasn't right, so once they'd paused in the shade of the stoop and the Russian had closed the door behind them, she said, "I don't get it, Frank. If he's just now signing the papers for that place, then why's he already moved in?"

Frank wasn't listening. Hands propped on his hips, he was staring off to the left, up the street. A woman about Tina's age stepped out of a doorway and began to run toward them. With a surprisingly menacing voice, she called, "*Frank!*"

First thought: *Is that Frank's wife?*

From the right, a man also ran toward them. His jacket swished from side to side as he galloped across the stones, and in his hand—a *gun.* What was *he,* then? But she didn't have time to follow her thoughts because she heard Roman Ugrimov's voice shouting down at them from above—yes, *everything* was suddenly converging—"*And her I love, you bastard!*"

Tina stepped forward, then back, because Frank was looking up at the sky. A punch of scream filled the air, then stretched out to a low wail that rose quickly in pitch, like a train speeding past.

The Doppler effect, her brain reminded her for no discernible reason.

Then she saw what was falling. Pink fluttering—brown hair—a body, a girl, *that* girl—Ingrid. And then—

At 10:27 A.M. Ingrid Kohl landed three feet from Tina. A thump and crunch, ruptured bone and flesh. Blood. Silence.

She couldn't breathe. Her body seized up. She couldn't even scream yet, not until Frank produced a pistol, shot three times, and fled. The woman—wife? girlfriend? thief?—bolted after him. Tina tripped and fell backward, hard, on the cobblestones. All she could do now was scream.

The other man, the one with the pistol, appeared at her side. He looked lost, staring at the mess of pink and red three feet from her. Then he noticed Tina, and briefly her screams ceased; she was afraid of him and his gun. But the screams came back of their own volition. *"I'm in labor! I need a doctor!"*

"I—" said the man. He looked in the direction where Frank and that woman had run; they were gone. He settled on the ground beside her, exhausted.

"Get a fucking doctor!" she shouted, and then they both heard three short cracks of a gun being fired.

The man looked at her again, as if she were a ghost fading away, then took out his cell phone. "It'll be all right," he said as he dialed. He spoke in Italian to someone. She recognized the word *ambulanza.* When he finally hung up—that's when she realized he'd been shot, somewhere in the chest. His shirt was almost black with shiny, fresh blood.

By then, though, a gush of maternal pragmatism had swept over her: It didn't matter that he'd been shot; he'd already called the ambulance. Her baby was as safe as it could be, given the circumstances. She calmed down, her contractions slowing, and the man, staring at her, gripped her hand tight, almost too tight, as if he hardly knew she was there. Down the street, the woman she'd later learn was named Angela Yates appeared again, crying. The man watched his accomplice sadly.

Tina said, "Who the hell are you?"

"What?"

She took a moment to regulate her breaths. "You've got a gun."

As if this were shocking news, the man released the pistol; it clattered to the ground.

"What," she said, then exhaled the pain of contraction through pursed lips, blowing three times. "What the hell are you?"

"I—" He squeezed her hand tighter, nearly choking on his words. "I'm a tourist."

6

Six years later, Janet Simmons noticed how the memory could still make Tina choke. Weaver's wife stared, mouth hanging open, at the coffee table, so as not to look at the woman asking all these questions.

"That, then, was Milo?"

Tina nodded.

Hesitantly, Simmons prodded: "What do you think he meant? That he was a tourist. In a situation like that, it's about the last thing someone would say."

Tina wiped her eyes with the side of her thumb and finally looked up. "The situation was that he had two bullets in his right lung and he was bleeding to death. In situations like that, probability goes out the window."

Simmons conceded the point, but that one word told her two things. First, that in 2001 Milo really had been a wreck, so much so that he was ready to admit to a complete stranger his ultra-secret job title. Second: Milo had recovered quickly enough so that Tina had no idea that it *was* a job title. "What was he doing there? In Venice. He told you, I guess. He had a gun, there was shooting, and the man you'd spent a day with had fled."

"Had been killed," Tina corrected. "Until that day, Milo was a field agent, and Frank—Frank Dawdle— he'd stolen three million dollars from the government."

"Our government?"

"Our government. That night, Milo put in his resignation. It wasn't about me, it wasn't about Frank. Not even about the Towers, which we learned about later. Milo's life had simply become unbearable."

"And there you were."

"There I was."

"Let's go back a second. You were both taken to an Italian hospital, and Stephanie was born. When did Milo show up again?"

"He never left."

"What do you mean?"

"When the doctors fixed him up, they put him in a room upstairs. As soon as he woke, he snuck into a nurse's station and found my room."

"He didn't know your name."

"We came in at the same time. He checked it by the hour. I'd passed out after the delivery, and when I woke up, he was asleep in a chair next to my bed. There was a TV, and the Italian news came on. I didn't understand what they were saying, but I knew what the World Trade Center looked like."

"I see."

"You *don't*," said Tina, the emotion back in her voice. "When I figured out what had happened, I started crying, and that woke Milo. I showed him what my tears were about, and when he got it, he started crying, too. Both of us, in that hospital room, wept together. From then on, we were inseparable."

While Simmons considered this love story, Tina looked up at the clock on the DVD player—after twelve. "Shit." She stood. "I have to pick up Stephanie. We're having lunch."

"But I've got more questions."

"Later," Tina said. "Unless you're planning to arrest me. Are you?"

"Can we talk later?"

"Call first."

Simmons waited for Tina to get ready. It took only five minutes. She reappeared, cleaned up in a light summer dress, and said, "What's the other level?"

"What?"

"Earlier, you said you were investigating Milo on two levels. We got distracted. One level was murder. What's the other?"

Simmons wished she hadn't brought it up. She wanted the time and space to get answers before Tina Weaver had an evening to think over some cover story. "We can talk about it tomorrow."

"Give me the Cliff Notes version."

She told Tina about the passport. "He's a Russian citizen, Tina. This is news to everyone."

Tina's cheeks flushed. "No, it's cover. Spies do that all the time. A cover for something he had to do in Russia."

"He told you about this?"

A quick shake of the head.

"Ever hear him mention the name Mikhail Vlastov?"

Again, Tina shook her head.

"Maybe you're right. Maybe it's just a misunderstanding." Generously, she smiled.

Down on Garfield, before splitting up, Simmons hesitantly broached what was for her the most important subject of their conversation: "Listen, Tina. I know what you told me up there about why you wouldn't run away with Milo, but I have to admit I don't buy it. The reasons are too practical. You said no for another reason."

Tina's face twisted briefly, heading toward a sneer, but halfway it gave up and relaxed. "You know why, Special Agent."

"You didn't trust him anymore."

A queer, offhand grin passed over Tina's features. She walked to her car.

As Simmons rounded the corner onto Seventh Avenue, her phone rang.

"Hold on to your socks," George Orbach said.

The phrase confused her a moment. "What?"

"William T. Perkins."

"Who?" She used a remote to unlock her car.

"Father of Wilma Weaver, née Perkins. Milo's grandfather. Lives in Myrtle Beach, South Carolina. Covenant Towers—assisted living community. Born 1926. Eighty-one years old."

"Thanks for the math," said Simmons, not betraying her excitement. "Is there a reason we never knew this before?"

"We never asked."

Incompetence, she supposed, went hand in hand with intelligence. No one had cared enough to find out if a grandfather was still breathing. "Can you send me the address, and tell Covenant Towers I'm coming?"

"When?"

She considered that as she got into the warm, stuffy car. "Tonight."

"Book a flight?"

"Yes," she said, then, checking her watch, made her decision: "Around six o'clock, and get three seats."

"Three?"

She got out of the car again, locked up, and walked back toward the Weavers' door. "Tina and Stephanie Weaver will be coming with me."

7

The truth, three lies, and some omissions. That was all Milo knew. The rest, Primakov had promised, would be taken care of. During that too-long week in Albuquerque, the old man had shared very little. Instead, he'd asked questions, just as Terence Fitzhugh was now doing. The story, from its beginning in Tennessee to its bloody end in New Jersey. He'd told it so often in New Mexico that he knew it better than his own life story. "Give me details," Primakov had insisted.

But he hadn't just asked about the story; he'd asked things Milo was not allowed to answer. Treasonable things. "You want my help, don't you?" So: the hierarchy of the Department of Tourism, the numbers of Tourists, the existence of Sal and his method of contact, the relationship between Homeland and the Company, and what the Company knew and didn't know about Yevgeny Primakov himself, which was very little.

Only after five days of this had the old man finally said, "I've got it now. Don't worry about a thing. Go in and tell them the truth. You will lie three times, and leave a few things out. I'll take care of the rest." What "the rest" consisted of was a mystery.

Did his faith falter? Certainly it did. It stumbled when he realized that he was being given the black hole treatment, and it nearly died when, that morning, John entered Room 5 with his briefcase full of terrible tricks. "Hello, John," Milo had said, but John wasn't such an amateur that he would be tricked into saying a thing. He placed his case on the floor, opened it to reveal the battery pack and wires and electrodes, and asked the two guards to please hold Milo's naked body down.

In truth, Milo's faith disappeared completely when the electric shocks were applied. They scrambled his nerves and his brain, so that he could feel no faith in anything outside that room. He could hear nothing when his body arched and shook on the cold floor. In the pauses between these sessions, he had wanted to scream the truth at them—no, he hadn't killed Grainger—that had been Lie Number One. But they never asked him a thing. The pauses were only for John to check Milo's blood pressure and recharge the machine.

The only thing that threatened to rekindle his faith made no sense to him. It was Lawrence, holding his ankles. As the pulses surged through his body, Lawrence let go of his feet and turned away, then began to vomit. John stopped his work. "Are you okay?"

"I—" Lawrence began, then climbed to his feet,

wiping his watery eyes. It hit him again, and he leaned against the wall, emptying his stomach.

John, unconcerned, reapplied the electrodes to Milo's nipples. Despite the pain, he felt a wash of relief, as if Lawrence's disgust might soon be shared by them all. He was wrong. Then Fitzhugh came in and showed him the photographs.

"You killed Grainger."

"Yes."

"Who else did you kill?"

"A Tourist. Tripplehorn."

"When did you kill Grainger? Before you killed the Tourist?"

"Before. No, after."

"Then?"

Milo coughed. "I took a walk into the woods."

"And then?"

"I was sick. Then I flew to Texas."

"Under Dolan?"

He nodded, now back on the sure ground of the awful truth: "I tried to get my wife and daughter to disappear with me," he said, telling Fitzhugh things he already knew. "They wouldn't—at least, Tina refused." He straightened with difficulty and looked at Fitzhugh. "I had no family, no job, and both the Company and Homeland were looking for me."

"A week followed," Fitzhugh said. "You disappeared."

"Albuquerque."

"What did you do in Albuquerque?"

"I *drank*. A lot. I drank until I realized it couldn't go on."

"Lots of people live their whole lives drunk. What makes you so special?"

"I don't want to live on the lam. Someday," he said, then stopped and began again. "I want to return to my family someday. If they'll have me. And the only way to make this happen was to turn myself in. Mercy of the court, and all that."

"Pretty far-fetched."

Milo didn't dispute this.

"That week in Albuquerque. Where did you stay?"

"The Red Roof Inn."

"Who with?"

"I was alone." Lie Number Two.

"Who'd you talk to? A week is a long time."

"Some waitresses—from Applebee's and Chili's. A bartender. But not about anything important." He paused. "I think I scared them."

They stared at each other, one clothed, one naked, and Fitzhugh finally said, "We're going to go through the whole thing, Milo. Sometimes it'll feel like a test of your memory, but it's not. It's a test of your truth." He snapped his fingers close to Milo's face. "You with me?"

Milo nodded, and the movement pained him.

"Two chairs," Fitzhugh said to no one in particular. The remaining doorman took it to be his order, and left. "John, keep yourself available."

John nodded curtly, lifted his case, and left looking like a blood-spattered encyclopedia salesman just after a sale.

The doorman returned with aluminum chairs and helped Weaver into one. Fitzhugh sat opposite, and when

Milo slipped to the side and fell off, he ordered a table as well. This helped, for Milo was able to collapse on its smooth white surface, streaking it with blood.

"Tell me how it started," said Fitzhugh.

That first day's debriefing lasted nearly five hours, chronicling the events lasting from the Fourth of July through the ill-fated Paris trip to Sunday, July 8, when Milo returned. He might have gotten the story out in less time, but Fitzhugh broke in often, questioning aspects of the tale. After the Tiger's suicide in Blackdale, Fitzhugh patted the table, annoyed that Weaver had slid down again, cheek against the blood-smeared Formica. "And this was a surprise, was it?"

"What?"

"Sam Roth, al-Abari, whatever. That he had been a Tourist."

Milo placed a soiled hand on the table, palm down, and rested his chin on it. "Of course it was a surprise."

"So let me get this straight. The Tiger—a professional with one of the world's stupider names—comes to this country solely in order to have a chat with you and then off himself."

Milo nodded into his knuckles.

"My question, I suppose, is: How did your file—your Tourism file, which should be resting in the upper stratosphere of top secret—how did this file end up in his hands?"

"Grainger gave it to him."

"Whoa!" Fitzhugh exclaimed, pushing back in his chair. "Let me be sure I heard you right. You're saying Tom was working *with* the Tiger? That's a big claim."

"I'm afraid it is."

"And Samuel Roth—you let him take his own life, right in front of you, when you knew the man was full of invaluable information."

"I didn't have a chance to save him. He was too quick."

"Maybe you didn't *want* a chance. Maybe you wanted him to die. Maybe—and this is interesting—maybe you *knew* he had the tooth cap and you reached into his mouth with your bare hands and pierced it for him. He was weak, after all, and your fingerprints were all over his face. It would've been a cinch for a strong man like you. Maybe you even did it on Grainger's orders—why not? You're blaming the poor man for everything else."

Milo answered with silence.

When they'd gotten to Grainger's briefing, the morning before he flew to Paris to test Angela Yates, Fitzhugh cut in again.

"So you *did* finally ask him about the Tiger."

"But he put me off," said Milo. "What was so hard about showing me the file? That's what I didn't understand. Not then. It took a long time before I got it. Too long."

"Got what?" Milo didn't answer, so Fitzhugh leaned back, crossed one knee over the other, and said, "I *know* he showed you the file, Milo. When you got back from Paris. So I hope you're not going to suggest that, because I hired Benjamin Michael Harris, I'm somehow connected to this. Poor recruitment skills still aren't a crime in this country."

Milo stared back, wondering if he should call this next part one of the lies or an omission. Sometimes the distinctions were baffling. "No. I knew that your involvement couldn't explain all the secrecy. Tom wasn't in league with you."

"Right. He was in league with the Tiger."

"Which is why it took so long to figure out," Milo explained. "Grainger gave me the file to put me off the scent; he wanted me sniffing in your direction."

Fitzhugh seemed satisfied with this.

It went on, Fitzhugh cutting in frequently for clarification, or to feign confusion. When Milo said he'd stayed on in Paris because of his suspicions, Fitzhugh said, "But you'd seen Einner's evidence. You saw the pictures."

"Yes, but what did they prove? Was she feeding Herbert Williams information, or was Williams feeding *her* information? Or was she being unwittingly pulled into someone else's game? Or was Williams spying on her to keep track of her investigation? Or was she actually guilty, and the man in the red beard just happened to be running both the Tiger *and* Angela, selling information to the Chinese? If so, who did he represent? It wasn't a single-person operation. Maybe the Chinese ran Herbert Williams as well."

"It's a goddamned Chinese puzzle."

"It sure is."

Fitzhugh answered his buzzing phone. He nodded to the caller, grunted a few times, then hung up. "Listen. It's been a long day, and you've done extremely well. We can delve deeper into the conspiracy tomorrow, okay?" He patted the table—his side, the clean side. "Excellent day's work."

"Then maybe I can get some food," said Milo.

"Sure. We'll also find you some clothes," Fitzhugh promised as he pushed back his chair and stood, smiling. "I really am pleased. And the details—they put a human face on all this miserable stuff. Tomorrow, I think, we should get a little more of that human face. Tina, for instance. Maybe we can discuss how you two are getting along. How things are with your darling stepdaughter."

"Daughter," Milo said.

"What?"

"Daughter. Not stepdaughter."

"Right." Fitzhugh raised his hands in an expression of defeat. "Whatever you say, Milo."

As his inquisitor left the room, Milo remembered Primakov's instructions. *Three lousy lies, Milo. You've lived your whole life lying, why change now?*

8

don't want you to be scared," Janet Simmons had whispered when Tina returned home. "We've located your grandfather-in-law, Milo's maternal grandfather, and I think it's only right you come along."

"That's impossible. They're all dead."

"Well, there's only one way to find out for sure."

Now, in a twin-engine Spirit Airlines flight from LaGuardia to Myrtle Beach, Tina held on to Stephanie, who had insisted on a window seat.

For her daughter, the sudden shift in agenda was exciting. An overnight trip to the beach, they'd called it. Christ, Little Miss was a good sport. How much had she suffered since two weeks ago, when, at Disney World, she'd woken to find a Homeland Security thug in her bedroom, looking for her father, who had suddenly disappeared? Why should she have to deal with any of this?

"How you doing, hon?"

Stephanie yawned into her cupped hand, staring at the leaden clouds. "I'm a little tired."

"Me, too."

"Are we really going on vacation?"

"Sort of. A short one. I just need to talk to someone. After that we can chill out on the beach. Sound all right?"

She shrugged in a way that worried Tina, but said, "Why's she coming?"

"You don't like Ms. Simmons?" Tina asked while, across the aisle, Simmons punched at her BlackBerry.

"I don't think she likes Dad."

A good sport, and smart to boot. Smarter, perhaps, than her mother.

Again, she wondered why she had agreed to this sudden trip. Did she really trust Special Agent Janet Simmons? Not entirely, but the carrot was too great: to finally meet a member of Milo's family. It was less about trust than curiosity. Really.

They landed a little before eight, and Tina roused Stephanie as they descended. From the window, they saw darkness marked by pinpoints of light that died out with the coastline. They weren't met by any special agents in the Myrtle Beach airport, and Simmons even had to take care of her own rental Taurus. She got driving directions from her BlackBerry.

It was Thursday evening, but it was also the height of summer, and they passed open-topped jeeps full of horny, shirtless college boys in knee-length shorts and stupid baseball caps, waving tallboys of Miller and Bud. Smiling at their attention, bottle-blondes gave them reasons to holler. Music spilled out from the clubs, though all they heard was the monotone *thumpa-thumpa* throb of dance music rhythms.

The Covenant Towers, nestled in a lush, wooded area on the north side of town, wasn't far from the beach, and it consisted of two long, five-story towers separated by grass and trees. "Pretty," Stephanie judged from her seat.

According to Deirdre Shamus, the pink-cheeked, perky director who had stayed beyond her regular shift to find out exactly why Homeland Security was interested in one of their residents, Covenant Towers was not a "nursing home," though medical facilities were on-site. "We encourage inde*pen*dence here."

William T. Perkins lived on the first floor of Tower Two, and Shamus brought them all the way to his door, greeting every resident they passed with overwrought enthusiasm. Finally, they stopped at number fourteen, a studio apartment. Shamus knocked, intoning, "Mr. Perkins! Your visitors have arrived!"

"Hold your fucking horses!" said an angry, rough voice.

Suddenly, Tina worried about Stephanie. What was behind this door? Her great-grandfather, maybe—she still couldn't quite believe that Milo wouldn't have known about him, and if he knew, he certainly would have told her. But what kind of man was he? She pulled Ms. Shamus aside. "Is there a place Stef can wait? I'm not sure I want her in there with us."

"Oh, Mr. Perkins is a firecracker, but he's—"

"Really," Tina insisted. "Like, a television room?"

"There's one down the hall.

"Thanks." To Simmons: "Be right back."

She walked Stephanie down three doors, and on the right found a room that held three sofas and a La-Z-Boy and seven elderly people staring at a rerun of *Murder, She Wrote*.

"Hon, you mind waiting here a little while?"

Stephanie waved Tina closer. "It *smells* here," she whispered.

"But can you take it? For me?"

Stephanie made a face to show just how bad it smelled, but nodded. "Not for long."

"Any problems, we'll be in room fourteen. Got it?"

On her walk back—number fourteen was now open, both Shamus and Simmons inside—Tina had a flash of paranoia. It was the kind of paranoia she'd lived with ever since Milo fled Disney World, ever since her own world had become populated by inquisitors and security agencies.

The paranoia spoke to her in Milo's voice: "This is how it goes down, Tina. Listen. They get you to send the child away. When you're done with your chat, the child's gone. Just vanished. The old people, they'll be on medication; they won't know what's happened. Simmons won't actually *tell* you she's got Stephanie. No. It'll all be inference and suggestion. But you'll be made to understand that she's got this document, a little thing. She'd like you to read it out for a camera. It'll say that your husband is a thief and a traitor and a murderer and please put him away for life. Do that, she'll say, and we might be able to track down dear Stephanie."

But it was just paranoia, she told herself. Just that.

She paused at the open door and looked in. Shamus was full of smiles, preparing to leave, and Simmons was settled on a chair beside a hairless, shriveled man in a wheelchair, his narrow face misshapen by age. His eyes were magnified by large, black-rimmed spectacles. The special agent beckoned her in, and the old man smiled, showing off yellowed dentures. "Meet William Perkins, Tina. William, this is Tina Weaver, your granddaughter-in-law."

Perkins's hand had been rising to shake hers, but it stopped. He looked at Simmons. "The *hell* are you talking about, woman?"

"Toodle-oo!" Shamus said as she left them to their privacy.

9

I t was hard for William T. Perkins to take. At first he claimed he had no grandson at all, then that he had none named Milo Weaver. His protestations were riddled with curses, and Tina got the impression that William T. Perkins had been a right bastard during his eighty-one years on the planet. He'd had two daughters, yes, but they'd left in their late teens without "so much as a single how-do-you-do."

"Your daughter Wilma, sir. She and her husband, Theodore, had Milo. Their son. Your grandson," Simmons pressed. Finally, as if these words represented incontrovertible evidence, Perkins slumped, admitting that, yes, he did have a single grandchild.

"Milo," he said and shook his head. "The kind of name you give a dog. That's what I always thought. But Ellen—she never gave a damn what I thought about anything. Neither of them did."

"Ellen?" said Tina.

"Trouble from the start. Did you know that in 1967, age seventeen, the girl took LSD? Seventeen! By eighteen, she was sleeping with some Cuban communist. José Something-or-other. Stopped shaving her legs, went completely off the board."

"Excuse me, Mr. Perkins," said Simmons. "We're not sure who Ellen is."

Perkins blinked his magnified eyes at her, confused a moment. "Ellen's my damned *daughter,* of course! You're asking about Milo's mom, aren't you?"

Tina inhaled audibly. Simmons said, "We thought Wilma was Milo's mother."

"*No,*" he corrected, exasperated. "Wilma took the baby—I guess he was four or five then. She and Theo couldn't have one of their own, and Ellen—Christ knows what she was up to then. She was all over the fucking map. Wilma wasn't talking to me either, but I learned from Jed Finkelstein—Wilma still deigned to talk to the *Jew*—that it was Ellen's idea. She was running around with some Germans by then. Midseventies, and the *police* were even after her. Guess she decided a kid would just slow her down. So she asked Wilma to take him." A whole-body shrug, then he slapped his knees. "Can you imagine? Just drop the baby off, and wash your hands of it!"

Simmons said, "Mr. Finkelstein—do you know where he is now?"

"Six feet under as of 1988."

"So, what was Ellen actually doing?"

"Reading Karl Marx. Reading Mao Zedong. Reading Joseph Goebbels, for all I know. In German."

"German?"

He nodded. "She was in Germany—the west one—when she gave up on motherhood. That girl always gave up on things once it got tough. I could've told her—being a parent is no walk in the park."

"But you didn't talk to her at all during this time."

"Now, that was *her* choice. Total silence for her flesh and blood while she went off with her Kraut comrades."

"Except her sister, Wilma."

"What?" Another moment of confusion.

"I said, *Except for Wilma*. She kept in touch with her sister."

"Yes." He sounded disappointed by this. Then he brightened as a memory hit him: "Finkelstein—you know what he told me? He was German, you know, and he read those newspapers. He said Ellen was picked up by the police. Put in jail. Know what for?"

Both women stared at him, expectant.

"Armed *robbery*. That's what for. She and her merry band of commies actually sank to robbing banks! Tell me, how does that help save the workers of the world?"

"Under her name?" Simmons asked sharply.

"Her name?"

"Was her name in the newspaper?"

He considered that, then shrugged. "Her picture was. Finkelstein didn't say—wait! Yes. It was some German name, wasn't it? Elsa? Yes, Elsa. Close to Ellen, but no cigar."

"What year?"

"Seventy-eight? No—nine. Nineteen seventy-nine."

"And when you learned this, did you contact anyone? The embassy? Did you try to get her out of jail?"

Silence returned like an unwelcome guest to William T. Perkins. He shook his head. "I didn't even tell Minnie. Ellen wouldn't have wanted that. She'd cut us off completely. Didn't *want* us to come to her rescue."

Tina wondered how many times in the last twenty-eight years this old man had repeated this to himself. His only justification for abandoning his daughter was weak, but it was all he had, like Tina's justifications for abandoning her husband.

When Simmons straightened, she looked to Tina like the consummate professional. Her face and tone were hard but not unbending. She was here for a reason, and she would only stay long enough to satisfy her needs. "Let me make sure I've got this right. Ellen leaves home and falls in with a bad crowd. Drug users, then political malcontents. Communists, anarchists, whatever. She travels a lot. Germany. In 1970 she has a baby. Milo. Around seventy-four or -five, she gives Milo to her sister, Wilma, and her husband, Theodore. They raise him as their own. Last you hear of Ellen is in 1979 when she's arrested for a bank robbery in Germany. Was she released?"

With the facts laid out so concisely, William Perkins seemed shocked by the story. In pieces, perhaps, it made sense, but lined up like this it became tragic, or simply unbelievable. The story was having the same numbing effect on Tina.

When Perkins spoke, it was a whisper: "I don't know

if she was released. Never checked. And she never contacted me."

Tina started to cry. It was embarrassing, but she had
no control anymore. Everything was turning up shit.

Perkins stared at her, shocked, then turned question-
ingly to Simmons, who shook her head for his silence.
She rubbed Tina's shaking back and whispered, "Don't
make any judgments yet, Tina. Maybe he doesn't even
know this. Remember: We're just trying to get to the
truth."

Tina nodded as if those words made sense, then
pulled herself together. She sniffed, wiped her nose and
eyes, and took a few breaths. "Sorry," she told Perkins.

"Not to worry, dear," he said and leaned forward to
pat her knee, which disturbed her. "We all need the wa-
terworks now and then. Doesn't make anyone a sissy."

"Thanks," Tina said, though she didn't know what
she was thanking him for.

"If we can," said Simmons, "let's get back to Milo."

Perkins sat straighter to show how much energy he
still had. "Shoot."

"Ellen disappears in seventy-nine, then six years
later, in 1985, Wilma and Theo die in a car crash. Is that
right?"

"Yes." No reflection, just fact.

"And then Milo was sent to an orphanage in Oxford,
North Carolina. Correct?"

He didn't answer at first. He frowned, ticking off his
memories beside what he'd heard, then shook his head.
"No. His father took him."

"Father?"

"You got it."

Tina stifled the next wave of weeping, but that only brought on nausea. Everything—*everything*—she knew about Milo's life was a lie. Which made a large chunk of her own life a lie. All facts were now up for debate.

"The father," said Simmons, as if she knew all about this—perhaps she did. "Now, he showed up just after the funeral, I suppose? Maybe at the funeral itself?"

"Wouldn't know exactly."

"Why not?"

"Because I didn't go to the funeral, did I?"

"Okay, so what happened?"

"I didn't want to go," he said. "Minnie kept at me. It was our daughter, for Christ's sake. Our daughter, who wouldn't speak to me when she was alive. So why should I talk to her when she's dead? And what about Milo? *He's our grandson,* she kept saying. *Who's going to take care of him now?* I said, *Minnie, we haven't been in his life for fifteen years; why do you think he wants us now?* But she didn't see things that way. And you could say she was right. Maybe." He held up his hands. "Okay, I can admit that now, but back then I couldn't. Back then I was stubborn," he said with a wink that brought bile to Tina's throat. "So she went. I stayed, and she went. Cooked for myself nearly a week before she came back. But she didn't have a kid on her arm, and she didn't even seem upset about it. I told her I didn't want to hear, but she told me anyway. That's how Minnie was."

"What did she tell you?" asked Tina, her sick body paralyzed.

"I'm getting to that," he said and sniffed. "Turns out

Milo's father had been watching the news, I guess, and he came to claim his son. That's according to Minnie. And get this—not only was he some absent father, but he was a *Ruskie*. Can you believe it?"

"No," Tina whispered. "I can't believe it."

Simmons had left doubt at the door. "What was this Russian's name?"

William T. Perkins squeezed his eyes shut and clasped his forehead, as if hit by a stroke, but it was only his way of dredging up memories that hadn't been touched in decades. He took away his hand, red-faced. "Yevy? No. Geny—yes. Yevgeny. That's what Minnie called him. Yevgeny."

"Last name?"

He exhaled a sigh, spittle white on his lips. "That, I don't remember."

Tina needed air. She stood, but the higher elevation couldn't help her get out of this cloud of sudden, brutal changes. Both looked at her as she settled down again and worked out the words: "Yevgeny Primakov?"

Simmons stared at her, shocked.

Perkins chewed his upper lip. "Could be. But my point is, this pinko pops up out of nowhere and talks Minnie into letting him have the boy."

Simmons cut in: "Didn't Milo have any say in it?"

"What do I know?" Then he conceded he might know something: "Way I see it, the boy didn't know Minnie, did he? This old woman shows up and wants him to come home with her. On the other hand, there's a Ruskie who *says* he's his father. You know how those Russians are. They'll convince you the sky's red. Probably filled his head with all kinds of stories of how wonderful Russia is and why doesn't he come enjoy it? If I was fifteen—God forbid—I'd go east with my daddy. Not head off with some old biddie obsessed with pot roasts and dusting." He paused. "That's what Minnie was like, if you must know."

"What about social services? Certainly they wouldn't just let this foreigner walk off with a fifteen-year-old boy. Would they?"

Perkins showed them his palms. "What do I know? Don't listen to me. I wasn't even there. But . . ." He wrinkled his brow. "These kinds of guys, they've got money, don't they? Money gets you everything."

"Not everything," Simmons insisted. "The only way Mr. Primakov would get him is the will. If your daughter put him in the will, giving him paternal rights."

Perkins shook his head. "Impossible. Wilma may not have liked us. She may have *hated* me. But she wouldn't've given the boy to some Russian. I didn't raise a stupid girl."

Simmons checked on Tina with a glance and a sly wink. She seemed satisfied by the talk, though Tina couldn't get her head on straight enough to understand what, exactly, she'd gotten. None of this helped Milo. Simmons said to Perkins, "Maybe you can tell me one last thing."

"Will if I can."

"Why did Wilma and Ellen hate you so much?"

Perkins blinked five times.

"What I mean is," she continued, as if running a job interview, "what exactly did you do to your daughters?"

Silence, then a long exhale that could have meant that the old man was preparing to bare his soul and sins to these strangers. It didn't mean that. His voice was suddenly young and full of venom as he pointed at the door: "Get out of my fucking home!"

As they left, Tina knew that she would tell Simmons everything. Milo was a liar, and at that moment she hated him.

It wasn't until they picked up Stephanie from the television room full of doting old people that she realized something else. "Oh, Christ."

"What?" said Simmons.

She looked into the special agent's eyes. "When we got back from Venice, Milo came with me to take care of Stephanie's birth records in Boston. He begged me to let him give her a middle name. I hadn't planned on one, didn't really care, and it seemed to mean a lot to him."

"What's her middle name?"

"Ellen."

10

About a half hour before they arrived, two doormen removed the Chinese takeout boxes, replaced his water bottle, and cleaned blood off the table, chair, and floor. It was a relief of sorts, because over the night, the stink of old kung pao and sweat had kept him on the edge of nausea.

Then Fitzhugh stepped inside, followed by Simmons. Milo hadn't seen her since Disney World, hadn't talked to her since Blackdale. She looked tired, as if she, too, had spent a sleepless night caged with her own stink.

Remember, Yevgeny had said, *Simmons is your salvation, but don't treat her that way.*

So Milo crossed his arms over his chest. "I'm not talking to her."

Simmons produced a smile. "Nice to see you, too."

Fitzhugh wasn't bothering with smiles. "Milo, it's not up to me, and it's not up to you."

"You don't look well," said Simmons.

Milo's left eye was swollen and purple, his lower lip broken, and one of his nostrils ringed with blood. The worst bruises were under his orange jumpsuit. "I keep walking into walls."

"So I see."

Before Fitzhugh could reach for it, she had taken his chair. He asked the doorman for another. They waited. During that minute and a half of silence, Simmons stared hard at Milo, and Milo returned the gaze without blinking.

When the chair arrived, Fitzhugh settled down and said, "Remember what we said before, Milo. About classified topics."

Simmons frowned.

"I remember," said Milo.

"Good," said Fitzhugh. "There's something I want to discuss first." He reached into his jacket pocket, but Simmons placed a hand on his lapel.

"Not yet, Terence," she said, then let go. "I want the story first."

"What's that?" Milo sat up. "What's he got in there?"

Fitzhugh took out his hand again, empty. "Don't worry about it, Milo. The story first. Okay? From where we left off."

Milo looked at him.

"You were just about to head to Disney World," Simmons said, proving that she'd at least been given an interview summary from yesterday. She opened her hands like a well-trained interviewer. "I have to say, your last-minute escape from there was pretty snappy. Nicely done."

"Is she going to talk like this the whole time?" Milo put the question to Fitzhugh, who shrugged.

"Just talk," said Simmons. "If I think sarcasm's appropriate, I'll use it."

"Yes," Fitzhugh agreed. "Get on with it." To Simmons: "And try to temper the sarcasm, okay?"

He told the story of Disney World as it had happened, with a single omission: Yevgeny Primakov's appearance at Space Mountain. Though he had lied to Tina about so much, he hadn't lied about the purpose of the old man's visit—he had wanted to know what had happened to Angela Yates.

It was easy to leave out that meeting, because it had no bearing on the cause-and-effect that is the one concern of interrogators the world over. This ease allowed him to observe how the two people across from him acted.

Fitzhugh sat rigid, straighter than he had the day before. Whereas yesterday he had seemed as if he had all the time in the world, today he was in a rush, as if the contents of the interview no longer mattered. Occasionally, he would say, "Yeah, yeah. We already know that."

Each time, though, Simmons would cut in: "Maybe I don't, Terence. You know how uninformed Homeland is." Then, to Milo: "Please. Go on." She wanted to know everything.

So Milo obliged. He told his tale in a slow, purposeful way, leaving no detail untouched. He even mentioned the color of Einner's Renault, to which Simmons said, "It was a nice car, was it?"

"This agent has good taste."

Later in the day, when Weaver finally got to his meeting with Ugrimov, Simmons cut in again and said to Fitzhugh: "This Ugrimov. Do we have him on our arrest lists?"

Fitzhugh shrugged. "I don't know anything about the guy. Milo?"

"No," said Milo. "He's never broken a law in the United States. He can come and go as he pleases, but I don't think he ever does."

Simmons nodded, then placed both her hands flat on the table. "Anyway, we'll get to this in a little bit, but one thing's been nagging at me. After making all these connections, you went and killed Tom Grainger, right?"

"Right."

"In a fit of anger?"

"Something like that."

"I don't buy it."

Milo stared at her. "I'd been through a lot, Janet. You never know how you're going to react."

"And, by killing your boss, you've obliterated the only evidence that might have proven at least some small part of your story."

"I never claimed to be a genius."

The silence was broken by Janet Simmons's ringing phone. She looked at the screen, then walked to the corner, a finger pressed against her free ear as she answered it. Both men watched. She said, "Yes. Wait a minute. Slow down. What? Yeah—I mean, no. I didn't do that.

Believe me, I had nothing to do with it. No—don't do that. Don't touch anything until I'm there. Got it? I'll be"—she glanced back at them—"a half hour, forty-five minutes. Just wait, okay? See you then."

She snapped her phone shut. "I've got to go right now."

Both men blinked.

"Can we pick this up again tomorrow?"

Milo didn't bother answering, but Fitzhugh stood, muttering, "I guess so."

Simmons looked around the interview room. "And I want him out of here."

"What?" said Fitzhugh.

"I've cleared a solitary cell at the MCC. I want him moved there by the morning."

MCC was the Metropolitan Correctional Center, a pretrial holding facility next to Foley Square in Lower Manhattan.

"Why?" asked Milo.

"Yes," said Fitzhugh, annoyed. "Why?"

She looked at Fitzhugh and spoke as if she were voicing a threat: "Because I want to be able to talk to him in a place you don't control completely."

The air seemed to escape the room as she, miraculously, held both their gazes. Then she left.

Milo said, "Looks to me like Ms. Simmons doesn't trust the CIA."

"Well, fuck her," said Fitzhugh. "She doesn't tell me when my own interrogation ends." He shoved a thumb over his shoulder. "You know why she's hot and bothered now, don't you?"

Milo shook his head.

"We've got a Russian passport with your face on it, under the name Mikhail Yevgenovich Vlastov."

Milo looked taken aback by that, because he was. Whatever plan Yevgeny had hatched, exposing his secret life couldn't be part of it. "Where'd you get it?"

"That doesn't concern you."

"It's a forgery."

"I'm afraid not, Milo. Not even the Company makes them this good."

"So what's it supposed to mean?"

Fitzhugh reached again into his jacket and took out some folded sheets. He flattened them on the table. Milo didn't bother looking at them; instead, he watched the old man's eyes. "What's that?" he said flatly.

"Intel. Compromised intel that ended up in Russian hands. Intel you had access to immediately before it was compromised."

Slowly, Milo's gaze moved from Fitzhugh's eyes to the papers. The first one read:

Moscow, Russian Federation
Case: S09-2034-2B (Tourism)

Intel 1: (ref. Alexander) Acquired Bulgarian embassy tapes (ref. Op. Angelhead) from Denistov (attaché) and will forward via U.S. embassy. 11/9/99

Intel 2: (ref. Handel) Recovered items from FSB agent (Sergei Arensky), deceased, include . . . copy

of tapes from Bulgarian embassy (ref. Op. Angelhead). 11/13/99

He knew from the concise style that Harry Lynch had
put this together. He really was an excellent Travel
Agent. In 1999, touring under the name Charles Alexander, Milo had acquired some secret embassy tapes from
the Bulgarian embassy in Moscow. The acquisition was
called Operation Angelhead. Four days later, another
Tourist—Handel—had come across a dead FSB agent,
or killed him, and upon his body found a copy of the
Angelhead tapes. Milo didn't know how the copy had
made it to the Russian.

He flipped through the rest, pausing a moment longer on the third one, which read:

Venice, Italy
Case: S09-9283-3A (Tourism)

Intel 1: (ref. Alexander) Track Franklin Dawdle,
under suspicion of fiscal fraud in amount of
3,000,000 USD. 9/10/01

Intel 2: (ref. Elliot) FSB source (VIKTOR) verifies Russian knowledge of the missing 3,000,000
via Dawdle, Frank, and the failed operation to
recover in Venice. 10/8/01

Fitzhugh read it upside down. "Yes, your last operation even made it to Moscow."

Milo turned the sheets over. "Are you really that

desperate, Terence? You can put a sheet like that together for any field agent. Information leaks. Did you
check how many pieces of intel ended up in French or
Spanish or British hands? Just as many, I'll wager."

"We don't have a French or Spanish or British passport with your face on it."

That was when Milo knew—Fitzhugh didn't care
about his confession anymore. Murder was small fish
when compared to being a double agent. It was the
kind of catch that would add a gold star to Fitzhugh's
record, and put Milo into either a lifetime of solitary or
a quick grave.

"Who gave it to you?"

Fitzhugh shook his head. "We're not telling."

No—Fitzhugh had no idea who had given it to him.
Milo had a pretty good idea, though, and it threatened
to atomize whatever faith he had left.

11

Tina had awakened that morning in Myrtle Beach and taken Stephanie out to the shore feeling lighter, almost forgetting about the tears from last night's poor sleep. She felt, she realized as she settled on a rented lounge chair and watched her daughter splash in the Atlantic, like a cuckolded wife, but the other woman couldn't be surveilled or attacked because the other woman was an entire history. It was not entirely unlike when she, in junior high school, started reading the alternate histories of her own country, finding out that Pocahontas had become a pawn in colonial power struggles and, after a trip to London with John Rolfe, died of either pneumonia or tuberculosis on the voyage back.

But where those broken national myths had filled her with youthful self-righteousness and indignation, her husband's broken myths humiliated her, made her feel stupid. The only smart thing she'd done, she realized, was deny Milo his last request that they disappear with him.

Her feelings intensified when they landed at LaGuardia, then took the airport shuttle into Brooklyn. The streets were claustrophobic, and each familiar storefront was another accusation from her old life. That was how she was beginning to see her life: old and new. The old life was wonderful because of its ignorance; the new life was terrible because of its knowledge.

Their bags weighed a ton as she followed Stephanie, who rattled the apartment keys as she ran up the stairs. She reached the door while Tina was still on the second landing, opened it, then came out again and pressed her nose through the guardrail. "Mom?"

"What, honey?" she asked, hiking the bags up onto her shoulder.

"Somebody made a big mess. Is Dad home?"

At first, when she dropped the bags and galloped that last flight, she was consumed by an inexplicable surge of hope. Lies or not, Milo had come home. Then she saw that the drawers in the table by the entrance had been pulled out and turned over, leaving a pile of loose change, bus tickets, takeout menus, and keys on the floor. The mirror over the table had been taken down and turned to face the wall, and the loose backing paper had been ripped off.

She told Stephanie to wait in the hall while she examined each room. Destruction, as if an elephant had been mistakenly let in. She even thought: *Come on, Tina, an elephant can't get up those stairs*. She realized she was getting hysterical.

So she called the number Simmons had left and listened to her calm voice insisting that this wasn't her doing, and she would be right over, and please don't touch anything.

"Don't touch anything," Tina called as she hung up, but Stephanie wasn't in the hall. "Little Miss? Where are you?"

"In the *bath*room," came the irritable answer.

How much more of this could Stephanie take? How much could *she* take? She hadn't told Stef about the sudden expansion of her family, the addition of a great-grandfather and a new grandfather she'd met in Disney World, but Stephanie was nobody's fool. In the hotel room this morning she'd started asking, "Who were you talking to in the old people's home?"

Tina, unable to keep lying to her own daughter, just said, "Someone who might know something about your daddy."

"Something to help him?" Despite having never been told, she knew Milo was in some kind of trouble.

"Something like that."

Tina took her out for Cokes at Sergio's, a pizza joint, and called Patrick. He sounded sober and clearheaded, so she asked him to come over.

He arrived before Simmons, and together the three of them returned to the apartment. The least-demolished room was Stephanie's, so they let her sort through her things while Tina told Patrick everything. Absolutely everything. By the time Simmons arrived, Patrick was in a state. Even during the height of his jealousy, he'd suspected none of this. Now he had to comfort Tina, who kept breaking down in tears. When Simmons stepped through the door, he turned on her.

"Don't tell us you didn't do it, okay? Because we know you did. Who else would've done it?"

Simmons ignored the blustering man and ranged through the apartment, stopping to smile and say hello to Stephanie, then took photos of each room with a little Canon. She stood in corners for multiple angles and crouched beside the disassembled television, the shattered vases (gifts, Tina explained, from her parents), the sliced sofa cushions, the small broken strongbox that had only held some family jewelry, though none of it had been taken.

"Anything missing?" Simmons asked again.

"Nothing." That, in itself, was depressing enough—after all this mess, no one had deemed her possessions worthy of stealing.

"Okay." Simmons straightened. "I've documented it all. Now it's time to clean up."

They got to work with broom and dustpan and Hefty bags Simmons had picked up from a convenience store. While she was squatting beside a broken mirror, picking up dozens of partial reflections of herself, she said, "Tina?" in her most friendly voice.

Tina was behind the television, trying to screw the rear panel back on. "Yeah?"

"You said some Company people came a few days ago. Two days before I visited. Remember?"

"Yeah."

Simmons walked over to the television, ignoring Patrick's accusing stare as he swept up shards of glass and pottery. "How do you know they were Company?"

Tina let the screwdriver drop to the floor and wiped her forehead with her wrist. "What do you mean?"

"Did they say they were Company, or did you just assume it?"

"They told me."

"Show you any ID?"

Tina thought about that, then nodded. "At the door, yes. One was Jim Pearson, the other was . . . Max Something. I can't remember his last name. Something Polish, I think."

"What did they ask you about?"

"You know what they asked about, Special Agent."

"No, actually. I don't."

Tina came out from behind the television while Patrick looked for the best defiant pose. By the time Tina settled on the sofa, he had found it: He moved behind her, a hand on each shoulder. "Do you really need to interrogate her again?"

"Maybe," Simmons said. She took the chair across from the sofa, the same place she'd sat during their first interview here. "Tina, it may be nothing, but I'd really like to know what kinds of questions they asked."

"You think they're the ones who did this?"

"Maybe, yes."

Tina thought about it. "Well, they started with the usual. Where was Milo? And they wanted to know what Milo had told me in Austin."

"When he asked you to leave with him," Simmons said encouragingly.

Tina nodded. "I told them the other Company people had already been through that—your people, too—but they said maybe I'd forgotten something that would help them. They were actually pretty nice about it all. Like high school career counselors. One of them—Jim Pearson—he went down a list of items to see if anything rang a bell for me."

"He had a list?"

"In a little spiral notebook. Names, mostly. Names of people I didn't know. Except one."

"Which one?"

"Ugrimov. Roman Ugrimov. You know, the Russian I told you about, from Venice. I had no idea why they'd bring him up now, so I dutifully said that I'd met him once, and that he'd killed a girl and I didn't like him. They asked when, I said 2001, and they said they didn't need to hear about it." Tina shrugged.

"What other names?"

"Foreign names, mostly. Rolf . . . Winter, or something like that."

"Vinterberg?"

"Yeah. And some, I guess, Scottish name. Fitzhugh."

"Terence Fitzhugh?"

Again, Tina nodded. The look on Simmons's face encouraged her to go on. "When I said I didn't know anything about him, who he was or otherwise, they didn't believe me. I don't know why. It was all right that I didn't know Vinterberg, but Fitzhugh?" She shook her head. "That, they didn't buy. They said things like, *Milo didn't tell you anything about Fitzhugh and some money?* I said no. They kept pushing. At one point, Jim

Pearson said, *What about Fitzhugh in Geneva, with the minister of*— But Max hit him in the arm and he never got around to finishing the question. Finally, once they saw I was really annoyed, they packed up their shit and left."

While she'd been talking, Simmons had again produced her BlackBerry. She was typing. "Jim Pearson and Max . . ."

"I don't know."

"But they had Company IDs."

"Yeah. They looked fine to me. I know Milo's pretty well—it keeps ending up in the wash."

"And they never said why they were asking about Fitzhugh?"

Tina shook her head. "I got the feeling Max thought they were saying too much." She paused. "You really think those are the guys who made this mess? They annoyed me, but I wouldn't expect this from them."

"Like I said, Tina. It wasn't Homeland. I'd have heard about it."

"And the Company?"

"Maybe, but I haven't heard anything from them either."

Tina grinned. "You're still in counseling, right?"

"Exactly." Simmons got to her feet. "Okay, let's get this place finished, and if you come across something that doesn't belong here, let me know."

They spent the next three hours reassembling electronics, picking up broken pictures, and restuffing cushions. It was frustrating work for all involved, and halfway through it, Patrick opened a bottle of vodka for general use. Simmons declined with thanks, but Tina poured herself a tall shot and drank it down in one go. Stephanie watched all of this wryly. She spent most of the time in her own room, repositioning dolls that had been taken from their proper homes. Around seven, as they were finishing, she came out of her room holding a cigarette lighter that advertised a Washington D.C., bar, the Round Robin, at 1401 Pennsylvania Avenue NW.

"How about that," said Simmons, slipping on a latex glove and turning it over in her hand.

"What is it?" asked Tina, a little bubble of adrenaline rising at the sight of physical evidence.

"Strange, is what it is." Simmons held it up to the light. "I know the place—big politicians' haunt. It might be nothing though."

"That's pretty bad tradecraft," said Tina. "Leaving something behind."

Simmons slipped the lighter into a ziplock bag and pocketed it. "You'd be surprised just how lousy most agents are."

"I wouldn't be," Patrick assured them all, and Tina almost smiled—the poor man was feeling left out.

As she prepared to go, Simmons's phone rang. She took it into the kitchen. Tina caught a momentary, uncharacteristic sound of glee from the special agent's lips. "You're kidding! *Here?* Perfect."

When she emerged from the kitchen, though, she was all business again, and after thanking Patrick for his help she pulled Tina into the hall and told her that, in the morning, she'd be meeting with Yevgeny Primakov. Tina's feet went cold. "He's in New York?"

"He'll be at the UN headquarters. It's a nine o'clock appointment. Do you want to meet him?"

Tina considered it, then shook her head. "I need to go to the library, take care of stuff I've let slip." She paused, knowing that Simmons could see through the lie—the truth was that she was terrified. "But maybe later, you could . . . I don't know . . ."

"I'll give you a full report. Sound all right?"

"Not really," said Tina, "but it'll have to do."

12

Fitzhugh ate at the same Chinese restaurant on Thirty-third they'd ordered Weaver's takeout from. He chose a table near the back to avoid interruptions, and to ponder the Nexcel message he'd received from Sal.

```
J Simmons sent request at 6:15 PM to
DHS acting director requesting li-
cense to access bank and phone rec-
ords of Terence A Fitzhugh. At present,
request is under consideration.
```

Over Szechuan chicken, he tried to think through this. It proved what he'd been sensing, that Simmons didn't trust him at all. It was in her tone, the entire way she dealt with him. Interagency rivalries were one thing, but this level of tension . . . she treated him as if he were the enemy. And now, she was asking Homeland's director for access to his records.

So he'd nipped it in the bud with a phone call. The request for access, he had been assured, would be denied.

Even so, he felt himself on the defensive, and that wasn't what he needed now. He should be leading the attack in order to control all possible damage by putting away Milo Weaver and ending this investigation.

The passport. That was his trump card. He still didn't know who had sent it. Forensics had only produced a single white hair: Caucasian male, aged fifty to eighty, a diet high in protein—but that described half of the intelligence world. He no longer cared who his benefactor was; his only concern was to wrap up this case before Simmons found a way to ruin all their hard work.

His thoughts were interrupted by a stranger who approached and said in French, "It's been so long," reaching out his hand to shake. Fitzhugh, stuck in the mental rhythms of his worries, was caught off guard. Staring up at the handsome, sixty-something face under wavy white hair, he took the heavy hand. Where did he know this man from?

"Excuse me," Fitzhugh said as they shook. There was something familiar in the face, but he wasn't sure. "Do I know you?"

The man's smile faded, and he switched to English—not his native language, but spoken in a kind of easy swing. "Oh. Bernard, right?"

Fitzhugh shook his head. "You have the wrong person. I'm sorry."

The man held up his hands, palms out. "No, my mistake. Sorry to bother you."

The man walked off, and though Fitzhugh expected him to return to a table, he actually left through the front door. He'd been so convinced Fitzhugh was his friend Bernard that he had come in from the street. French? No—in his accent he'd caught Slavic traces. Czech?

Eleven blocks uptown, on the twenty-third floor of the Grand Hyatt, Simmons was sitting on her stripped bed, typing queries into the Homeland database, looking for the record of a Company agent, Jim Pearson. It came up empty. She tried variations on the name, then sent a message to Matthew, her plant inside Tourism, asking him to check the Langley computers, in case Jim Pearson's records hadn't made the trip to Homeland.

While waiting for the answer, she looked for whatever she could find on Yevgeny Primakov. In the morning, she would meet him in the lobby of the UN's General Assembly building, which, as George had put it, was "un-fucking-believable."

Unbelievable, indeed. From what she read on the United Nations site, Yevgeny Primakov worked in the financial section of the Military Staff Committee of the Security Council, with an office in Brussels. An accountant? She doubted that. Was his presence in New York a beautiful coincidence? Or had he made sure to be there in case he was called upon by the United States to answer questions about his son?

She accessed a secure section of the Homeland site, and her searches turned up a skeletal history of Yevgeny

Aleksandrovich Primakov, onetime colonel. He was inducted into the KGB in 1959, and in the midsixties began his travels. Known destinations: Egypt, Jordan, West and East Germany, France, and England. When the KGB morphed into the FSB after the fall of the Soviet Union, Primakov stayed on, heading a department of military counterintelligence until 2000, when he retired and began a new career with the United Nations.

They had little more on him, though in 2002 the U.S. representative to the UN requested a background check on Primakov. No reason given, and the resulting report was not available.

During the last years, Homeland had been absorbing FBI files connected to terrorism, past and present. It was within this clerical subsection that she found a single sheet on Ellen Perkins, who was convicted in absentia for being an accomplice in two crimes: the 1968 robbery of a branch of the Harris Bank in Chicago, and, in early 1969, the attempted arson of the Milwaukee police's District Seven headquarters. Last spotted in Oakland, California, before disappearing completely.

Given what William Perkins had told her about Ellen—robbing banks in Germany—she was surprised to find nothing else under her name, or under Elsa Perkins. It took a Google search—*Elsa Perkins Germany armed robbery*—to come across a site dedicated to the history of seventies' German terrorist groups. Baader-Meinhof, the Red Army Faction, the Socialist Patients' Collective, and the Movement 2 June, which counted among its members one Elsa Perkins, American. According to the webmaster,

Perkins joined the Movement 2 June in October 1972. By most estimates, she was seduced into the Movement by the charismatic Fritz Teufel. She lasted longer than most members, but was arrested in 1979 and sent to Stuttgart-Stammheim Prison. In December of that same year, she committed suicide in her cell.

Milo's door opened. Three doormen stepped in, and he noticed that the swelling around Lawrence's eye was beginning to subside. It was Lawrence who held the manacles, which he attached to Milo's wrists and ankles; then the three of them went with their shuffling prisoner down the corridor to the elevators, where they used a special keycard to access the parking lot on the third underground floor.

They took Milo to a white van not unlike armored police vans seen in movies. In the rear, two steel benches stretched its length, punctured by holes through which Lawrence threaded the chains. Once they were out on the street, heading south, Milo could see through the tinted rear window that it was nighttime, and asked if it was Friday or Saturday. Lawrence, sitting across from him, checked his watch. "Still Friday, just about."

"And the eye? Looks better."

Lawrence touched it. "I'll survive."

In Lower Manhattan, the van arrived at Foley Square, took a side street around the Metropolitan Correctional Center, then descended into the secure underground lot. The driver showed his identification and prisoner-transfer order to the guards, who raised the gate and let them through. They parked beside a steel elevator and waited until the doors had opened before unlocking Milo and moving him to it.

"They have room service here?" Milo asked innocently.

The two other doormen stared uncomprehendingly at him, but Lawrence smiled. "Private cells, at least."

"Like I didn't have that before."

"Come on, man."

Simmons's mail program bleeped for her attention, and she read Matthew's reply. The last record of a Company agent by the name of Jim Pearson was in 1998, when the forty-year-old agent with that name died of a congenital heart defect.

So Jim Pearson wasn't a Company agent—no real surprise there. All the ruse took was a fake badge. There was also no Jim Pearson in Homeland. What, really, did she have? Of course: the cigarette lighter that Stephanie had found in her room. Round Robin. A haunt of Washington politicians and their entourages.

She opened two browser windows, one to the House of Representatives, one to the U.S. Senate. In each she found the personnel directories and typed *Jim Pearson*. The House gave up nothing, but the Senate had a single Jim Pearson, who worked as an "assistant scheduler" to Minnesota Republican Nathan Irwin. There was no photograph, just his name. She followed links to Nathan Irwin's page and studied the list of twenty aides in his employ. There again was Jim Pearson, and a few lines above him was Maximilian Grzybowski, "legislative assistant." One of those unfamiliar Polish names that could easily slip a harried woman's mind.

At ten, when his phone rang, Fitzhugh was back at the Mansfield Hotel. He'd brought a bottle of scotch back to the room, but tried not to drink too much of it. "Carlos?" said the senator. His voice sounded tense.

Fitzhugh cleared his throat. "It's taken care of?"

A pause. "There never was a request."

"Wait a minute. Say that again."

"I'm saying, Carlos, that you made me look like a fool. I'm talking to the top man, and when he calls me back he tells me no one ever asked anything about you. Nothing. You may not understand this, but you only get a few favors from these kinds of people. I just wasted one of mine."

"If there was nothing," Fitzhugh began, but the senator had already hung up.

He felt like he was going to be sick. Not because of Nathan Irwin's anger—he'd worked in Washington long enough to know a senator's anger lasts only until the next good deed you do for him. What upset him was that Sal's message, sent through the proper channels, had been wrong. For the past six years, Sal had been Tourism's best source inside Homeland Security. His information was never contradicted. This time he'd made a mistake.

Or perhaps, Fitzhugh worried as he plunged deeper into the scotch, Homeland had uncovered Sal, and was now using him to feed disinformation into Tourism. Was that possible?

He set his scotch aside and dragged out his laptop. It took a moment to power it up and access the Nexcel account, but as soon as he did he drafted a quick e-mail to Sal:

```
Information proved wrong. Is it a mis-
take, or were plans changed? Are you
compromised?
```

He sent it off with a hard click on the trackpad button, only afterward realizing his mistake. If Sal were compromised, then Homeland would be watching his account. What would they do? Write back in his name? Probably. What reply, then, would prove he was compromised? That is, what would Homeland want him to believe?

13

The taxi worked its way through the morning traffic up First Avenue, then let her off on Raoul Wallenberg Walk. She hurried across the lawn, passing plainclothes security men and New York troopers. It was nearly nine. She cut through a long line of tourists that led to metal detectors and showed her Homeland ID to a Vietnamese guard. He passed her to two uniformed women who patted her down and went over every inch of her body with a handheld explosive detector.

The United Nations General Assembly building has a long, sixties-modern lobby, littered with paintings of past secretaries general, low leather couches, and placards with slogans and lists of upcoming events. Simmons found a spot beneath the suspended Foucault pendulum, knowing that Yevgeny Primakov would have to come to her, since she didn't have a photo of him. He apparently had one of her—this meeting place, according to Orbach, had been his idea.

As she stood there, looking expectant, the faces of the world passed by in the form of assistants and interns from all the UN countries. She remembered her last visit, not long after her divorce, when she thought that there was something special about this place. The warmth of internationalism had filled her, just briefly, and she'd even considered working for this amalgam of nations. Like most Americans, though, in the years that followed she heard more about its failures than its successes, and when the Department of Homeland Security came calling, and the recruiter described how this new department wouldn't be hogtied by the red tape that plagued so many institutions, she succumbed to her innate patriotism.

"Look up," said an old man, smiling. His accent was Russian.

She peered up at the gold-plated sphere that swung directly from a wire.

"It's a nice thing to have around," said Primakov, clasping his hands behind his back and staring up with her. "It's the physical evidence that the planet rotates, despite how things feel where we're standing. It reminds us that what our eyes see and our senses feel isn't always the complete truth."

She stared at the mechanism a moment longer, just for politeness, then stuck out a hand. "I'm Janet Simmons, Homeland Security."

Instead of shaking, he brought her knuckles to his mouth; he kissed them. "Yevgeny Aleksandrovich Primakov of the United Nations, at your service."

When he let her hand go, she slipped it into her blazer pocket. "I wanted to ask about your son, Milo Weaver."

"Milo Weaver?" He paused. "I have two wonderful daughters—around your age, I believe. A pediatric surgeon in Berlin and a litigator in London. But a son?" He shook his head, smiling. "No son."

"I'm talking about the son you had with Ellen Perkins in 1970."

His broad, confident smile didn't falter. "Are you hungry? I missed my breakfast, which in America is a crime. The diner breakfast is America's great contribution to world cuisine."

Simmons nearly laughed. "Sure. Let's get some breakfast."

Together, they crossed the lawn again, Primakov sometimes nodding at others heading in the opposite direction, toting briefcases. He was in his element, a man at ease with his position in the world, even under the threat of a Homeland Security agent dredging up old secrets. He had a single nervous gesture, though: He sometimes raised a fleshy finger to his cheek and swiped at it, as if ushering away a fly. Otherwise, he was all old-world elegance in his tailored gray suit, blue tie, and perfectly fitting dentures.

The diner he'd promised turned out to be an overpriced nouveau-American restaurant with a separate breakfast menu. When the hostess offered a window seat, Primakov licked his lips, swatted at his cheek, and suggested a booth in the rear of the restaurant.

He ordered the "Hungry Man" plate of scrambled eggs, toast, sausage, ham, and home fries, while Simmons stuck with coffee. Playfully, he accused her of trying to lose weight, "which is baffling, because you have a perfect figure, Ms. Simmons. If anything, you should add a few kilos."

She wondered when a man had last talked to her this way. Not in a while. She called over the waitress and ordered an English muffin.

Before the food came, they went through some of Primakov's particulars. He openly admitted to having risen to the rank of colonel in the KGB, staying on during its transformation into the FSB. By the midnineties, though, he had become disillusioned. "We kill our own journalists, you know that?"

"I've heard."

He shook his head. "It's a pity. But from inside, there's little you can do about it. So I considered my options and in 2000, the new millennium, decided to work for the world at large, rather than my own nation's petty interests."

"Sounds commendable," she said, remembering her own brief thoughts in that direction. "But the UN must be frustrating."

He raised his bushy brows and conceded with a nod that this was true. "The failures are what reach your newspapers. The successes—those are just boring, aren't they?"

The waitress returned with two warm plates. Once

the old man had begun eating, Simmons said, "I want you to tell me about it. I'm not interested in digging up dirt. I just want to know who Milo Weaver really is."

Chewing, Primakov stared at her. "Right. That Milo person you mentioned."

She gave him the most endearing a smile she knew how to make. "Yevgeny. Please. Let's start with Ellen Perkins."

Primakov looked at her, then at his food, and then, with an exaggerated shrug, set down his utensils. "Ellen Perkins?"

"Yes. Tell me about her."

The old man flicked something from his lapel—a woman's hair, it looked like—then snatched at his cheek. "Because you're so charming and beautiful, I have no choice. Russian men are like that. We're too romantic for our own good."

One more endearing smile. "I appreciate it, Yevgeny."

So he began.

"Ellen was special. You have to know that first of all. Milo's mother wasn't just another pretty face, as you say in America. In fact, she wasn't really that beautiful, physically. In the sixties, the revolutionary cells of the world were full of long-haired angels. Hippies who stopped believing in peace, though they still believed in love. Most of them had no real conception of what they were doing. Like Ellen, they were from broken homes. They just wanted a new family. If they had to die, so be it. At least they'd die for a reason, unlike those poor boys in Vietnam." He used his fork to point at Simmons. "Ellen, though—she saw through the romance. She was an intellectual convert."

"Where did you meet?"

"Jordan. One of Arafat's training camps. She'd spent the last few years being radicalized in America, and when I met her she was inspired by the PLO and the Black Panthers. She was a bit ahead of her time, you see. At that time—sixty-seven—there was no one in America she could talk to. So, with a couple of equally disenfranchised friends, she showed up in Jordan. She met Arafat himself, as well as me. She was far more impressed by Arafat."

He paused, and Simmons realized she was supposed to fill in the silence. "What were you doing there?"

"Spreading international peace, of course!" A wry smile. "The KGB wanted to know how much money to spend on these fighters, and who we could recruit. We didn't really care about the Palestinians; we just wanted to stick a thorn in America's great Middle Eastern ally, Israel."

"Ellen Perkins became a KGB asset?"

He swiped at his cheek. "That was the plan, wasn't it? But Ellen saw right through me. She saw that I didn't care as much about world revolution as I did about keeping my job. The more names I added to my roster of friendly warriors, the more secure my pension became. She saw that. She called me a hypocrite!" He shook his head. "I'm not kidding. She started listing the atrocities the Soviet Union had committed. The Ukraine famine, trying to starve West Berlin, Hungary in fifty-six. What could I say? I dismissed the Ukraine as a madman's mistake—Stalin's, that is. For Berlin and Hungary, I talked up counterrevolutionaries from the West, but Ellen had no time for my excuses. *Excuses*—that's what she called them."

"So she wouldn't work with you," Simmons said, thinking she understood.

"Quite the contrary! As I said, Ellen was smart. Jordan was just foreplay. If you understand my meaning. Her little ragtag group would learn to shoot and blow things up, but afterward they would need support. At the time, Moscow was generous. She wanted to use me. I, on the other hand, was failing in my duty already. You see, I'd fallen in love with her. She was ferocious."

Simmons nodded, as if all this made sense to her, but it didn't. She was too young to have known the nuances of the cold war, and her parents' stories of the revolutionary sixties made it sound like the Decade of Cliché. Falling in love with a revolutionary meant falling in love with a suicide bomber chanting disconnected verses from the Qu'ran. That was a few steps beyond her imaginative abilities. "Her father, William—Ellen didn't talk to him, did she?"

All the good humor bled from Primakov's face. "No, and I never would have encouraged her to do so. That man is a true shit. Do you know what he did to Ellen? To Ellen and her sister, Wilma?"

Simmons shook her head.

"He deflowered them. At the age of thirteen. It was their coming-of-age present." Decades on, the anger was still with him. "When I think of all the good people who died, who were killed by my people and your people over the last sixty years, I find it humiliating—yes, *humiliating*—that a man like that continues to breathe."

"Well, he's not living well."

"Living at all is too good for him."

14

She wouldn't make Weaver's ten o'clock interview at the MCC, so she excused herself and called from beside the cash register. Fitzhugh answered after two rings. "Yes?"

"Listen, I'm running late, maybe a half hour."

"What's going on?"

She almost told him, but changed her mind. "Please, just wait for me in the MCC lobby."

By the time she returned, Primakov had finished half his breakfast. She apologized for the interruption, then pushed on: "So. You became Ellen's lover."

"Yes." He wiped his lips with a napkin. "In the fall of 1968, for about two months, we were lovers, to my delight. Then, one day, she was gone. She and her friends had simply vanished. I was in shock."

"What happened?"

"Arafat himself told me. They'd tried to sneak out

that night. They were caught, of course, and held in a little room on the outskirts of the camp. He was called to make a judgment. Ellen explained that she and her friends were taking the fight out of the Middle East and into America. They would attack U.S. support for Israel at its roots."

"You mean, kill Jews?"

"Yes," said Primakov. "Arafat believed it and let them go, but Ellen . . ." He raised and shook his hands in evangelical praise. "What a woman! She'd fooled one of the world's great liars. She wasn't interested in killing Jews—Ellen was no anti-Semite."

After a year in a PLO training camp, daily indoctrination, and maps of Israel marked up with targets? Simmons wasn't sure she believed that. "How do you know?"

"She told me herself. Six months later, in May 1969."

"And you believed her."

"Yes, I did," he said, and his sincerity almost made her believe as well. "By then, I'd been transferred to West Germany to look into those revolutionary student groups that were just starting to destroy banks and department stores. One day in Bonn, I heard that an American girl was looking for me. My heart leapt—really, it did. I wanted it to be her, and it was. She was alone now, on the run. She and her friends had robbed a bank and set fire to a police station. She fled to California, for help from her beloved Black Panthers. They told her she was insane. Then she remembered Andreas Baader and Gudrun Ensslin's bombing of the Schneider department store the previous year. She thought she'd find some common sentiments in Germany." He sighed, licking his lips. "And that, my dear, she did. Then, within a few weeks of her arrival, she heard about a chubby Russian asking a lot of questions."

"Chubby?"

He looked down at his thin frame. "I didn't worry enough in those days."

"How did the meeting go?"

Primakov rocked his head, smiling at this thought or that. "At first, it was all business. As Ellen would say, *sexual affairs that obstruct the normal processes of the revolution are nothing more than destructive bourgeois sentimentality.* Maybe she was right, I don't know. All I know is that I was even more in love with her, and when she demanded an outline of West German revolutionary activity, I obliged instantly. I introduced her to some comrades who, generally, thought she was a wreck. They thought some of her more radical views showed signs of imbalance. You see, German freedom fighters worked as a family, but by then Ellen was rejecting even the *notion* of family as bourgeois. Anyway," he said, "we became lovers again, then she got pregnant. Toward the end of sixty-nine. She was on the Pill, but I suppose it slipped her mind occasionally. She was, after all, very busy planning the overthrow of all Western institutions."

Primakov stroked his cheek again, and Simmons waited.

"She wanted an abortion. I argued against it. I was becoming increasingly bourgeois in those days, and I wanted a child to bind us together. But with that shit as a father, how could she ever view families in a positive light? So I said, *If revolutionaries don't have children, how is the revolution to continue?* I think that finally convinced her. The name Milo was her idea. I later learned that Milo had been her beloved dog when she was young. Strange. That was also when she changed her own name to Elsa. It was partly for security—I supplied new papers—but it was also psychological. A baby was her entrée into a new revolutionary world. She felt she should be reborn as a liberated woman."

"You stayed together?"

Again, he rocked his head. "That's the irony, you see. I wanted Milo because I thought he would pull Ellen closer to me. But now, she was one hundred percent liberated. I was just a petit-bourgeois male. An occasional penis—that's what she called me. She had other occasional penises at her disposal. I became one of a crowd."

"That must have hurt."

"It did, Special Agent Simmons. It truly did. At best, I was an occasional babysitter, while she went off with her comrades to start their famous trail of destruction. I'd gained a son, but I'd lost her. Finally, in a fit of frustration, I demanded—*demanded,* mind you—that we get married. What was I thinking? I'd made the final bourgeois compromise, and she didn't want her son poisoned by my wicked ideas. By then it was seventy-two, and the Red Army Faction was in full swing. Moscow was breathing down my neck to get control of these kids. When I told them it was out of our hands, they recalled me." Primakov opened his hands to show that everything was out of them. "I was desperate by then. I even tried kidnapping Milo." He laughed quietly. "Really, I did. I assigned two of my best men to the task, but by then a new agent from Moscow had started sniffing around. He notified the Center, and they abruptly changed my agents' orders. My own men were now to take me, at gunpoint, back to Moscow." He took a long breath and let it out loudly, staring across the now-busy restaurant. "That, my dear, is how I left West Germany in disgrace."

"What do you know about what followed?"

"A lot," he admitted. "I still had access to reports. I followed Ellen's career the way little girls follow their favorite pop singers. The RAF trials were headlines all over Europe. Ellen wasn't picked up, though. I heard that she had fled to East Germany with her baby, then that she had returned to join the Movement 2 June. And then, in 1974, police discovered the body of Ulrich Schmücker in the Grunewald, outside Berlin. He'd been killed by his own Movement 2 June comrades." He paused, frowning. "Was Ellen there? Did she take part in Schmücker's execution? I don't know. But within three months she resurfaced in North Carolina, at her sister's house. She asked Wilma to take Milo as her own. Ellen must have known that things wouldn't end well for her, and this was the only way to protect him. She made no demands for a radical education, only insisted that he not be brought, ever, to his grandparents. And he never was."

"She was arrested."

Primkov nodded. "In 1979. Later that year she hung herself with her own pants."

Janet Simmons leaned back, overcome by the feeling

that she'd just listened to an entire life. A mysterious life, full of holes, but a life nonetheless. Her desire, at that moment, was to sit down with Ellen Perkins and ask *why?* for each decision she'd ever made. She couldn't understand Primakov's love for such an obviously unbalanced woman, but the fascination . . . She shook herself free of these thoughts. "So, Milo was in North Carolina with his aunt and uncle. Did he know who they were, who his mother was?"

"Yes, of course. Wilma and Theo were honest people, and Milo was four when he came to them—he remembered his mother. But it was a secret. Ellen believed— maybe rightly—that if the authorities knew who Milo was, they'd use him as leverage to get at her. So Wilma and Theo told everyone they'd gotten him from an adoption agency. Wilma told me that Ellen would sometimes arrive under a false name to visit Milo. Usually, they'd only learn about the visit afterward. She'd tap on Milo's window, he'd climb out, and they'd go walking through the night. It terrified Wilma. She worried that Milo would go with anyone who tapped on his window. Then, of course, the visits stopped when he was nine."

"Did they tell him what happened?"

"After a while, yes. He already knew about me. Occasionally—maybe once a year—I visited. I didn't try to bring him back with me. He was an American. He had no need for another father—Theo was a good man. Only at their funeral did I learn that I'd inherited custody. If I had any doubts, they disappeared when I met Minnie, Milo's grandmother, who kept making excuses for why her husband, Bill, hadn't come to his own daughter's funeral. I wasn't going to let them take him."

"So he did go to Russia."

"Yes," said Primakov, then narrowed his eyes. "He didn't put that on his Company application, did he? Not on his school transcripts either. That was my idea. Back then, we still thought of the world as divided between East and West. A different East and West from now. I didn't want that working against him in the future. So we settled on a little fiction. Three years in an orphanage after his aunt and uncle's death. There was no need for anyone to know they weren't his real parents. For all purposes, they *were* his parents."

"It's a bit much to ask a kid," Simmons suggested. "To lie about three years of his life."

"Most kids, maybe. But not Milo. Remember, he received visits from a mother who was a wanted criminal. Each visit, Ellen reminded him that their relationship was a secret. He already had a special place in his brain for a secret life. I just added a few things to it."

"But the cold war ended," she insisted. "You could have set the record straight."

"Tell that to him," said Primakov. "I did. But Milo asked me how his employers would react if they knew a twenty-year-old kid had pulled the wool over their eyes? Milo knows how institutions work. Point out their flaws, and they'll bite you for the favor."

This, Simmons had to concede, was true.

"He hated Russia, you know. I tried—I tried every day to show him the beauty of Moscow and his Russian heritage, but he'd spent too long in America. All he saw was the corruption and dirt. He actually told me, right in front of my daughters—and in flawless Russian, which only made it worse—that I worked for the People's Oppressors. But what really hurt was when he said I wasn't even aware of my crimes, that I was stuck in a petit-bourgeois cocoon." He paused, brows raised. "See what I mean? I suddenly felt as if Ellen were standing there, shouting at me."

The irony made even Janet Simmons smile. "But you didn't leave him alone, did you? Two weeks ago, you crashed his vacation. Why?"

Primakov chewed the inside of his mouth as if re-aligning his dentures. "Ms. Simmons, you're obviously getting at something with all this. I've been open with you because I know Milo is in your custody, and I don't believe any of this will harm my son. Like you say, it's not the cold war anymore. But if you want me to go on, I need something from you. I need you to tell me what's going on with Milo. I saw him at Disney World, yes, but since then I haven't seen or heard from him."

"He's being held for murder."

"Murder? Who?"

"Among others, Thomas Grainger, a CIA officer."

"Tom Grainger?" he said, then shook his head. "I don't believe it. Tom was as close to a father figure as Milo, as an adult, ever had. Certainly more than I was."

"He's confessed to the murder."

"Did he say why?"

"I'm not at liberty to share that."

The old man nodded, a finger grazing his cheek. "Of course, I did hear about Tom's death. I'm not saying this because he's my boy, you understand. I'm bourgeois enough to believe in fair punishment for a crime."

"I don't doubt that."

"I just don't think . . ." He paused, looking into her cool eyes. "Forget it. I'm an old man, and I talk a lot of tripe. Disney World. That's what you wanted to know about."

"Yes."

"Simple. I wanted to know what had happened to Angela Yates. She was an excellent agent, a real compliment to your great nation."

"You knew her?"

"Sure," he said. "I even approached Miss Yates with the offer of a job."

"What kind of job?"

"Intelligence. She was an intelligent woman."

"Wait a minute," Janet began, then stopped. "Are you telling me you tried to *turn* Angela Yates?"

Primakov nodded, but slowly, as if measuring how much he could say. "Homeland Security, the CIA, and NSA—they all try to turn members of the United Nations every hour of every day. Is it so unforgivable for the United Nations to try the same?"

"I—" Again, she had to stop. "You talk as if you've got some intelligence agency here."

"Please!" Primakov exclaimed, again showing his hands. "The United Nations has nothing of the sort. Your country, for one, wouldn't abide it. Of course, if someone wants to share some knowledge with us, we'd be foolish not to accept it."

"What did Angela say?"

"An unequivocal no. Very patriotic, that one. I even tried to sweeten the pot. I told her the United Nations was interested in going after the Tiger. But still, she refused."

"When was this?"

"Last year. October."

"Do you know how much work she did tracking the Tiger after that?"

"I have some idea."

"How?"

"Because I fed her information whenever I had it to share."

They watched each other a moment, then Primakov continued. "Look. We didn't want the credit for catching the Tiger. We only wanted him stopped. His assassinations were disrupting European economies and causing unrest in Africa. Usually, she didn't know the information came from us. She considered herself extremely lucky. You can argue she was."

"What about Milo?"

"What about him?"

"Why didn't you feed him information? He was following the Tiger."

Primakov thought about his answer before speaking: "Milo Weaver is my son. I can love him, yes. I can make sure my parentage doesn't ruin his career. But I also know that, as my son, he has my own limitations."

"Such as?"

"Such as not being as clever as Angela Yates. He caught the Tiger, yes, but only because the Tiger *wanted* to be caught." Primakov blinked at her. "Don't get me wrong, Ms. Simmons. Milo's very clever. He's just not quite as smart as his old, now dead, friend."

Primakov took a bite of cold egg, and Simmons said, "You really are very well informed, Yevgeny."

He inclined his head. "Thank you."

"What do you know about Roman Ugrimov?"

Primakov dropped his fork; it clattered on the plate. "Excuse me, Ms. Simmons, but Roman Ugrimov is as much of a shit as Milo's grandfather. Another pedophile—did you know? Some years ago he killed his underaged *pregnant* girlfriend in Venice simply to make a point." He pushed away his plate, his appetite now completely ruined.

"You know him personally?"

"Not as well as you do."

She drew back. "Me?"

"The CIA, at least. The Company makes the strangest bedfellows."

"Wait," said Simmons. "He may have crossed paths with some employees, but the Company doesn't work with Roman Ugrimov."

"Please, don't pretend," the old man told her. "I've got photographs of him dining happily with one of your administrators."

"Which administrator?"

"Does it matter?"

"Yes, actually. It does. Who met with him?"

Primakov pursed his lips, thought, and shook his head. "I don't remember, but I can send over a copy of the pictures if you like. A year old. Geneva."

"Geneva," Simmons whispered, then straightened. "Can you have it sent over today?"

"Whenever you like."

She produced a pen and a notepad and began writing. "I'll be at the Metropolitan Correctional Center. Here's the address. Your people can just give it to security, with my name on it." She ripped off the sheet and handed it over.

Primakov read, squinting, then folded it in half. "It will take a few hours to track down. Will one o'clock suffice?"

"Perfect." She checked her watch—it was a quarter after ten. "Thank you very much, Yevgeny." They stood, and he held out his hand. She placed hers in his and waited as he brought her knuckles again to his lips and kissed them.

"The pleasure has been all mine," he told her, very seriously. "Remember Foucault's pendulum, Ms. Simmons. My son may say he's guilty of murder, but despite years apart, I know him better than you do. He'd never kill his father."

15

The interview room at the MCC was much like the one in the Avenue of the Americas building, with one crucial difference: a window. It was small, high, and secured with bars, but it gave Milo his first glimpse of sunlight in three days. He hadn't realized how much he had missed it.

Still in manacles, he had been secured to his chair by a polite guard named Gregg, and after five minutes they entered. While Simmons remained the consummate professional, Fitzhugh seemed off his game. There were fresh bags under his eyes, and he kept his arms crossed defensively over his chest. Something was up.

Milo continued with his story. Landing at JFK, the car rental, driving to Lake Hopatcong, parking a half mile away, and walking through the woods. Simmons didn't let the narrative move too quickly, picking at details as they came.

The conversation with Grainger came out in summary. "He was scared. I could tell that right away. At first, he claimed he had nothing to do with Tripplehorn meeting Ugrimov and the Tiger. Then he admitted he knew something about it, but the orders hadn't come from him. They'd come from above him."

"From whom?"

He shook his head, glancing at Fitzhugh, who was chewing the inside of his mouth. "Wouldn't say," Milo told her. "He tried to make it into a conspiracy. High reaches of power, that sort of thing. He said that it was all part of a plan to disrupt China's oil supply."

"You believed him?"

He hesitated, then nodded. "Yes, I believed in the aims of what was happening. But I think the buck stopped with him. In fact, I know it. I already talked about how upset he was that Ascot had taken over the Company."

"Yes," said Simmons. "I read the transcript of that."

"Tom was terrified. At the time, I thought he was just worried about his section, that a lot of people would get the axe. Maybe he was, but it wasn't enough to upset him that much. He was afraid his little side project would become derailed. Who kept the Tiger's file from me? Tom. Who made sure Angela and I never worked together to catch him? Tom."

"Yes," Simmons admitted. "And who gave the Tiger your file, assuring that he'd come to you at some point?" When Milo didn't answer immediately, she answered the question herself: "Tom."

Milo shook his head. "That backfired. He made sure

the Tiger had my file, and hoped the Tiger would come and take care of me himself."

"Tom thought the Tiger would kill you."

"Yes."

"Go on."

Milo explained that Grainger was desperate to dig himself out of his hole. "What's the best way to do that? You shift the blame to those above you."

"People like Mr. Fitzhugh here?" Simmons suggested, smiling.

At first, Fitzhugh didn't smile, then he did, forcefully, and leaned forward. "Yes, Milo. Did Grainger try to soil my good name?"

"Sure he did. But what else could he say? He accused everyone he could think of. Everyone except himself."

"And so you killed him," Fitzhugh said, urging the story on.

"Yes. I killed him."

Simmons crossed her arms over her breasts and stared at Milo a moment. Then: "Inside the house, just inside the front door, someone else died. Blood everywhere. Also, three windows were broken. In the stairs to the second floor we found seven slugs."

"Yes. That would be Tripplehorn."

"You killed this man?"

"I interrogated Tom for a few hours on Monday night. I don't know how he did it, but somehow he made contact. Maybe he'd already expected me and had prepared. But in the morning Tripplehorn arrived. He trapped me on the stairs, and I was lucky to get him."

"Where was Tom when this occurred?"

"In the kitchen. I guess he broke the windows, looking for a way out—"

"A way out?" Simmons interrupted. "But the windows were broken from the outside."

Milo paused, looking uncomfortable, but he was glad Simmons had a clear memory for details. "Like I said, I don't know. All I know is, Tom got out. I was next to Tripplehorn's body when I saw him running past. I didn't even think. I was furious. I took Tripplehorn's rifle, aimed, and shot twice."

"Once in the forehead, once in the shoulder."

Milo nodded.

"He was running away?"

"Yes."

"Yet he was shot from the front."

Milo blinked, trying not to show his pleasure. Primakov had been right about everything. "I shouted his name. He stopped and turned back."

Her expression suggested she knew this already. "One thing's strange, though."

Milo, staring at the table, didn't bother asking what that strange thing was.

"You got rid of Tripplehorn's body, but not Grainger's. Why'd you do that, Milo?"

He shook his head, not meeting her eyes. "I thought that if I got rid of Tripplehorn, then ballistics would match the bullets to his gun. The hunt would shift from me to him. What I forgot was that he doesn't really exist. He was black ops."

"You mean, a Tourist?"

Milo raised his eyes to meet hers, while Fitzhugh

shifted in his seat, saying, "What're you talking about, Janet?"

"Let's cut the bullshit, okay? We've known about your special field agents for years. Just answer the question."

Milo looked to Fitzhugh for guidance, and the older man, chewing his cheek, finally nodded.

"Yes," said Milo. "He was a Tourist."

"Thank you. Now that that's out of the way, can we go on?"

He told them about disposing of Tripplehorn's corpse in the mountains near Lake Hopatcong, but claimed not to remember exactly where. Then he'd sent a coded e-mail to Tina from an Internet café.

"The barbecue party," Simmons said with a grin. "That was good. Only figured it out after Tina told us."

"Then you also know that it was a failure. She wouldn't leave with me."

"Don't take it personally," said Simmons. "Not many people would just drop everything and disappear."

"Either way, I was stuck. I didn't want to leave without my family, and my family wouldn't leave with me."

"So you drove to Albuquerque," Fitzhugh cut in. "Stayed at the Red Roof Inn."

"Yeah."

"This is verified?" asked Simmons.

Fitzhugh nodded, then looked up at the sound of someone knocking on the door. He opened it a crack. The voice of a guard wafted in: "This is for Special Agent Janet Simmons."

"Who's it from?" asked Fitzhugh, but Simmons was

already on her feet, pulling the door open and taking the flat manila envelope from the guard.

"Just a sec, guys," she said, then stepped into the corridor.

Fitzhugh looked at Milo, sighing heavily. "It's a hell of a thing."

"What is?"

"All this. Tom Grainger. Did you have any idea he could be so manipulative?"

"I hardly even believe it now."

Simmons returned with the envelope under her arm. Her cheeks, both men noticed, were nearly fuchsia.

"What's the news?" asked Fitzhugh, but she ignored him and returned to her chair.

She stared hard at Milo, thinking something over, then placed the envelope flat on the table, her hand on top of it. "Milo, I want you to explain the Russian passport."

He wanted to know what was in that envelope, but said, "Terence mentioned it. It's a forgery, or a trick. I'm not a Russian citizen."

"But your father is."

"My father's dead."

"Then how did he show up in Disney World two weeks ago to have a secret meeting with you?"

"*What?*" said Fitzhugh.

Simmons ignored him. "Answer me, Milo. Your wife might not be the kind of person to disappear with you, but she's just as human as the rest of us. You introduced her to Yevgeny Primakov without ever telling her that she was meeting her father-in-law. And two days ago, we went to see your grandfather on your mother's side. William Perkins. Ring any bells?"

The air went out of Milo. His scalp buzzed. How had she done it? *Trust me,* his father had said, but this couldn't have been part of any plan, exposing all this. He turned to Fitzhugh. "There's nothing to say about this. I'm devoted to this country and the Company. Don't listen to her."

"Talk to *me,*" said Simmons.

"No," said Milo.

"Milo," Fitzhugh began, "I think you better—"

"No!" he shouted, and started jumping in his chair, the noise of rattling chains filling the small room. "No! Get out of here! This conversation is over!"

The guards were already inside, two of them, holding Milo's shoulders, kicking his feet off the floor and pressing him down. "Get rid of him?" one asked Fitzhugh.

"No," said Simmons, standing. "Keep him there. Terence, come with me."

They left, and Milo calmed beneath the guards' hands. This had not been part of any plan—his outburst had come from somewhere else. It was the nervous reaction to that secret place being cracked open. Now they knew. Not just them, though, but Tina.

He slumped until his forehead settled on the table. Tina knew. She knew now what her husband was and had always been. A liar.

Did any of this even matter anymore? All he'd wanted was to go home again, and now, probably, that was one place he was no longer welcome.

Without knowing it, he began to hum. A melody.

Je suis une poupée de cire,
Une poupée de son

He stopped himself before it broke him completely.

Through the closed door, he heard Fitzhugh shouting something indecipherable, then footsteps leading away. Simmons entered alone, the envelope under her arm, the flush in her cheeks fading. She spoke to the guards: "I want you to turn off the cameras and microphones. Got it? All of them. When you've done that, knock three times on the door but don't come in. Yes?"

The two men nodded, glancing down at the prisoner, then left.

She took her seat across from Milo, placed the envelope on the table, and waited. She said nothing, and Milo said nothing, only shifted for a better position, the chains making a little noise. He decided not to speculate on what was going on—speculation was killing him. When, finally, they heard three clear knocks on the door, Simmons allowed herself a soft smile. She used the friendly voice she'd first used in Blackdale, Tennessee, the one she'd been taught in interrogation training, and leaned forward, the better to close the psychological distance.

She pulled out the photographs one by one until the three were beside each other on the table, facing Milo. "Do you recognize these men, Milo?"

It was a restaurant, Chinese. Two men shaking hands. He gritted his teeth, finally understanding.

You'll know. You'll know when it's time for the Third Lie.

When he spoke, his voice was crackly from his shouting fit. "Light's not too good."

She considered this statement, as if it had basis in fact; it didn't. "Well, that one looks like Terence, doesn't it?"

Milo nodded.

"The other man—his friend—does that face look familiar?"

Milo made a show of examining the face. He shook his head. "Hard to say. I don't think I know him."

"It's Roman Ugrimov, Milo. Surely you remember his face."

Milo wouldn't admit to anything. He pursed his lips and shook his head.

She collected the photographs and slipped them back into the envelope. Then she pressed her hands together, at her cleavage, as if in prayer. Her voice was sweetness and light. "We're all alone here, Milo. Terence is out of the building. He's out of the picture now. You can stop protecting him."

"I don't know what you're talking about," he answered, but it was a whisper.

"Cut it out, okay?" she said softly. "Nothing will happen to you if you simply tell me the truth. I promise."

Milo considered that, looked ready to say something, then changed his mind. He took a raspy breath. "Janet, despite our personal issues, I do trust that you'll stick to your promise. But that might not be good enough."

"For you?"

"And others."

Janet sat back, eyes narrowing. "Who? Your family?"

Milo didn't answer.

"I'll take care of your family, Milo. No one's going to touch them."

He flinched, as if she'd touched a nerve.

"So stop protecting him, okay? He can't do anything. He can't even hear us. You and me, Milo, we're completely alone. Tell me the real story."

Milo considered this, then shook his head. "Janet, none of us are ever alone." He exhaled, glanced at the door, and leaned close so his whispered Lie Number Three would be better heard. "I made a deal with him."

"Terence?"

He nodded.

She watched him a moment, and he waited to see if she could fill in the details herself. "To take the rap for Grainger's murder," she speculated.

"Yes."

"And blame Grainger for everything else?"

Milo didn't bother confirming this. He only said, "I was promised a short jail term, and he . . ." Milo swallowed. "And he would leave my family alone. So if you plan on doing something about this, you had better be ready to protect them with your life."

16

H e'd known, even before walking into that interview room off of Foley Square, that things were sinking fast. It was the note from Sal:

```
Not compromised. My last communica-
tion was about JS's trip to DT HQ. How
is it wrong?
```

It was a tragic reply, no matter how he looked at it. There were three possibilities.

1. It was not Sal on the line. He had been exposed, and someone at Homeland was writing him confusing e-mails, using Sal's name.
2. Sal was there, but again, he was compromised, and his new masters were telling him what to say.

3. Sal was there, but didn't know he was compromised. Someone had decided to slip Fitzhugh an extra message and watch him sweat it out.

All three possibilities were bad news.

But he'd collected his wits before the interview. The truth was that nothing could connect him to the Tiger, the death of Angela Yates, or even Grainger. The whole operation had been run through Grainger, who was dead, which meant that, other than Milo Weaver, there was nothing left to threaten him. It was a dead case—it *should* be a dead case.

Self-assurances can only take you so far. Simmons had first thrown him off guard with that revelation about Weaver's parentage—how had they not found this before? Then she asked him into the corridor.

"Tell me why two aides to Senator Nathan Irwin were questioning Tina Weaver about you. Can you do that?"

"What?" He'd never heard anything about this before. "I don't know what you're talking about."

Janet Simmons's cheeks were brilliant in their flush, as if they'd each been slapped hard. "You told me before that you didn't know anything about Roman Ugrimov. That's correct?"

Fitzhugh nodded.

"Which I guess means you've never met him."

"That's exactly what it means. What's this about?"

"Then what's this?" She let him open the envelope himself. He pulled out three page-sized photographs. A Chinese restaurant, shot from a wide-angle hidden camera pointed at a small rear table.

"Wait a minute," he began.

"You and Ugrimov look pretty friendly to me," said Simmons.

His vision fogged as he thought back to the previous night. Just a mistake, a man who mistook him for someone else. He tried to get Janet Simmons in focus. "Who gave you these?"

"It doesn't matter."

"Of course it does!" he shouted. "This is a setup, don't you see? This was taken last night! The man—he thought I was someone else . . . that's what he said. He shook my hand, then apologized because he thought I was someone named . . ." He tried to remember. "Bernard! That's it! He said Bernard!"

"These were taken last year in Geneva." Her quiet voice contrasted with his hysteria.

Then, finally, he understood. It was her. It had always been her. Janet Simmons and the Department of Homeland Security had come gunning for him. Why, he didn't know. Maybe in retaliation for Sal. All this—her pretense of wanting Milo Weaver behind bars, of being frustrated by Tom Grainger—it was all a ruse to distract him from her real aim, which was to bury Terence Albert Fitzhugh. *Christ,* he thought. They didn't even *care* about the Tiger or Roman Ugrimov. Bait and switch. It was all about him.

Finally, some words had come to him. "Whatever you think you know, it's just fantasy. I don't know Roman Ugrimov. I'm not the guilty party here." He pointed at the door. "*That's* the guilty party, Janet, and you can falsify all the evidence you like. It won't change a thing."

He'd stormed out and found his way to this bar full of tourists, not far from his hotel. Scotch had always been his drink, because that's what his father and his grandfather had sworn by, but all around him idiots from south of the Mason-Dixon guzzled beer, while their women sipped wine coolers and laughed at their men's stories.

How could it have gone so bad, so quick? What had he done wrong?

He tried to pull back, to see the situation from a distance, but it was hard. He knew, if only from his good work in Africa, that a few well-placed acts could be interpreted in any number of ways. Was he interpreting correctly? Was he in touch with the underlying truth of the evidence in front of him?

After six, someone at the jukebox put on Journey, which felt like his cue to leave. He slipped into the movement of weekend tourists heading to Broadway shows, wanting to be just another part of their anonymous body, but at the next corner, spotting a pay phone a block from the Mansfield, he realized he couldn't. He needed help.

He shoved in coins and called the number he tried not to abuse, and Senator Irwin answered on the fifth ring with a wary "Hello?"

"It's me," said Fitzhugh, then remembered what he was supposed to say: "Carlos. It's Carlos."

"Well, how are you, Carlos?"

"Not well. I think my wife's got me figured out. She knows about the girl."

"I told you, Carlos, you've got to cut that out. It does no one any good."

"And she's heard about you."

Silence followed.

"It'll be all right," Fitzhugh insisted. "But I might need some help. You know, someone to cover for me."

"Want me to send someone?"

"Yeah. That would be great."

"You still meeting her at the hotel?"

"Yes," said Fitzhugh, pleased by the senator's patience. "I'm meeting her there at . . ." He checked his watch in the light of the setting sun. "She'll be there at ten this evening."

"Better make it eleven," Senator Irwin told him.

"Sure. Eleven."

The senator hung up first, and Fitzhugh settled the dirty receiver in the cradle and wiped his hands on his pants. A bellboy recognized him with a smile and a nod, and Fitzhugh returned the greeting. He had about five hours to get sober, so he went to the Mansfield's M Bar and ordered coffee. But after a half hour and a few words with the twenty-year-old bartender, a pretty aspiring actress, he changed his mind. A little buzz wouldn't ruin him. Three more scotches, and he stumbled up to his room.

What to do about Simmons? The senator had enough pull to transfer her to one of those dreary regional Homeland offices, up around Pierre, South Dakota, perhaps. Simply keep her away until the investigation could be completed and Weaver sentenced to prison for killing Grainger. He no longer placed his bets on Weaver being a Russian mole—that was a bird in the tree. The bird in the hand was murder, and Weaver's beautiful confession. He might change his story at the last minute, of course, but with Simmons out of the way Fitzhugh could work with the story already recorded. Really, he assured himself, finding what was left of his scotch beside the bed and pouring himself one more shot, it was just a matter of removing Simmons from the present equation—that would make everyone, even the irritated senator, happy and safe.

Punctually at eleven, a knock on the door woke him. He'd slipped off into an easy nap without realizing it. Through the spy hole was a man as old as himself, gray on the sides, one of the senator's aides. He opened the door and offered a hand, but when they shook the man didn't offer his name. That's how these special men were; they didn't use names. Fitzhugh locked the door, turned on the television for covering noise, and offered the man a drink from Grainger's bottle. The man politely refused.

"We should get down to business," the man said. "Tell me everything."

17

Special Agent Janet Simmons arrived on Monday, July 30, the morning after Milo's third night at the MCC. The path to Milo Weaver had begun the previous morning, Sunday, when her cell phone buzzed her awake at 5:00 A.M. It was the local Homeland office, which thought she might be interested in some 911 chatter. She was, and took a taxi over to the Mansfield Hotel.

She spent three hours looking over the room and all Fitzhugh's personal effects. She used her Canon to photograph the note he'd left behind. She had a long talk with the homicide inspector, a twenty-year veteran who had seen it all. This was just another sad man in a city that, when it wasn't ecstatic, slipped into a too-easy depression. A Company representative arrived on the scene at nine and thanked her for her swift appearance, but insisted her help was no longer needed.

She'd returned to the Grand Hyatt feeling numb but hungry, ate a large breakfast in the Sky Restaurant, and thought back over the trail of information she'd collected during the previous four days. In her room, she gazed at the photograph of Terence Fitzhugh and Roman Ugrimov in Geneva, then made a call to Washington. Immigration, she was told, did have a flight plan for one Roman Ugrimov, who had flown into JFK on Thursday, July 26, and flown out again on a late flight Saturday, July 28. Yesterday.

She called George and asked for photographs of one Jim Pearson and one Maximilian Grzybowski, aides to Senator Nathan Irwin from Minnesota. An hour later, they were in her in-box.

By four, she had reached Park Slope, but this time she didn't bother parking out of sight of the apartment. She found a spot on Garfield, near the front door, and rang the bell to warn Tina there was a visitor. Because of the broken pieces that had to be thrown away, the apartment was airier now, lighter. A pleasant place to spend a Sunday afternoon. Simmons had picked up a box of cookies on the way over to reward Stephanie for finding the cigarette lighter, and the girl seemed pleased Simmons had even remembered. Then they sat on the sofa and Simmons opened her laptop and shared the pictures of Jim Pearson and Maximilian Grzybowski. Though she'd half expected it, Tina's shaking head and insistence that these men were complete strangers still made her feel as if she'd opened a box full of despair.

Afterward, Tina wanted to hear everything about Yevgeny Primakov. Simmons saw no point in hiding

Milo's heritage from her, so she told the story in its entirety. By the time she finished, all three of them were in awe of this woman, Ellen, and the life she had lived. "Christ," said Tina. "That's so rock and roll."

Simmons laughed. Stephanie said, "Rock and roll?"

Back in her hotel, Simmons spent most of the night in a fit of anger. When the surprise (and even admiration) had faded, anger was all she was left with. The virgin would have again referenced her megalomania. Megalomaniacs cannot abide the idea that they are not personally in control of every variable. It becomes worse when they realize that not only are they not in control, someone else is, someone who has been directing all of their movements.

In the midst of her fury, she used the hotel phone to call the United Nations operator and demanded Yevgeny Primakov's New York number. The operator told her that Mr. Primakov had left New York that morning. According to her information, he was on vacation, but should be reachable through the Brussels offices from September 17. Simmons nearly broke the receiver, slamming it back into the cradle.

Eventually the anger did fade, if only because of exhaustion. She remembered the fresh energy she'd had in Blackdale, Tennessee. Her engine had first been revved there and had sustained its intensity over the length of an entire month. It had to run out of gas; that only made sense.

In the morning, she took the subway south to Foley Square, went inside the Metropolitan Correctional Center, suffered through security by emptying her pockets of her entire life, and asked to speak to Milo Weaver.

They brought him up in manacles again. He looked tired, but healthy. The signs of the beating he'd gotten in the Avenue of the Americas offices lingered only as bruises, and he actually looked as if he'd put on a pound or two. His eyes were no longer bloodshot.

"Hello, Milo," she said as the guard, on his knees, attached his chains to the table. "You look fit."

"It's the excellent food," he said, smiling at the guard, who grinned back as he stood. "Is it solid, Gregg?"

"Indeed it is, Milo."

"Fantastic."

Gregg left them alone and locked the door behind himself, but waited by the reinforced window to keep an eye on the situation. Simmons took a seat and wove her fingers together on the table. "You get any news in here?"

"Gregg smuggled in the Sunday *Times*," he said, then lowered his voice. "Don't let that get around, okay?"

Simmons used an imaginary key to lock her lips, then tossed it away. "Fitzhugh's dead. Body discovered in his hotel room yesterday morning."

Milo blinked at her, surprised—but was he surprised? She had no idea. She had read his file and uncovered the hidden nooks of his past, but Milo Weaver was still an enigma. He said, "How about that?"

"Yes. How about it?"

"Who did it?"

"The coroner says suicide. The pistol was licensed to him, and there was a note."

He showed more surprise, and again she wondered. He became serious. "What did it say?"

"A lot of things. It was a rambling note, bad writing, probably written while drunk. He had a fifth of scotch in him. A lot of it was for his wife. Apologies for being a bad husband, that sort of thing. But he did devote a few sentences to the case. He said he was responsible for Grainger's death. He said he'd been running Grainger from the beginning. Really, all the things Grainger told you. The things you said you didn't believe."

"Are you sure it was suicide?"

"There's nothing to suggest otherwise. Unless you know something else you're not telling me."

Milo stared at the white surface of the table, his breaths audible, thinking. What was he thinking about?

She said, "There's one thing I only figured out late Saturday night, probably around the time Fitzhugh died. It does kind of throw everything into question, and I'd planned on following up on it today."

"What's that?"

"The day after you came back to the Avenue of the Americas, Fitzhugh received an anonymous package— that Russian passport of yours. It was real, but the question he never answered was: Who sent it?"

"I'd like to know that, too."

She smiled. "But you already know, don't you? Your father, Yevgeny Primakov. He sent it so that, if I wasn't already, I would start to question your entire history, find your grandfather, and be led to Yevgeny himself."

Milo didn't answer. He just waited.

"It was smart. I'll admit that. He could've sent it to

me directly, but he knew I wouldn't trust an anonymous package. Instead, he sent it to Terence, knowing he would be happy to share it. Terence thought it would bury you, but it did the opposite. It led me to Primakov, who just happened to have a photograph of Terence with Roman Ugrimov—Roman, who just happened to be in town, too. Amazing coincidence, don't you think?"

"I think you're imagining conspiracies, Janet."

"Maybe I am," she said agreeably, because a part of her wanted to believe that that's all it was—her imagination. Like Milo weeks before, she didn't like the feeling that she'd been led by the nose. Still, she knew it was true. "There's a certain beauty to it," she said. "Your father sends something that has the potential to expose you as a Russian spy, but instead it leads to evidence condemning Fitzhugh. Your father must love you very much to stick his neck out like that."

"That's ridiculous," said Milo. "How could he know that you'd follow that exact path?"

"Because," she said quickly, the answer already on her lips, "your father knew—if only because you told him—just how bad the relationship between Homeland and the Company is. He knew that if I smelled a mole, I would start to dig deep in order to squeeze the Company. As it turned out, they never had a mole, just an agent with a secret childhood."

Milo considered all this while staring at his cuffed hands. "Maybe that's possible, Janet—in your paranoid world, at least—but you never got enough to really nail Fitzhugh, did you? It was all circumstantial stuff. Yet Fitzhugh still shot himself. No one could predict that."

"If he really shot himself."

"I thought you believed he did."

"Fitzhugh," said Simmons, "was too much of an old fox to do that. He would've fought every step of the way."

"So, who killed him?"

"Who knows? Maybe your father took care of that. Or maybe my investigation was making someone above Fitzhugh nervous. He made it very clear in his note that the buck stopped with him. You believe that? Do you believe that Fitzhugh was just a rogue administrator who decided to destabilize African countries in order to disrupt China's oil supply?"

Milo's shoulders slumped in an attitude of dejection. "I don't know what to think, Janet."

"Then maybe you can answer a question."

"You know me, Janet. I'm always happy to help."

"What did you do during that week in Albuquerque?"

"Like I said, I drank. I drank and ate and shat and thought. Then I took a plane to New York City."

"Yeah," she said, standing. She'd had enough of this. "That's what I thought you'd say."

THE BEGINNING
OF TOURISM

MONDAY, SEPTEMBER 10 TO
TUESDAY, SEPTEMBER 11, 2007

1

He knew from the beginning how it would end, despite all the fear and doubt brought on by the strict prison regimen. It was tailor-made to encourage doubt in anything involving the outside world, even an old Russian fox. The prison said: *At this hour, you wake; at that hour, you eat. Midday is time for physical exercise in the Yard.* In the Yard, your mind may begin to wander outside the walls, to postulate and speculate on what might be happening at that very moment, but you're soon disrupted by the minutiae of prison socialization. A Latino gang suggests basketball isn't your game, a black gang tells you this is its bleacher. The skinheads explain that you'll run with them, because you're a brother; you're white. If, as Milo did, you reject them all out of hand, claiming that you belong to none of their cliques, then your wandering mind is again sucked back inside the walls, devoted to staying alive.

Over the first three weeks of Milo's month-and-a-half incarceration, there were three attempts on his life. One was by a bald fascist who thought his hands were weapons enough, until Milo crushed them in the bars of a neighbor's door. On two separate occasions others came at him with knives made of sharpened dining utensils, while their friends held Milo still. They landed him in the infirmary with his chest, thighs, and buttocks marked up.

Two days later, the second attacker, previously a hired fist for a Newark crime syndicate, was discovered dead—quietly suffocated, not a print on him—under the black gang's bleachers. A wall of silence sprang up around Milo Weaver. He was a thorn in their side, they said among themselves, but sometimes it's best to just let a thorn stay where it is, lest it start to infect.

Periodically, Special Agent Janet Simmons came to visit. She wanted to verify details in his story, sometimes about his father, sometimes focusing on Tripplehorn, whose body had been discovered in the Kittatinny mountain range, west of Lake Hopatcong. He asked about Tina and Stephanie, and she always said that they were fine. Why didn't they come to see him? Simmons became uncomfortable. "I think Tina feels it would be difficult for Stephanie to take."

After three weeks, while he was resting in the infirmary to repair some wound or other, Tina finally came. The nurse wheeled him out to the visitation room, and they talked through phones, separated by bulletproof plastic.

Despite the circumstances (or because of them? he wondered), she looked good. She'd lost a few pounds, and that accentuated her cheekbones in a way he'd never seen before. He kept touching the separator window, but she wouldn't be lured into this mawkish expression of desire. When she spoke, it was as if she were reading from a prepared statement.

"I don't understand any of this, Milo. I don't pretend to. One moment you tell everyone that you murdered Tom, and the next moment Janet Simmons tells me you didn't. Which one is the lie, Milo?"

"I didn't kill Tom. That's the truth."

She grinned. Perhaps the answer was a relief; he couldn't tell anything from her face. She said, "You know, the funny thing is that I could take that. If you killed Stephanie's godfather, I really could take it. I've kept a big store of faith in you for many years, and I could believe that you killed him for the best of reasons. I could believe murder was justified. You see? That's faith. But this other thing. Your father. *Father*, Milo. Jesus!" Whatever prepared statement she had was crumbling now. "How fucking long were you going to wait to tell me about this? How long before Stephanie found out she had a grandfather?"

"I'm sorry about that," he said. "It's just . . . I've lied about it since I was a kid. I lied to the Company. After a while, it was as good as the truth to me."

There were tears in her eyes, but she wasn't crying. She wouldn't let herself break down, not in the visiting room of a prison in New Jersey. "That's not good enough. You understand? It's just not good enough."

He tried to change the subject: "How's Stef? What does she know?"

"She thinks you're on a job of some sort. A long-term job."

"And?"

"And, what? You want me to say she misses her daddy? Yes, she does. But you know what? Her real father, Pat, has risen to the challenge. He picks her up from the sitter's, and he even cooks. He's turned out to be a pretty good guy."

"I'm glad," Milo said, though he wasn't. If Patrick made Stephanie happy, then that was fine, but he didn't trust that Patrick would remain around long enough. He was not a constant kind of person. Despite himself, he asked the worst imaginable question: "Are you and he . . . ?"

"If we were, it wouldn't be your business anymore. Would it?"

That was really all he could take. He started to stand, but the knife wound in his chest barked back. Tina noticed the pain in his face. "Hey. Are you all right?"

"I'm fine," he said, hung up the phone, and called for a guard to help roll him back to the infirmary.

On September 10, a Monday, he got his final visit from Special Agent Janet Simmons. She told him that, finally, the evidence had been pieced together. She wouldn't say why it had taken so long. The blood in Grainger's house had matched the corpse found in the hills. She'd pulled in some favors with the French and gotten a DNA match connecting the corpse to the bottle of sleeping pills in Angela Yates's Paris apartment.

"I don't understand, Milo. You were innocent. You didn't kill Grainger or Angela. As for the Tiger, I still don't know what to think."

Helpfully, Milo said, "I didn't kill him either."

"So, okay. You killed no one. And one thing I know for sure is that you never made a deal with Fitzhugh to protect your family—that was just window dressing."

Milo didn't answer.

She leaned closer to the window. "The question follows: Why couldn't you be up-front with me? Why the parade of misinformation? Why did your father have to manipulate me? It's fucking humiliating. I'm a reasonable person. I would've listened."

Milo thought about that. During those hours on the nineteenth floor, he'd wanted to do just that. But, again, he remembered why. "You wouldn't have believed me."

"I might have. Even if I didn't, I would have checked on your story."

"And found no evidence," he said, then remembered what the Tiger had told him two months and a lifetime ago. "I had to be elusive, because no decent intelligence agent believes anything she's told. The only way I could make you believe it was if you discovered it on your own, while thinking that I never meant to lead you to the truth."

She stared at him, perhaps feeling manipulated, perhaps feeling stupid, he didn't know. These days, he knew so little. Finally, she said, "Okay. Then what about this senator? Your father sent a couple guys posing as aides to a senator, Nathan Irwin, who were then posing as Company men. Why lead me to a senator?"

"You'll have to ask him that."

"You don't know?"

Milo shook his head. "I suppose the senator's connected to everything, but my father never told me."

"What did he tell you?"

"He told me to trust him."

She nodded slowly, as if trust were a difficult concept to swallow. "Well, I guess it worked, eventually. And tomorrow, once the paperwork's finished, you'll be free."

"Free?"

"You've been cleared, haven't you?" She leaned back in her chair, the phone pressed to her ear. "I'm giving the warden an envelope with some money. Not a lot, just enough for a bus ticket to wherever you're going. Do you need a place to stay?"

"I've got a little place in Jersey."

"Oh, right. The Dolan apartment." She looked at the frame of the separation window. "I haven't talked to Tina in a while. Are you going to see her?"

"She needs more time."

"You're probably right." She paused. "You think it was worth it?"

"What?"

"All the secrecy about your parents. It's put a halt to your career, and Tina is . . . well, you might have ruined your marriage."

Milo didn't hesitate in his answer, because he'd thought of little else in that prison. "No, Janet. It wasn' worth it at all."

They separated with polite words, and Milo wen

back to his cell to pack his few belongings. Toothbrush, a couple of novels, and his notebook. It was a small bound pad in which he'd begun to turn myth into reality. On the inside cover he'd scribbled THE BLACK BOOK.

Had they bothered to examine it, the guards would've been baffled by the five-digit numbers that filled it— they referenced pages, lines, and word counts from the prison library's edition of a Lonely Planet travel guide. The jaunty tone of the decoded version would have surprised anyone who knew Milo Weaver:

What is Tourism? We know the pitch—Langley will tell you that Tourism is the backbone of their readiness paradigm, the immediate response pyramid, or whatever they've rebranded it this year. That you, as a Tourist, are the pinnacle of contemporary autonomous intelligence work. You're a diamond. Really.

All that may be true—we Tourists are never able to float so high above the chaos to find the order in it. We try, and that's part of our function, but each fragment of order we find is connected to the other fragments in a meta-order that is controlled by a meta-meta-order. And so on. That's the realm of policymakers and academics. Leave it to them. Remember: Your primary function as a Tourist is to stay alive.

2

Among the possessions returned to him upon his release was his iPod. One of the guards had used it occasionally during the past two months, so it was fully charged. On the bus, Milo tried with no success to rouse himself with his French mix. He went through a few seconds each of all those pretty girls who made the sixties look like they might have been fun, ending with "*Poupée de cire, poupée de son*." He couldn't even manage to listen to all of that one. He didn't cry—that was past now—but these optimistic melodies had no bearing on his life, such as it was, anymore. He scrolled through the artist list and tried something he hadn't listened to in a long time: the Velvet Underground.

That, then, seemed to reflect his world.

He didn't go to the Dolan apartment yet. Instead, he got out at Port Authority and took the subway up t

Columbus Circle. He picked up some Davidoffs and wandered directionless through Central Park. He found a bench among other benches and families and children, tourists scattered among them, and smoked. He checked his watch, judging the time, and made sure to put the cigarette butt in a trashcan. Paranoia, perhaps, but he didn't want to be picked up for littering.

He'd noticed his shadow on the bus. A young man, twenties, with a mustache, a thin neck, and a phone from which he sent a number of text messages. He'd followed Milo off the bus and down into the subway, at some point chatting on his phone to give an update to his masters. He didn't recognize the man, but he supposed that in the last month the Department of Tourism would have been gutted and restocked with plenty of fresh faces. The existence of his shadow didn't really bother him, because the Company just wanted to make sure he was put to bed. They wanted no more trouble from Milo Weaver.

In his head, Lou Reed sang about shiny boots of leather.

Now, as he walked east along the southern edge of the park, the shadow was a half block behind him. A good agent, he thought. Don't crowd your subject. Milo left the park and, after two blocks, descended into the Fifty-seventh Street station, where he took the F train downtown.

He had time, so he didn't mind that the F was local the whole way, stopping continually on its way to Brooklyn. People wandered on and off, though his shadow, perched by the rear of his car, stayed where he was.

The only movement he made was to take a newly freed seat, though he made sure to sit in it when Milo wasn't looking.

Milo finally stood as the doors slid open at the Seventh Avenue stop, and, when he glanced back, he was surprised to see his shadow was already gone. Had he gotten out earlier? Milo stepped onto the platform and felt a bump against his side as someone rushed to get into the train. He looked up as the train doors were sliding shut again. His shadow stared back at him through the scratched plastic windows. In fact, the man was smiling at him, patting his jacket pocket. The train started to move.

Confused, Milo patted his own pockets and felt something new. He withdrew a small black Nokia he'd never seen before.

He took the stairs and approached along Sixth Avenue, hurrying across Garfield. He was lucky—no one called out to him. Finally, he reached the Berkeley Carroll School.

It was nearly time, the streets backed up with cars in a two-block circumference around the school. He ignored the other parents grouped on the sidewalk, chatting about jobs and maids and grades, and found an inconspicuous spot beside a weary, sunstroked elm.

As the school's release bell rang and a visible flutter of movement went through the crowd, the phone rang.

He checked the display and, as expected, it said PRIVATE NUMBER. "Hello?"

"You all right?" his father said in Russian.

Milo didn't feel up to it. He spoke his side of the

conversation in English. "I'm still breathing." Across the street, children with adorable backpacks spilled out into the crowd of parents.

"It shouldn't have taken so long," said Primakov. "But I had no control over that."

"Of course you didn't."

"Did they say anything about a job?"

"Not yet."

"They will," his father assured him. "You understand, don't you, that you'll be demoted back to Tourism. It's the only thing they can do. You're cleared of murder, but no company likes to have their failures pointed out to them."

Milo was on the balls of his feet, staring. Among the children he'd picked out Stephanie. Her bob had grown out, so that no physical evidence of her Independence Day performance remained. She really was beautiful, so much more than his prison-stunted memory had allowed. He fought the urge to cross the street and scoop her up.

"Milo?"

"I know all this," he said, irritated. "And I know to accept the offer. Are you satisfied?"

Stephanie paused, pivoting to look around, then brightened as she saw someone she knew. She ran toward . . . Patrick, climbing out of his Suzuki.

"Listen," Primakov said into his ear. "Milo, are you listening? I didn't want it to turn out like this. But it's the only way. You can see that, right? Grainger was small, Fitzhugh was small, too. The problem isn't a couple of rogue men; it's institutional."

Patrick had picked her up and kissed her and was walking her back to the Suzuki. Milo spoke in a flat voice: "So what you want is for me to bring down the entire CIA."

"Don't be ridiculous, Milo. That would never happen, and I don't even want it. All I want is a little international cooperation. That's all any of us want. And since you don't want to just take a job with the United Nations . . ."

"I'm not going to be your employee, Yevgeny. Just a source. And you'll only get what I decide should be known."

"Fair enough. And if there's anything I can do to help you. I can talk to Tina. She could be brought into the circle. She's smart; she'd understand."

"I don't want her to understand."

"What? What are you talking about?"

"Her life's too unbalanced as it is. I don't want to curse her with knowing that much."

"Don't underestimate her," his father ordered, but Milo wasn't listening anymore. He'd had a whole week of the old man's words in Albuquerque, his scheming and deal-making. What was he left with now?

The Suzuki was part of the parade of cars carrying children home, and he noticed a gift-wrapped box in the back, for his daughter's birthday.

"Milo? You there?"

But Milo only heard the Bigger Voice, the one that spoke in his mother's strange intonation. Endlessly in that cell on the nineteenth floor, it had told him that everything he was doing was wrong, but he hadn't lis-tened. Now: *There goes the last of your hope.*

He heard Einner: *I'll bet the Book has something to say about hope.*

And he: *It tells you to not get hooked on it.*

Then it was six years ago to the day, and he was bleeding all over the sun-baked Venetian cobblestones. A pregnant woman screamed, while inside her the child beat and scratched to come out. He'd thought it was the end, but he'd been wrong. All of it—all the things that mattered, they were just beginning.

A strand of Tourist philosophy came to him, and for once he talked back to that disappointed voice that lived inside him: *We don't need hope, Mother, because there is no end.*

"What was that?" asked Yevgeny.

The Suzuki turned the corner. They were gone.

Read on for an excerpt from

THE NEAREST EXIT

—the next Milo Weaver novel,
available soon from St. Martin's Paperbacks:

There are three emergency exits on this aircraft. Take
a few moments now to locate the one closest to you.
Please note that, in some cases, the nearest exit may
be behind you.

THE LAST FLIGHT OF HENRY GRAY
MONDAY, AUGUST 6 TO TUESDAY,
DECEMBER 11, 2007

1

When DJ Jazzy-G hit the intro to "Just like
Heaven," that Cure anthem of his youth, Henry
Gray achieved a moment of complete expat eu-
phoria. Was this his first? He'd felt shades of it other
times during his decade in Hungary, but only at that
moment—a little after two in the morning, dancing at
the ChaChaCha's outdoor club on Margit Island, feeling Zsuzsa's lips stroke his sweat-damp earlobe . . .

only then did he feel the full brunt and stupid luck of his beautiful life overseas.

Eighties night at the ChaChaCha. Jazzy-G was reading his mind. Zsuzsa was consuming his tongue.

Despite the frustrations and disappointments of life in this capital of Central Europe, in Zsuzsanna Papp's arms he felt a momentary love for the city, and the kerts—the beer gardens that Hungarians opened up once they'd survived their long, dark winters. Here, they shed their clothes and drank and danced and worked through the stages of foreplay, and made even an outsider like Henry feel as if he could belong.

Still, not even all this sensual good fortune was enough to bestow upon Henry Gray such intense joy. It was the story, the one he'd received via the unpredictable Hungarian postal service twelve hours before. The biggest story of his young professional life.

His career as a journalist thus far had rested on the story of the Taszár Air Base, where the U.S. Army secretly trained the Free Iraqi Forces in the Hungarian countryside as that unending war was just beginning. That had been four years ago, and in the meantime Henry Gray's career had floundered. He'd missed the boat on the CIA's secret interrogation centers in Romania and Slovakia. He'd wasted six months on the ethnic unrest along the Serbian-Hungarian border, which he couldn't give away to U.S. papers. Then last year, when the *Washington Post* was exposing the CIA's use of Taliban prisoners to harvest Afghan opium and sell on to Europe—during that time, Henry Gray had been mired in another of his black periods, where he'd wak up stinking of vodka and Unicum, with a week missing from his memory.

Now, though, the Hungarian post had brought him salvation, something that no newspaper could ignore. Sent by a Manhattan law firm with the unlikely name of Berg & DeBurgh, it had been written by one of its clients, Thomas L. Grainger, former employee of the Central Intelligence Agency. The letter was a new beginning for Henry Gray.

As if to prove this, Zsuzsa, who had been standoffish for so long, had finally caved to his affections after he read out the letter and described what it meant for his career. She—a journalist herself—had promised her help, and between kisses said they'd be like Woodward and Bernstein, and he had said of course they would.

Had greed finally bent her will? In this moment, the one that would last a few more hours at least, it really didn't matter.

"Do you love me?" she whispered.

He took her warm face in his hands. "What do you think?"

She laughed. "I think you do love me."

"And you?"

"I've always liked you, Henry. I might even love you someday."

At first, Henry hadn't recalled the name Thomas Grainger, but on his second read it had dawned on him— they had met once before, four years ago when Gray was following leads on the Taszár story. A car had pulled up beside him on Andrássy utca, the rear window sliding down, and an old man asked to speak to him. Over coffee, Thomas Grainger used a mixture of patriotism and bald threats to get Gray to wait another week before filing the story. Gray refused, then returned home to a demolished apartment.

July 11, 2007

Mr. Gray,

You're probably surprised to receive a letter from someone who, in the past, has butted heads with you concerning your journalistic work. Rest assured that I'm not writing to apologize for my behavior—I still feel your articles on Taszár were supremely irresponsible and could have harmed the war effort, such as it is. That they didn't harm it is a testament to either my ability to slow their publication or the inconsequence of your newspaper; you can be the judge.

Despite this, your tenacity is something I've admired. You pushed forward when other journalists might have folded, which makes you the kind of man I'd like to speak to now. The kind of journalist I need.

That you have this letter in your hands is evidence of one crucial fact: I am now dead. I'm writing this letter in order that my death—which I suspect will have been at the hand of my own employer—might not go unnoticed.

Vanity? Yes. But if you live to reach my age, maybe you'll be able to look upon it more kindly.

Maybe you'll be able to see it for the idealistic impulse I believe it is.

According to public records, Grainger had run a CIA financial oversight office in New York before his fatal heart attack in July. Then again, public records are public for a reason—they put forth what the government wants the public to believe.

Around three, they fought their way off the dance floor, collected their things—the seven-page letter was still in his shoulder bag—and crossed the Margit Bridge back to Pest. They caught a taxi to Zsuzsa's small Eighth District apartment, and within an hour he felt that, were his life to end in the morning, he could go with no regrets.

"Do you like that?" Zsuzsa asked in the heavy darkness that smelled of her Vogue cigarettes.

He caught his breath but couldn't speak. She was doing something with her hand, somewhere between his thighs.

"It's tantra."

"Is it?" He gasped, clutching the sheets.

This really was the best of all possible worlds.

I will now tell you a story. It concerns the Sudan, the department of the CIA I preside over, and China. Unsurprisingly for someone like you, it also concerns oil, though perhaps not in the way you imagine.

Know too that the story I'm about to tell you is dangerous to know. My death is evidence of this.

From this point on, consider yourself on your own. If this is too much to bear, then burn the letter now and forget it.

Afterward, when they were both exhausted and the street was silent, they stared at the ceiling. Zsuzsa smoked, the familiarity of her cigarettes mixing with the unfamiliarity of her sex, and said, "You will bring me along, right?"

All day, it hadn't occurred to her that the story had nothing to do with Hungary, and Hungary was the only country where her language skills were of any use. He would have to fly to New York, and she didn't even have a visa. "Of course," he lied, "but you remember the letter—it's dangerous."

He heard but didn't see her snort of laughter.

"What?"

"Terry is right. You are paranoid."

Gray propped himself on his elbow and gave her a long look. Terry Parkhall was a hack who'd always had an eye for her. "Terry's an idiot. He lives in a dream world. You even suggest the CIA was in some way responsible for 9/11 and he hits the ceiling. In a world with Gitmo and torture centers and the CIA in the heroin business, how's that so unimaginable? The problem with Terry is that he forgets the basic truth of conspiracy."

Self-consciously, she rubbed at her grin. "What is the basic truth of conspiracy?"

"If it can be imagined, then someone's already tried it."

It was the wrong thing to say. He didn't know why,

because she refused to explain, but a definite coldness fell between them, and it took a long time before he was able to fall asleep. It was a staccato sleep, broken up by flashes of Sudanese riots under a dusty sun, oil-streaked Chinese, and assassins from Grainger's secret office, the Department of Tourism. By eight he was awake again, rubbing his eyes in the poor light coming in from the street. Zsuzsa breathed heavily, undisturbed, and he blinked at the window. There was a pleasant ache in his groin. He began to have a change of heart.

While Zsuzsa couldn't be much use tracking down the evidence behind Grainger's story, he resolved all at once to make her his partner in it. Did tantra change his mind? Or some indefinable guilt over having said the wrong thing? Like her reasons for finally sleeping with him, it didn't matter.

What mattered was that there was a lot of work ahead; it was just beginning. He began to dress. Thomas Grainger himself had admitted that his story was shallow. "As yet I have no solid evidence for you, except my word. However, I'm hoping for material very soon from one of my subordinates." The letter ended with no word from his subordinate, though, just the reiteration of that one crucial fact, "I am now dead," and a few real names to begin tracking down evidence: Terence Fitzhugh, Diane Morel, Janet Simmons, Senator Nathan Irwin, Roman Ugrimov, Milo Weaver. That last one, Grainger claimed, was the only person he could trust to help him out. He should show the letter to Milo Weaver, and only Milo Weaver, and that would be his passage.

He kissed Zsuzsa, then snuck out to the yellow-lit

Habsburg morning with his shoulder bag. He decided to walk home. It was a bright day, full of possibility, though around him the morose Hungarians heading to their mundane jobs hardly noticed. His apartment was on Vadász utca, a narrow, sooty lane of crumbling, once beautiful buildings. Since the elevator was perpetually on the blink, he took the stairs slowly to his fifth-floor apartment, went inside, and typed the code into his burglar alarm.

He had used the money from the Taszár story to buy and remodel this apartment. The kitchen was stainless steel, the living room equipped with Wi-Fi and inlaid shelves, and he'd had the unstable terrace that overlooked Vadász reinforced and cleaned up. Unlike the homes of many of his makeshift friends, his actually reflected his idea of good living, rather than having to compromise with the regular Budapest conundrum: large apartments that had been chopped up during communist times, with awkward kitchens and bathrooms and long, purposeless hallways.

He flipped on the television, where a Hungarian pop band played on the local MTV, dropped his bag to the floor, and took a leak in the bathroom, wondering if he should begin work on the story alone or first seek out this Milo Weaver. Alone, he decided. Two reasons. One, he wanted to know as much as possible before sitting down to whatever lies Weaver would inevitably feed him. Two, he wanted the satisfaction of breaking the story himself, if possible.

He washed up and returned to the living room, then stopped. On his BoConcept couch, which had cost him an arm and a leg, a blond man reclined, eyes fixed on a dancing, heavy-breasted woman on the screen. Henry's mouth worked the air, but he couldn't find any breath as the man turned casually to him and smiled, giving an upward nod, the way men do to one another.

"Fine woman, huh?" American accent.

"Who . . ." Henry couldn't finish the sentence.

Still smiling, the man turned to see him better. He was tall, wearing a business suit but no tie. "Mr. Gray?"

"How did you get in here?"

"Little of this, little of that." He patted the cushion beside him. "Come on. Let's talk."

Henry didn't move. Either he wouldn't or couldn't—if you had asked him, he wouldn't have known which.

"Please," said the man.

"Who are you?"

"Oh, sorry." He got up. "James Einner." He stuck out a large hand as he approached. Involuntarily, Henry took it, and as he did so James Einner squeezed tight. His other hand swung around, stiff, and chopped at the side of Henry's neck. Pain spattered through Henry's head, blinding him and turning his stomach over; then a second blow turned out the light.

For a second James Einner held Henry, half elevated, swinging from that hand, then lowered it until the journalist crumpled onto the renovated hardwood floor.

Einner returned to the couch and went through Henry's shoulder bag. He found the letter, counted its pages, then took out Henry's Moleskine journal and pocketed it. He went through the apartment again—he had done this all evening but wanted a final look around to be sure—and took Gray's laptop and flash drives and all his burned CDs. He put everything into a cheap piece of luggage he'd picked up in Prague before boarding the train here, then set the bag beside the front door. All this took about seven minutes, while the television continued its parade of Hungarian pop.

He returned to the living room and opened the terrace doors. A warm breeze swept through the room. Einner leaned out, and a quick glance told him the street was full of parked cars but empty of pedestrians. Grunting, he lifted Henry Gray, holding him the way a husband carries his new wife over the threshold, and, without giving time for second thoughts or mistakes or for casual observers to gaze up at the magnificent Habsburg facade, he tipped the limp body over the edge of the terrace. He heard the crunch and the two-tone wail of a car alarm as he walked through the living room to the kitchen, hung the bag over his shoulder, and quietly left the apartment.

2

Four months later, when the American showed up at Szent János Kórház—the St. John Hospital—on the Buda side of the Danube, the English-speaking nurses gathered around him in the bleak fifties corridor and answered his questions haltingly. Zsuzsa Papp imagined that, to an outside observer, it would have looked as if a famous actor had arrived in the most unexpected place, for the nurses were all flirting with him. Two of them even touched his arm while laughing at his jokes. He was, they told Zsuzsa later, charming in the way that some superstar surgeons are, and even those few who didn't find him attractive felt compelled to answer his questions as precisely as possible.

They began by correcting him: No, Mr. Gray hadn't come to St. János in August. In August he'd been taken to the Péterfy Sándor Kórház with six broken ribs, a punctured lung, a cracked femur, two broken arms, and a fractured skull. It was there, over in Pest, that he'd been pieced back together by an excellent surgeon ("trained in London," they assured him) but had not woken afterward. "The fracture," one explained, touching her skull. "Too much blood."

The blood had to drain away, and though the doctors held out little hope, they transferred Gray to St. János in September to be observed and cared for. A small, wiry-haired nurse named Bori had been his primary caregiver, and Jana, her taller friend, interpreted everything she told the American. "We have—had—hope, you understand? The damage to the head is very bad, but his heart continue to beat and he can breathe on his own. So no problem with the small brain. But we wait to see when the blood will leave his head."

It took weeks. The blood did not completely drain away until October. During that time, his bills were paid by his parents, who came from America only once to visit but made regular bank transfers to the hospital. "They want to take him to America," Jana explained, "but we tell them it's impossible. Not with his condition."

"Of course," the American said.

Despite his condition stabilizing, the coma persisted. "These things, they are sometimes a mystery," another nurse explained, and the American gave a sad, understanding nod.

Then Bori blurted out something and raised her hands happily. "And then he wakes up!" Jana translated.

"That was just a week ago?" the American said, smiling.

"December fifth, the day before Mikulás."

"Mikulás?"

"Saint Nicholas Day. When the children get boots full of candy from Nicholas."

"Fantastic."

They called his parents to deliver the good news, and once he was able to talk they asked if he wanted to call someone—perhaps the pretty Hungarian girl who'd come to visit once a week?

"His girlfriend?" the American asked.

"Zsuzsa Papp," said another nurse.

"I think Bori is jealous," said Jana. "She falls in the love with him."

Bori frowned and asked rapid, embarrassed questions that everyone refused to answer with anything but laughter.

"So Zsuzsa came, did she?"

"Yes," another nurse said. "She was very happy."

"But he was not," Jana said, then listened a moment to Bori. "I mean, he is happy to see her, yes, but his mood. He was not happy."

"What?" asked the American, confused. "He was sad? Angry?"

"Frightened," said Jana.

"I see."

Jana listened to Bori, then added, "He tell his parents not to come. He say they are not safe, he will come home hisself."

"So that's where he went? He went home?"

Jana shrugged. Bori shrugged. They all shrugged. No one knew. After four days of consciousness, just

two days before this charming American arrived looking for his friend, Henry Gray disappeared. Not a word
to anyone, not even a good-bye to the heartsick Bori.
Just a quiet escape in the late afternoon, once all the
doctors had gone home and Bori was in the break room
eating her dinner.

The memory of losing her favorite patient wet Bori's
eyes, and she tried to hide them with a hand. The American looked down at her and placed his own hand on her
shoulder, provoking jealousy in at least two of the nurses.
"Please," he said. "If Henry does get in touch with you,
tell him that his friend Milo Weaver is looking for him."

That was the way Zsuzsa understood the event when
Bori called her at the offices of *Blikk,* a popular local
tabloid, to pass on the information about the friend.
Then Zsuzsa went to the hospital and approached Jana
and the others for their versions.

Had the hospital visit been the only sighting, she
would have tried to find this Milo Weaver. As it was,
he kept appearing, and what struck her was that each
time he appeared, though his questions remained the
same, his manner and history changed.

With the nurses, he was a friend of Henry's family, a
pediatrician from Boston. At Pótkulcs, Henry's favorite bar, the two Csillas talked of Milo Weaver, a chain-
smoking novelist based in Prague who had come down
to crash at Henry's place. To Terry and Russell and
Johann and Will and Cowall, all of whom he'd easily
tracked down at their regular café haunts on Liszt Fe-
renc Square, he was Milo Weaver, AP stringer, following up on a story Henry had filed last summer on the

economic tensions between Hungary and Russia. From a Sixth District cop, she learned that he had even arrived to speak with his chief, representing Henry's parents' law firm, and wanted to know what had been learned about their son's disappearance.

Before his vanishing act, Henry had made it clear to her: Trust no one except Milo Weaver, but tell him nothing. It was a riddle—what use was trust if it meant silence?

"You mean you don't trust him?"

"Maybe. Look, I don't know. If someone can toss me out of my window only hours after I got that letter, then what protection can any one man offer? I just mean that you should talk to him, but don't tell him where I am."

"How can I? You won't tell me where you're going."

Despite what Henry might have thought, Zsuzsa wasn't about to follow his words blindly. She was a good journalist—a better journalist than dancer—and knew that Henry, for all his momentary fame, would always be a hack. Fear kept objectivity an arm's length from him at all times.

So when her editor called to tell her that an American film producer named Milo Weaver had come to the office looking for her, she reassessed her position. "Did you tell him how to find me?"

"Jesus, Zsuzsa. I'm not completely corrupt. He left a phone number."

It was a way. The safety of the telephone would allow her all the distance she needed for a quick vanishing act, as quick as Henry's had been.

Even so, she didn't call. This man named Milo

Weaver had too many professions, too many stories. Henry's golden letter had said to trust him, but there was a world of difference between Milo Weaver and a man calling himself Milo Weaver. There was no way for her to know which was which.

There was some information on him; she'd scoured the Internet months ago, after Henry's attempted murder. A CIA employee, an analyst at a fiscal oversight office—assumedly the same clandestine Department of Tourism that Thomas Grainger had run.

At the time of Henry's attack, though, Weaver had been in a prison in New York State for some financial fraud—"misappropriation" was the most specific word she could track down. There were no photographs anywhere.

So she settled on silence, which was just as well since she had nothing to tell. That Henry had woken from his months of sleep with weak muscles and a dry mouth and the utter conviction that *They* would soon be after him—yes, she could share these facts, but anyone looking for Henry would know them already. The details of his attack? Henry had run through what he remembered many times to be sure she had it all. He'd even begun exposing his own flaws, crying as he apologized for having lied to her: He never could have used her on the story.

"You think I didn't know that?" she'd asked, and that finally ended the embarrassing tears.

She stayed at a friend's house in the Seventeenth District, took the week off from work, and even skipped her regular weekend slot at the 4Play Club. She avoided all the places she knew, because if he was any good, this Milo Weaver would already know them, too.

Despite the measure of paranoia, her exile was refreshing, because she finally had time to read, which she mistakenly devoted to Imre Kertész. With a secret agent looking for her and Henry gone, reading the Nobel Prize winner just made her think of suicide.

On the fourth day of what she was starting to think of as her vacation from life itself, she had coffee with her friend, then watched from his window as he left for work. She left the Kertész novel by the television and showered, then dressed in some fashionable sweats. She'd decided to go out—she would have her second coffee in a nearby café. She packed her phone and Vogues in her purse, grabbed a coat, and used the house keys on the front door. Standing on the welcome mat, silent, was a man about six feet tall. Blond, blue-eyed, smiling. "Elnézést," he said, and the perfectly pronounced Hungarian *Excuse me* distracted her briefly from the fact that he matched the nurses' lush descriptions of Milo Weaver.

It came to her, but too late. He'd reached out, hand tight over her mouth, and shoved her against the wall. With a backward kick he closed the door. He glanced to each side as she tried in vain to bite his fingers, then struck him with her purse. She shouted into his palm, but nothing useful came out, and with his spare hand he ripped the purse from her and threw it at the floor. He only needed one hand on her mouth to keep her still; he was remarkably strong.

In English, he said, "Calm down. I'm not here to hurt you. I'm just looking for Henry."

When she blinked, she felt tears running down her cheeks. "My name is Milo Weaver. I'm a friend. I'm probably the only useful friend Henry has now. So please, don't scream. Okay? Nod."

Though it was difficult, she did nod.

"Right. Here goes. Quiet, now."

He released her slowly, twitching fingers hovering in front of her face, ready to go in again. She felt the tingle of blood flowing back into her sore lips.

"I'm sorry about that," he said as he rubbed his hands together. "I just didn't want you to panic when you saw me."

"So you attacked me?" she said weakly.

"Good—you speak English."

"Of course I speak English."

"You all right?"

He reached for her shoulder, but she turned before he could touch her again and headed into the kitchen.

He was right behind her the whole way, and as she took out a can of Nescafé and a box of milk with her unsteady hands, he settled against the door frame and crossed his arms over his chest, watching. His clothes looked new; he looked like a businessman.

"What's the story for me?" she asked. "Pediatrician? Novelist? Lawyer? Right—film producer."

When he laughed, she turned to face him. The laugh was genuine. He shook his head. "Depends on the situation. With you I can be honest." He paused. "I can can't I?"

"I don't know. Can you?"

"What did Henry tell you?"

"About what?"

"About the letter."

She knew blocks of the letter by heart, because for those few days in the hospital, after waking, Henry had demanded she help him remember. His fractured memory had bonded with hers, and they had been able to reassemble enough of it. For reasons of oil, the Department of Tourism, which employed brutal "Tourists" like this one, had killed a religious leader—a mullah—in the Sudan, which had sparked last year's riots. Eighty-six innocents had been killed.

Yes, she knew plenty, but she still wasn't sure about Milo Weaver.

"Just that there was a letter," she said. "There was a story in it. Something big. Do you know what it said?"

"I have an idea."

She said nothing.

"The man who wrote the letter was a friend. I was helping him uncover evidence of an illegal operation, but he was killed. Then I was kicked out of the Company."

"What company?"

"You know what Company."

To avoid his heavy stare, she turned away and set water to boil, then found a bowl of brown sugar cubes.

He said, "The letter told Henry to trust me."

"Yeah. He did say that."

"And what about you?"

"The letter wasn't meant for me," she said to the

spoon she dipped into the Nescafé granules, measuring them into cups and spilling some on the counter. He didn't answer, so after a moment she turned again, then dropped the spoon. It clattered against the tiles. He had a pistol in his hand, a small thing no bigger than his fist, and it was aimed at her.

He spoke quietly. "Zsuzsa, you have to understand something. The truth is that if you don't answer my questions, things could turn very bad. I could shoot you in the extremities. I mean your hands and your feet. If you still didn't want to talk, I could keep shooting, a little farther in each time, until you passed out. But you wouldn't die. I'm no doctor, but I do know how to keep a heart beating. You would wake up in your friend's bathtub, in cold water. You'd be scared, and then you would be more scared because of the knife I'd take from that drawer behind you to make more pain. This could go on for days. Trust me on this. And in the end I'd get all the answers I needed. The answers that would only help Henry."

His easy smile returned, but Zsuzsa's knees went bad—first one, then the other. They buckled, and she sank to the floor, her limbs useless. Nausea hit her, and she leaned over, waiting for her breakfast to come up.

Staring at the tiles, which were filthy this close and sprinkled with coffee, she heard something click against the floor, then a rattling, scratching sound. The pistol slid into view and stopped against her hand.

"Take it," she heard him say.

She covered it with her right hand, then used her left

to push herself up. He was still in the doorway, still leaning casually, still smiling.

"It's yours," he said. "I'm not going to do anything at all to you. I just want you to know that I can be trusted. If you think at any point that I'm fucking with you, just raise that and put a bullet in my head. Not in my chest—I might get you before you pull the trigger again. In my head," he said, tapping the center of his forehead. "That way, it'll all be finished." He got off the door frame. "I'll be waiting in the living room. Take your time."

It took twenty minutes for her to gather her wits and face him. She considered calling for help, but her friend didn't have a landline, and one glance into the corridor told her that Milo Weaver had picked up her purse on his way. When she passed the front door, she saw the deadbolt was locked and the key had been removed. So she emerged with a tray of two coffees, sugar, milk, and a pistol. She found him on the couch, flipping through the Kertész. "Baffling," he told her.

She placed the tray on the coffee table beside her purse and house keys. Then, remembering, she took back the gun and slipped it into the front pocket of her sweatshirt.

"Kertész? You know him?"

"The name, sure. But I mean your language." He looked at the page again and shook his head. "I mean, where does it *come* from?"

"The Urals, they think. No one knows for sure. It's a great mystery."

He closed the book and placed it on the table, th

dropped a sugar cube into his coffee. He sipped at it. He had all the time in the world.

"You want to know about Henry."

"I want to know where he is."

"I don't know."

He took a long breath, then drank more. He said, "I know you were at the hospital before he ran off. Four days in a row, staying hours each time. And you're telling me he didn't mention he'd be leaving?"

"He did say that. He didn't say where."

"Certainly you have some idea."

"He called someone."

"There's something," said Weaver. "Who?"

"I don't know."

"What phone did he use? Yours?"

She shook her head. "One of the nurses'. He wouldn't use mine."

"Why not?"

"The same reason he wouldn't tell me where he was going. He didn't want to put me in danger."

Weaver thought about that, then grinned as if something were funny.

"What?" she said, worried.

"I just don't know how he's going to follow the story alone. Doesn't he want my help?"

She had been standing all this time, the small gun remarkably heavy in her pocket—or perhaps it was just the weight of her fear of it. She didn't like this Milo Weaver. He had none of the charm or sexiness everyone se talked about. Perhaps this was just how CIA men re. They were motivated by their missions, and whatever slowed them down—a terrified lover, perhaps—could be kicked around as needed.

Still, she did have the gun, didn't she? That was something. That, in CIA language, was trust. As she settled on a chair, she took the pistol from her pocket and placed it on her knee.

"Of course he wants your help," she said, "but he said that no one man can help him now. Not when the whole CIA is trying to kill him. He doesn't expect your help anymore."

Weaver seemed confused. "What does that even *mean*?"

"You tell me. Maybe you can also tell me why it took four goddamned months for you to come here and offer help. Can you do that?"

Weaver thought about it, his face settling into a blank stare. Then he set the cup back down on the tray. He stood. Zsuzsa stood, the pistol in both hands.

"Thanks," said Weaver. "You have my phone number in case he gets in touch?"

She nodded.

"Don't underestimate me, and make sure he doesn't either. I can help him get to the bottom of this, and I can protect him. Do you believe that?"

Despite everything, she did.

"Can I have my gun back now?"

She wasn't sure.

His smile returned, and she thought she caught a measure of that famous charm.

"It's not loaded. Go ahead and shoot me."

She stared at the pistol, as if by looking she could

know. Then she pointed it vaguely in his direction, but pulling the trigger was a far thought. Finally, Weaver stepped forward and snapped the pistol from her hand. He pressed the barrel into his own temple and pulled the trigger. Twice. Zsuzsa flinched as two loud clicks cut through the room, and later she would realize that the most frightening thing that morning was that Milo Weaver didn't flinch at all. He knew the gun was empty, but still . . . not flinching seemed somehow inhuman.

He scooped up the keys and let himself out. She watched him from the window as he left the apartment building and crossed the dead grass. He was speaking on a cell phone, no expression, no hesitation in his stiff shoulders or his relentless gait. He was like a machine.

Olen Steinhauer's
Milo Weaver series continues with

AN AMERICAN SPY

Now available in trade paperback
from St. Martin's Griffin!